HIDDEN HEIR WITH HIS HOUSEKEEPER

HEIDI RICE

THE FORBIDDEN BRIDE HE STOLE

MILLIE ADAMS

MILLS & BOON

First published in Great Britain 2024
by Mills & Boon, an imprint of HarperCollins*Publishers* Ltd,
1 London Bridge Street, London, SE1 9GF

www.harpercollins.co.uk

HarperCollins*Publishers*, Macken House, 39/40 Mayor Street Upper, Dublin 1, D01 C9W8, Ireland

Hidden Heir with His Housekeeper © 2024 Heidi Rice

The Forbidden Bride He Stole © 2024 Millie Adams

ISBN: 978-0-263-31996-5

02/24

MIX
Paper | Supporting
responsible forestry
FSC™ C007454

This book is produced from independently certified FSC™ paper to ensure responsible forest management.
For more information visit: www.harpercollins.co.uk/green.

Printed and Bound in the UK using 100% Renewable Electricity at CPI Group (UK) Ltd, Croydon, CR0 4YY

HIDDEN HEIR WITH HIS HOUSEKEEPER

HEIDI RICE

MILLS & BOON

To Rob, let's go back to the Italian Riviera soon!

CHAPTER ONE

MASON FOXX STOOD at the eighty-foot-long champagne bar, carved out of a single piece of mahogany, and nursed a luke-warm glass of 1959 Dom Perignon. He gazed at the guests making pointless small talk and gorging themselves on the free cordon bleu canapés in the cavernous warehouse space below, decked out in fake greenery to launch a male fragrance which smelled like mould, in his humble opinion.

The former power station on the South Bank of the River Thames had been gutted and rehabbed a few years ago, and eventually converted into this stunning entertainment venue.

His lips quirked in wry amusement. Funny to think this ultra-modern, minimalist palace of steel and concrete was within spitting distance of the hole where he'd grown up.

He rubbed his thumb over the scar on his eyebrow—a habitual gesture which reminded him of his childhood, and how hard he'd fought to ensure he never ended up back in that hole again.

His smile became tinged with contempt.

Not one of these pampered narcissists knew what it was like to fight for every single thing you needed to survive. Then again, the hotel empire he had worked his backside off to create came with social commitments like this one, which were nowhere near as much of an adrenaline rush as living by your wits on the mean streets of Bermondsey. Truth was, he'd almost rather be getting a kicking at The Dog and Duck—where fortunes had changed hands faster than the packets of little pills with smiley faces on—than sipping overpriced bubbles, bored out of his skull.

Of course, The Dog and Duck had been bulldozed ten years ago, and Bermondsey was now as gentrified as the rest of Southwark, while the villains he'd been terrified of as a boy were all banged up or dead. But at least those criminals had personality, unlike the array of dull, talentless nepo babies, corporate suits and limelight hoggers who turned up at these events like clockwork.

He placed the fancy flute on the bar. Time to head back to the empty penthouse suite he kept at The Foxx Grand in Belgravia, or his equally soulless loft apartment at Foxx Suites overlooking Tower Bridge, if he was getting sentimental about the bad old days—and the villains who had once made his life a misery.

'Would you like a fresh glass, sir?' the eager-to-please young barman asked.

'No, thanks, mate, I'm driving. And don't call me sir,' he replied.

The kid blushed and let out a forced laugh. But then the barman's eyes widened as he caught sight of something over Mason's left shoulder.

'Wow,' the boy murmured, his expression awestruck. 'She's even more stunning in the flesh.'

Mason turned, expecting to be underwhelmed by whoever the kid was staring at.

He'd dated his fair share of stunning women, and in his experience looks were overrated—because they often came with zero personality. But then he spotted her too.

His mind blanked and his heartbeat slowed—then ramped up to about five thousand beats per second. Stunning didn't even begin to cover it.

In a fragile, floaty sky-blue gown which clung to her subtle curves and sparkled in the million and one fairy lights which lit the warehouse's exclusive balcony bar, the girl had the sort of regal beauty guys a lot classier than he was would once have written sonnets about.

He wondered if her skin could be as soft and luscious as it appeared.

The urge to plunge his fingers into the blonde curls perched on top of her head in an expertly constructed hairdo kicked him in the gut.

What the hell?

He shoved his fists into his trousers pockets. He might be more than happy to indulge his baser instincts, but even he had never wanted a woman with this much intensity at first sight. He didn't like it, because it reminded him of the feral kid he'd once been—always on the outside looking in at other people's perfect lives.

Her gaze coasted towards him, almost as if she could sense him watching her from the other side of the bar. And he got an eyeful of her delicate, perfectly symmetrical features.

Damn.

Her face was as striking as the rest of her. Her bone structure was like a work of art while the smoky gunk around her eyes made them look huge... And strangely guileless.

Which had to be an act. No woman who carried herself with such effortless sensuality would be unaware of the challenge her I'm-too-perfect-to-touch appearance would present to every heterosexual bloke in the place.

Her tongue flicked out to moisten her lips in a nervous gesture which would have been endearing if it weren't so hot.

It had the desired effect though, directing his voracious gaze to her mouth. Her plump, dewy lips glistened, and looked so kissable his throat became drier than the Gobi Desert.

He swallowed and sucked in a breath, annoyed to realise the rush of blood draining below his belt was making him lightheaded. But despite his disintegrating brain power, or maybe because of it, he could not stop staring.

But then those big doe eyes widened as her gaze finally connected with his, and she jolted.

What was that about? However goddess-like she appeared, surely she couldn't read his filthy mind from twenty paces? Before he could decide how to react—still spellbound by her artless beauty—she turned and disappeared.

For several heartbeats he stood like a dummy, staring at the place where she'd been, trying to figure out if she had been real—or a figment of his sex-starved imagination. He hadn't dated for over a month, after all. Not since Della had started making noises about moving in with him.

'Wow,' the barman whispered. 'Why do they call her the Ice Queen when she's so hot?'

'Who is she?' Mason demanded, wishing for once he took an interest in celebrity gossip.

'Th… That's Beatrice Medford,' the guy stuttered. 'Lord Henry Medford's daughter.'

Medford's daughter? Seriously? He knew Medford, in passing. He'd met the guy a couple of times at the exclusive Mayfair club Mason had joined a few years back, mostly just to piss off the posh nobs who hung out there. The man was a pompous ass who had inherited a fortune and then lost most of it… Because he wouldn't know a good investment if it sucker-punched him in the gut.

How could a woman that stunning have come from Medford's inbred gene pool?

'She's also Jack Wolfe's sister-in-law,' the barman supplied. 'They were engaged a few years ago, but he ended up marrying her older sister, Katherine, of Cariad Cakes. It was all over the tabloids,' the barman finished, falling over himself to answer Mason's question.

Mason stared some more at the empty spot across the bar. *Wolfe*. He knew Jack Wolfe a lot better than Medford. They came from similar working class backgrounds. And, like Mason, Wolfe was smart and ambitious and a ruthless businessman. Or at least he had been, until he'd got married and had a kid, and softened right up.

He'd met Wolfe's wife too. And while the woman had an earthy, voluptuous, force of nature kind of beauty, which had obviously enslaved Wolfe, Mason would not have put Katherine Wolfe in the same gene pool as the goddess he'd just stripped naked with his thoughts either.

'Is that right?' he said to the barman, with an insouciance he didn't feel. Desire was still pumping through him in a way he hadn't felt in far too long. Maybe right back to when he'd been a teenager and had craved the kind of human contact he'd only ever found in sex.

The thought made him uneasy.

So, the goddess was a daughter of the aristocracy. If she were priceless antique porcelain, that would make him the knock-off kitchenware you could buy in bulk at any South London street market.

It figured. That had to be where the regal grace came from—wealth, privilege and a sense of superiority he had always found a pain in the arse.

Then again, it had been a long time since he'd enjoyed

the thrill of the chase and maybe knocking a princess off her pedestal would salvage this evening's entertainment.

Strolling over to the balcony, he searched the crowd. He spotted her instantly, her blonde hair like a beacon.

The warehouse lights dimmed and a world-famous DJ opened his set from a stage at the far end of the cavernous space.

Mason headed down the winding metal staircase leading to the dancefloor, already full of people moving to the beat. The music pulsed, while multi-coloured lasers slashed through plumes of artificial smoke, ramping up the throb of anticipation in his gut.

Of course, it was doubtful he'd still want Medford's untouchable daughter after having a conversation with her—given his low tolerance for snooty society princesses—but there was only one way to find out.

He spotted the blonde chignon taking the stairs opposite him. Was she heading for the exit? So soon?

Not so fast, love…

Who was that guy? Looking at me as if he wanted to gobble me up in a few greedy bites…

Beatrice Medford lifted the hem of her designer gown and shot up the stairs towards the first-floor balcony.

She really ought to be outraged. Bar Guy's gaze had roamed over her body with an insolent entitlement she'd never encountered before. Men usually gazed at her with awe, or adoration. Because all they ever saw was the sheen of class, the shield of respectability, the sexless and untouchable grace which was all part of the façade her father had created.

But she hadn't been outraged at all—if she were being entirely honest with herself, what she'd actually been was… well, turned on.

Which was seriously weird for two reasons: she didn't get turned on by male attention. Because she got enough of it to know it had no real connection to who she was inside. And also because she had no desire to even be here, wearing this far too revealing dress and uncomfortable five-inch heels, simply because her father had demanded it of her.

She shouldn't have let him bully her into 'being seen' at tonight's event. Because she knew exactly what his decision to hire her a stylist and a designer gown at vast expense and demand she come to the Cascade Scent launch was really all about. It was just another of Henry Medford's increasingly desperate attempts to shore up his flagging finances by hooking his daughter up with the nearest eligible billionaire.

This afternoon, in his study, he'd even given her a short-list of men he thought it would be suitable for her to 'engage with' tonight—his cold, assessing glare raking over her with a chilling mix of calculation and contempt. If that hadn't been enough of a wake-up call to his demeaning intentions, his preposterous list had included a three times divorced investment banker who was older than he was, and a boutique hotel magnate who'd dragged himself out of a notorious South London council estate and was well known for dating and dumping beautiful women with the same ruthless efficiency he'd acquired his property portfolio,

Gee, thanks, Daddy, why not tell me you're pimping me out without telling me you're pimping me out?

She sighed as she reached one of the venue's many secret bars and gazed at the throng of gyrating bodies blocking her route to the exit.

She should have told her father to take a hike this time. The way her sister Katie had been suggesting she do for years. Instead of allowing herself to be parcelled up like a

mannequin in shoes that made her arches ache and a prac-
tically transparent dress and deposited at an event where
she would rather fade into the high-end furnishings than
'engage with' one of the men her father had suggested, who
were no doubt just like him.

As if one unconscionable overbearing bastard in her life
wasn't enough!

She'd been terrified of her father once… Back when she
was twelve years old and she'd watched him rant and rave
and kick her sixteen-year-old sister out of the house. It still
disgusted Bea that she had done not one thing to help Katie,
because she'd been too busy cowering in a corner with her
hands over her ears, pretending to be invisible.

But she'd discovered in the past few years, ever since
she'd asked Katie to dump the fiancé her father had lined
up for her—because Bea had been completely overwhelmed
by Jack Wolfe's forceful personality—and then watched her
brilliant, beautiful and entirely independent sister make a
life with Wolfe instead, it was past time she got a life of
her own.

Which meant no longer kowtowing to her father's
agenda—or relying on his money.

She wasn't terrified of him any more—and she had options now. She'd spent the last two years, on the afternoons
she was supposed to be at the beauticians or the gym or
'lunching' with the 'friends' she had never really liked from
her finishing school in Lausanne, attending classes which
Katie had paid for. She had a natural ability for learning
languages, her ear attuned to the nuances of pronunciation,
her mind fascinated by the intricacies of grammar and verb
constructions. And she hoped one day to make a career out
of her skill. Although she hadn't quite figured out how yet.

Katie, of course, had also offered her a place to stay with

her and Jack and their toddler son, Luca, at their home in Mayfair. But there was only so much of Katie's charity Bea could accept without destroying what was left of her pride.

Unfortunately, knowing she had no intention of attracting the nearest billionaire so he could shore up her father's ailing finances tonight was a lot easier than saying no to him...

She would find a way out from under her father's influence *eventually*, she told herself staunchly. But she had to do it under her own steam. Unfortunately, planning and thinking and then overthinking her options was one of Bea's super powers. Taking direct action, not so much.

She edged through the bar full of ravers getting into the groove on the throbbing retro disco beat.

Case in point: she'd totally convinced herself, while sitting in her father's leased car being driven to this event, that she would seduce the first unsuitable guy she met to show her father her love life was not his concern and manipulating it not a sound investment strategy. But as soon as Bar Guy had managed to kick-start a sex drive she didn't even know she had with one searing I-want-to-see-you-naked look, she'd totally lost her nerve.

Fabulous. So much for Bea the man-killer! More like Bea the virgin prevaricator.

No wonder her father thought her love life was still his to control, when she'd never had a proper boyfriend, except Jack Wolfe—and she hadn't even had the guts or the inclination to sleep with him before she'd got Katie to ditch him by proxy.

It would actually be mortifying she was still a virgin at twenty-two, still living at home and still relying on her father to support her—because learning five different languages without finding a way to make a living from them didn't count—if it weren't so pathetic.

She reached the other side of the bar and entered another long corridor.

Why had Bar Guy's searingly hot look had her flight instinct kicking in this time?

Because his attention had seemed different from other men she'd dated?

He was very handsome, in a rough, rugged sort of way, his tall, muscular frame perfectly displayed in the expertly tailored designer suit as he dominated the bar. But it was the dark knowledge in his gaze which had disturbed her the most—burning over every inch of exposed skin and making her pulse points pound in unison with her accelerating heartrate.

That hot look had been so exhilarating and its effect on her so surprising—because wow, she actually had a libido. But then his attention had become too exhilarating, and felt like far too...*much*.

She slowed her pace, still breathless but more than a little annoyed now with her latest display of total capitulation.

Bar Guy hadn't approached her. He hadn't really even acknowledged her. All he'd done was look.

So why are you running away from him, exactly?

Was this just another instance of her failure to stand her ground? And engage with life.

She gathered some deep breaths into her burning lungs to calm the sensations pulsing in her abdomen when a figure appeared at the end of the corridor.

Her heartbeat jumped, then shot to warp speed as he walked towards her.

Him.

Had he followed her?

'Hello there, Beatrice,' he murmured, the rumble of amusement almost as disturbing as the sensations now throbbing in time with the bass beat from below. 'What's the hurry?'

He stopped in front of her, close enough for her to detect the scent of laundry detergent and sandalwood over the aroma of sweat and stale liquor from the bar behind.

How tall was he? Because at five foot eight, she didn't usually have to look up to guys. But even in her skyscraper heels, he had a good few inches on her.

'How do you know my name? Do I know you?' she asked, then wanted to kick herself.

Why did she sound so pompous and defensive? Of course he knew her—most people did after her break-up with Jack two years ago. Because her former fiancé's whirlwind marriage to her sister a few months later had been forensically examined by every celebrity gossip column and blog from here to Timbuktu.

His sensual lips twisted into an ironic semblance of a smile.

'We haven't been formally introduced,' he said, although she'd already figured that out, because if she had met him, no way would she have forgotten him. 'But, according to the barman,' he added, 'you're the Medford Ice Queen.'

She winced. 'You have no idea how much I hate that name,' she shot back. Especially as, for once, it couldn't be further from the truth. She felt as if she were about to spontaneously combust.

He chuckled, a deep rusty sound which reverberated in her torso.

'Yeah, I'm not surprised,' he murmured. 'It doesn't suit you.'

Heat mottled her cheeks. But before she had a chance to respond to *that* comment, he added, 'Why did you run off like that?'

She frowned, mortified. How did he know their non-encounter in the bar opposite had spooked her? She might be a virgin, but she was usually an expert at faking the aloof sex goddess act... Just ask the celebrity hack who had crowned her the Medford Ice Queen.

'I don't know what you mean.' The lie would have been more convincing if she hadn't shivered involuntarily when she said it, and the industrial-strength blush hadn't spread up to her hairline.

One scarred eyebrow lifted. 'Sure you do,' he said. 'Did I freak you out?'

'I... I wasn't freaked out,' she scoffed, or tried to, not easy when her heart was now jammed between her thighs and busy doing the rumba.

The sarcastic smile only looked more assured.

She was so totally busted.

'I really don't know what you're talking about,' she soldiered on, attempting to climb out of the massive pit of embarrassment she'd dug for herself.

Perhaps shut up now, Bea, you're protesting way too much.

She pursed her lips.

'Then let me introduce myself,' he said smoothly. 'Mason Foxx.'

Foxx? Where had she heard that name before?

But then it registered. He was the rough diamond hotel magnate who had hit number one on her father's *Billionaires to Pimp Bea Out to Tonight* shortlist.

Shock was swiftly followed by another nuclear blush to lay over the first. Unfortunately, discovering his identity didn't dim the endorphin rush in the least.

She studied the hand he'd offered by way of introduction. His fingers were long and surprisingly elegant, despite the scars on his knuckles. The tattoo of a bird of prey in flight etched across the back was even more intriguing.

She cleared her throat and shook his hand, because it would be rude not to.

'Bea Medford,' she mumbled, the feel of his work-roughened palm making yet more intoxicating sensations streak up her arm.

'Bea, huh? That doesn't suit you either,' he said, with way too much familiarity.

But she was already getting the impression Mr Foxx didn't stand on ceremony much.

'Well, it's been a pleasure, Mr Foxx,' she said, trying for dismissive—but not remotely pulling it off thanks to the streak now sprinting from her arm into her breasts.

She tugged her hand free.

'Has it really?' he asked, not buying her I-am-so-not-affected-by-your-nearness act. 'Because I got the impression you would rather injure yourself than make my acquaintance from the way you sprinted off in those ankle-breakers,' he said, glancing at her heels.

'Which begs the question why did you follow me?' she managed, the streak now heading straight for her panties.

'You admit it then,' he said. 'I *did* spook you in the bar.'

'I'm so not answering that question on the grounds it will totally incriminate me.'

He laughed, the twinkle in his dark eyes full of genuine amusement for the first time. It had a weird effect on the rumba in her panties, which rose to wrap around her ribs. Why did she get the impression he didn't laugh often, and very rarely without that sarcastic edge?

He dropped his head to one side, his all-seeing gaze searing her cheeks, but this time it didn't disturb her, it only excited her. Which disturbed her even more.

'Why did I freak you out?' he asked again, the tone of his voice managing to be both coaxing and curious.

She shrugged and looked at her heels, trying to buy some time.

How on earth did she answer *that*? When she didn't know the answer herself.

She flexed her toes, aware of the pain in her feet.

On impulse, she eased her sore feet out of the shoes. Relief came first, followed by the sudden sense of freedom— and a single moment of devastating clarity.

She didn't have to be the Medford Ice Queen, or her father's puppet—any more than she had to wear the painful heels his stylist had chosen to 'engage' the interest of this man.

'That's better,' she sighed. 'High heels are the work of the Devil.'

The heady pulse in her abdomen accelerated when she looked up to discover she'd just increased his height advantage by another five inches.

'I'll take your word for it,' he said. 'I hardly ever wear them.'

She laughed, because the comment was so incongruous. From the little she knew about Mason Foxx, the last thing she would have expected him to be was remotely charming or self-deprecating.

But then he skimmed a knuckle under her chin to tip her face up.

A sizzle of awareness shot through her as his eyes narrowed.

'Why won't you answer my question?' he said, the mocking light dying—as if her answer mattered but he wasn't expecting to like it. 'Why did you run away from me?'

She stepped back, and he let his hand drop. But something about the tiny glimpse of vulnerability had her blurting out the truth. 'Because when you looked at me, I really liked it.'

Fire flashed in his eyes, then echoed in her sex. Alarmingly. Strictly speaking, his identity should have been a massive turn-off. But, judging from the streak now doing the macarena in her panties, that wasn't happening.

'And that's a problem, why, exactly?' he asked with the directness of a man who knew what he wanted and had no qualms about going after it.

His arrogance was intoxicating, though, because it spoke of a confidence she had always lacked. And suddenly she didn't want to be that gutless princess any more, who wore uncomfortable shoes because her father demanded it.

Or the Medford Ice Queen, scared of her own desires.

Or the woman who would rather second-guess herself a thousand times than step outside her comfort zone.

Or the girl who had been so averse to any form of confrontation for so long she'd ended up at this event, primed to attract this man for her father's benefit instead of her own.

Her father wasn't here.

He never had to know she'd met Foxx and had found him... Extremely hot. So why on earth did it matter whether Foxx was at the top of his hit-list?

Mason Foxx was the first man to ever make her feel this fizzy, sparky, delicious awareness. How could she ever make a life for herself, take command of her future, if she didn't even have the courage to own her own libido?

The way he clearly did.

'I guess it's not a problem,' she found herself saying. 'Per se.'

'*Per se?*' he said, that mocking eyebrow shooting back up his forehead. But the devilishly naughty light dancing in his dark eyes only tempted her more, to do something so daring, so shocking, so wicked, it might finally dynamite her out of her comfort zone for good—and turn her into a woman as bold and brave and cool as Katie.

Go for it, Bea. After all, where has staying within your comfort zone ever got you but doing your father's dirty work in really uncomfortable shoes?

'What does the *per se* mean?' he teased.

'It means it's not a problem if you like me too,' she managed.

Then cringed. Did that sound too forward? Too desperate? Too needy? Perhaps she should have taken lessons in flirting as well as languages, because she clearly had no clue how to throw herself at a guy with any degree of finesse.

But then the mocking light in his eyes died, to be replaced by something a great deal more volatile… And even more compelling.

Had she shocked this unshockable man? And why did that feel so powerful?

He placed his hand on the wall above her head, trapping her in the space. His gaze roamed over her, and she had the vague thought she had unleashed a force she had no idea how to handle.

But rather than scaring her, his thorough perusal felt exhilarating. Especially when she spotted the edge of another tattoo against the open collar of his shirt—and saw his pulse throbbing heavily in his neck. He was exhilarated too.

She gulped down the ball of heat forming in her throat as he leant closer and whispered against her earlobe.

'FYI, I want to kiss you senseless right now, Beatrice. And there's no *per se* about it.'

She choked out a raw laugh, the confidence she'd struggled to locate for so long firing through her system like a drug. She lifted her arms and clasped his broad shoulders. Then ran her fingernails across his nape, thrilled by his shudder of response.

'FYI,' she whispered back as she pulled his head down to hers. 'Why don't you, then?'

He chuckled. And she felt like a superhero, before his mouth found hers…

His tongue slid across her lips, caressing, insistent. She opened for him instinctively, her heart punching her ribs in sharp staccato beats as his tongue thrust deep, exploring, exploiting, devastating…

The adrenaline kick throbbed between her thighs and her breasts swelled. She arched her back, desperate to alleviate the vicious ache in her nipples.

His fingers thrust into her hair, to hold her steady for the delicious torment. She'd never been kissed before with such hunger, such purpose, such determination and demand. And it was staggering and scary and mind-blowing all at once. But as her tongue tangled with his and she kissed him back with equal fervour, the passion locked inside her for so long burst free. And every thought bar one went up in smoke.

The Medford Ice Queen is toast at last.

Mason dragged his mouth from Beatrice Medford's lips, his pulse pounding ten to the dozen and the desire flowing through his system threatening to affect his ability to walk.

He searched the woman's stunning face in the shadows, saw the dazed expression in the pale blue of her irises as her eyes opened. Triumph and adrenaline hurtled through his body.

She had been as blown away by that kiss as he had.

There was nothing he enjoyed more than the unexpected. And Beatrice Medford, the Ice Queen with the artless smile and the hottest lip action this side of the universe, was the unexpected on steroids.

He cradled her cheek, ran his thumb over her translucent skin.

Yup, as soft and luscious at it looks.

She jolted, her skin blazing, and he grinned.

Wow, she was so responsive it was actually kind of ridiculous—and strangely endearing. Even though those wide innocent eyes had to be an act—because no one was this transparent, especially not a society princess who kissed with so much passion.

'How about a drink?' he murmured, framing her face in his palms, unable to stop touching her skin, the texture so fine, so delicate. He gathered a ragged breath and captured a delicious vanilla scent which was sweet and sultry and addictive all at once. 'At the bar opposite,' he added.

The last thing he wanted was to take her where people could see them, but the pressing need to cool down before he exploded was at the forefront of his mind—and stripping her naked in a nightclub corridor was probably out.

But if she didn't stop staring at him with the sheen of passion dilating her pupils to black, he was not going to be able to walk very far.

She licked her lips, making the pain pulse in his groin.

'Could we…? Could we go somewhere private?' she said.

His mind blanked for a second. And the pain surged.

It was the last thing he'd expected her to say. But then she'd been much more forthright than he'd anticipated already.

'How about my place?' he said, before he could second-guess himself.

She had to know going somewhere private was going to create temptations they would have a hard time resisting. But even he didn't usually move this fast. That said, it had been a long time since he'd been blown away by a simple kiss.

'FYI, though, that could be dangerous,' he added, to make it absolutely clear where this was headed if they ended up anywhere alone.

She blinked, her eyes still dazed with passion and something that looked weirdly like determination.

'Dangerous is what I want,' she said, the husky whisper promising so much heaven, he was sure he'd go straight to hell if he didn't take her up on it.

'Understood,' he said, and scooped her into his arms.

She yelped. 'Mr Foxx, what are you doing?' she said, forced to throw her arm around his shoulders.

'*Mr?* Seriously, Princess? Don't you think we've gone beyond that?' he asked, enjoying her indignation—a lot.

He marched down the corridor towards the exit, with her squirming deliciously, the backless gown sending a whole new level of torture through his system.

'*Mason*,' she said, sending him a stern look, which did not slow his heartrate one bit. 'You don't have to carry me...'

'Sure I do. It's quicker, it's safer—because you're barefoot—' he said, pleased he could make a reasoned argument when his brain was starting to disintegrate. 'And I like the feel of you in my arms.'

'Really?' she said, with that odd combination of awareness and surprise. Why was that so captivating? When it couldn't be genuine.

'Yeah, really.' He glanced down as he bumped open the door to the emergency staircase with his backside and caught her staring—avidly—at the barbed wire tattooed on his collarbone, which he'd once thought was cool.

He had come to hate the low-rent design, had considered having it removed for years, but as he saw the fascination in her eyes, he knocked it right off his to-do list.

'Stop wriggling,' he added. 'I wouldn't want to drop you on your very nice backside.'

She huffed, but tightened the arm looped around his shoulders as he jogged down the stairs.

When they reached the ground floor, he was forced to carry her back into the fury of the dancefloor. The DJ was pumping out a club classic. But as he toted her through the crowd, he became aware of camera phones lighting up as people noticed them.

'You can put me down now,' he heard her shout, but allowed the words to get swallowed by the music.

He didn't want to put her down. Didn't want to risk losing the adrenaline rush of anticipation which was making him ache.

At last, he stepped onto the building's forecourt and the night air hit—helping to cool the increasingly problematic heat. His shiny new SUV appeared, and the valet leapt out to whisk open the passenger door.

He was forced to relinquish her, and deposit her in the front seat.

'Buckle up, Beatrice,' he said, not even winded despite the fact he'd just carried her the length of the building. He pulled his wallet from his jacket and handed the valet a fifty-pound tip. 'Cheers, mate.'

'Thank you, Mr Foxx. Have a great evening,' the teenager said.

Oh, I intend to, he thought, the anticipation starting to choke him.

He skirted the bonnet and climbed into the driver's seat. Then turned to his guest. The spurt of pride and possessiveness shocked him a little as he took stock of her, looking serene and elegant and yet so perfect sitting in his car.

But as he closed the door and started the ignition, he forced himself to get the foolish spurt of pride under control.

Just a one-night booty call, Mase.

And not a foregone conclusion at that, because this woman had more class than he could even dream of.

He shifted into gear and roared away from the kerb.

The lights of old warehouses which had been turned into luxury flats flickered over the car's new paintwork as they drove along the river. These same warehouses had been derelict when he was a boy, the broken glass and rubble becoming his own personal adventure playground. Their newly pointed facades and gleaming glasswork reminded him he was no longer that feral kid, but a rich man in control of his own destiny.

So what if he wanted Beatrice Medford…*a lot*? Didn't mean he needed her. At all.

CHAPTER TWO

MASON SLOTTED THE SUV into one of his reserved spaces in Foxx Suites' underground car park. Anticipation and arousal charged through his veins as he turned to his passenger—which was daft, the woman had agreed to a nightcap, nothing more.

She hadn't spoken during the ten-minute drive from Bermondsey. Perhaps she was regretting what he had guessed was a rash decision the minute she'd made it.

He'd seen the spark of rebellion in her eyes, and had found it almost as captivating as the flush still heating those high cheekbones. Her bright blue eyes were sheened with an intoxicating combination of determination... And innocence.

What *was* that about? Surely it had to be a trick of the light? Or the clever glitter of make-up which made her eyes look so huge?

Because she couldn't be innocent. She was in her twenties by his reckoning, and had been engaged to Jack Wolfe once upon a time. And if there was one thing he knew about Wolfe, the guy wasn't the type to offer marriage without making sure he was compatible with his fiancée in bed.

'If you've changed your mind, I'll take you home,' he said abruptly, irritated by the wave of disappointment...

And the spurt of jealousy at the thought she had once belonged to Wolfe.

Why should he care? He wasn't the possessive type.

And he preferred his women to have experience, to know
what they wanted, so he could give it to them. Assuming,
of course, he was going to get lucky tonight, which did not
look likely any more, when her teeth dug into her bottom lip.

Heat surged into his groin, which annoyed him more.

He shifted in his seat, perplexed to realise her indecision
was actually turning him on more, not less.

'I don't want to go home,' she said.

He nodded. And the need did a victory lap in his groin.

Climbing out of the car, he took a moment to get a hold
of himself. He wasn't an untried kid. Not any more. And
he didn't lose his cool with women, no matter how captivating or classy they were.

She probably just saw him as a bit of rough. A guy who
was much more basic and straightforward than the posh
boys she usually dated.

Of course, the fact she'd been engaged to Wolfe meant this
wouldn't be the first time she'd lowered her social standards.

He frowned as he rounded the front of the car.

*Stop getting hung up on Wolfe. And the fact she's a lot
posher than you are.*

Since when had he ever cared about all that class crap?

He reached the passenger door, intending to open it for
her—he could mind his manners if he felt like it—when it
swung open and her bare foot appeared.

'Hey.' He stepped in front of her before her feet could
land on the cold, filthy concrete. 'Not so fast, Princess.'

Her bright blue gaze snapped to his face. 'I'm not a princess. I'm merely the daughter of a lord. And not even a very
impressive one'

He chuckled. He couldn't help it. How could she look even more stunning when she was telling him off?

'Duly noted,' he said, then lifted her off the seat before she could object.

'Mason, what are you doing?' she demanded as he strode towards the lift.

'Getting you from A to B,' he said, grinning down at her perturbed face as he inhaled another lungful of the glorious scent he'd noticed in the club. It reminded him of the cupcake stall under the railway arches near where he'd grown up. He'd loved going there every Sunday, to help out Mrs Archer, the nice lady who owned it, so he could earn a few bob and stuff himself with the leftovers she hadn't sold at the end of the day.

'Just for the record... I don't need you to carry me everywhere,' she said. Awareness surged through him again at her perplexed expression.

'Yeah, I know,' he said. 'But I like carrying you, remember,' he finished, surprised to realise it wasn't a joke.

He'd enjoyed having her cradled in his arms as they'd made their way across the dancefloor. And not just because she'd been all soft and fragrant and wriggly—but because he'd liked the attention from the crowd. For once, he hadn't minded people taking photos, because they had assumed Beatrice Medford was his...

'Well, thanks,' she huffed, not impressed with his compliment.

It was his turn to frown, though, as the lift doors opened and he stepped inside with her.

Why had he wanted complete strangers to assume he was dating Beatrice Medford?

He didn't need to impress anyone with the women he dated. And she wasn't even his. Not yet anyway.

He put her down, and her bare feet landed on the lift's luxury carpeting.

'Plus, I wouldn't want you getting your feet dirty,' he added, to cover the gaff.

'My feet really aren't that delicate,' she said. 'But thank you, I appreciate your chivalry,' she added, looking more disturbed than thankful.

Chivalry? Yeah, right.

The compliment was so inaccurate, he didn't know whether to be amused or appalled. He pressed his key card to the reader to access the penthouse—and give himself a moment to calm down.

Something about her polite thank you, though, had irritated him too.

Had he read her wrong? Had the spark of anticipation in her expression when she'd suggested going to his place all been in his head, thanks to an inferiority complex he hadn't even realised he had until about five seconds ago?

He stabbed the penthouse button. The lift whisked upwards.

She dragged in an audible breath as the glass box surged out of the basement complex and climbed the outside of the old wharf building which Foxx Group had remodelled five years ago. The scenic lift gave them an enviable view of the London skyline at night.

Across the river, the Tower of London's majestic turrets were spotlit in the red and blue of the Union flag. It looked stoic and forbidding, its walled garden dwarfed by the sprawling office complexes that surrounded it. In the foreground, the centuries-old architectural splendour of Tower Bridge winched upward to let a boat pass through the Pool of London and continue its journey up-river.

'Wow! That's…amazing,' she murmured.

He'd grown used to the spectacular view over the last couple of years but, as her face brightened, pride and achievement swelled in his chest.

This was *his* city, its history and elegance now as much a part of his life as its squalor and violence had been nearly twenty years ago. And this part of it—this breathtaking view—was something he'd worked to earn, right from the day he'd got his first proper job using a fake ID, aged fourteen, to work as a bellboy in the Jones Tower Hotel next door, named after the bridge's designer Horace Jones. And renamed the Foxx-Jones five years ago, when it became his.

'Yeah, not bad,' he said with deliberate insouciance.

She glanced over her shoulder and sent him a grin which had his heart bobbing.

She was even more stunning when she smiled.

The lift glided to a stop, but he couldn't seem to detach his gaze from hers.

Her skin glowed in the half-light and he could see her pulse pounding in the delicate well of her collarbone. Her blonde updo had come undone during their exit from the club, the escaped tendrils clinging to her neck and accentuating its swanlike grace. His gaze dropped to the glimpse of cleavage above the provocative neckline of the gossamer gown.

What would she taste like if he kissed her there? At the base of her throat where her pulse fluttered. Would she be rich and sweet, like Mrs Archer's cupcakes on a hot summer day, or fresh and exotic, like the icy pineapple juice she'd given him to wash them down with?

Awareness flared in the pure cerulean blue of her eyes, along with the spark of determination and anticipation. And suddenly he knew. She wanted him with the same intensity.

The lift doors opened, but did nothing to break the spell.

He directed her into the lavish open-plan space he had helped design himself. The sparsely furnished room was dominated by a glass wall leading to a terrace which ran the length of the building and made the most of the view across the Thames.

'After you, Princess,' he murmured, but the mocking name came out on a husky breath.

Because what he saw as she stepped into his home, still clutching her shoes, the dress clinging to her in all the right places, wasn't an Ice Queen but a flesh and blood woman, eager to explore their chemistry.

He took off his jacket and dumped it on one of the leather sofas, the tailored fabric suddenly feeling like a straitjacket. Undoing the cuffs of his shirt, he rolled up the sleeves and crossed to the bar, more than ready now to explore that livewire connection too.

'So, what's your poison, Princess?' Mason Foxx asked in that low voice which seemed to hold a thousand and one promises Bea couldn't quite fathom. But also didn't want to ignore.

Was he toying with her? Perhaps she ought to be more cautious? After all, she'd never been alone with a man like him, a man so forceful and rugged and assured he made no bones about what he wanted. Plus, all she really knew about him was that her father had asked her to seduce him, and his kiss had the power to make her forget everything but the feel of his lips on hers.

But despite all the potent sexual energy which emanated from him, she sensed Mason Foxx had a core of pride which made her positive he wouldn't take advantage of her.

Even though she had already asked him to.

She'd been in his arms twice already. And, despite her

protests, she'd loved the surge of adrenaline, the shudder of awareness, as he'd carried her with that audacious sense of entitlement.

Surely the kinetic energy which made her body feel alive and languid at one and the same time was what Katie had told her about? The 'sex is incredible when you do it right, sis' thing Bea had convinced herself she would never experience.

Odd to think she should feel it for this man. Why would her libido finally awaken for Mason Foxx? Perhaps because he was so overpowering. Hot enough to thaw out an Ice Queen—even one who had begun to believe she might be asexual.

One thing was certain. It didn't matter any more that he was one of the men on her father's list. Because she had no intention of telling her father about tonight. Sleeping with Mason Foxx to satisfy her own desires—rather than her father's investment opportunities—suddenly felt like the ultimate act of rebellion. The perfect way to stake a claim to her own sex life for once. Or at least it had in the club, when she'd asked him to bring her here…

'A glass of wine would be great,' she said, licking her lips nervously, aware of his gaze straying to her mouth.

'White or red?'

'Um…' The question threw her, because she rarely drank. 'White, I guess,' she said, deciding something chilled would probably be a good idea, given that her body felt as if it were on fire.

He nodded, then opened a fridge beneath the bar which held an array of expensive-looking bottles. He selected one, uncorked it—using one of those minimalist corkscrews she'd only ever seen waiters use—then poured the golden liquid into a long-stemmed glass.

He handed it to her, then poured himself a glass too. She took a sip. The fresh buttery flavours burst on her tongue.

'What do you think?' he asked.

'Delicious.'

'Good.' He swirled the wine in his own glass, took a taste, then smiled as she took another gulp, mostly to keep her hands busy. 'It's a Montrachet Grand Cru,' he said. 'It ought to taste good—it goes for over a grand a bottle at the bar in the Foxx-Jones Hotel next door.'

'It...*what*?' she sputtered, then coughed. 'You're joking?' she wheezed as he patted her back.

'Nope,' he said, smiling.

'Oh, God, I think I just choked on at least a hundred pounds' worth,' she said.

He laughed, that rich, throaty, rare laugh which made her heart bounce.

'Not a problem,' he said. 'I've got a whole case of it.'

'That's not even funny,' she said, although she couldn't help smiling back at him.

'So, you and Jack Wolfe—what was *that* about?' he asked, the change of subject so abrupt she almost got whiplash. 'Because I can't see you shackled for life to a reprobate like him,' he added in an easy, jokey tone which did nothing to disguise the sharp look in his eyes.

Which were dark green, not brown, as she had originally assumed.

'Jack's not a reprobate,' she said, struggling not to drown in the vivid emerald hue of his irises, which reminded her of the chalk hills near Medford Manor in Wiltshire in spring.

'So, you've still got feelings for him?' he commented, the tone still conversational, but the sharp look intensifying.

'Heavens, no!' she blurted out, and his sensual lips curved, the cynical half smile tinged with something that seemed a little smug. 'I mean, I never really had feelings for him.' She scrambled to justify her reaction. 'Not *those* feelings, anyway. He's very happily married to my sister Katie. He's a forceful person. And so is Katie, which makes them perfect for each other.'

She took a gulp of the wine, feeling exposed under that patient gaze. Why was she explaining herself to him? Her relationship with Jack—or rather the lack of one—was not his business.

'So why were you ever engaged to him?' he asked.

She wanted to be outraged at the intrusive question. Tried to feel indignant.

But, before she could find a reply, he hooked a tendril of her hair behind her ear. His thumb glided down her cheek, making her skin sizzle, and then stroked the pulse point in her neck, completely disarming her.

Her breathing gathered painfully in her lungs as he tucked his hand back into his pocket. But the damage was already done.

The proprietary touch should have disturbed her, but all it did was energise her and make her rampaging pulse get wedged between her thighs. Her gaze seemed to be locked with his. She didn't need his approval, so why did what he thought of her seem to matter so much? Enough for her to search for an answer which wouldn't reveal the humiliating truth—that she had been engaged to Jack Wolfe to please her father.

'I... I don't really know,' she lied. 'Jack asked me and I was hopelessly flattered, so I said yes.'

She looked away from his probing gaze, embarrassed by her not entirely truthful answer. But as she imagined what he might think of her lame response, she became brutally aware of the different paths their lives had taken.

Mason Foxx had never bowed to anyone else's wishes but his own. While she'd always taken the easy option, obeying her father because it had been so much less stressful than standing up to him, the way Katie had done. What would this man think of her, if he knew that about her? A man who, by all accounts, had been given nothing, and fought tooth and nail for every single thing he possessed. While she'd been born into privilege, had been handed everything on a silver platter, and owned virtually nothing of any value.

She planned to change that, had convinced herself that honing her language skills would eventually help her find a way out, but the truth was her life at this point was a mere shadow of what it could have been if she'd been less of a doormat.

He hadn't said anything, hadn't responded to her answer. Maybe because he knew it was a lie.

She stared at the magnificent skyline—the majesty of Tower Bridge, the austere beauty of the Tower of London—and finally confronted the full weight of her own cowardice.

'I knew as soon as I said yes to him, it was a colossal mistake,' she murmured, wanting to be as honest as she could without exposing the sordid truth about her choices. 'I knew Jack would consume me, and I could never make him happy. That I wasn't enough for a man like him.'

She blinked furiously, aware of the pity tears she couldn't let fall—because that would be hopelessly self-indulgent.

She was the only one to blame for her pathetic life, her lack of any concrete achievements. Yes, her father was a bully but she could have escaped him long ago, if she'd had Katie's courage. Or the drive and ambition of Mason Foxx, a man who was determined to make his mark no matter the odds he faced.

She turned to find him watching her—the emerald-green

eyes glittering with passion and purpose and an intensity which would have been disturbing if it weren't so... Well, so exciting.

What he saw was the illusion, of course—of a serene, privileged woman in charge of her own life. Instead of a hopeless fake, in charge of nothing of any significance.

But, for once, Bea wanted to live up to the image, the hype. Maybe if a man like Mason Foxx could see something to admire in her, she could see something to admire too.

'What makes you think you're not enough for any man, Beatrice?' he asked softly, sounding genuinely curious.

Because I know I'm a fake. But I intend to remedy that. Starting now.

She placed the half-empty glass of expensive wine on the bar. And met that dark, possessive gaze. She smiled, stupidly touched by his faith in her. Or at least in the illusion. And became mesmerised by the gold shards in his irises which were alight with a promise she now understood.

He could take her places she had never been before, never even wanted to go. If she let go of that frightened girl and embraced the woman she could be. The woman she had always wanted to be.

She lifted on tiptoes to cradle his cheek. His jaw tensed as he sucked in a breath and the day-old stubble rasped deliciously against her palm.

His eyes flared with longing. And the excitement in her gut surged, along with the potent feeling of power. And purpose.

'Would you kiss me again, Mason?' she asked.

Glass shattered as he went to place his wine on the bar and missed.

Triumph echoed through her heart at the thought she had so much more power than she had ever realised.

He clasped her hips in strong hands to drag her closer, until the hard line of his body moulded hers. Her nipples tightened painfully, pressed against his chest, the scent of soap and man intoxicating as it enveloped her.

He tucked a knuckle under her chin and bent his head towards her mouth.

But then he rasped, 'You need to be sure, Princess.' The mocking nickname was like an endearment, his hot breath feathering her cheek. 'Because if I kiss you again, we might not be able to stop.'

She swallowed heavily. It was a warning, one that a frightened girl would once have heeded. She was unleashing something bigger than herself, something she knew nothing about. But in this moment, all his warning did was make the adrenaline spike and the ache in her core become painful.

Mason Foxx wanted her, and she wanted him. That was what mattered now.

So she nodded.

His mouth captured her sob of surrender, his lips firm, seeking and voracious. She opened for him again and let him lead the kiss, but as their tongues tangled she found herself making demands of her own.

The kiss became desperate and all-consuming, but also tender. She drove her fingers into his hair and dragged him closer still—his hunger sending her senses into a tailspin of need.

His hands clasped her bottom, pressing her to him, until she became brutally aware of the thick ridge revealing the effect she had on him, which he couldn't hide.

As they came up for air, his harsh pants matched her ragged sobs.

He swore softly, then boosted her into his arms. 'Wrap your legs around my waist,' he rasped.

She did as he asked, unable to deny the dizzying rush of emotion at the realisation he was protecting her bare feet from the broken glass. She clasped his face, kissed his cheeks, his chin, his forehead, loving the feel of his skin on her lips and the harsh murmur of his breathing.

He carried her down a corridor at the back of the space and entered a huge bedroom.

A vast picture window on the far side looked out across the Thames Estuary towards Rotherhithe and the docks—the view was less romantic but somehow more real than the one at the front of the building.

He put her down and her bare toes sank into thick carpeting.

'I want you naked, Beatrice,' he said, the gruff demand in his voice impossibly seductive.

But the raw request made her hesitate.

No man had ever seen her naked before. She'd always been self-conscious about her body, knowing her boyish figure was at its best displayed in designer couture. Would he be disappointed, appalled even, when he saw her virtually flat chest, her narrow hips, her thin frame? She didn't want to risk all her newfound confidence evaporating before they got to the main event.

But she forced herself to nod. As he reached for her, though, she evaded him.

'I want you naked too,' she said.

Perhaps if they were both naked, she would feel less exposed.

His eyebrows lifted, but then he laughed. 'All right, Princess.' The words were mocking, but when he began to unbutton his shirt, revealing the tattoo of barbed wire that looped around his collarbone, her self-consciousness faded, washed away on a surge of heat.

He stripped off the shirt and flung it away.

Oh...my.

If she'd thought the view from the lift had been spectacular, it was nothing compared to the sight of Mason Foxx's naked torso.

Her gaze raked over the defined slabs of muscle, the hair-dusted pecs, the ridges of his six-pack, the muscles which arrowed towards his waistband. And the many small scars and two other tattoos—one crude, one intricate—all evidence of the uncharmed life he'd led.

He flipped open the button on his trousers, revealing a pair of black boxer shorts, but just as the rush of moisture flooded her mouth...and her panties...he paused.

'What are you waiting for?' he said, the teasing note doing nothing to disguise the rasp of urgency. 'I thought we were in this together?'

'Oh, yes. Of course,' she said, the last of her self-consciousness incinerated by that playful, provocative tone. She found the side zip of the designer gown with clumsy fingers, slid it down, then paused as he kicked off his shoes, stripped off his trousers.

'You need some help with that?' he asked as he stepped closer.

She nodded because she couldn't seem to move.

His quick grin was feral as he used one fingertip to edge a strap off one shoulder. She shuddered as he eased the other strap down, and the silky dress slid over her body to pool at her feet. She shivered, but she wasn't cold. Not even close.

He stepped back and cleared his throat. 'You're beautiful, Beatrice,' he murmured, his voice so rich with appreciation and approval she felt beautiful for the first time in her life.

'Your hair...' he said, glancing at the elaborate chignon. 'I've been wanting to mess it up all night.'

She wasn't sure if he was asking her permission, but she nodded anyway, loving the thought of him destroying the hairstyle an exclusive stylist had spent over an hour creating.

He located the first pin, dragged it loose. Then another and another. She sighed when the heavy mass tumbled down.

'Shake it,' he demanded. She did as he asked, letting it bounce off her shoulders, aware of his gaze scorching her face, her collarbone and then dipping to her breasts, confined in the strapless bra.

He did a twirl with his finger. 'Turn around.'

Again, she followed his instruction, spellbound by the desire darkening his eyes.

She focused on his tall shape behind her, reflected in the glass wall, illuminated by the low lighting. She jolted as her bra snapped open, the sound like a gunshot in the quiet room.

He peeled off the lace and threw it away. Large hands cupped her breasts from behind. Rough calluses stroked over her engorged flesh, making it tighten and swell. She arched into his touch as firm lips captured the throbbing pulse in her neck. His fingers plucked at her tender nipples, and a ragged moan burst out.

She had never realised she was so sensitive there. But he seemed to know just how to caress and entice her, to drive her passion to fever-pitch as she writhed against his hold.

Too much and yet not enough.

'Look at yourself, Beatrice,' he said, his voice hoarse, his desire as urgent and fierce as her own.

She stared at the woman in the glass, shocked by how wild and uninhibited she seemed, as his hand left her naked breast to glide down her torso. She noticed the bird of prey etched on the back, became mesmerised by the design as his fingers slid into her panties and found the slick folds of her sex.

'You're so wet for me, Beatrice,' he said.

'Yes.' She bucked against his sure touch, her moan becoming a full-throated groan. Bowing back, she reached up, curling her hand around his neck to anchor herself. Panting now, in gasps of need.

'Please…' she begged as he continued to tease and incite, retreating then returning, tempting her swollen flesh.

He swore softly against her neck, then feasted on the pulse point, his other hand still playing with one engorged nipple.

Arrows of sensation darted down, turning the heat at her core into a raging inferno.

The waves of pleasure built with each pass of his thumb, too close and yet not close enough, each swirl of that devious fingertip taking her to the edge, but retreating before she could reach the peak.

'Oh… God.' She gripped his hair, tugged hard, riding his hand now, desperate to release the tension building at her core, vaguely aware of the spectacle she was making of herself but not able to stop, not even able to care.

She bit into her lip as he found the very heart of her.

'Come for me,' he said.

The pleasure centred in her sex—burning, bright, beautiful—then blew apart, sending her shooting over that high ledge. She cried out as the fierce pleasure crested, caught his grunt of triumph through the hurricane in her ears.

And let herself soar. Just like that bird. At last.

Fierce need enveloped Mason as he scooped Beatrice's limp body into his arms and carried her to the bed.

Had he ever made love to a woman before who was so responsive to his touch? He didn't think so. He had always considered himself skilled at bringing women to climax. He liked sex. A lot. But having her reach for him, feeling the sting as she'd grabbed a fistful of his hair and let herself shatter had been something else…

Urgency charged through his veins, the ache in his groin painful as he laid her out and watched her eyelids flutter open.

She looked dazed and a little confused.

'Hey there,' he said, the emotion scraping against his throat shocking him. 'You okay?'

'Yes. Absolutely,' she said simply. Then she smiled, that sweet, mesmerising, weirdly innocent smile that brightened her whole face and made her look young, in a way he was sure he'd never been.

Her transparent joy and the sense of achievement in her expression made him feel as if he'd just taken her somewhere she'd never been before. Which *had* to be his ego talking, but, even so, he couldn't ignore the swelling against his ribs, or the powerful press of the erection stretching his boxers.

He needed to finish this before he lost what was left of his mind.

'Hold that thought,' he said, forcing an easy smile to his lips that he didn't remotely feel.

He hooked her panties, eased the scrap of lace down long slender legs and breathed in the musty scent of her arousal. Standing, he stared down at her lean body, the small but perfect breasts, the cascade of hair which halloed around her striking face. She was staring back at him, the flush of awareness turning to…

What was that? Because it almost looked like embarrassment.

But then she glanced pointedly at his boxers. 'I thought we agreed we were in this together?' she said in an unsteady voice, despite the snark.

He chuckled, her audacity easing the tension in his chest. Why was he making this a big deal?

'Fair point, Princess,' he said as he dragged off his boxers and threw them away.

Her eyes widened and the unyielding erection swelled as the last of the blood drained out of his head.

Women had looked at him before and commented on his size, usually with appreciation. But when those wide blue eyes met his again and her teeth chewed her bottom lip, he thought he saw panic flit across her features.

Okay. *Unexpected.*

Did she think he was some kind of brute? That he wouldn't treat her with the care and attention she deserved?

He dismissed the thought, shoved it back into the box marked 'newly discovered inferiority complex' and climbed onto the bed, remembering at the last minute to reach into the bedside table. He'd never brought any of his dates here because this was his home base, so he was more than a little relieved when he found a condom.

He ripped open the foil envelope with his teeth then sheathed himself, frantic to get back to where they'd been moments before, when she'd come apart in his arms, before he'd had to worry about practicalities.

He lay down and stroked her cheek, then leant forward to devour those plump lips again. She lifted into his kiss, responding to him eagerly. And the panic receded, to be replaced by pride, smugness even, and pure unadulterated lust.

This was good, this was right. They had incredible chemistry. That was all. No biggie. A connection he intended to enjoy before she left in the morning. But they had a whole night to indulge themselves.

Even so, the desire to rush overwhelmed him as he reached down to find her ready for him. She bucked against his touch, her gasp one of surprise and surrender, which was more than enough to make his hunger spike.

'Can I touch you too?' she asked as he caressed her, her voice thick with arousal, but still oddly hesitant.

'You don't have to ask for permission,' he managed, touched by the request.

But when she nodded, then reached down to curl slender fingers around his thick shaft, her touch was devastatingly intense even through the condom, and he realised his mistake.

As she stroked him, her caresses somehow both clumsy and bold, the climax built at the base of his spine, threatening to rage out of control... He could only stand it for a few seconds before he grasped her wrist and tugged her fingers away.

'I need to be inside you, Beatrice.'

'Oh... Okay,' she said.

He nodded, then rolled on top of her and grasped her hips in his hands to angle her pelvis. 'Lift your knees,' he groaned as she grasped his shoulders.

He probed at her entrance and held her firmly to press home in one hard thrust.

She tensed, her fingernails digging into his shoulders. And he stopped abruptly. He groaned, the feel of her—so tight, so exquisite—almost more than he could bear. But had she just winced?

She was trembling and panting—but, as his own pleasure built, he could see hers slipping away.

'Am I hurting you?' he asked, determined not to move until he was sure, clinging to the last threads of his control. 'You're so tight,' he managed as he struggled to hold off the urge to drive deeper.

He wasn't a small man, he knew that, which was why he was always careful. But with her maybe he hadn't been careful enough.

Shame washed over him as he waited, still lodged inside her, aware of her muscles contracting around him as she struggled to adjust.

'Look at me, Beatrice,' he demanded, his hand shaking as he cupped her cheek. 'Are you good?'

She met his gaze at last. 'Yes,' she said. But he didn't believe her entirely.

Her pupils had dilated to black, a sure sign of her arousal, but he could see the shock too. And feel the tension.

Moving his hand, he dragged it down her torso to locate the place where they joined, determined to bring her pleasure back. She jerked as he rubbed the hot nub.

'Shh,' he soothed, stroking, inciting, watching as her face began to relax. The tight clasp of her body softened as she relaxed enough to allow him to sink to the hilt.

He gave them both a moment to absorb the sweet shock, but he couldn't control the urge to move for long.

He rose up, adjusting her hips so his pelvis would rub her clitoris on each thrust. He heard her soft pants as the pleasure built again, flowing towards him in furious waves.

She clung to him, her fingers slipping on his shoulders, her panting breaths spurring him on as the coil at the base of his spine tightened, the exquisite sensations furious and raw.

He thrust harder, faster, and she matched his moves, riding into the storm with him.

The wave slammed into him just as her body clenched around his, the climax exploding through him and into her. He threw back his head, the shout one of fury and pleasure beyond bearing as the mind-blowing orgasm crashed over him. He rode the furious wave, pumping everything he was, everything he had into her as he felt her shatter too.

CHAPTER THREE

Wow.

Bea floated in a pool of bliss as Mason collapsed on top of her with his erection still firm, still huge inside her.

Her lungs heaved as she began to swim towards full consciousness—and she became more aware of all the places her body ached.

She felt… New. Different somehow. More sensual, more aware, braver, bolder. And more herself at last.

Or was that just the afterglow?

She focused on a pinprick of red light winking on the ceiling. Peering past Mason's muscular shoulder, she spotted a plane flying across the night sky before it disappeared, probably on its way to City Airport.

The inane observation dragged her the rest of the way out of her blissful bubble and into uncomfortable reality.

She gave Mason a soft shove, then flinched when he moved off her… Moved *out* of her. A moan escaped.

He rose over her, his expression difficult to decipher in the shadows, but she heard his uneasiness when he cradled her cheek.

'What's wrong? Did I hurt you?'

She shook her head, foolish tears stinging her eyelids. She covered his hand and dragged it away from her face, terrified by the emotion swelling in her throat.

It *had* hurt, a little bit, at first. She had no yardstick to measure him against, but she was pretty sure he was not your average guy. She guessed it stood to reason given his height. She'd actually been quite worried when she'd seen that prodigious erection in all its glory for the first time.

But he had been so careful with her, so attuned to her distress—something she really hadn't expected. Or been prepared for.

Just like she really hadn't been prepared for how overwhelming it would be, not just having him inside her, but having him give her another, even more powerful release as they'd strained to reach their release together.

Was that why her emotions felt so raw? So wobbly and tender. She'd waited such a long time to have sex, had convinced herself she might never even want it, so the intensity of the orgasms he'd given her had seemed significant. When they really weren't.

His shoulders relaxed and his forehead touched hers. 'Good,' he murmured.

She swallowed, far too aware of his concern for her.

He rolled away and sat on the edge of the bed.

Awareness spread as he stood with his back to her, holding his shorts, then crossed to a door on the other side of the room. She grabbed the sheet to cover herself—suddenly self-conscious—as he switched on the light in the adjoining room. She got a glimpse of a glass shower and quartz tiles—and an eyeful of his magnificent body, and the red marks on his shoulder blades where her nails had dug into his skin. A Celtic design etched across his lower back drew her gaze to his magnificent glutes—and had heat pooling in her abdomen—before he disappeared into the bathroom and shut the door.

She lay on the bed, listening to the water switch on and eventually off.

Her heartbeat was threatening to choke her by the time he finally reappeared—which seemed to take hours.

Thank goodness he had put his boxers on, although she could still make out the outline of his sex—which looked, if not fully erect, then certainly not limp either.

Goodness, was he already interested in doing it again?

He cleared his throat. 'Up here, Beatrice.' Her gaze shot to his face.

His wry tone was belied by the frown on his face. The guilty blush—because he had caught her staring at his crotch—bloomed across her collarbone and flooded her cheeks.

She tried to concentrate on his frown and interpret it as he perched on the bed next to her.

Had he been expecting her to get dressed and leave while he was in the bathroom? She had no idea what the etiquette was for a one-night stand, a hook-up. She sat up abruptly, clasping the sheet to her breasts. Why hadn't she made her getaway while he was showering? Now she looked as clueless and unsophisticated as she actually was.

Time to find her panties and scram.

'I should probably make a move,' she murmured. But as she scooted away from him, he snagged her upper arm.

'Not so fast, Beatrice. I have a question.'

'Oh? Okay,' she said, trying to sound nonchalant, not easy when her face had to be glowing brightly enough to be seen from space and he could probably feel her shaking. 'What…what question?'

'Why didn't you tell me you were a virgin?'

'How did you know?' she blurted out.

Then wanted to slap herself when his gaze sharpened. Why hadn't she lied, played dumb?

She felt so exposed now, the sheet doing nothing to hide the blush, which had exploded.

'I guessed,' he said, letting go of her arm. 'So, it's true. I'm the first guy you've ever slept with.'

She wanted desperately to lie, but how could she when she'd totally outed herself already? Anyway, wouldn't lying make her seem even more unsophisticated?

'Well...yes. But it's really not a big deal,' she said, although of course it was.

Awkward, much. Could she actually seem more clueless and immature?

'Why me?' he asked, his voice gentle but his gaze acute.

'I just... I just wasn't ready before. But with you...' She hesitated.

If only she knew what he was thinking. Was he annoyed? Freaked out? Embarrassed for her? Did he think the fact she'd waited so long, to then do it with a man she barely knew was sad, or funny, or simply pathetic?

It was impossible to tell, because his expression was completely unreadable.

'But with me... What?' he prompted.

She turned away from his probing gaze. The stunning view of the Docklands—laid out before them like a carpet of wonders—did nothing to make her feel any less silly and insignificant.

He took her chin in his hand to turn her face to his.

'Out with it, Beatrice. I want to know why you didn't sleep with the guy you were engaged to, but you slept with me.'

She heard it then, the edge in his voice.

Why was he so interested in her engagement to Jack Wolfe, when it felt about a million years ago now?

Although she supposed he did have a point. She wasn't sure she had an answer for him though. Not a coherent one anyway, because she didn't really know *why* she'd been so eager to leap into his arms this evening—when she'd never been reckless or impulsive or even turned on really, by Jack or any other guy, until now.

If only she knew why Mason looked so wary and tense.

He'd stopped calling her Princess. Even though she'd disliked the nickname at first, she missed it now. Because it had seemed light and teasing and affectionate, even if he had been mocking her. And for a moment it had made her feel like his equal.

She stared at her hands, the knuckles whitening as she clutched the sheet.

She'd never felt more powerless in her life. And that was saying quite a lot, considering she'd been under her father's thumb for most of it.

She shrugged, but the movement felt brittle and stiff. 'I guess with you I felt safe.'

Which sounded ludicrous when she said it out loud. But he didn't laugh at her, which was something.

'And really turned on,' she continued.

If she was going to tell him the truth she might as well tell him the whole truth, even if the blush rising up her neck was liable to set fire to her cheeks any second. 'There's a reason they called me the Ice Queen. And that's the reason, right there.'

His frown became a fissure. 'I don't get it—what reason?'

'I'm basically frigid.' She pushed the words out.

But, instead of agreeing with her, his dark brows rose,

and then he laughed. 'Hell, Beatrice, I don't know who told you that...or who *they* are...' His gaze skated over her, making her skin prickle. 'But they're wrong. I've never met anyone hotter or more responsive.'

'Really?' she said, stupidly pleased with his verdict, even though it made her look like even more of a fool.

He cupped her cheek, clasped her neck to pull her towards him, then dropped his forehead to hers. She could hear him breathing. Feel the tension in him rising as her own body melted in response. That delicious, provocative, exciting tension which they'd released together so spectacularly less than ten minutes ago.

'Yeah, really,' he muttered, then he kissed her.

The kiss was gentle but also possessive. Her heart thundered, the relief making her light-headed.

Whatever had just happened, he didn't despise her and he wasn't angry with her...

He broke off the kiss, but his thumb continued to stroke the pulse hammering against her collarbone, making her aware of the heat pooling between her thighs, but also the discomfort.

'I'm honoured that you chose me,' he said, surprising her not just with the blunt statement, but also the way it made the ache in her ribs increase. 'Would you like to stay tonight?'

She nodded because she was finding it hard to speak.

She was unbearably touched by his candid admission, especially as she suspected he wasn't a man who revealed his feelings easily. Or would admit to being honoured very often.

'Do you want to grab a shower?' he asked.

She nodded again. He found a robe in the wardrobe, which dwarfed her when she put it on. But she was grateful for the chance to cover her nakedness, feeling self-conscious again as she darted into the bathroom.

She took her time—trying not to think about the way her heart was all but choking her.

His reaction wasn't what she'd expected. At all. He'd been perceptive and understanding when she had expected him to be appalled—making her glad she'd chosen to trust him with her first time.

When she returned to the bedroom he was stretched out on the bed, looking hot and delicious and... Her gaze snagged on the pronounced ridge in his boxer shorts. *Dangerous.*

'I'm not sure I can do it again tonight,' she admitted, even as the heat surged. 'I'm a bit sore.'

He chuckled, the rough sound alluring.

'Don't worry. We're gonna have to take a rain-check anyway because we have a situation with the condoms. How about I just hold you? You might want to grab a T-shirt from the dresser, though, to stop me getting any ideas.'

'I'd like that.' She grinned, his thoughtfulness making the emotion swell again.

After finding an oversized T-shirt which covered all the essential bits, she climbed onto the bed and he tugged her into his arms. Her body relaxed into the warmth of his and she inhaled the delicious scent of pine soap. But then her mind snagged on something he'd said.

'What's the situation with the condoms?'

His fingers, which were stroking her arm and setting off all kinds of interesting sensations, stopped. He cleared his throat. And she glanced round to find him staring at her.

'Turns out they're older than I thought. You're the first woman I've brought here in...' He shifted slightly, and if she knew him better she might have thought he seemed embarrassed. 'Well, ever, actually. I guess I must have stashed them in the drawer four years ago when I moved in.'

She folded her arms across her chest, rather enjoying his discomfort. After all, didn't they say turnaround was fair play?

'Four years?'

She was the first woman he'd brought here? Why did that feel so significant, and flattering?

'I should have checked the date on them, but I was too desperate to have you...'

She grinned. She couldn't help it—this was getting better and better.

'Okay, well, I guess if we're going to do this again...' She paused, realising she really, *really* wanted to. With him.

They didn't have a future together. They were far too different and she was about to leave the kind of social circles he moved in. Plus, his wealth would be a barrier to the new life she wanted to establish for herself—as an independent, self-sufficient woman. But having just discovered she had a libido, she didn't want to bury it again yet.

'You'll have to buy some new ones,' she finished. 'Or I could?'

'So, you're not on any form of birth control?' he asked, his expression becoming pained.

'Not yet. No.'

'Crap,' he murmured. 'Okay, then we do have a bigger problem. The condom we just used burst.'

Embarrassment flooded her cheeks and she lifted off his chest. Of course, that was what he'd been alluding to. Exactly how stupid was she that she hadn't figured it out sooner?

'It's okay, Beatrice.' He sat up abruptly and grasped her arm. 'Don't panic. Where are you in your cycle?'

She tried to focus on the question, not easy with the crippling embarrassment. 'I had my last period about three weeks ago.'

'That's good,' he said, trying to be reassuring, while all sorts of eventualities were charging into her head now... None of them good.

How could she not have protected herself? Good grief, she hadn't even thought about contraception until he'd produced a condom—a faulty, out-of-date condom.

'You're not right in the middle of your cycle, at least,' he added.

'No, but I could still get pregnant. That's a bit of a myth. Unless one of us is infertile.' Although she could not imagine Mason Foxx firing blanks, and she suspected she was unlikely to be infertile either.

After all, hadn't Katie fallen pregnant after her first encounter with Jack Wolfe? It was why her sister and Jack had had a shotgun wedding only a few months after Bea had broken off her engagement to him.

Of course, Jack and Katie were blissfully happy together now. But it had been really tough for them for a while. And Katie had the kind of guts and fortitude Bea could only dream of. Plus, she couldn't imagine Mason Foxx being happy about becoming an accidental father after a one-night booty call.

But instead of looking worried, he smiled. Was this funny? Because it didn't feel very funny.

'Yeah, I guess it is a myth,' he said. 'But I'm a firm believer in not panicking until there's actually something to panic about. I'll make you an appointment with my doctor tomorrow and we can check out our options, just in case...'

'But what if...?'

He placed his finger over her lips. 'Don't get spooked again, Princess,' he said.

The return of the affectionate nickname soothed her anxiety, a bit.

'We can't figure out anything until morning,' he added. 'But then we can take whatever precautions we need to make sure this is not a problem.'

His calmness, and the way he said *we*—making it clear, however reckless they had been, they were in this together—helped her to relax more.

'Come here,' he said, propping himself against the pillows and dragging her back into his arms.

She allowed herself to be held, the rollercoaster of emotion she'd been on all night catching up with her in a rush.

She guessed that was what losing your virginity, having two titanic orgasms when you thought you were frigid, then discovering you could be accidentally pregnant could do to you…

'We'll figure it out tomorrow, okay? I swear,' he said, his voice forceful and so reassuring it made her heart hurt.

Of course, they had options. Lots of options. This didn't have to be a catastrophe.

She nodded against his chest. She shouldn't rely on him too much. But, just for tonight, would it be so wrong to bow to his pragmatism? To let him take charge?

'Now, go to sleep, you're exhausted,' he added.

'I know…' she said, cracking a huge yawn. 'You exhausted me.'

She closed her eyes, feeling at least a little bit kickass again when his rough chuckle lured her to sleep.

CHAPTER FOUR

MASON SPRINTED UP the building's back staircase in his running gear, his headphones blaring out a favourite R&B classic and the fresh pastries he'd bought at the bakery round the corner slung under his arm.

But despite the three-mile run he'd taken all the way to the London Eye and back along the Embarkment, endorphins were still rioting through his system. Because one of the most captivating women he'd ever met was lying in his bed, waiting for him—after a night of insanely good sex.

Insanely good, even though she had been a virgin. He slowed to a jog as he reached the top floor, then shoved open the fire door with his shoulder—still not one hundred percent sure how he felt about that.

When he'd first figured out the truth in the bathroom, while also discovering the condom he'd used wasn't fit for purpose, he'd been stunned.

Why would a woman like Beatrice—classy, beautiful and more sensitive than he'd first realised—choose a man like him? He was hardly known for his sensitivity. Nor did he have a great track record when it came to relationships.

He wasn't a guy who had ever worn his heart on his sleeve. If he even had a heart any more...

He'd jettisoned the need for love a long time ago—and he didn't regret it. Because it had made him tougher and more resilient. His emotional self-sufficiency, the ability to trust in his own judgement, had helped him to build a multi-billion-pound global hospitality brand in the space of a decade.

But when she'd blurted out the truth, confirming his suspicions about her lack of experience, instead of being annoyed, or wary, or freaked out, what had surged up his torso had felt a lot like pride. It was the same feeling of validation he remembered from the day he'd signed the lease on his first property—a crumbling bedsit in Hoxton which he'd rehabbed himself over one long hot summer and turned into his first boutique hotel—at the age of twenty-one.

He'd never quite managed to replicate that spurt of fierce joy and pride in his accomplishments—until he'd woken up this morning, with Beatrice curled around him, fast asleep, wearing one of his old T-shirts. Her breath had feathered his collarbone, her scent—vanilla and female arousal—had filled his lungs and his body had been raring to go again in seconds.

Hence the need for a three-mile run.

He didn't know why she'd trusted him with something so precious, but he was glad she had. It had stunned him, but it had also humbled him...in a way he hadn't been humbled in a long time. And while he was still grappling with the fallout from her decision—and why it had affected him so deeply—one thing he was sure of. He didn't want to let her go. Not yet.

He took a deep breath and ignored the constriction in his chest.

Okay, Foxx, get real. This is just about the insanely good sex—and your gargantuan ego.

If he didn't do love, he sure as hell didn't do love after one night.

He walked into the apartment's open-plan living space

and took a moment to admire the way the spring sunshine gleamed off the expensive furniture a world-class interior designer had spent a fortune selecting for him and sparkled on the water outside.

As the mighty Thames snaked through the magnificent view, the light feeling in his chest refused to subside.

He had a good life. A great life. A life he'd spent seventeen years working like a dog to create for himself. But until last night, when Beatrice had fallen asleep in his arms and that odd feeling of possessiveness had settled into his gut, it had never even occurred to him there could be more. That maybe he'd spent so much of his life striving to achieve the next milestone on his journey to world domination of the hospitality industry, he'd never taken the time to create something which couldn't be bought and paid for.

Until last night, he had never valued anything he couldn't put a price on. But her trust in him meant something. Even if he wasn't entirely sure what.

He placed the fresh pastries on a plate and walked to the main bedroom to check on her. Her slight shape lay curled under the duvet on the far side of his bed—had she even moved? Boy, he really had exhausted her last night.

His ribs tightened again, even as his heartbeat plunged into his shorts.

He headed to the guest bedroom to shower and change so he wouldn't wake her. After washing away the sweat from his run, he switched the dial to frigid to get himself under control.

She was going to be sore this morning. Which meant there was going to be no repeat performance, however much he might want one. But his disappointment—at the thought he was going to have to wait to make love to her again—faded at the thought of getting the chance to talk to her.

Because there were so many things he wanted to know about her.

She'd been more candid than he'd expected about her engagement to Wolfe. He could admit now he had been wildly jealous of that previous attachment—another new experience for him. But the green-eyed monster had died as soon as he'd discovered she'd never let Wolfe make love to her.

He grinned. *Neanderthal, or what?*

After tugging on a pair of sweats and a T-shirt, he grabbed his work mobile off the chest of drawers, to discover numerous messages from his PA Joe McCarthy and more from Jackson White, the head of the PR company he used to manage the Foxx Group's public profile. After a cursory glance, he clicked through to a tabloid article attached to one of Jackson's messages—and winced at the cheesy headline: *Has Hotel Hottie Foxx Melted the Medford Ice Queen?*

Then he enlarged the shot of him and Beatrice leaving the club the night before which illustrated the piece. He chuckled, because apparently nothing was going to sour his good mood this morning.

Not bad, he decided. They looked good together, with her cradled in his arms as if she belonged there. Jackson had attached the screenshot of the article to a message which simply read:

WTH Mace?! We need to talk about your new girlfriend.

Cheeky sod.

But then he and Jackson went way back, to the early days.

He'd catch up with him later today because Beatrice wasn't his girlfriend. *Yet.* But Jackson's question had him picturing her on his arm for the social events he usually found a major chore. His heart bobbed in his chest at the realisation she would make those boring events a lot more entertaining. The fact that her classy beauty would not do the Foxx brand any harm at all was not lost on him either.

Getting way ahead of yourself again, bro.

He dialled his PA, because before he and Beatrice had a conversation about their future he needed to make her an appointment with his doctor as he'd promised.

As he waited for Joe to pick up—because it was still only seven a.m. on a Saturday—he realised he was surprisingly ambivalent about the possibility of an unplanned pregnancy. Of course, they had a lot of options if his condom *faux pas* led to that. But even after he'd discovered the tear in the condom last night—something which would have bothered him big time with any of the other women he'd dated—the panic hadn't come.

Children weren't on his radar. Never had been. He really wasn't the paternal type. What did he even know about family, or being a dad, when his mum had done a runner when he was still little more than a baby and his old man had been such a loser? But when he'd confronted Beatrice with the problem and she'd panicked, he'd been surprisingly calm—and weirdly turned on—because he couldn't quite get past the delicious thought of Beatrice's slender body round with his child.

He closed his eyes briefly as a renewed surge of desire fired through his system.

'Hey Mason.' Joe picked up at last. 'How are you? I didn't expect to hear from you this morning. Especially after who you pulled last night.' Joe let out a wry laugh, because he was also a mate. 'How was the Medford Ice Queen? Not too chilly, I hope,' he added, still with that teasing tone.

Mason frowned, not liking it, or the nickname which

couldn't have been further from the truth. And which he had begun to suspect had left Beatrice with a ton of hang-ups.

'Don't call her that, Joe.'

'All right. No problem, bro,' Joe replied, the jokey tone sobering.

'Actually, I need you to contact Dr Lee. Make an appointment for Beatrice today. Out of hours.'

He trusted the people he employed to keep his business confidential. But after last night's headlines he needed to protect Beatrice from any more unwanted attention while they were figuring out their relationship. Perhaps he could persuade her to fly with him to New York tomorrow night? On Monday he was due to start scoping out sites for the Foxx Group to expand into the US, so he could totally make the case for it business-wise. And it would give them a chance to get away from the British media and have a time out to talk about last night. And what they wanted to happen next. He'd never considered having a mistress because he thought the whole concept was tacky and old-fashioned, but he could totally get behind the idea of having Beatrice at his beck and call for a while.

'Okay,' Joe said. 'Can I tell Dr Lee what it's about?'

Mason hesitated. 'Just a standard check-up,' he prevaricated. Then wondered why he was prevaricating. There was nothing wrong with taking responsibility for the burst condom. 'Plus, we need to discuss birth control options. And get Beatrice a pregnancy test.'

Joe gasped, then cursed. 'So you *did* thaw out the Ice Queen. That's fast work, even for you.'

'I thought I told you not to call her that,' Mason said, annoyed.

'Yeah, but… Mase…' Joe sounded concerned, which

seemed like a massive overreaction. 'Are you sure you want to date her for real?'

'What's that supposed to mean?' he asked, his happy buzz turning into genuine irritation. Did everyone have an opinion on his sex life? And Beatrice's. No wonder she had so many hang-ups.

'You do know her old man has targeted you as a possible son-in-law?'

'What?' he murmured, irritation turning to shock as the happy buzz he'd woken up with imploded.

'Medford. It's not that big a secret he's been looking to hook his youngest daughter up with an advantageous match for years. It's why she was engaged to Wolfe a while back. Rumour is Wolfe lent him a ton of money, then swallowed the loss when he got hitched to the older sister and broke it off with Beatrice. She does what her old man wants, unlike Katherine.'

Mason sank down onto the edge of the bed, his knees too shaky to hold him. So many thoughts and feelings were bombarding him he couldn't seem to differentiate any of them. Except the hole opening up in the pit of his stomach, which he remembered from when he was a kid.

He cut off the memories.

Not going there. Not ever. That was ancient history. He'd been a skinny boy back then, still kidding himself his mum would come back one day and his dad wasn't a bad guy, just a man with an addiction he couldn't control.

But he wasn't that gullible, stupid kid any more, had stopped being him when he'd left that life behind.

He thrust his fingers through his hair, appalled to realise his hand was shaking. He clenched his fingers into a fist to stop the pathetic reaction. And noticed the phoenix in flight he'd had inked onto the back of his hand when he was fourteen years old. The night he'd promised never to let anyone use him again.

'What makes you think Medford has *me* targeted as a possible son-in-law?' he asked, surprised his voice was steady when his stomach was so jumpy he felt nauseous.

Was that why she had chosen him? To take her virginity. It had never been about him, or the livewire sexual connection he had thought was genuine… She had never really been into him. She'd been told to come on to him by her old man.

'Just stuff I've heard in the last few days,' Joe said, sounding increasingly uncomfortable. 'When I saw the pictures online last night, of you and her leaving the Cascade launch, I figured you knew. That you were playing her.'

So last night had been a big fat lie that he'd fallen for. Enough to be all bright-eyed and bushy-tailed this morning at the thought of dating her. Of making her his.

'I'm not that desperate to get laid, Joe,' he said, but he could hear the bitterness in his own voice. And the shame.

Because he was exactly that desperate. Or why would he have fallen for her act so easily? He'd even told her he had been honoured she'd chosen him to be her first, like some romantic fool. Instead of a man who had always known the score. That women like her thought they were above guys like him.

Which was really ironic. Because, for all her airs and graces and that plummy accent, she was no better than the women who used to leave their calling cards in the broken phone boxes around Bermondsey when he was a boy. The big difference being those women hadn't had a choice. Had been driven by desperation, poverty, coercion and/or addiction. He'd always had sympathy for them. He had no sympathy for Beatrice Medford, though. Because she hadn't been forced to play him last night. She probably thought she was better than those working girls too, except she wasn't. Because she wasn't desperate, she was just spoilt and entitled. And greedy.

'Right. Well, thanks for letting me know,' Mason murmured.

'You still want me to make that appointment with Dr Lee?'

He frowned. And swore softly.

Hell, she could be pregnant. Had she planned that too? Maybe not. After all, he was the one who had supplied the faulty condom. But she hadn't even mentioned birth control. Her panic last night must have been an act too, he decided. Because surely a pregnancy would fit right in with her father's get-your-hooks-into-Mason agenda.

And if she were pregnant he would be stuck with her, because one thing he would never do was desert his own flesh and blood, the way his mother had.

'Yes,' he said, thrusting his fingers through his hair, his anger at her and himself—for being such a chump—starting to consume him. 'But tell Lee I'll want her to persuade Ms Medford to agree to a pregnancy test ASAP.'

If there were consequences, he would deal with them. His way.

He ended the call with Joe, then sat staring at the view he'd been so proud of five minutes ago—the view which had assured him he had finally arrived, and had become the man he had always wanted to be. Not just successful, but worthy of success.

The view which now looked flat and dull and ostentatious.

Because he'd just been taken for a colossal mug. By Beatrice *and* her old man.

But even as he nursed his resentment and nurtured his fury—so he could fill up the hole in his gut—an empty space remained.

Reminding him there was still some of that dumb kid inside him—the kid who could be hurt. The kid he thought he'd killed a lifetime ago. The little boy who had waited for his mum to return for months, until he'd finally wised up and realised she was never coming back. But somehow Beatrice Medford had found that kid and exploited him.

'Hi, Mason, are you here?' her voice called from the living room, shy and unsure.

He forced himself to get off the bed.

He spotted her standing by the coffee machine as he walked into the living area. And had to brace against the visceral jolt of heat. How could he still want her? When she had played him so comprehensively.

But when she swung round and he saw the vivid blush slashing across her cheeks and the shy smile lifting lips still red from last night's kisses, he knew exactly why. Wearing nothing but the old T-shirt which skimmed her thighs and showed off her mile-long legs to perfection, her hair a mess of unruly curls and her ragged breathing drawing his gaze to the way her unfettered breasts peaked beneath the worn cotton, she looked so fresh and appealing and guileless his mouth watered.

Cynical fury twisted inside him as he rode the wave of want. Because it was fake.

Or mostly fake. Their livewire connection had been real, because she sure as hell hadn't faked those orgasms. But she had also bartered her virginity and risked a pregnancy to hook him.

Somehow, though, as the fury engulfed him, the possibility didn't seem like a total disaster any more. Maybe there would be benefits from having Beatrice Medford on his arm for a price. At least he wouldn't have to deal with all the hearts and flowers nonsense.

On his arm she could give him a class he'd always secretly yearned for. And while he'd never seriously considered becoming a father, he had thought vaguely about his legacy. And about one day, in the distant future, passing it on.

If that time turned out to be now, who better to spruce up his bloodline than the daughter of a lord?

And, best of all, he'd be in control. Because he had something she and her father needed. Money. And now he knew the truth about her, she wouldn't be able to dynamite that stupid kid out of hiding a second time.

'Good morning, Princess,' he said, careful to keep the edge out of his voice as he climbed onto a stool at the breakfast bar. The endearment which had been a joke last night wasn't really a joke any more, though.

He sent her one of his fake smiles, the kind he used when he wanted to lull the competition into thinking he was all charm and no substance.

'How you doing this morning?' he asked, pouring on the bad-boy-made-good schtick, even though he felt empty inside.

So what if their relationship would be just another transaction? All that mattered now was that, like all the other deals he'd made in his life, he came out on top.

'Good, thank you,' Bea said politely as she noticed the tattoo which roped around Mason's biceps and flexed under the short sleeve of his T-shirt. And tried not to notice the wobble in her stomach, which had been getting worse ever since she'd woken up in his bed, feeling warm and languid and well-rested.

That would be the wobble which had just gone into over-drive when he had strolled towards her in jogging bottoms and a T-shirt, with his feet bare and his damp hair raked into haphazard rows.

In the daylight, the expensive, starkly modern apartment and the devastating view of Tower Bridge looked even more intimidating... But nowhere near as intimidating as the man himself—her lover—in his natural habitat.

She took a careful breath, aware of his glittering green gaze roaming over her face... Except... What had happened to the warmth from last night? Why did the look in his eyes suddenly seem a little impatient?

Perhaps he hadn't expected her to still be here? Should she have left already? Unfortunately, she knew even less about morning-after etiquette than she did about one-night stand etiquette.

But something was definitely off. Because the Princess endearment seemed less like an endearment now too. And she was sure she could detect the sparkle of resentment in his gaze.

But perhaps that was just her insecurity? The insecurity which had stopped her living her best life—or any life at all really—for so long.

She forced herself to smile and crossed her arms over her chest. She wished she had found something less revealing to wear before she'd walked out here in search of coffee... And him. But it was too late to stress about that.

Things had become far too heavy last night, thanks to her virginity and his busted condom. But she didn't want to appear anxious or nervous, or as if she was expecting some kind of commitment. Because she really wasn't.

He probably already thought she was clueless and gauche and over-sensitive. So she needed to bring her A-game now and create a much better impression. She wanted to appear smart and empowered and worldly—and not as if her emotions were all over the place, even if they were.

But for that, she definitely needed coffee.

She turned her attention to his state-of-the-art espresso machine. 'I'm afraid I may need a degree in nuclear physics to figure out how to work this.'

'I'll do it,' he said. 'I guess you're not used to making your own coffee.'

She heard the note of judgement, but was certain that *had* to be her projecting.

He joined her by the machine, but as she stepped aside to give him room—far too aware of his scent—he gave a rough chuckle.

'Why so jumpy, Princess?' he asked.

She glanced at him, the heat exploding in her cheeks—because she'd definitely heard an edge this time, as if he found her nervous reaction vaguely pathetic.

'I'm… I'm not,' she stuttered, as the wobble stamped around in her stomach like a jumping bean wearing hobnailed boots.

'Sure you are,' he said with a certainty which made her feel embarrassed about her lie. 'How about we try this?' he added, then leaned back against the countertop. Placing a hand on her waist, he tugged her between his outstretched thighs.

She braced her hands on his chest. Her gaze was level with the tantalising ring of barbed wire on his collarbone, her lungs full of the smell of him, fresh from the shower— sandalwood and pine soap. But while his scent had been intoxicating the night before, it bothered her that she couldn't control her reaction to it. Not just the surge of endorphins, but also the nerves playing havoc with the booted jumping bean in her belly.

He lifted her chin, forcing her to meet that assessing, pragmatic gaze. He placed a kiss on her nose, the gesture just casual enough to be condescending.

'There's no need to be nervous. I'm happy to take a rain check before round two, Princess.'

She stiffened. She wished he would stop calling her that. She didn't like it any more. Because the nickname seemed to be loaded with the brittle cynicism she'd noticed when he'd first stepped into her path at the club, but had convinced herself had never been aimed at her. Now she was a lot less sure.

'What makes you think round two is a foregone conclusion?' she murmured, finally getting up the courage to assert herself, at least a little bit.

'Yeah? Why wouldn't it be?' The penetrating gaze skated over her—kicking off those blasted endorphins again—but she didn't feel confident and empowered any more, she felt hopelessly exposed... And unfairly judged. 'Is it because I haven't proposed marriage yet?' he added, his voice thick with derision now. 'Or because you need to let Daddy know you've got me on the hook first before you put out again?'

Her jaw dropped as she lurched out of his arms, not sure she'd heard him correctly. Or understood what he was implying.

'I'm sorry, what did you say?' she managed to murmur around the boulder in her throat.

He laughed again, but the caustic chuckle held no humour at all.

'Come on, Princess, you can drop the act now. I know why the Medford Ice Queen deigned to jump me last night. The virginity was a nice touch, by the way—cute and original. And I'll admit the condom was my bad, although I'm sure we can figure out a way to make any consequences work for both of us. But I'm not as dumb as you seem to think I am. Nor am I as gullible or as easily impressed as Jack Wolfe.'

She stumbled back another step, so horrified she couldn't breathe, couldn't even really process what he had just said. There were so many unfair and unjust accusations to unpick, she couldn't seem to grasp hold of any of them.

But what was far worse was the way he was looking at her... As if she were...*nothing*. Because the cruel resentment and the rigid fury in his gaze threw her back to that terrible night when her father had ranted and raved and thrown Katie out of the house. Then turned to her and told her to stop whimpering and get out of his sight.

And she'd done exactly what he'd told her.

But Mason's ruthless demolition of her confidence was so much worse because, instead of shouting or screaming, he looked so calm, so cold, so confident. And, unlike her father, who had never been able to control his temper, Mason knew exactly how much damage he was doing.

'Okay,' she said calmly, without any clue as to why she was so calm when he had just sliced apart her self-esteem in a few scalpel-sharp strokes like a surgeon extracting a donor's heart, each cut deeper and more efficient than the last.

But this was no bloodless evisceration, she realised as soon as she managed to gather enough oxygen for her lungs to start functioning again, because the injury felt all too real.

She walked into the bedroom on autopilot. After discarding his T-shirt, she found her dress and yanked it on, then located her shoes, all as the suffocating memories from that night so long ago—and from last night—pressed down on the gaping wound in her chest.

The only thing that mattered now was getting out of here before the pain became too debilitating.

'I should go,' she said, again with perfect politeness, as she crossed the living room.

He stood by the counter, staring at her as if she had lost her mind. But it was a sign of how far gone she was that his cynical frown seemed like a win compared to the blank indifference of moments before.

'So, you're going to sulk now? Because I figured out your little act?' he asked.

She didn't reply, because it took all her strength to keep putting one foot in front of the other. Once she got out of the loft apartment she dashed to the emergency stairs, knowing she couldn't wait for the lift in case he followed her.

She had to hold it together, had to get out.

But as she scrambled down the stairwell she couldn't hold back the indescribable pain any longer. Or the silent, self-pitying tears, so reminiscent of the night when she had watched her sister being evicted from her life... And done nothing.

She scrubbed her cheeks, sucking in jerky breaths, the vague thought circling around and around in her head that these tears were just as futile and pointless and cowardly now as they had been when she was twelve. When her world had fallen apart the first time.

CHAPTER FIVE

'HELLO, MRS GOULDING, is my sister at home?' Bea bit into her lip, determined to hold back the crying jag which had demolished her during the cab journey from Tower Bridge to Katie and Jack's house in Mayfair.

Clare Goulding, her sister's housekeeper, was a professional, so her expression barely changed as she took in Bea's bedraggled appearance. But Bea could see the pity in the older woman's eyes when she replied.

'Why, yes. Mr and Mrs Wolfe are in the dining room having breakfast with Luca. Do come in.' She held the door wide, not asking for an explanation. 'I'll let them know you're here.'

'Thank you, but could I borrow some money first to pay the cab driver who brought me here?' Shame washed over her at the thought of the cabbie she had begged a lift.

'I'll handle it, Miss Beatrice,' the housekeeper said. 'Don't worry.'

Guilt twisted in Bea's stomach, adding to the wave of humiliation which had been building ever since she had run out of Mason Foxx's penthouse loft half an hour ago.

Panic had assailed her in the cab, finally drying the futile tears as she'd realised she couldn't return to her father's house or everything Mason had accused her of would be true.

Maybe she had been driven by an attraction, an excitement which had been totally real to her as Mason had kissed and caressed and eventually possessed her last night. But how could she claim to be her own woman, able to make her own decisions, when sleeping with Mason had also been what her father wanted?

She wanted to hate Mason for pretending to care about her, even a little bit, the night before. Because it had brought back all the old yearnings—to matter to someone, to be special and cherished, the way she could vaguely remember her Welsh granny had once cherished her… But did she really have the right to be angry that Mason wasn't who he had pretended to be when she wasn't either? And, frankly, what had she ever done to deserve to be cherished by anyone, anyhow?

Mason Foxx had just said this morning what everyone else already knew but were too polite to say. She was a parasite.

'I'm sure Mr and Mrs Wolfe will be overjoyed to see you,' the housekeeper added, scooping up her purse from the side table. She headed out to pay for Bea's cab.

Will they? Why?

Bea stood dumbly in the lobby, wanting desperately to run down the hall and recount all the cruel things Mason Foxx had said and done, then cry on Katie's shoulder and let her big sister make it all better somehow.

As she had done so many times before.

Because whenever Bea had screwed up, whenever she needed a respite from their father's demands and ultimatums, or whenever she just needed a fix of her adorable nephew Luca, she would rush over here and let Katie comfort and console her and make her feel better about herself and her refusal to do anything concrete to change her life.

How would this time really be any different?

The sound of Luca's giggles, followed by the rumble of Jack's deep voice and her sister's laughter filtered from the room down the hall. Yearning ripped through Bea's chest, but right behind it was disgust, with herself and her self-ishness.

She should not have come here.

Jack and Katie both had busy careers which made their quality time with their son Luca incredibly precious. Not only that, but Katie was in the first trimester of her second pregnancy, and Bea knew her sister was suffering again from morning sickness. She would never turn Bea away. But what right did Bea have to add to her sister's responsibilities, to ask her to fix another of the stupid mistakes Bea had made, when all Bea's problems were entirely of her own making?

Seeing Katie's gym bag beside the hall table, she grabbed it.

She needed a change of clothing, and while Katie and she were hardly the same shape, they *were* the same shoe size. She scribbled out a note on the pad in the hall, apologising for borrowing the clothes and promising to pay Katie back. Then she forced herself to add the sentence she should have written years ago.

I've decided to leave London. Thank you for all your support over the years, but I've finally got this now. Love B x

Maybe if she wrote it down, she could begin to believe it.

She could still hear Jack's and Katie's voices, and their son Luca giggling, as she headed out of the house, her guilt and humiliation joined by misery and panic.

A part of her knew the reason she wanted to leave London and disappear wasn't just because she couldn't continue to lean on her sister, but also because Mason Foxx lived here.

Strike two to Bea the coward!

The hope, the bubble of confidence, the excitement and exhilaration at her own boldness last night, had never been anything other than desire. She understood that now. Mason hadn't needed to be so cruel. But she was the one who had wilfully believed a fairy tale. She was the one who had let him hurt her—because she had once again been looking to someone else to give her life substance and meaning.

Her heart tore in her chest as she walked down the front steps, leaving the only people who really cared about her behind.

Mrs Goulding was still chatting to the cab driver at the end of the driveway as Bea slipped through the garden gate unseen. She headed down the mews behind the palatial Georgian townhouse. The beautifully appointed home where her sister had made a life for herself with Jack Wolfe—through hard work, honesty, integrity, courage, perseverance and an independent spirit Bea had always lacked.

She took off her heels and slipped on her sister's gym shoes and her sweatshirt over the revealing dress. It was only a couple of miles to the bank where she had an account containing the small inheritance her mother had left her, as well as a safety deposit box with the Irish passport she'd been able to apply for a year ago—thanks to an Irish grandfather—with some fanciful notion of one day using her language skills to start a new life in Europe. One of the many, many things she'd never had the courage to actually do.

The bank was open until noon on a Saturday.

She broke into a run, adrenaline helping to cover the fear clawing at her throat.

She wasn't brave or smart or determined like her sister. She had always been pathetic and insecure and indecisive. But if she was ever going to turn herself into someone she could be proud of, she had to begin somewhere. And hitting rock bottom for the second time in her life felt like the perfect place to start.

Two days later

'Mr Foxx, there's a Katherine Wolfe here to see you. She doesn't have an appointment but she's quite insistent.'

'Send her up. And hold my calls,' Mason said to the receptionist, then shoved his phone into his back pocket. He strode through the suite of rooms that he kept at his flagship hotel in Belgravia and used as a London base for his business.

He'd spent two days trying to track Beatrice Medford down after she'd run out of his loft. He would have preferred to hear from her, but her sister would have to do. For now.

The fury, though, which had been building all weekend, tightened its stranglehold on his throat. He forced himself to breathe through it.

Don't let her see you give a damn. That's the only way to deal with these people.

But what the hell was Beatrice playing at? And where had she gone? Because her father didn't even know.

The old bastard had shown up at the Foxx Grand in Belgravia on Sunday morning, after Mason had been forced to contact him in an attempt to locate his daughter. Medford had been all obsequious smiles and bonhomie, believing Mason and his daughter were now an item. It had taken

Mason about ten seconds to realise Medford had no idea where she was. And once Mason had told him he hadn't seen her since Saturday morning, the old man's pale blue eyes had filled with irritation—but no sign of affection or concern.

It had given Mason pause.

But the moment of hesitation—about the way he'd spoken to her—was swiftly quashed.

She'd obviously gone off in a huff. Because Mason had figured out the truth. Perhaps she hadn't been home yet because she didn't want to break the bad news to her old man that there would be no marriage proposal from their latest billionaire mark—but there might be an unplanned pregnancy. Unfortunately, that didn't alter the fact she could even now be carrying his child, which meant he needed to find her. Pronto.

He paced in front of the lift, waiting for her sister to appear.

He was going to give Beatrice hell when he finally located her—for putting him in the untenable position of having to contact Jack Wolfe's wife to ask her where her sister was, like a lovesick fool. Instead of a man who lived up to his responsibilities.

He dismissed the memory of her face, the pale skin pallid with shock, her huge blue eyes sheened with distress while she shot out of his apartment as if her feet were on fire.

A memory which had resurfaced at regular intervals since Saturday morning. But which he refused to dwell on.

If she hadn't wanted him to call her out, she shouldn't have come on to him in the first place. And made him think she had given him something precious, when her virginity had just been another bargaining tool.

The lift bell pinged, but as the doors slid open he found

himself straightening, taken aback by the fierce look in Katherine Wolfe's eyes as she marched out.

'Mason Foxx, I presume,' she remarked with enough derision to be insulting. 'You bastard. Where is my sister?' she demanded, her glare hot enough to melt lead.

'I don't know,' he replied, raising his voice to match hers.

Unlike her father, though, who had been indifferent to his younger daughter's whereabouts, Katherine Wolfe looked ready to start ripping his place apart to find her sister.

'You must have some idea,' she countered. 'Because, other than my housekeeper, you appear to be the last person to have seen her. And if you don't want me calling the police in the next ten seconds...' she jerked her phone out of her purse 'and demanding they question you, you'd better tell me what you did to her on Friday night.'

'Are you nuts?' he shouted, the prickle of unease at the mention of the police only infuriating him more. Once upon a time he'd been terrified of the law. Scared the things he'd once had to do to survive might come back to destroy his new life... But not any more. 'If I knew where Beatrice was,' he added, 'why the hell would I have contacted you?'

'Oh, yes,' she sneered, stuffing her phone back into her purse. 'Your very cryptic message about needing to get in touch with her ASAP. Why do you need to get in touch with her?'

'That's between me and Beatrice and none of your business.'

'Well, I'm making it my business, Romeo. Did she spend Friday night with you?'

'Yes,' he said, damned if he would lie about that. He had nothing to be ashamed of.

'And then you just kicked her out the next morning after

you slept with her, is that it?' Katherine Wolfe's glare narrowed. 'Of all the heartless...'

'I didn't kick her out. She left,' he said, beyond furious now. Who did this woman think she was? And what exactly was she accusing him of?

'But you must have said something, *done* something, to have upset her,' she demanded again.

'Why must I?' he replied, getting royally sick of the third degree. But, even so, a prickle of unease crawled up his back. The memory of Bea's devastated expression the next morning—and the feel of her body, relaxed and trusting against his when he'd woken up, coming back full force.

'Because my housekeeper said she arrived at our place on Saturday morning, bedraggled and distraught,' Katherine Wolfe replied. 'She left me a weirdly cryptic note that didn't make a lot of sense. And then she disappeared.'

'She...*what*?' he asked, his fury fading as another unwanted memory blindsided him. Of when he'd thrust heavily inside her, and she'd flinched.

He hadn't meant to hurt her. Hadn't known she was a virgin. Because she hadn't told him. But why hadn't she contacted him since that night? It had been over forty-eight hours and he hadn't been able to get in touch with her.

'She disappeared...' her sister said again, then gave a deep sigh.

Her shoulders wilted, the fierce expression fading. She paced to the large bay window which gilded the suite in spring sunshine. With her back to him, he could see the temper draining away, until all that was left was tension.

'Bea can be flaky at times, but one thing she would never do, unless she was having a major crisis, is cavort around London while not looking her best,' she said, her voice trembling slightly. 'Appearances are important to her because she hasn't got a lot else to bolster her self-esteem, thanks to our pig of a father.'

'What did you mean, she's disappeared?' he asked, his stomach twisting.

He hadn't *meant* to hurt her when they'd made love, that much was true, but he *had* meant to hurt her the next morning, and he was feeling less comfortable about that now.

Katherine Wolfe turned to face him.

'She's not at our father's place. And her phone has been switched off since Saturday night, because Jack pulled a few strings to get the mobile company to check it. I discovered this morning that she's emptied her savings account and the safe deposit box where she was keeping her ID documents. But I've contacted all her friends…or, rather, her acquaintances, as Bea doesn't really have any close friends…and no one's seen her.'

Katherine sighed, the vulnerability in her eyes reminding Mason of Beatrice for the first time.

The Medford sisters were nothing alike physically. Katherine was shorter, with an abundance of curves and a shock of in-your-face red hair—while Beatrice was slender and tall, her naturally blonde hair giving her a fragile grace. But as Katherine stared back at him, looking scared, he could see a definite resemblance… Because, like Beatrice, when he had unloaded on her and she'd said nothing, Katherine had the same hopelessness in her eyes.

'I've been begging her to get away from our father for years, so maybe this is a good thing,' she murmured. 'Our father would have seen the press pictures from the Cascade launch, so he will have had expectations about your relationship. Expectations he would have tried to bully Beatrice into fulfilling for him, because that's the way he operates.' She tugged her bag strap in a nervous gesture as the last of her temper deflated. 'She definitely hasn't contacted you since she left you on Saturday?'

Mason's stomach churned. The picture Katherine Wolfe had just painted of Beatrice's dysfunctional relationship with her father was not the one he had assumed.

'No, she hasn't,' he murmured—which was the truth. But not the whole truth.

He had to find her and speak to her. To make sure she wasn't pregnant.

But he could see now that the reason she hadn't contacted him might be more complicated than he had assumed. Maybe she wasn't just sulking or trying to enhance her bargaining position.

Had he overreacted on Saturday morning because he'd always hated being taken for a mug? It triggered stuff from way back. But had he let that baggage from his childhood cloud his judgement where she was concerned? Because he hadn't given her much of a chance to explain herself...

'I need to get back.' Katherine glanced at her phone. 'If she does contact you, would you let me know? Or, better still, get her to contact me. Or I'll worry.'

'Sure,' he said, although he knew Beatrice wasn't going to contact him.

'Look, I'm sorry I went off at you,' Katherine added, the easy and apparently genuine apology surprising him even more. 'But I've been frantic. I've always looked out for her. She's my baby sister.' She sighed heavily. 'But maybe it's time I let her stand on her own two feet.'

'Actually, there is something,' he said as she turned to leave.

'Which is?' Katherine asked, a flicker of impatience joining the concern. But for some reason it didn't annoy him as much now.

The two sisters obviously had a close relationship. The sort of relationship he had never experienced and didn't really understand. But which he could probably use. Because if Beatrice was going to contact anyone, it was likely to be this woman.

'She may be pregnant,' he said.

'She… *How*?' Katherine Wolfe replied, the searing look back with a vengeance. 'Do you mean to say you didn't use protection?'

'I used a condom,' he said before she could work her way back up to a full head of steam. 'It burst.' He decided not to mention that he hadn't checked the use-by date, because none of this was any of her business. 'I made an appointment for her with my doctor. If she is pregnant, I want to know about it.'

'Which is code for what, exactly?' Katherine's voice rose as she got way ahead of herself again. 'That you plan to make her have a termination?'

'Did I say that?' he snapped back, as the anger he'd managed to bank returned. He didn't explain or defend his actions or his choices to anyone, not any more. 'The point is, I have a pressing reason to find her too. So if *you* locate her, you need to let *me* know.'

Katherine's eyes narrowed, but then she swore—a word he wouldn't have expected to hear from the mouth of a member of the British aristocracy. But then Katherine Wolfe was turning out to be almost as much of a surprise as her sister.

'Fine.' She sighed again. '*If* Bea contacts me, I will tell her you wish to speak with her. But that's all I'm prepared to do. It appears my little sister has finally decided to start making her own decisions, and the least I can do is respect that,' she said, each word loaded with a thinly veiled warning. 'I think the least you owe her is to respect her choices too,' she added pointedly, before sweeping back into the lift and stabbing the button.

As the doors closed behind her, Mason tugged out his mobile and tapped out a text to his PA.

Hire the best private detective you can find. Cost not an issue. Beatrice Medford has done a runner and I need to locate her ASAP. NO STONE UNTURNED.

He pocketed the mobile as soon as he got Joe's thumbs-up emoji. But as he headed back into his office he knew he wasn't going to get any work done today as the vague feeling of unease intensified.

Yeah, he'd respect Beatrice's choices. But only if her choices didn't involve never contacting *him* again. He needed to know if she was pregnant. But, more than that, he realised now, he also wanted to know why she'd run.

CHAPTER SIX

One week later

'*SIGNORINA*, YOU MUST be careful—do not get any more rides with strange men,' the kindly old farmer said in gruff Italian as Bea reached for the door handle of his truck.

Good advice from Signor Esposito, given what had happened with the last strange man she'd accepted a lift from, Bea thought wryly.

Then admonished herself for thinking about *him* again.

She pushed a weary smile to her lips as she shouldered her rucksack.

'Thank you, Signor Esposito, and don't worry, I will be very careful,' she replied in fluent Italian as she hopped out into the tourist bustle at the seafront in Rapallo.

The familiar pulse of panic was joined by a surge of loneliness as she watched him drive off. Signor Esposito had been a godsend, giving her a lift all the way to the Italian Riviera when he'd found her attempting to hitchhike for the first time in her life just outside Bobbio. His kindly, avuncular manner had made her feel safe after a terrifying few days. She'd never travelled alone before. And certainly not without considerable funds. It had been an eye-opener to discover how tough it was to get anywhere without the benefit of her father's money, a personal tour operator or a mobile phone because she'd had hers pinched in the Gare du Nord.

She hefted her pack onto her shoulders with a perkiness she didn't feel but was determined to fake.

Buck up, Bea. Being on your own and incommunicado is a good thing. You need to learn independence and self-reliance.

The last ten days had certainly been a baptism of fire—as she'd wound her way through France, into the Swiss Alps and eventually through the north of Italy—while becoming increasingly aware of her dwindling funds.

But her solo travels had taught her some valuable lessons already. Such as: you get a much better choice of hostel bed if you arrive early; long hair is a massive pain to wash in coach station toilets; two-euro sunblock does the same job as a two-hundred-euro designer brand; and only accept rides from men old enough to be your granddad.

She swiped her hair behind her ears, disconcerted by the savagely short cut which she still hadn't got used to after getting it hacked off by a Turkish barber in Bern. See lesson *numero due* in Bea Medford's Lessons Learned While Panic Backpacking Around Europe.

She took a moment to absorb the bustle of the port town on the Santa Liguria peninsula—and the beauty of her surroundings. Cafés and restaurants lined the road in between the palm trees, the tables already packed with tourists months before the start of the summer season.

She'd had no destination in mind when she'd left London on the Eurostar over a week ago—back when she'd thought she could afford to splash out on train tickets. She'd been desolate and despondent—courtesy of her one glorious

night with Mason Foxx and the horrific morning after—
and had boarded the first train out of the UK.

She'd only ended up in Rapallo because this had been
Signor Esposito's destination when he'd offered her a lift.
But as she made her way along the waterfront the rich scent
of roasting garlic and seafood filled her senses and the sun
warmed her skin. Lavish villa hotels and resorts dotted
the hills above, contrasting with the haphazard terraces of
pastel-coloured houses which lined the harbour. She stared
enviously at the clear blue sea lapping against the array of
fishing boats and luxury yachts docked in the bay.

Surely the Italian Riviera was as good a place as any to
change her life.

Firstly, it was several hundred miles away—both figu-
ratively and geographically—from her former life in London and *him*. And it was a tourist hotspot. She needed to
find work—and quickly. A tall order for someone who had
never had a proper job.

She had realised, while sitting wide awake during the
twelve-hour coach ride from Bern to Milan, she didn't know
how to *do* anything. Except speak five European languages,
not all of them fluently. So a tourist resort ought to be the
best place to begin looking. She hoped.

After plucking up her courage and pushing way outside
her comfort zone to ask for work at each café on the seafront, she soon realised the stupidity of that assumption.
Apparently, if you had no experience you were about as
useful as an ex-London socialite with a backpack when it
came to securing bar or restaurant work. But in the last café
she tried, a young barista took pity on her and informed
her the resort hotels around Portofino would be recruiting
housekeeping staff for the summer.

She had no idea what 'housekeeping' entailed, but as she

started the trek along the coastal path to Portofino, with her pack digging into her shoulders and the tiredness making her legs feel like overcooked spaghetti, she decided she had time to figure it out.

'You must change sheets, towels, yes?' Signora Bianchi, the housekeeping manager of the old-fashioned resort hotel tucked into the cliffs above Portofino, rattled off instructions in Italian as she led Bea into a palatial suite.

The view from the room's *terrazzo* was stunning, taking in the glint of a pool below and the stepped terraces leading down to a private beach and dock. Bea got precisely two seconds to admire it before she was led into the suite's bedroom.

'Vacuum and polish until everything shines,' the woman added, indicating the many marble surfaces and the worn carpet. 'Then you must clean the bathroom, top to bottom, and replenish all toiletries. You have experience, *si*?'

'Oh, yes, absolutely,' Bea lied, having never scrubbed a toilet in her life. But this was her new life, she decided, a life she was in control of at last. And supporting herself, however she could, was the first step on the ladder to becoming the new woman she wanted to be. And no longer the sort of woman men like Mason Foxx despised.

You're not doing this for him. You're doing this for yourself. Remember that.

'The rate is eight euros an hour. Shifts start at six a.m., finish at three,' the housekeeping manager continued. Bea nodded again. The rate was below minimum wage because the job offered room and board in a shared dorm, but that would be a major boon to her budget. 'You will have to work on every weekend for the first two months. *Bene?*'

'*Sì, bene, molto bene*,' she said, maybe a little over-enthusiastically when the older woman sent her a curious frown.

The *signora*'s gaze glided over the cheap summer dress and sneakers Bea had purchased in a discount store just outside of Paris. 'We have uniforms—find one which fits in the storeroom, the cost will be taken out of your first pay packet.' She checked her watch, all business. 'Your probation lasts two weeks and can start now.'

'*Grazie*, Signora Bianchi. I won't disappoint you, I promise,' Bea said, determined to make it so as they made their way out of the suite and down the staff staircase. It would be hard work, harder than anything she'd ever done before, but a heady sense of anticipation took hold as she was shown her cart and took a quick shower before getting dressed in the hotel's tailored uniform.

She was feeling considerably less buoyant when she finished her first shift four hours later, and crashed onto her bunk in the staff quarters she would be sharing with six other women. Her knuckles were raw, her shoulders felt as if someone had been pummelling them with a hammer and her legs hurt, because kneeling on marble floors was hell on your knees. But as she lay, staring at the clean but worn mattress of the bunk above, a feeling of pride and validation blossomed. And the panic and devastation from that morning a week and a half ago, when Mason Foxx had looked right through her, finally began to ease.

She wasn't doing this to make Mason Foxx think she was worthy. Because she would never see him again.

No, she was doing this for herself. And for that girl who had always believed she couldn't be anything more than a decoration, a distraction, a vacuous, insubstantial, flaky airhead whose looks and appearance and ability to attract male attention were her only worth. Something her father had taught her but Mason had reinforced, because all he had ever seen—or ever *wanted* to see—was the illusion her father had created.

Ironically, she actually *had* been invisible today to the guests at the resort—as she'd wheeled the cumbersome cart in and out of the vacant bedrooms in her maid's uniform. But for every toilet she'd made shine, every room she'd tidied and polished, every bed she'd smoothed fresh sheets onto and tucked with the precision her fellow maid and new best friend Marta had taught her, her confidence in her previously undiscovered work ethic increased.

Today, she'd achieved something of real value for the first time in her life. A day's work for a day's pay.

It was a surprisingly good feeling—despite her complete and utter exhaustion.

She held her hands up, frowning as she examined the chipped nails and sore, reddened skin. That said, she was investing in a pair of heavy-duty rubber gloves with her very first pay package.

As she fell into sleep, her life seemed full of new possibilities. New horizons. New dreams. Which were a lot more prosaic than the ones she'd once had—of finding someone to love her and value her, the way her father never had. But so much more achievable. Because now all she had to do to make her dreams come true was learn how to scrub a toilet properly.

It wasn't until three weeks later that Bea discovered she hadn't made her last catastrophic error of judgement, not by a long shot, and that her new life was not destined to be anywhere near as simple as she had assumed.

And that Mason Foxx would always be a part of her life now... Whether she got up the guts to contact him again or not.

CHAPTER SEVEN

Four months later

'SIGNOR FOXX, the Presidential Suite is being made ready by our new housekeeping manager. Do you wish to order food or...'

'I just want to crash,' Mason interrupted the Portofino resort manager's welcoming spiel. He was shattered after the flight from New York to Genoa and the drive along the coast—a journey he'd undertaken on the spur of the moment because the private eye Joe had hired five months ago had finally got a whiff of Beatrice Medford's whereabouts.

He probably should have rented a driver as well as the luxury convertible at Genova City airport, but he'd needed time to clear his head after the long flight. And the update from the PI.

Apparently, the man had managed to track Beatrice's movements as far as Rapallo ten days after Mason had last seen her—but then her trail had gone cold.

She was probably holed up at one of the luxury hotels in the region, because the Italian Riviera was just her style.

Off course, there was no guarantee she was still here. But Mason had been too wound up to wait any longer for more news, after having waited months already for this much, so he'd broken off delicate negotiations in Long Island to buy a chain of motels so he could fly all the way to Italy.

But as he'd driven along the coast, the picturesque coastline had done nothing to improve his mood.

How could the woman have disappeared so completely? And why had she? And how come he hadn't been able to look at another woman, let alone date one, since she'd walked out on him?

Because it had begun to feel that his determination to find her was about more than just the need to confirm she wasn't pregnant.

Not just every time he woke up, hard and ready for her, his heart beating ten to the dozen and his body yearning to touch her again. But every time the memory of her distraught face when she'd walked out on him crept into his consciousness—which had really started to annoy him.

He didn't agonise over his past behaviour, because dwelling on it only led to regrets and indecision and, worst of all, weakness. And, anyway, Beatrice was the one who had nixed her chance to explain herself with her little disappearing act.

But as he waved off the bellboy to tote his own bag, the niggling thought that his search for Beatrice had become an obsession persisted.

'Shall I instruct the housekeeper to finish the room later, *signor*?' the manager asked as he swung open the door to the Presidential Suite.

The sitting area was bright and airy and scrupulously clean, and the view across the bay impressive. But the suite's furniture was worn and fussy, its design features stuck firmly in the nineties. From what Mason had seen so far, the whole place could do with a refresh.

'Nah.' Mason dumped his bag on the couch in the main

room. 'She can finish. But then I don't want to be disturbed,' he added, dismissing the guy.

He just wanted to be left alone now. Maybe once he'd had a refresh himself, he could figure out what the hell he had been thinking, flying to Italy to chase down a woman he hardly knew but remembered far too vividly.

He slipped off his shoes, then carried his bag to the bedroom and opened the doors to a *terrazzo* that looked onto the coast.

The sea air overlaid the scent of lavender polish and potpourri. The August sun peeped through the clouds, the weather fresher than usual for this time of year. He stood for a moment to take in the view. The cluster of brightly painted houses that overlooked the harbour were defiantly picturesque. Incongruous super-yachts dwarfed the tourist boats and a few fishing vessels which bobbed in the blue-green water. But while the old *castello* which had been converted into this hotel had an enviable position above the Ligurian Sea, he noticed the cracks in the plasterwork and the fading grandeur of the terrace below, where a smattering of tourists braved the sea breezes lounging beside an old-fashioned pool.

Definitely ripe for development, although business wasn't at the forefront of Mason's mind… Just like it hadn't been for five months, because he'd been distracted and out of sorts ever since that night in March.

That needed to stop now. Perhaps that was why he'd raced all the way here, not to chase the shadows from that night which had refused to die, but to finally put an end to this unhealthy, irrational obsession once and for all. Beatrice couldn't be pregnant, because she would have let him or her sister know, so she could hose him for support payments.

It was past time to let the fallout from that night, and her attempt to trick him into a commitment, go.

The sound of a toilet flushing dragged him out of his navel-gazing and an unseen woman's voice began humming a pop tune. The sweet, seductive melody floated into the bedroom from the en suite bathroom, making adrenaline spike in Mason's groin.

Seductive? What the…?

He tensed, shocked by his physical response, as the maid sang the words to the chorus in English. In an English accent.

Okay, he was officially losing his mind, because her voice sounded like…

Then the maid stepped out of the bathroom, her head bent, carrying a bucket and mop.

He couldn't see her face, only the short cap of blonde hair cropped close to her head. But the tailored lines of the hotel's blue uniform did nothing to disguise her slender figure, or her rounded belly as she turned to close the bathroom door.

The spike of adrenaline became a wave, slamming into Mason with devastating force. Why did the maid remind him so much of Beatrice? When her hair was too short. And the society princess he'd met that night would never be seen dead working for a living. Perhaps because this woman's pregnant bump reminded him of the dreams which had tortured him, ever since that night, of his child growing inside her…

He thrust his fingers through his hair. Damn, was he actually losing his mind for real?

But then the vanilla scent hit him, and the wave of confusion turned into a blast of heat… Potent, provocative and devastatingly familiar.

'Beatrice?' he murmured, sure he had to be dreaming now or going mad.

The maid's head lifted. She dropped the bucket, splashing dirty water onto the carpet.

'Mason!' she whispered, looking almost as shocked as he felt.

Recognition slammed into him, and all but knocked him off his feet, as his gaze shot from her flushed, beautiful face—only made more striking by the boyish haircut—to land back on that tell-tale bump.

It *was* her. How was that even possible?

But then all he could seem to focus on was her belly. And his astonishment was overtaken by a visceral mix of anger and disbelief... And something that felt disturbingly like desire.

'Is that mine?' he ground out on a rusty gasp of fury.

That?

Indignation barrelled through Bea's body, overriding the cocktail of other emotions battering her—shock, panic, guilt, arousal—*arousal*, seriously?

Her hand cupped the place where her baby grew, instinctively protecting it from the emerald glare of the man not ten feet away from her—who she'd convinced herself she wouldn't have to see again, until she was ready.

'No, *that* isn't yours, it's mine,' she said, her voice surprisingly calm given she had just been dropped into a waking nightmare.

What was Mason Foxx doing in Portofino, in the Presidential Suite of her hotel? Was he the Very Important Guest her manager, Fabrizio, had told her about half an hour ago?

Or was his presence in front of her an apparition? A terrible manifestation of her guilty conscience, which she'd been studiously ignoring for months. For four months and twenty-one days, to be precise, ever since the lovely Dr Rossi had confirmed she was pregnant. Had this illusion been sent by the Do-the-Right-Thing Fairy to force her to stop avoiding the inevitable and contact the father of her child?

But the tall, broad-shouldered man in worn jeans and a T-shirt, his jaw covered in beard scruff, his dark chestnut hair finger-combed into waves, his eyes stark with shock and his tanned features flushed with outrage, looked far too real and solid and forbidding to be a figment of her guilty conscience.

The searing emerald gaze narrowed dangerously.

'Answer the question. Am I the father?' he said, throwing out a hand to indicate her belly but not shifting his gaze from hers—as if the evidence of her pregnancy was like Medusa, and if he looked at it directly he would turn to stone.

The indignation protecting Bea from her shock at seeing him again—alive and well and as much of a judgemental bastard as she remembered—was joined by a healthy dose of disgust.

A part of her wanted to lie, to tell him no, this baby wasn't his. Because he seemed less than pleased at the prospect. And her baby deserved the best of everything, including a father who wanted it to exist.

Discovering she was pregnant four and a half months ago had been an enormous shock, because she had totally convinced herself the early signs of her pregnancy were all phantom ones. That her tiredness, her one light period and her tender breasts were just a result of the shock to her once pampered system of having to get up before dawn and do manual labour for eight hours straight.

But the confirmation of her condition and the options available to her—delivered in Dr Rossi's measured voice—had also been a massive wake-up call. Because, as she'd come to terms with her new reality and realised she didn't want a termination, she had also realised that every single cowardly, self-serving, foolish, reckless, impulsive mistake she made from now on would have consequences. Not just for her, but also for her defenceless child.

She'd been determined, before that life-changing moment in Dr Rossi's office, to prove she could make a life for herself here. But discovering she was going to have a child had nearly broken her resolve. She'd been so close to calling her sister to beg for her help. She had even considered—in a particularly low moment during a gruelling shift cleaning up after a debauched party in the Honeymoon Suite while battling low-grade morning sickness—returning to her father's house in London. But somehow, she had powered through the panic and the anguish, and the physical exhaustion of early pregnancy, and come out the other side a better, more focused person.

She'd worked slavishly in the months since, enough to get a temporary promotion when Signora Bianchi had to take some time off, and she had even managed to move out of the bunk room into a place on the hotel grounds. She was no longer the society princess Mason Foxx had treated with such contempt. Nor was she the pathetic, easily cowed girl who had allowed herself to be bullied her whole life, and who had run away rather than stand up for herself.

She was a stronger, more determined person now. Maybe she still didn't have a long-term plan for her life—and her baby's life. And maybe she still struggled to deal with confrontations, which was why she hadn't contacted Mason months ago. But she had made the decision to have this baby. Alone. So she did not need him to be a part of its life.

So, while it would be wrong to lie to him about his part in making this child, she could give him a way out.

'You don't have to be the father,' she said, reasoning desperately. 'If you don't want to be.'

The frown on his face became furious. 'What the hell is that supposed to mean? Either I'm its…' He paused, looking unsure of himself for the first time since she'd met him. His Adam's apple bounced as he swallowed, as if he was struggling to even say the word *father*… 'Either I got you pregnant, or I didn't,' he continued. 'So, which is it?'

'If you're asking me if your sperm created *my* child,' she said, pressing her palm over her belly to protect her bump from that judgemental glare. 'Then yes, it did.'

He swore again, making her stiffen.

'But, as far as I'm concerned, that's where your involvement ends,' she added. But her voice was no longer steady, all her resolve and determination—and the courage she'd worked so hard to earn over the last five months—fading in the face of his fury.

'Like hell it does.' His gaze raked over her belly, then he scrubbed his hands down his face. 'There'll be a kid walking around in this world with my DNA. That makes me involved.' She noticed the tremor in his fingers before he jammed his hands into his pockets. Something about the evidence of his panic downgraded her own.

This man had treated her appallingly all those months ago. And she hadn't deserved it. He'd never given her a chance to defend herself. So what right did he have to behave like the injured party now?

'When were you planning to let me know you were having my kid?' he demanded, but she could hear the tremor in his voice too.

And suddenly she understood. He was trying to hide his fear behind a wall of outrage. She'd had months to get used to the news, he'd only had five minutes. While she didn't believe he was a good man, after the way he'd discarded her so callously, it occurred to her that he was probably in shock.

The knot in her belly loosened, and the weightless feeling of inadequacy—which had marred so much of her childhood and adolescence whenever she'd appeased her father—dissolved a little more.

'I don't know,' she said honestly. 'When I was ready to face your anger, I guess.'

His brows shot up his forehead and he swore again, but colour slashed across his cheeks before he marched through the terrace doors.

Was that shame she had seen in his face? Or was she projecting?

She followed him onto the *terrazzo*, surprised to find him sitting on one of the loungers, his forearms perched on his knees, his gaze fixed on the horizon. He didn't look angry any more, or even shocked. He looked shattered.

'I'm not angry.' His gaze met hers, then drifted down to focus on her bump. When his gaze returned to her face, she saw something in his eyes that shocked her even more than his surprise appearance at the Portofino Grande.

Uncertainty. Confusion. And awareness.

'I'm just…' He raked his hair back from his face and stared out at the bay again, the blank stare making her sure he couldn't see the famous harbour, or the verdant coastline framing the sea. 'Hell, I don't even know what I'm feeling right now.'

She sat on the lounger opposite him, the spurt of sympathy surprising her. But she understood how scary it was not to be able to process your emotions—because she'd spent so much of her life unable to process her own. And she had the sneaking suspicion that Mason Foxx rarely even examined his emotions, let alone processed them. So there was that.

'I understand,' she said. 'I was shocked too when the doctor confirmed the test results.'

His head swung round, the accusatory stare destroying the brief truce. 'And when was that, exactly?'

Her pulse rate leapt and the tension in her stomach returned. She stood and brushed shaky palms down her uniform, determined to steady herself. She needed to fortify herself before she dealt with his anger—because she was probably in shock too.

Making this baby had been an accident, but it was one she was more than prepared to live with.

'Perhaps we could meet again later to discuss all this?' she offered, not prepared to be subjected to his inquisition before she'd had a chance to properly adjust to his presence in Portofino. She glanced at the water stain on the carpet where she'd dropped the bucket. 'I need to clean up the mess I made, and then finish my shift.'

But as she attempted to walk away, he leapt up and grabbed her wrist. 'Not so fast.'

The shock of his touch shot up her arm, before she could tug it loose. 'Please don't touch me.'

He frowned but released her. 'Okay.' He tucked his hand back into his pocket. 'But I want answers *now*. And I'm not prepared to wait.'

She scowled at him. 'Well, tough, because I have work to do.'

He let out a bitter chuckle. 'Is this some kind of a joke?'

He flicked his finger to indicate her uniform. 'Since when do you work for a living?'

The muscles in her spine stiffened and it was her turn to glare.

He'd accused her of being a freeloader before, of having no pride or self-respect. And at the time he had been partly right. But he wasn't right any longer, and she refused to allow him, or anyone else, to belittle or denigrate what she did for a living, or what she had achieved in the past five months. Maybe being a chambermaid wasn't the pinnacle of human endeavour, and maybe her income was a minute fraction of his, but she had a prodigious work ethic now, and she happened to be exceptionally good at what she did.

'Since I decided to start supporting myself,' she replied as calmly as she could manage while her insides were tying themselves in knots. 'So I no longer had to be at the mercy of men like you.'

She walked back into the main living area and knelt down to clean the carpet with the stiff dignity of a queen.

The mocking sound was impossible to ignore when he followed her into the room, but she didn't look up. She needed to regroup, rethink, figure out what all of this meant. But one thing she refused to do was be judged or bullied by him again.

But then she heard him speaking into the house phone. 'Hi, send another maid up to clean the room.'

He'd slammed the phone back down before she could object.

'How... how dare you?' she spluttered, getting to her feet. 'I'm perfectly capable of finishing the job. Of all the high-handed, overbearing... You had no right to...'

'I have every right,' he interrupted her, slicing through her indignation with a nonchalance which was meant to enrage—and didn't fool her for a second, because his tanned skin was flushed with temper. 'I happen to be a paying guest. And I don't want you cleaning my damn carpet when I've spent thousands of pounds trying to locate you—not to mention torpedoing an important project in the Hamptons yesterday to catch the red-eye here—with the vague hope of finding you and talking to you.' His gaze skated over her belly again. 'And that's before we even get to the fact you're gonna have my kid, and you chose to hide out here playing chambermaid instead of telling me that.' His voice rose in anger. 'For five solid months.'

She flinched, then hated herself for the show of weakness.

She opened her mouth to shout back at him. But had to shut it abruptly when Marta appeared at the door to the suite, looking anxious and flustered.

'Signor Foxx, I am here to clean your room. Signor Romano wishes to know if there is a problem with Beatrice's work,' she said, sending Bea an apologetic look.

Marta knew what it was like to deal with difficult guests. And she had always covered for Bea, especially in the early days when her pregnancy had exhausted her far too easily. But Marta's 'don't worry, I've totally got your back here' look only made the tangle of nerves in Bea's belly tie themselves into a knot.

Marta couldn't help her with this situation.

'There's no problem with her work,' Mason barked in reply. 'But tell Romano he's giving Beatrice the rest of the day off.'

Marta coloured but managed to hide her surprise admirably. 'Yes, *signor*.'

He turned to Bea, who was momentarily speechless in the face of his arrogance.

'You've got half an hour to change and meet me by the red two-seater in the forecourt. Don't make me come and find you...again,' he added, before stalking into the bathroom and slamming the door.

Bea stood, shaking, her insides churning so hard now she couldn't think, let alone move. But worse was the creeping feeling of panic and inadequacy which she'd thought she'd tamed after five months of surviving on her own.

Marta's hand touched her shoulder. 'Who is this man? Are you scared of him?'

Bea shook her head. She wasn't scared of him. That much, at least, was true.

'Is he the father of the baby?' Marta asked, flooring Bea for a moment. How did her friend know? Was it that obvious?

But she found herself nodding again.

'And he did not know of its existence?' Marta added.

Again, Bea was forced to nod.

'So, this explains his temper, yes?'

'Tantrum, more like,' she murmured, but Marta's observation had forced her to face one uncomfortable fact. She really should have contacted Mason months ago.

'He is very rich and powerful according to Fabrizio,' Marta murmured, her lips quirking. 'And very hot. But if you do not wish to go with him, I will tell him you are sick. And cover for you with Fabrizio until he is gone.'

Bea blinked, then wanted to hug Marta for being such a loyal friend.

If only she could take her friend up on the generous offer to cover for her so she could flee. But where would she go? She had established a life here. And she had the baby to think about too. Also, with Mason in his current master of the universe mood, she would be putting Marta's job at risk as well as her own if the other maid tried to defy their Very Important Guest. And Marta didn't deserve to be put in the middle of her drama with Mason just because she'd had the bad judgement to befriend her.

Bea was forced to shake her head. 'It's okay.'

Mason was right about one thing, at least. They did need to talk.

Strictly speaking, this was a conversation she should have had the guts to have months ago. And avoiding it any longer would not make it any easier.

'*Grazie*, Marta.' She gave her friend a hug of thanks. 'I need to go with him and get this over with…' Although she had the feeling that this conversation was unlikely to be the end of anything. 'But if you could keep the fact I'm spending the afternoon with Mr Foxx quiet, I'd appreciate it.'

The hotel had a rule about fraternising with guests. But somehow the thought of breaking it felt like the least of her worries. That said, it was just more proof of how little consideration Mason had given to her situation by basically ordering her to spend the afternoon with him.

But, frankly, what did she expect from a man who wore his arrogance like a badge of honour and clearly still thought she was beneath his contempt?

Marta nodded, but then her lips quirked. 'Make sure you wear your best dress.' She glanced at the bathroom door, behind which they could hear the shower running. 'A man like this deserves to be kept waiting. So he will know—just because you are a maid you are no pushover.'

Beatrice nodded. But as she took the back stairs she had the awful feeling that Marta was wrong. Bea the pushover was still lurking inside her, just waiting to reappear in a crisis.

* * *

A good forty minutes later, Bea headed back through the hotel grounds to the forecourt. After considerable debate, she had donned a light summer dress with sunflowers on it, which was too tight around her breasts and the bump, but otherwise flattered her figure.

Mason's tall frame dwarfed the expensive sports car as he leant against it. He'd folded his arms over his broad chest in an impatient stance which highlighted the tattoo circling his biceps. His eyes were shaded by a pair of aviator sunglasses which had probably cost more than her monthly salary—but she could still feel his scowl.

'You're late,' he remarked.

She dug her teeth into her tongue to control the knee-jerk apology for her tardiness which almost popped out of her mouth. Mason sneered at politeness, she already knew that. And, anyway, she didn't have anything to apologise for—give or take the odd secret pregnancy.

'I don't take orders from you,' she replied, pleased when he stiffened and drew himself up to his full height.

If he thought he could still intimidate her, she would be sunk. So she would just have to fake a confidence she didn't feel. Until she did feel it. *Easy.*

His brows flattened. But as he yanked open the passenger door she could see she'd surprised him with her ballsy response. Good.

Welcome back, Bea the badass.

'Get in,' he said.

She glared at him for two long seconds to make it clear she would get into the car when she was good and ready, then folded herself into the passenger seat.

He slammed the door with enough force to make the car shake.

Strike two to Bea the badass.

For once, she didn't care about inciting a man's temper. The thought was surprisingly liberating as she watched him climb into the driver's seat without a word, the dark frown radiating his disapproval.

Unfortunately, as the car fishtailed out of the hotel forecourt, spraying gravel onto the lawn, and he accelerated down the short driveway and onto the coast road, her newfound confidence disappeared into the rear-view mirror as she was forced to grab the expensive leather seat in a death grip.

CHAPTER EIGHT

'PLEASE SLOW DOWN.'

Mason glanced at his passenger, but before he could tell her he didn't take orders from her either, his gaze snagged on her belly. And his pulse rate shot straight back into the danger zone.

She seemed calm, her short hair plastered to her head and accentuating that stunning bone structure, the simple cotton dress flattened against her breasts. Why did they seem fuller than when he'd last seen her? Was that a result of her pregnancy too? Just one of the changes to her body caused by his child?

His child.

He swallowed convulsively, surprised by the urge to ask her about every detail of the pregnancy.

Then he noticed her fingers white-knuckling on the car's upholstery.

He eased his foot off the gas to take the next bend, as the car wound its way along the coastal road back towards Rapallo.

Killing them both—and the bump—was not going to improve this situation.

Or lower his heartrate.

Or help him to think coherently. His mind had gone

AWOL ever since he'd spotted her in the hotel room in that maid's outfit.

But that was no excuse to behave like an idiot.

He shifted into first to take the fork in the road, which led to an exclusive cliff-top restaurant at the top of the peninsula. He'd located the Michelin-starred *trattoria* on his phone while he'd been waiting for her, then offered them a small fortune to secure a table, cancel all their other bookings for the rest of the afternoon and compensate their guests.

He considered it money well spent. Because he didn't trust himself to be alone with her while they had this discussion, but nor did he want an audience of tourists taking snaps of them together and posting it on social media.

And, frankly, twenty grand was a drop in the ocean compared to what he'd already shelled out on the private investigator to facilitate this conversation.

They arrived at the restaurant, perched on the brow of the hill, with only one table set on the terrace which looked out over the point.

The maître d' rushed out to greet them. 'Signor Foxx, we are delighted to welcome you to Del Mare,' he said, bowing as he opened Beatrice's door. 'I am Giovanni. All is prepared as you requested.'

'*Grazie*,' Mason murmured as he climbed out of the car and threw the keys to the parking attendant.

But as he placed his palm on the small of Beatrice's back to escort her into the restaurant behind Giovanni, she stiffened and stepped away from him.

'I can't… I can't eat here, Mason,' she whispered, a stubborn frown on her face.

'What's the problem?' His gaze flicked to her belly. 'Is it the seafood?' he asked, as it occurred to him that he knew absolutely nothing about what pregnant women could and could not eat.

Her eyes widened, and then she let out a nervous laugh—which didn't exactly make him feel any better about all the stuff he did not know about her condition.

'No... It's not... I'm fine with seafood. It's just...' She glanced at the maître d', who was waiting a respectful distance away. Then she leaned closer, giving him a lungful of that intoxicating vanilla scent. 'I can't afford to eat here.'

He stared at her for a moment. Was she joking? But she didn't look as if she were joking, from the embarrassed flush on her cheeks.

'I'm paying,' he said flatly.

'But I don't want you to pay,' she insisted. 'I'd like to go Dutch.' She held out her hands to encompass the exclusive restaurant, the terrace framed by wisteria vines which afforded them a breathtaking view of the coastline. Silver cutlery and crystal stemware sparkled in the sunlight on the solitary table set especially for them. 'But this is way outside my budget,' she added. 'Could we please find somewhere a bit cheaper? I know a great pizza place in Rapallo that does lunch for under ten euros.'

It was his turn to frown. She *was* actually serious.

For a moment, he was lost for words.

What had happened to the society princess, the Medford Ice Queen, a woman used to living in the lap of luxury and expecting other people to pay for it? Because this was not the woman he had slept with all those months ago.

Or at least, not the woman he had assumed he'd been sleeping with.

Of course, maybe he should have expected this. After all, he had just found her scrubbing toilets for a living in a second-rate hotel.

He'd convinced himself while waiting in the car park that her menial job had to be a trick to garner his sympathy. But he was starting to doubt that conclusion. Exactly how long had she been working at the Portofino Grande? Because, according to Romano, she was the housekeeping manager, and as far as he knew she'd had no experience with any kind of work when they'd met five months ago.

But then his surprise turned to irritation.

If she'd needed cash, she'd had another good reason to contact him. And yet she hadn't.

Her new financial independence wasn't the only big change, though. She'd held her own when he'd freaked out in the suite. She hadn't cried or wilted or cowered or sulked, the way he would have expected. She'd stood up for herself. He'd seen glimpses of that woman five months ago, but apparently Beatrice Medford was now a fully-fledged Valkyrie.

A part of him—a *large* part of him—didn't like this new, improved Beatrice—because getting her to do what he wanted was going to be tougher. But another part of him had a grudging respect for what she had achieved.

And seeing her spirited response to him had been a major turn-on too. *Go figure*.

Of course, it was beyond stupid for her to have holed herself up here, trying to earn a living in a minimum-wage job when he was more than capable of supporting her—and he certainly intended to tell her that. But while he'd already decided she couldn't work at the Grande any longer, he couldn't quite bring himself to demand she do as he said.

He'd crushed her spirit once before. And he was beginning to realise he didn't feel nearly as justified about doing that as he once had.

Of course, changing restaurants was non-negotiable, but

perhaps he could figure out a way to get her to agree to eat here without stomping all over her pride.

'I don't want to eat somewhere too public, Beatrice,' he explained. 'If the press get hold of photos of us together, we're going to have a problem on our hands…'

On top of the massive one we've already got—that you chose to hide out in Portofino instead of letting me know I was your baby daddy.

She blinked as if the thought had never occurred to her, as he tried to cut off his resentment while another thought reverberated in his head.

Did she ever intend to tell me about the pregnancy?

'Don't you think you're being a little paranoid?' she said, but the stubborn tilt of her chin had softened. 'I doubt there are any British tabloid journalists hanging out at Pizzeria di Rapallo. And I'm not news any more. The Medford Ice Queen is dead and gone. And good riddance.'

The comeback surprised him, but not as much as the vehemence with which she announced the demise of the woman she had once been. Or, rather, the woman the press and her father had pretended she was. Not for the first time, he wondered how he had never thought to question that image.

'You're noticeably pregnant,' he said, still trying to be persuasive, even though this discussion was getting them nowhere. 'And if any photos end up on social media of the two of us having a heart-to-heart, precisely five and a half months after the last time we were splashed all over the internet together, it won't take long for the press to figure out whose baby it is,' he continued.

The bitterness stuck in his throat again.

Why *hadn't* she told him? Did she think he wasn't good enough to be her baby's father? Was that it?

'We've got this place to ourselves for the rest of the afternoon,' he added. 'So we can discuss this without an audience.'

'How did you manage that?' she asked, her eyes widening as she set off on another pointless tangent. 'This restaurant is always booked out months in advance.'

'I wanted privacy for this conversation,' he said, his frustration and impatience torpedoing his desire to be reasonable. Time to cut to the chase. 'And I was prepared to pay for it. If you want to go Dutch on the cost, you can take out a loan another time. But right now we're wasting time and money. And I'm beginning to think this is just another of your tactics to avoid telling me why you decided scrubbing toilets in Portofino made more sense than letting me know I was going to become a father.'

She stiffened, but he could see the flicker of guilt in her eyes.

Bingo. Maybe she genuinely wanted to pay her way, but she was also not keen on having this conversation.

Well, tough.

'That's not true,' she said at last, but the tremble in her voice told a different story.

'Then prove it and stop arguing about nothing. I've been trying to find you for five months, Beatrice. And I'm entitled to know why you didn't contact me as soon as you knew about junior,' he said, forcing himself to look directly at her bump. Which, thankfully, was now only hitting a solid seven on the freak-out scale.

He could see she still wanted to argue, but as she gripped the strap on her purse, her head swinging between him and the maître d', he could also see her indecision. Because Beatrice was nothing if not completely transparent. Thank God that was one thing about her which hadn't changed.

Her gaze finally met his, and she sighed. 'Okay, fine. But if we ever share a meal again, I'm paying.'

'Agreed,' he snapped, then cupped her elbow and led her into the restaurant.

As they followed Giovanni to their table he noticed how the pulse on the inside of her arm battered his thumb. And how her vanilla scent added a rich sultry note to the refreshing aroma of summer blooms and sea air.

She swept her hands over her bottom to sit down, and a rush of blood hit his groin.

There was no *if* about it. They *would* be sharing a meal again, because one thing was for damn sure—he had no intention of letting her out of his sight any time soon.

Bea listened to the waiter reel off a list of special dishes, grateful for the interruption. She sat ramrod-straight and stared at the horizon, unnerved by the luxury of the deserted restaurant, which felt like revisiting another life—and the intense scrutiny of the man opposite her. She could *feel* his gaze on her and sense his forceful presence across the table. Which was unnervingly reminiscent of their one night together.

His attention had been so exhilarating then, and it still had the power to make her skin prickle and her heartbeat throb low in her abdomen even now.

If only she could read him as easily as he seemed to be able to read her.

She knew he was furious with her for not contacting him about the baby. She also understood that reaction and had been ready to confront it. But somehow his silent assessment now made her more uneasy than his temper had earlier.

She picked up the menu—to stop her hands trembling—and made herself glance his way.

Just as she had suspected, he was watching her, but his fierce expression was more thoughtful than hostile.

She let go of the breath clogging her lungs. It would be better if this didn't have to be a confrontation.

She was glad she'd spoken up about his choice of restaurant, though, even if he had steamrollered over her objections. Because she had sensed a willingness to negotiate which hadn't been there when he'd demanded she go to lunch with him.

Progress? Of a sort.

The waiter stopped talking and she picked the only entrée she could remember from the list. Mason ordered the same.

The waiter took the menus and left. But as Bea went to place her now unoccupied hands in her lap, Mason leaned across the table and snagged her wrist.

His touch, as always, was electric, and she couldn't control the instinctive shudder as he opened her fist and ran his thumb across the calluses on her palm.

She tugged her hand free, feeling stupidly embarrassed when she had nothing to be embarrassed about. She worked for a living now. Why should she be ashamed of that?

'How long have you been working as a maid?' he demanded.

Her cheeks heated. 'I'm not housekeeping staff any more. I'm the housekeeping manager.'

His lips quirked, the half-smile making the muscles in her spine stiffen. Maybe she'd overestimated his newfound respect for her.

'Okay, how long have you been the housekeeping manager?'

'Not long, only since Signora Bianchi had to take leave when her husband had a stroke,' she said. 'I stepped up because Marta didn't want the extra responsibility,' she added, eager to fill the charged silence, and give him more of an insight into who she was now. 'Marta has two young children and Fabrizio was only offering an additional five euro an hour to take the position for the rest of the summer.' She barrelled on. 'It means having to organise the rotas, ensure all the rooms are ready each day before three and train new staff,' she continued. 'Plus, I have to ensure the cleaning supplies are always sufficiently stocked and arrange the laundry...'

He held up his hand and she hesitated, ready for him to say something contemptuous or dismissive, but instead he murmured, 'You sound like you know a lot about the job.'

'I... I do. I like it,' she offered, surprising herself with the admission.

Over the past five months she'd learned so much—how to ensure the marble didn't streak when you rinsed it, how to fold the bed sheets until they bounced, and all the other cleaning hacks which earned her good tips and made sure her rooms were scrupulously clean and delivered on time. A lot of the work was drudgery and not something most former society princesses would aspire to, but she was immensely proud of the temporary promotion. She liked the greater responsibility. And the extra money had also been very welcome. She lived frugally, but it was difficult to keep within her means and she needed to save more for when the baby arrived—because she hadn't worked long enough in Italy to qualify for more than the most basic maternity benefits.

'Really?' His scarred eyebrow lifted. 'You actually enjoy cleaning up other people's mess?'

And there it was, the contempt she had been expecting. It upset her to realise it hurt more than it should. His opinion of her didn't matter. It never had.

'I was talking about the promotion,' she shot back. 'But actually, no, I'm not ashamed of cleaning. It's a job. And it means I'm not dependent on anyone any more.'

He gave a slight nod, his gaze narrowing as if he were seeing something he had never noticed before.

Pride swelled in her chest.

Even though his approval didn't matter, it felt important he see how much she had changed from that clueless, eager-to-please girl who had thrown herself at him. And convinced herself that losing her virginity to a man like him would somehow validate her as a woman. When she was the only person who could do that.

'I get it,' he said eventually, tapping his fingers on the table. 'Is that why you chose to hide out here and you didn't tell me about the pregnancy? Because you wanted to prove you could survive on your own?'

His tone was surprisingly non-confrontational, coaxing even, but she could hear what he hadn't said—that he thought she had been playing at being independent just to annoy him.

She took a deep breath, eased it out slowly to keep her temper in check.

The waiter appeared with a bottle of sparkling water, some freshly baked focaccia and a saucer of olive oil to dip it in, giving her a chance to gather her thoughts.

She had prepared a hundred persuasive answers to the question of why she hadn't contacted him sooner over the last five months, but she could see now, every one of them had been riddled with half-truths and blatant lies, as well as assumptions about how he would respond to the news of her pregnancy, which she didn't know him well enough to make.

He'd been incredibly cruel to her that morning—not just in the judgements he'd made about her, but the way he'd spoken to her… But the night before, he had been very different, treating her with care and tenderness, while taking responsibility for the burst condom. She still didn't know which of those men was the real Mason Foxx—the arrogant, overbearing bastard who had accused her of terrible things or the man who had held her in his arms and shown her a pleasure she had never even believed existed.

She eased another steadying breath out through tight lungs, attempting to quell the burst of awareness. She needed to focus, because his nearness had always had the potential to derail her common sense.

She dropped her head, stared at the hands clasped tightly in her lap. She examined the reddened skin on her knuckles, the small burn on her thumb from when she'd ironed her uniform for the first time—and gulped down the shame which threatened to gag her.

'I guess that's part of it,' she admitted, forcing herself to meet that probing gaze.

The truth was, she *should* have contacted him as soon as she'd known she was pregnant. And he deserved an honest answer. Or as much of an honest answer as she was capable of giving him.

'You… You accused me of things which weren't true. I hadn't intentionally seduced you to get a marriage proposal out of you for my father's benefit,' she managed, hating the defensiveness in her voice and the way his eyes sharpened.

Did he still think her virginity had been a trick to snare him? Why should she care if he did? What he'd said had been ugly and hurtful, but by protesting her innocence was she giving him permission to make those accusations in the first place?

But he didn't say anything, didn't challenge her, so she forced herself to continue and say what needed to be said.

'But you *were* one of several men on a list my father had given me that afternoon.' She gulped down the ball of humiliation in her throat, sickened again by how easily she had once allowed herself to be manipulated. And how little she had done to fight against—or even call out—her father's cynical agenda. 'He told me he wanted me to…' she lifted her fingers to do air quotes '…*engage with* you. That's why he hired a stylist and an expensive designer gown and a chauffeur-driven car to take me to the event. So you were right about his intentions. But when I met you, I didn't know who you were, and when you told me your name…' The heat seared her collarbone, but she made herself continue. 'I already felt…*something*… With you. And it had nothing to do with his list or fulfilling his agenda.'

'Something, huh?' One dark brow lifted, the scepticism in his expression not letting her off the hook for a second. 'I think you're going to have to do better than that, Beatrice.'

Bother. Apparently, he was not going to be satisfied with euphemisms. But then why would she have assumed he would be? Mason Foxx was nothing if not direct. It was one of the things she had once found so attractive about him.

She cleared her throat.

Why was it so hard to talk about that livewire connection, when they'd made a baby together? It was just sex after all, and chemistry. It had only been a big deal for her because it had been her first time, her *only* time. But the emotional connection she had kidded herself they'd shared that night had all been in her head.

'Well, you were very hot, and I responded to you in a way I hadn't thought I'd ever respond to anyone…' She hesitated to take a gulp of the fizzy water. 'Sexually speaking,' she continued, impossibly grateful suddenly that he'd probably paid a king's ransom to empty the restaurant. 'My father created the Medford Ice Queen to snare men like you and Jack Wolfe.' She stared at her hands again. 'And, although I had been unhappy for a long time, and had even taken language lessons with the vague idea of coming to Europe and breaking away from his influence, I had let him believe I was willing to be that person. And I'd never explicitly disabused him of that fact.'

She raised her head to find him watching her, but the accusation had gone, to be replaced by a disturbing heat she recognised.

She looked away again, across the cliffs, determined to ignore it. Surely this continued attraction was nothing more than an inconvenient leftover from the physical sensations she had never been able to forget from that night?

Don't fall into the trap of mixing insane chemistry with intimacy and affection again—because that will only make you vulnerable.

Maybe Mason Foxx wasn't as unreasonable or unstable as her father, but he was still a powerful man who didn't do soft or tender. Having a relationship with a man like him would always have been a disaster.

She met his gaze. 'I didn't really have a plan when I left London,' she continued because he hadn't said anything, his reaction impossible to decipher. 'I just knew I needed to change. *Everything.* I ended up in Rapallo by accident. And the job at the Grande was pretty much the only one I could get without any experience. But after a while, things just started to fit.'

The waiter reappeared, accompanied by a female assistant holding a tray aloft. After laying two plates on the table, he whipped off the silver covers to reveal heaped helpings of the seafood linguini they'd ordered.

Her stomach knotted with apprehension. The scent of

garlic, roast tomatoes and chargrilled langoustine filled Bea's senses. But she'd never felt less like eating anything in her entire life.

As the waiting staff left, Mason picked up his fork and began twirling the pasta. As he swallowed the first bite, still not responding, she felt irritation collide with the bundle of nerves in her stomach.

She coughed, loudly.

He glanced up from shovelling the pasta into his mouth, swallowed. 'Why aren't you eating?' he asked.

Seriously?

'Because I'm not hungry. I can't eat. Until I know what you have to say.'

'About what?'

She threw her hands up, exasperated. 'About everything, Mason. About becoming a father. About finding me again. About what I just told you… Stuff like that!' she huffed, so frustrated now she could scream.

Was he playing some kind of game with her? Trying to unnerve and antagonise her?

But when he placed his fork back on his plate, his demeanour didn't appear manipulative or confrontational. Good to know she could read that much at least.

'The way I see it…' The tight muscle in his jaw started to twitch, but she had the strangest feeling his fury wasn't directed at her any more. 'Your father is a bully, who doesn't give a damn about you, except what he can get out of you. He showed up at my office the day after you disappeared, and straight away I recognised the type. Because my old man was the exact same, just without the peerage and the posh accent and the expensive suits. A sewer rat willing to sell his own kid to the highest bidder. I don't blame you for wanting to escape from that.' The barely leashed aggression shocked her a little, but not as much as the pulse of compassion at the glimpse into his childhood.

It was all part of the Mason Foxx myth, that he'd had a rough start in life. But the details had always been deliberately vague, steeped in rags-to-riches romanticism to make the Foxx Group's CEO seem invincible while also being a brilliant brand ambassador for aspirational luxury.

But as he ran his thumb over the scar on his brow, and she glimpsed the barbed wire tattoo on his collarbone which had fascinated her that night—and fascinated her still—she wondered about the reality of his rough start. What price had he paid to become a success? What experiences had given him the drive and ambition to escape? And had he really been able to leave that boy behind? Because beneath the anger and bitterness directed at the father who had exploited him, she also detected an odd note of regret, even guilt, which didn't fit at all with the myth he had created for himself.

'I'm glad you broke free of that bastard,' Mason continued, dropping his hand from his face as if he had just noticed the habitual gesture. 'I also owe you an apology for the way I reacted that morning. Which I can see now had as much to do with baggage from my childhood as it did with finding out about your old man's agenda.'

'What baggage?' she asked, astonished not just by his forthright apology, but also the way it made her feel—both vindicated and seen.

'Just…stuff.' He shrugged, clearly unwilling to elaborate.

Had he said more about his past than he'd intended?

She quashed the foolish burst of compassion and hope. She'd allowed herself to get emotionally invested before, when she was lying in his arms that night, kidding herself the physical intimacy they'd shared had meant something more.

She couldn't make that mistake again. Because there was so much more at stake now. Not just for her, but also her baby.

Their baby.

She let the thought sink in. It had been so easy not to engage with Mason's place in her child's life while she was working her backside off to create a new life for herself. It was a lot less easy while he was sitting across from her, his broad shoulders stretching his T-shirt and his stubbled jaw reminding her of the feel of his lips on her...

She pushed down the unwanted blast of heat.

Focus, Bea, for Pete's sake.

'It's not important,' he said evasively, the intense gaze becoming hooded. 'The point is,' he continued, lifting his fork again, to wind it into the pasta, 'I guess I can understand why you ran off, but that doesn't explain why you didn't tell me that...' He ducked his head to indicate her belly. 'That our night had consequences.'

That? It? Junior? Your condition? The pregnancy? Consequences?

Was it significant that whenever he referred to their baby, he used impersonal terms? He'd made a massive deal about the fact she hadn't informed him of the pregnancy, but at the same time he hadn't given her any hints about what he felt about becoming a father.

'I intended to tell you, eventually,' she said, determined to believe that was true. She'd come so far. Enough to know she wasn't a coward any more. But contacting him had seemed overwhelming.

'I guess I kept putting it off to focus on other things... Like making a living,' she added, which was mostly true. 'And because I was scared about how you would react to the news.' Which was absolutely true. Her emotions whenever she thought about telling Mason had swung violently between panic and fear and guilt, so it had been simpler not to think about telling him at all. 'So I took the easiest option and just kept putting it off. And for that *I* owe *you* an apology,' she said, finally getting to the point.

Whatever his views on fatherhood, she hadn't had the right to keep this pregnancy a secret.

She'd made the decision to have this baby—*their* baby— without involving him, and she refused to regret it because she still didn't know how he would have reacted if she'd told him straight away. But it didn't matter what he might have said and done then, because it was academic now.

His brow furrowed with disapproval. But instead of berating her again for failing to contact him sooner, he shoved the pasta into his mouth. He chewed and swallowed, then gave her a stiff nod.

'Okay. Apology accepted,' he said, his tone tight, and a little grudging, but his gaze direct. 'I guess we both made mistakes.'

Relief washed through her. The knots in her stomach loosened.

Maybe this didn't have to be as hard as she had thought it would be.

But then he shot a pointed glance at her untouched food. 'Eat up before it gets cold. Then we need to discuss next steps.'

Next steps? What *next steps?*

Was he going to make demands and ultimatums? To dictate what would happen now? Because she was not about to compromise the independence she'd worked so hard for to kowtow to a man—even the scorching-hot billionaire who was the father of her child…

Scorching-hot? Where did that come from? So not the point, Bea.

Her skin flushed as she lifted her fork and concentrated on her food to beat back the latest wave of anxiety.

Mason Foxx was still a virtual stranger. She needed to get to know him better before she made any more assumptions about him. Good or bad.

They'd both apologised for past hurts, the wrongs they'd done each other. She had no idea what he could possibly mean by 'next steps'. But the fact it sounded so ominous could have more to do with her own insecurities, and the huge power imbalance between them, and that heat which would not die, than any malign intent on his part.

She still didn't even know what he felt about the pregnancy—other than angry she hadn't told him sooner. So it made sense to nurture this tentative truce.

And to avoid getting hung up on his scorching hotness! *Sheesh*.

Unfortunately, as they ate in silence—him demolishing the tasty pasta dish, while she picked at hers—the knot in her stomach and the hot brick in her abdomen refused to get the memo.

CHAPTER NINE

'*YOU WERE VERY HOT, and I responded to you in a way I hadn't thought I'd ever respond to anyone... Sexually speaking.*'

Mason polished off the last of the seafood linguini, his voracious appetite for food covering his voracious appetite for something else entirely—as the words Beatrice had murmured about their night five months ago spooled through his head on a loop. And forced him to acknowledge something he'd been refusing to engage with for five solid months.

He still wanted her. *A lot.*

Their unfinished business wasn't just sexual any more, might not *ever* have been just sexual—but sex was the one thing he felt comfortable focusing on. Her confirmation that her reasons for choosing him to take her virginity had never had anything to do with her father only made him eager to focus on it more.

Because that volatile sexual chemistry—which he had felt the first moment he had laid eyes on her—hadn't dimmed in the slightest.

It also explained a lot of things which had been confusing him for five months. Why he hadn't been able to forget her. Why he'd spent a fortune tracking her down. Why he'd dropped everything and flown out to the Italian Riviera.

Where the weird kick of joy as well as shock had come from when he'd spotted her in the maid's uniform and discovered she was pregnant with his baby.

On some basic, elemental level he just wanted her to be his.

He didn't believe in fate, or kismet, or love at first sight, or any of that other romantic stuff people used to justify their basic instincts. But he did believe in biology and chemistry. Which had to be why he had staked a claim to Beatrice that night, which couldn't now be broken.

The baby was an abstract concept to him in a lot of ways. He had never thought of becoming a father, probably would have laughed in the face of anyone who had suggested he would ever *want* to get a woman accidentally pregnant. But with Beatrice, he couldn't suppress the thought that their current situation didn't feel like a trap so much as an inevitability.

An inevitability he could use.

He had no idea how long the need, the yearning, the urge to possess her and protect her would last. After all, he'd never felt this way about anyone before—as if he had a sexual connection with them that was so strong and real and intense it might actually go beyond the physical. But one thing was certain—after five months of being desperate to find her, he planned to explore it.

As he watched her pick at her food, though, he could sense her nerves.

However hard she had worked to reinvent herself, one thing remained the same—she was still vulnerable. Much more vulnerable than she probably realised.

She had been blindsided by their intense physical connection that night too. Which was even less of a surprise. She had been a virgin, plus she had spent her life up to that point being bullied and coerced by her father. He hadn't lied when he'd told her he knew what that felt like. How it could destroy your self-esteem. Although he wished he hadn't revealed quite so much.

Thank God he had managed to stop himself blurting out the truth about his mum too.

She didn't need to know about the things he'd done to survive, to escape. Because then she might start questioning whether she wanted him within fifty feet of this baby.

Their baby.

He swallowed the last bite of pasta as the waiter arrived, disturbed to realise that Beatrice's reaction to his past might matter to him. He'd always been determined to curate his own story, but now, more than ever, he was glad he'd kept the sordid details of his past out of the public eye.

He certainly did not want her to know that his mum had abandoned him—or she might wonder why she had. Which was something he'd asked himself a thousand times over the years… And the only answer that made sense was that there was something in him his mother had been unable to love.

He didn't need Beatrice's love, but he was beginning to realise he wanted a commitment from her. So, letting her know that even his own mum hadn't wanted to stick around was not a smart move.

'*Il dolci*, Signor Foxx?' the maître d' asked.

'No desserts, thanks, Giovanni, we're finished here,' he announced. 'Charge my credit card and add a five-hundred-euro tip and, thanks, it was delicious.'

Giovanni beamed, then whisked the plates away. As the man disappeared, Mason dropped his napkin on the table and stood.

'But Mason, we… We haven't discussed next steps yet?'

Beatrice's face was a mask of confusion, but he could see her apprehension too.

He was glad she was off-kilter, because that could work in his favour. But he also needed to get her to relax enough to be amenable to what he had to say.

He knew how to negotiate, but he was used to negotiating from a position of power. And he didn't have all the power here. Thanks to his irrational behaviour five months ago, and his freak-out an hour ago. Plus, he'd never wanted anything as much as he wanted Beatrice Medford back in his bed.

The pregnancy could be a boon or a bust in that respect, he wasn't really sure which. And her newfound independence was another obstacle which could go either way. She couldn't really enjoy scrubbing toilets for a living but, at the same time, he could see that earning her own wage—after spending so long under her father's thumb—had to be seductive.

And the truth was, even their sexual connection wasn't necessarily going to work in his favour, as Beatrice seemed oblivious to exactly how powerful and rare it was.

'Let's head back to the Grande to have that discussion,' he said.

Until he figured out how to deal with all the variables, he wasn't about to play his hand. Which meant stalling. For now.

Her eyes widened. 'I… I don't think that's a good idea. If Signor Romano sees me going to your suite, he'll want to know why.'

He frowned. He didn't give a damn about Romano. As far as he was concerned, her job was over now anyway. She couldn't keep working as a maid—he drew in a breath—or even a housekeeping manager. Not now he'd found her.

But he forced himself not to lose his cool. Because it would be totally counter-productive when it came to Operation Get Beatrice to Relax.

'Then let's head back to your place. Where do you live?' he asked, suddenly realising he was curious.

She frowned. She wasn't too keen on that idea. But he could also see she didn't want to risk breaking their truce. 'I live on the grounds of the hotel. I guess we might be able to sneak to my trailer without being seen.'

A trailer? She was living in a mobile home... What the actual...?

He bit his tongue, schooled his features. 'Terrific,' he said. 'Let's go.'

But as they made their way back to the car, he could feel his hackles rising again. What had she been thinking?

As he drove down the coast road at a more sedate pace, he promised to do whatever it took to make Beatrice see sense.

Because no way in hell was he going to allow the mother of his child to live in squalor, doing manual labour for pennies, hundreds of miles away from where he could keep an eye on her.

'Watch your step, it's rocky here,' Bea said, aware of Mason's pricey high-tops as he followed her through the grove of gnarled lemon trees.

He hadn't said much on the drive back, but she had sensed his disapproval when she'd directed him to the unpaved road which led to the overgrown terraces banked into the cliffs above the hotel. But her heart lifted as they came out of the old orchard and approached the mobile home Marta and her husband had helped her to tow up here a month ago.

With rent in this area way out of her price range, she'd spent the last of her inheritance buying the third-hand mobile home after spotting it in a car park in Rapallo. She'd negotiated with Fabrizio to let her park it on the unused land, hooked up the electricity and water supply to the kitchen below and spent all her spare time cleaning, repairing and decorating it. She had a spectacular view from the porch she'd constructed from old crates and planted with flowers and herbs in a cluster of pots. Stringing solar-powered fairy lights through the branches of the surrounding lemon trees had turned her new home into an enchanted citrus-scented oasis—and she loved sitting here in the evenings, doing translation work for the nearby tourist bureau to supplement her income.

Space was at a premium inside the trailer, with a tiny box shower and composting toilet, a compact lounge/kitchenette and a bedroom at the back taken up entirely by her one extravagance—a queen-sized bed—but she had everything she needed.

This was *her* place. She no longer had to share the bunk room with the seasonal staff.

She fished the key out from under a pot of fresh basil and opened the door, aware of Mason's silence.

She hadn't wanted to bring him here. The man was a billionaire who had walk-in wardrobes bigger than the home she was so proud of. But as she entered the neat, scrupulously clean and well-ordered kitchen and lounge area, she refused to let it bother her.

'Would you like a cup of tea?' she asked from behind the counter.

'Sure,' he said without enthusiasm.

He had to duck to get in the door. And with his head

skimming the low ceiling, his presence instantly made her home look more cramped than compact.

'How long have you lived here?' he asked, his gaze gliding over the bright, colourful furnishings which she had borrowed or sourced at local markets and thrift stores—and convinced herself were vintage and eclectic.

'Just over a month,' she said, busying herself with the tea-making. 'I love it. It gives me privacy and freedom, and it's affordable. Signor Romano takes a peppercorn rent and the utility fees off my wages and the evenings are stunning here, with the scent of bougainvillea and lemons in the air and the heart-stopping view across the bay towards Portofino.'

'Uh-huh,' he said with a distinct lack of enthusiasm as he settled on the two-seater couch which made up her living area. The old frame creaked under his weight, and when he stretched out his long legs, his feet almost touched the opposite wall.

She waited for the water to boil, aware of the huge chasm which existed between their lives. But she couldn't resist the opportunity to watch him, unobserved. His shoulders were impossibly wide as they stretched across the back of the couch. His hair was shorter than it had been that night, when she'd fisted her fingers into the silky waves and held onto him as he sank into her.

And made a baby.

She blinked and concentrated on the tea, the flush of heat so intense it was uncomfortable. And embarrassing. But as she poured the boiled water into her teapot and arranged a tray with two mugs and some freshly baked amaretto cookies, the hot brick in her abdomen continued to pulse. How come she could smell him over the almond scent of the amaretti and the citrus from the trees outside? That intoxicating aroma of woodsy cologne and laundry detergent and sandalwood soap which had her remembering far too forcefully the feel of him, making her his.

Not his, Bea. You belong to no one now but yourself and your baby.

But then she frowned at the tea tray. She added a bowl of sugar and a jug of milk—and tried to contain the foolish wave of emotion at the thought that she had made a baby with this man but she had no clue how he liked his tea.

Which is why you allowed him to come here. Because you need to know him better.

Heat scorched her cheeks.

Just not in the biblical sense, even if your sex-starved body is comprehensively contradicting you on that score.

Which had to be the pregnancy hormones. Totally.

She started to lift the tray.

'Wait, I'll get that,' he said, and rose so swiftly from the couch the trailer rocked.

Then he was next to her in the tiny kitchen, his strong body close enough to touch. And smell not just the delicious woodsy cologne and the soap, but also the tantalising aroma of salt and man she remembered from that night.

He went to lift the tray just as she tried to step aside, and their bodies collided. Her breath caught in her lungs, her gaze trapped in his, her whole body alive with sensations she'd tried to forget. But hadn't. Awareness and passion darkened his eyes to a mossy green, and made her insides clench.

She couldn't seem to move. Almost as if in slow motion, he raised his hand and brushed his thumb down the side of her face. She shivered, her tongue darting out to moisten her lips, her throat so dry she felt as if she were attempting to swallow a boulder.

'I still want you, Beatrice,' he murmured, his rough voice barely audible above the blood rushing in her ears. 'I never stopped wanting you.'

His hand slid down to cup the back of her neck.

She should say something. *Anything*. But she couldn't find the words to protest as his head bent to hers, his breath feathering across her lips.

'If you don't want this too, you have to tell me now,' he murmured.

But instead of calling a halt to this madness, her sob of surrender sounded like a gunshot in the cramped space.

His lips captured hers—claiming, branding—and his fingers threaded into her hair to cradle her head and anchor her mouth for his possession. The hot rock in her stomach plunged between her thighs and throbbed, the hunger and heat so familiar and yet different.

More demanding, more intense, so much more overwhelming.

Their tongues tangled, the dance of seduction both fierce and forthright and unstoppable, the heady haze of need descending so fast she couldn't think. All she could do was feel.

She kissed him back with a fervour she couldn't control. She grabbed his T-shirt to drag him nearer, until her bottom hit the counter and his lean abs pressed against the tight mound of her belly.

Hard hands grasped her waist and lifted her onto the counter, until she was perched on the edge, her legs splayed around his hips.

They broke apart. She needed air, she needed time to

think. What was she doing? Giving in to this insane desire was not smart.

But then he pressed marauding lips to her neck, forcing her head back against the cupboards, and palmed her breast.

Sensation spiralled down to her core with devastating purpose, and a moan escaped as he eased the front of her dress down, releasing one engorged nipple.

His lips captured the yearning peak, which was so much more sensitive now. She clasped his head to her chest, urging him on, as his palms trailed up her thighs, pushing her dress to her waist.

He swore softly and released her nipple from the delicious torment. The breeze from the open door made her aware of her bared breast, the nipple damp from his kisses, drawing tight. But then he shifted back, and her gaze locked on the thick ridge in his jeans.

Their eyes met, the flush of arousal slashing across his cheeks like the fire burning across her collarbone.

'Is this okay?' he asked, his hand hovering on the buttons of his jeans.

The harsh demand registered, but she couldn't seem to process what he was saying through the heady fog of desire.

'Will it harm the baby?' he asked again, as he stroked the thick length, desperation turning his gaze to a rich emerald.

All she could do was shake her head dumbly, while her every thought was obliterated by the throbbing need to feel him inside her again.

He grunted, then dragged her panties down her legs, before finding the swollen nub of her clitoris with his thumb. She braced her hands on the counter, dropped her head back and gave herself over to his sure, devastating touch as he worked her into a frenzy.

She was panting, sobbing, as she flew to her peak, but

just as the pleasure broke over her, she heard him fumbling with his jeans and releasing the thick erection.

Hooking her legs over his hips, he dragged her forward and entered her to the hilt.

She clung to his shoulders as his forehead touched hers, his harsh breathing matching her own. He gave her time to adjust to the overwhelming pleasure, the exquisite sensation, the intense connection. Then he began to move, drawing out, thrusting back, slowly, carefully but with a purpose, a determination which sent her careering back to that terrifying peak. The pleasure rose to crest again—so fast, too furious—the sensations consuming her vicious and unstoppable now.

The molten pleasure exploded along her nerve-endings as she let out a feral cry of completion, shattering one last time. She heard him shout out, and fly over right behind her.

What the hell did I do?

Mason clasped Beatrice's bare hips and pressed his face into her fragrant hair, trying desperately to level himself. To take stock. To think past the bone-melting climax which had left him weak and shaky and strung out.

But he couldn't seem to battle his way out of the thick fog of afterglow. Couldn't seem to feel anything but the tight clasp of her body, massaging him through the last of his orgasm, and her hands, limp and trembling, as she clung to him. And couldn't hear anything but the thunder of his own heartbeat and the ragged pants of her breathing.

He'd just taken her like an insane person.

One minute they'd been standing too close in the cramped space, and the next he'd been dragging off her panties and thrusting heavily into that tight, wet heat.

His chest heaved as enough of his faculties returned to

dump him off the glittering cloud and plunge him into brutal reality.

He shifted back, felt her twitch as he moved away from her.

She looked shell-shocked, dazed, her breathing uneven, her nipple reddened where he had mauled it moments ago. He braced against the swift spike of desire as she banded an arm across her chest to cover her nakedness.

Shame engulfed him as he stuffed himself back into his jeans.

He bent to pick up her underwear, brutally aware of her struggling to repair her own clothing. He clasped her elbow to help her get down from the narrow counter. As she landed on her feet, she tugged her arm free, and shame closed his throat.

What could he say to make amends? He'd planned to be smart, sophisticated, pragmatic, to reason with her about her living conditions, to persuade her to give up her job and let him support her… And then, eventually, to show her that whatever they'd shared in London wasn't over.

But, instead of that, he'd jumped her as soon as he'd scented her arousal and got close enough to touch.

He handed her the scrap of lace.

She grabbed it and slipped her panties back on.

'Thank you,' she said, the polite reply incongruous.

'I didn't use a condom,' he murmured. 'I'm sorry.'

Her gaze finally connected with his, but the vivid blush on her cheeks only made her seem more innocent. More vulnerable. And made him feel like more of an animal.

Where had all his cool points gone? Before Beatrice he'd always strived to be, if not charming, at least generous with women in bed. He knew he was rough around the edges, but he never wanted any women to be able to say he wasn't aware of their pleasure too. But with Beatrice, sex had always been different. It had never been fun, or light, or recreational. It had always been basic and elemental—a force of nature he couldn't control. He'd come close to losing it completely just now, and it shocked him.

'It's okay,' she said, running her fingers through her short cap of curls and breaking eye contact. 'Luckily, I don't think you can get me pregnant twice,' she added with a dry wit which might have been funny—if he hadn't felt so raw and exposed.

The comment brought the baby back to the forefront of his mind, the way it hadn't been as soon as she'd given him the go-ahead earlier.

The shame kicked up another notch.

She went to step around him, and he laid a hand on her waist to hold her in place.

'I haven't slept with anyone else since that night,' he said. 'And I've never taken a woman without protection before now,' he added, not even sure why he felt compelled to defend himself.

But when her eyes widened at his admission, the look in them doubtful, he knew why.

He'd accused her of using him that night, but the truth was, it had always been the other way around. He'd used *her*. Because she'd responded to him with an innocent enthusiasm which had made him feel connected to her in a way he'd never felt connected to any other woman. But he needed to be able to control it or he was in danger of becoming that feral kid again, looking for validation where there was none.

'Okay,' she said, sounding wary now.

He blocked her path as she tried to step around him again. 'Are you okay?'

Her brow furrowed, as if the question puzzled her. He'd bet he was the only bloke she'd ever slept with. He couldn't imagine her sleeping with other men when she was pregnant with his child, and all he'd shown her so far was hunger, and heat. The urge to show her tenderness, though, only confused him more.

'I had several orgasms,' she said, her cheeks flaming but her gaze unflinching. 'If that's what you're asking.'

He cleared his throat, the husky confession doing things to his self-control he didn't need.

'Actually, it's not.' He cradled her cheek, slid his thumb over the abraded skin he'd kissed too enthusiastically. 'The baby?' he managed. 'Will it be okay? I didn't mean to be so rough.'

She shifted away from him. And he was forced to release her.

He needed to get a grip and ignore the scent of sex filling the tiny kitchenette—not to mention the remnants of that mind-blowing orgasm still echoing in his groin—which were doing weird things to his libido.

'The baby's fine, Mason. You weren't that rough. I enjoyed it. I guess there was still some pent-up…stuff between us. But I…' She ran her hand down her face, clearly flustered. Why did he find that arousing too? 'I definitely don't think we should do it again,' she added. 'Because that will just complicate things.'

Everything inside him rejected the statement.

'Beatrice, they're already complicated,' he said, because there wasn't much point in avoiding the obvious. 'You're going to have a baby, which means you can't stay here doing this job. You do realise that?' he added, because he might as well get it out there. He had planned to be subtle, coaxing, persuasive, but he'd already torpedoed that approach.

He'd seen the way she'd beamed with pride when she'd walked into this broken-down trailer. And heard the sense of achievement in her voice when she'd talked about her job at the resort. But she needed to see sense now.

'Not when it's my child you're having,' he added. 'I won't allow it.'

He knew he'd made a major tactical error the minute he'd said it when she sucked in a sharp breath. He blamed it on the fact that all his brain cells had just been incinerated.

'That's outrageous, Mason,' she announced, her expression going from flustered to horrified in a heartbeat. 'You don't get to decide what I'm allowed to do just because I'm pregnant.'

When it's my kid, yes, I damn well do.

It was what he wanted to say, but he managed to hold onto the knee-jerk counter-attack as a few of his brain cells worked their way back out of his boxers.

The truth was, he wasn't entirely sure where the fierce desire to protect her and his child came from. Perhaps it was wrapped up in the shock of finding her pregnant—after having dreamed about it so often. Maybe it was the far too revealing revelations they'd shared at lunch, or the explosion of endorphins which he was still trying to get a handle on… But understanding his fierce need to stake a claim on this woman and ignoring it were not the same thing.

He couldn't ignore it, not any more. He'd tried for the last five months and all it had done was leave him on edge—which had to explain why he'd gone off like a powder keg as soon as he'd been alone with her in a confined space.

'That came out wrong,' he said, trying for conciliatory now his cognitive function wasn't a total bombsite.

'Yes, it flipping well did,' Beatrice concurred, looking appalled.

'I just meant… I want you to come back to London. With me. I can buy you a place.' He let his gaze glide over the home she was so proud of, but which would never be good enough—for her or his baby. 'Which would be much more suitable than this one. And I want you to have the best healthcare.' Plus, she would finally be where he needed her to be, for his sanity, if nothing else. 'I screwed up with the condom, so you and the baby are my responsibility.'

'That's ridiculous, Mason. No, we're not,' she said, but she sounded more exasperated now than appalled—which felt like progress.

He'd made a total balls-up of this conversation in every possible way. But something about her expression made him glad he'd finally broached the subject of her returning to London. He'd never been a sophisticated guy—especially with her—so subtle would always have been a stretch.

'I chose to have this baby, not you,' she continued. 'I had options when the doctor confirmed I was pregnant, but I didn't take them.'

He sighed, but the tension in his ribs released as it occurred to him he was glad she hadn't.

'And I'm really not ready to uproot my life again,' she added. But when she chewed on her bottom lip in that distracting way she had, two things occurred to him. Not all her cognitive abilities were fully functioning yet either. And she was more anxious and less sure than she seemed.

Both things he could take advantage of, once he'd worked out a coherent strategy. But to do that he needed time to get his brain function fully operational again.

'Why don't we take a rain check on this discussion?' He cupped her chin and planted a kiss on her lips, satisfied when her mouth softened instinctively. 'I need to grab a shower first,' he continued, suddenly feeling lighter than he

had in a while. Five months, to be precise. 'And so do you,'
he added, sniffing the air, which was still heavy with the
scent of sex. 'Or that smell is liable to turn me on so much
I may have to christen the bed in this place too.'

'Mason, what the …? That's *not* funny,' she cried, sounding outraged as she slapped his hand away.

But he could see the stunned arousal turning the pale
blue of her irises to black. And he knew she was no more
immune to the scent of him on her skin than he was.

'We can go to the pizza place you mentioned in Rapallo,'
he said, his regenerating brain cells starting to work over-
time. 'And you can pay. What's it called?'

'Pizzeria di Rapallo,' she said, drawing out the words to
emphasise her uncertainty. 'We can go for dinner and discuss this more. But I'm not giving up my life here, Mason,'
she added. 'Or coming back to London with you. I can't.
And I don't want to.'

Yeah, you can, and you will.

Because he was going to do everything in his power to
convince her.

'I'll pick you up at seven,' he said as he backed out of the
trailer, leaving her standing in the doorway looking deliciously rumpled and delightfully confused.

As he headed back to his car through the citrus grove,
he dug his phone out and fired off a text to Joe.

Found B Medford in Portofino. Pregnant. Baby mine. @
Pizzeria di Rapallo tonight. Tip off press.

That took care of the stick.

He hated the tabloid press but she had to realise that,
sooner or later, they would find her here, and when they

did her life would be untenable. He was just speeding up the inevitable.

Now, all he had to do was come up with a persuasive carrot.

She'd mentioned studying languages, and he'd heard her speaking fluent Italian, making him wonder if she were a polymath. Plus, she knew more about the sharp end of hospitality now than most of his executives. Finding her a position in London that would satisfy her desire for independence and utilise her skills, while also giving her a much better salary and career prospects, would make it even harder for her to resist the inevitable.

He dismissed the tiny ripple of guilt as he shoved the phone back into his pocket. He had always been ruthless. It was a skill he'd developed to get over his mother's desertion and escape his father's failures without a scratch.

He frowned, climbing into the car. Or at least not any emotional ones.

Of course, that was also why he was unlikely to be a good father in the traditional sense.

But his ruthlessness was how he'd built a billion-pound legacy which his child and Beatrice could benefit from—even if he wasn't cut out to become a permanent part of their lives.

He began to whistle as he reversed the car down the rutted track, feeling sure of himself again for the first time in five months.

The residual hum of desire pulsed in his lap as he remembered their frantic lovemaking in her trailer.

The fringe benefits of having Beatrice exactly where he wanted her, preferably somewhere less cramped and a lot closer to home, would be a perk they could both enjoy. Until their volatile sexual chemistry had worn off—which would, no doubt, be some time before she gave birth to his child. But when that time came, he planned to have fulfilled all his responsibilities to her and the baby—which would at least make him a better parent than the two useless people who had given birth to him.

CHAPTER TEN

THE FOLLOWING MORNING, Bea woke feeling tired and unsettled, and still tender from yesterday afternoon's jump-fest in her kitchen—which had made sleeping all but impossible.

Every time she closed her eyes she could see Mason's face again, his eyes glittering with arousal and purpose, and feel him thrusting heavily inside her—taking her to places she had only ever been with him.

Her heart bobbed in her chest. And the familiar desire surged again.

She glanced at her alarm clock and groaned, then threw back the sheet. She had half an hour before her shift started.

But as she dragged herself out of bed she recalled their dinner date over pizza at the bustling eatery on the seafront, the tables packed as the sun edged towards the sea on the horizon—and her frustration increased.

Their conversation in Rapallo had been a lot less productive than their lunch date.

Because Mason had resolutely refused to listen to her. She didn't want to leave Portofino just because he felt responsible for their baby, or so they could have lots more great sex, or so he could offer her an amazing job—after questioning her extensively about her language skills... Because, as annoyingly tempting as all those offers were, she knew they were just bribes to bend her to his will.

It had taken her a while to get her heartbeat under control when he'd turned up at seven to collect her. And it had become harder and harder to say no. Because being in his company had brought back all those unwanted urges. *Again.*

It was lowering to realise that, despite a five-month separation, and the person she had become in that time, this man still had a powerful hold over her.

She should not have had sex with him. And not just any sex, but frantic, no-holds-barred, mind-blowing orgasmic sex. But during their meal she had managed to forgive herself for jumping him.

Mason Foxx was charismatic, edgy, ruggedly handsome, phenomenally successful and stunningly hot. Why wouldn't he make her weak at the knees? Even Marta had noticed his charms and she'd been happily married for five years and had two children under four. Plus, Mason was the father of her baby. Maybe it wasn't just her weak impulse control where he was concerned which was to blame, but also the biological imperative of seeking out the one person who could help protect her child?

Maybe that also explained the clenching sensation in her ribs when he had told her he wanted her to come back to London.

After taking a quick shower and donning her hotel uniform, she headed into the kitchen and began making herself her morning coffee—while resolutely trying not to relive yesterday's jump-fest again.

She really hadn't expected him to want to support her. The most she had hoped for was that he wouldn't hate her, for taking the choice away from him to become a father. But when he had laid out his plan, determined to give her and their baby whatever they needed to thrive, she had felt her wayward emotions getting the better of her again.

Which had made her even more wary of accepting his offer.

She didn't want to risk falling into her old habit of subjugating her needs to someone else's wishes. And she couldn't give up her independence. Not for anything. Or anyone.

The one thing Mason hadn't said, the one thing he had refused to be drawn on even, was whether or not he wanted to be an active part of this baby's life after it was born.

She frowned, her thoughts scattering as she noticed the ripples forming in her coffee. A strange rumbling developed. The sound became deafening, the vibrations so violent it made the cupboards rattle and the whole trailer shake.

She rushed to the door of the trailer.

Was this an earthquake? Did they have earthquakes on the Italian Riviera?

She flung the door wide, in time to see an enormous black shape darken the sky above, then glide over her head and drop down towards the terrace below.

What on earth...?

Then she noticed the Foxx Group logo emblazoned on the machine's side as it landed on the hotel lawn.

She was still staring at the helicopter when Mason marched through the citrus orchard, with an intent look on his face. Her heartbeat shot straight to warp speed, because she remembered that look from yesterday afternoon, when they'd made love in the trailer... And yesterday evening, when he'd walked her back here in the twilight, and she had resisted the powerful urge to ask him in for a nightcap— because she had known exactly where that would lead.

'You need to pack. We have to leave,' he said without preamble as he reached her.

'Why?' she asked, startled not just by the urgency in his

voice but the desire to obey him without question—which could not be good.

'The press is here,' he said.

She heard it then, the commotion below them—a cacophony of shouts and pops no longer masked by the chopper's engines.

'Pictures of us together at the pizzeria last night are all over the internet,' he continued. 'Romano and the staff are having to hold them off until the security guards I've hired arrive.'

Shock came first, swiftly followed by guilt. He'd warned her this might happen when she'd first suggested eating at the pizzeria in Rapallo. Why hadn't she listened to him?

'I can't believe they still care,' she said inanely, struggling to adjust to the situation—and the wrenching realisation that her choices had just narrowed considerably.

She would have to leave. The Grande's clientele came here looking for a peaceful vacation, not to be besieged by paparazzi and journalists. Plus, she had just made Marta and Fabrizio and everyone else's jobs impossible.

'Of course they care,' he said, sounding surprisingly magnanimous, given the untenable situation she had created for everyone.

He had been right. Hiding out in Portofino indefinitely and pretending her past didn't exist had never been a viable option for the long term.

'Society Princess runs off to Italy to become a maid and have a billionaire's kid alone and in secret,' Mason added. 'It makes a great story.'

A story which he would be the villain of, she realised, as the last of her delusions about her situation came crashing down.

Why had she never considered how her choices would

reflect on him? And the reputation he'd worked so hard to build. He'd said nothing last night about the negative press her situation would attract. But she should have realised how it would look if the press ever discovered she was living in Italy, doing a menial job while pregnant with his child.

'I've spoken to Romano,' he said, gently herding her back into the trailer. 'And your friend Marta. He's going to write you a final cheque and she'll meet us by the bird to say goodbye.'

She blinked furiously, devastated—at having to leave her life here so abruptly—but also stupidly touched that he had arranged everything so quickly.

She hadn't wanted to accept his help before. Had been determined to resent the loss of independence that would represent. But perhaps she should have realised she had already lost that by choosing to have his child.

She'd proved something incredibly important to herself during the last five months. That she wasn't useless, or pathetic, that she could thrive and prosper if she worked hard and showed initiative. But she had to face the reality now— of her situation, but also of his.

'But we need to go now,' he added, crowding her trailer again with his presence.

'Okay,' she said.

His eyebrows flew up. 'Really? No more arguments?'

'No, I understand,' she said.

All he'd wanted was to do the right thing. For her and their baby. And she needed to let him.

As she set off to pack up as much of her life in Italy as she could carry, it occurred to her that her confidence in her own abilities had never depended on where she was, or what she did for a living. Or even who she was with—even if that person was as overwhelming as Mason. All it had ever depended on was her own courage and determination.

As she said a hasty goodbye to Marta and Fabrizio and the other hotel staff by the Foxx Group helicopter—while the press shouted intrusive questions from the hotel car park, threatening to break the barricade being manned by Mason's security guards—a pang of regret and sadness pierced her chest.

She had found a home in Portofino. But she needed to move on and build a home for her baby as well now, which ought to include its father...

She settled into the helicopter as Mason spoke to the pilot. But as she strapped herself into the seat, instead of feeling compromised, or wary, her heart did a giddy two-step.

She didn't know if they could make this relationship work. She wasn't even sure they would still want to by the time the baby was born. There were so many things about Mason she didn't know, she frowned, including how he took his tea. But trusting to luck and her own judgement didn't seem anywhere near as scary as it had when she'd arrived in Rapallo five months ago.

She caressed her bump, remembering the explosion of hormones which had occurred in her trailer yesterday... The pulse in her abdomen became wild and insistent as Mason strode out of the cockpit, then folded his muscular body into the seat next to her.

'All good?' he asked as the helicopter's blades whirred above their head.

She nodded. 'Yes. And thank you.'

'What for?' he asked.

She smiled, enjoying his puzzled frown. For such a forceful guy, he wasn't always as sure about everything as he seemed.

'For rescuing me,' she said, nodding towards the press hordes still trying to clamber over the barricades. 'From that.'

His gaze intensified, then dropped warily to where her hand rested on her belly. 'Having got you into this mess,' he said, 'it was the least I could do.'

She wondered what mess he was talking about.

Then realised that might be why he hadn't wanted to talk about fatherhood. Because he simply didn't know yet how he felt about it.

But then the rest of his reply registered. And it occurred to her that other men would have done a lot less.

Why did it matter if he was unsure about his role in this baby's life? They had four months to figure it out now. Together.

Mason wasn't a bad man. And the desire between them was still as vibrant and exciting as ever. So why shouldn't they explore that too?

Her heart lifted in her chest as the big bird rose off the ground and the noise from the blades drowned out further conversation.

The smile on her lips sank into her heart as the sun shimmered over the deep blue of the sea below, dazzling her... She and Mason and their baby *might* have a bright future ahead of them—as a family—something she'd always yearned for, but never thought she truly deserved... Until now. But how would she ever know if she didn't make the most of this chance to find out?

She waved goodbye to the first real friends she'd ever had, before the lush beauty of the Italian Riviera—where she had finally discovered the real Bea Medford—disappeared under the clouds.

But her heart continued to float on the flight to Genoa, and the journey on the Foxx company jet back to the UK—lightened by hope and determination and the promise of all the possibilities ahead of her, which she couldn't wait to explore.

CHAPTER ELEVEN

THE SCENIC LIFT travelled up the outside of the Foxx Suites building—Tower Bridge looking suitably imposing as it spanned the river—while Bea grappled with the realisation that she had basically come full circle in five months.

She'd built her life back up from that low point—built it back better and stronger. She wasn't that panicked girl any more, but it still felt strange, and emotionally a little overwhelming, to be back at Mason's London penthouse again.

'Hey, you okay?' Mason asked, his hand stroking her back.

She glanced over her shoulder and sent him a tired smile. He'd asked that question constantly since the helicopter had left Portofino. And he couldn't seem to stop touching her, which—while kicking off those unruly desires—had also felt protective and comforting, sort of.

'Yes, it just feels weird. Being back here again. When I feel like a different person.'

He tugged her gently into his arms until her belly rested against his waist. 'I guess you're two different people now,' he joked.

She chuckled, grateful that he could joke about the baby. 'Yes, I suppose we are.'

As they walked into the lobby area he dumped the rucksack she had stuffed with all her most precious possessions several hours ago on the breakfast bar. Still a little dusty from her journey through Europe to get to Portofino and made of cheap nylon, her pack looked out of place on the sleek marble surface.

But then she felt totally out of place in the stunning designer bachelor pad.

She gulped down the tickle of anxiety in her throat.

Mason strolled to the kitchen area and poured her a glass of chilled water from the gleaming double wide refrigerator. She chugged it down gratefully. The throb in her abdomen returned when he tucked a short curl of hair behind her ear, the look in his eyes a mixture of bossy, possessive and intense.

Which was also super-hot. *Damn him*.

'If there's anything you need, just text,' he said, while she continued to drink the cold water. 'I can get the rest of your stuff in Portofino shipped over. I've had all my things cleared out, so the place is all yours.'

'You won't be sleeping here too?' she asked.

His lips quirked and she realised how needy she sounded.

But she'd assumed—had hoped, in fact—that they would be living together. She wanted to get to know him. Not just how he felt about the baby, about them, but everything, because he fascinated her—on so many different levels.

'Not sleeping, no,' he answered, the sensual smile suggesting he was enjoying her discomfort. 'I prefer my own space. But I'm hoping that won't preclude us sharing the bed here on a regular basis.' His gaze heated, and hot blood charged into her cheeks, while turning the throb in her belly into a definite hum. 'Or the kitchen counter. Lady's choice.'

'I see,' she said, or rather croaked, her throat having dried to parchment. She took another gulp of the icy water.

She could tell him she didn't want to continue their sexual relationship. But that ship had already sailed and hit an enormous iceberg on her kitchen counter in Portofino. Plus, the hum was making it clear a sexless relationship wasn't what she wanted.

But his decision to live elsewhere was more problematic. How could she get to know him if he was hardly ever here?

'Why do you need your own space?' she asked, because it occurred to her that could be even more of an issue when the baby was born. Not that she expected him to live with them, exactly, if he wasn't comfortable with that. But perhaps it was time to start asking more direct questions about how he envisioned his place in this child's life.

He shrugged. 'I guess I've never been good at sharing,' he said cryptically. 'Plus, I'm a workaholic. I do a lot of travelling. I sleep, at most, five hours a night. And I've never had to tell anyone where I am or what I'm doing. Joe, my PA, knows my schedule. But that's it.'

'You've never lived with *anyone*?' she asked, a little astonished by the revelation—and the insight it gave her into his life.

She had known he was a lone wolf. It was all part of the Foxx brand. But had he always been alone, and why did that seem a little sad somehow? He'd mentioned the dysfunctional relationship he'd had with his father, but what about his mother? Or other carers and relatives? And why had he never lived with any of the many women he'd dated? She guessed commitment issues weren't uncommon in workaholic billionaires in their thirties. But what would that mean when he became a dad?

He shrugged again, but the movement was less relaxed. 'Not since I was a kid,' he said. 'And even then, I was always much better off on my own,' he clarified.

'Okay,' she said, feeling oddly bereft for him.

She'd always had Katie—even when her big sister was sofa surfing round London as a homeless teenager she'd kept in touch. And when Bea was really small, she'd had her Welsh grandmother too. She could still remember the cottage in Snowdonia where Angharad Evans had lived, and which Katie had eventually inherited. The warmth of the wood-burning stove on a rainy day, and the cosiness of the big brass bed upstairs where their *Nain* had told them bedtime stories about the mother who had loved them but had died too young.

Why would any child be better off without the security of being loved? Unless the people who were supposed to love them never had.

'Hey… It's not a big deal,' he said, taking the glass out of her hand and placing it on the breakfast bar. 'It's just easier if I don't live here.' Leaning against the marble bar, he took her hips in his hands and tugged her towards him. She braced her palms against his chest and felt his pectoral muscles flex and quiver—which sent sensation shooting into her panties. 'I don't want to keep you up at night waiting around for me… Unless I've got plans for you that don't involve sleeping.'

The suggestive gleam in his eyes had her choking out a laugh. And dispelled the moment of melancholy, which she was sure was his intention. But she let it go. She had time, lots of time, to find out more about his past and to quiz him about his plans for the future.

'Is everything always about sex with you?' she asked with mock outrage, as she threaded her fingers into his hair and tugged his lips closer.

'Pretty much,' he said, not sounding remotely apologetic as his devilish lips found the pulse point in her neck.

Before she could protest about his distraction techniques, or question him further, he boosted her into his arms.

'Come on, Princess,' he said, the old endearment making the throb in her abdomen rise to wrap around her heart.

'Practicalities later,' he declared. 'Naked fun now.'

As he marched down the hallway, she couldn't find the will to resist him.

Surely sex was a good way to increase the intimacy between them—and help them both relax and enjoy this new phase of their relationship, she reasoned.

And as his devious hands cupped her bottom, then sank into her panties, her anticipation peaked, and she concluded that sex certainly couldn't hurt.

Much, *much* later, she lay in a boneless heap, her body giddy with afterglow, on the bed where they had once made a baby, what felt like a lifetime ago, as he levered himself off the mattress.

She watched him dress, his muscular frame—and those fascinating scars and tattoos—gilded by the evening sunshine, while she resisted the pull of exhaustion and ignored the pang of dismay and regret.

Once he was fully clothed, he tucked her under the duvet, kissed her forehead and murmured, 'Later.'

But as the sound of his footsteps disappeared down the hallway and lulled her into a dreamless sleep, a thought drifted through her semi-consciousness…

They'd had lots of naked fun, but they hadn't sorted out any practicalities—except that his mouth was as versatile and inventive as the rest of him when it came to giving her multiple orgasms.

CHAPTER TWELVE

One month later

'MASON, WE'VE GOT a table for you and Ms Medford for the Phoenix fundraiser tonight—just wanted to know if you're likely to attend,' asked John Taverner, Foxx's far too eager publicity manager. 'Joe told me to confirm directly with you.'

That was because his PA knew his social schedule was mostly blank now, Mason mused, taking in the view of Tower Bridge as the lift climbed to the top floor. Because he preferred to keep his evenings free—for booty calls with Beatrice.

He frowned. Booty calls, and too much more.

'We won't be there,' Mason murmured into his phone as the lift reached the penthouse. 'Give our apologies and add an extra hundred grand to the donation,' he finished, then cut off the call and shoved the phone into his pocket.

He'd escorted Beatrice to several events the first few weeks they'd been back in London. He'd enjoyed showing her off, plus he'd been convinced her presence on his arm— as the mother of his child—would enhance the Foxx brand. But he'd grown bored with that charade quickly, especially after he'd become aware how tired she got in the evenings.

At six months, her pregnancy was starting to take a toll on her energy levels, so it made sense not to parade her around tonight—and the press intrusion was always intense, so why encourage it?

He tore off his tie as the lift's doors opened. But as he dumped his briefcase on the hall table, unease skittered up his spine.

When exactly had he become such a homebody, more eager to spend time with her than promote his business?

He tried to shake off the uncomfortable thought, but as he stepped into the living area of the penthouse, his frown deepened and the muscles in his neck tightened.

He'd ensconced Beatrice here four weeks ago—specifically so he could keep his life separate from hers—but had spent pretty much every night since rushing back here to join her for dinner and sex after they both finished work.

He had always loved going to work, but the struggle to leave Beatrice at dawn every morning—so he had time to return to his suite at Foxx Belgravia and prepare for the day—was real. And what the hell had happened to his work ethic these days?

He'd barely been able to concentrate on the string of meetings he'd had today about the new Foxx Motel chain they were building in the Hamptons, had even delegated the site visit to his New York executive team because he didn't want to spend time away from her. The whole project had begun to feel like a chore because his mind was always elsewhere. Such as this morning, when he had been fixated on the memory of Beatrice's breasts peeking over the duvet as she lay virtually comatose when he'd left.

Why couldn't he control the constant desire to be with her?

He'd started to look forward to their evenings together

for a host of reasons and not just the sex. He loved hearing her eager observations about her new job—and was stupidly proud of what she had achieved in such a small space of time.

When he'd told his acquisitions team to find her a position which would utilise her language skills and had a competitive salary and benefits, he'd envisioned the job being busy work which would fulfil the promises he'd made to her in Portofino. But Beatrice had the work ethic of a Trojan and was a genuine polymath—according to her boss Jenna, who adored her—so she'd quickly made herself indispensable.

He appreciated her unique insights into his business initiatives too, in the conversations they shared about each other's day over takeaway food, or their latest culinary disaster—because neither of them had any aptitude in the kitchen and he didn't want to hire staff when he wanted to be alone with her. He'd even started to enjoy her snippets of information about the pregnancy, perhaps because he had become unbearably curious about the life inside her too. Even though he shouldn't be.

He shrugged off his jacket and dumped it on the statement sofa—where he had brought her to a screaming orgasm last night after they'd watched one of the romcoms she loved. But he couldn't seem to shrug off the troubling direction of his thoughts.

How had he become so dependent on spending time with her? And why, when he found it so easy to deflect any probing questions about his past and their future, was he finding it a lot less easy to justify those deflections?

Perhaps because he'd become so aware of the eager hope in Beatrice's eyes—every night he turned up back here again.

She wanted more than he could give her, he already knew that.

He should start preparing her for the time *after* the baby was born, when he wouldn't be around so much, if at all. Fatherhood was something he would suck at. So why couldn't he just tell her that?

'Beatrice?' he shouted, pushing the troubling thoughts to one side.

He still had three months to get round to that conversation. So what if he was enjoying spending time with her? He'd worked hard for years to get where he was today. And Beatrice had put in quite a shift herself since getting pregnant. The baby's arrival would put an end date on this interlude once and for all. So why shouldn't they enjoy it while they still could?

But when she didn't answer, his neck muscles tensed. Was she in the study again, working late?

He had come close to calling her boss Jenna today and demanding she ease up on Beatrice's workload, because he'd found her crouched over her computer yesterday evening. If Jenna had dumped a load more translations on her he wasn't going to hold off any longer—to hell with his decision not to interfere in her career...

But when he swung open the study door, he found the room empty.

He rubbed the back of his neck, in a vain attempt to massage away his frustration—and the tiny ripple of panic. So where was she then?

Hopefully not in the guest room, where she was setting up the nursery he had insisted on paying for but had been avoiding.

He headed down the hall towards the main bedroom.

But as he opened the door, he heard the shower running

in the en suite bathroom. And the tension in his neck shot straight into his groin.

He walked silently into the bathroom, propelled by the familiar kick of arousal.

Perhaps all he'd really needed was to get laid. *Again*.

She stood in the glass cubicle with her body in profile, her face tilted into the stream. The treated glass gave him a clear view, despite the plume of steam rising from the hot jets. The flare of her hips and the curve of her breasts—which were getting heavier by the day—only added to the allure of her generous belly and her flushed skin, covered in soap.

A loud groan escaped as the kick of need sank deep.

Her head swung round. And their gazes locked.

Her face relaxed into a seductive smile—as she turned towards him, so he could look his fill. He drank in the sight like a man about to die of thirst. The water cascaded down her back and ran in rivulets over her full breasts. She cupped the heavy orbs, lifted and squeezed them, as if offering them to him, then grazed her thumbs over the engorged nipples.

He began shedding the rest of his clothing in a frantic rush. But as his cognitive abilities made a speedy exodus from his head, a new panic surfaced.

Why couldn't he stop wanting her? All the time. Seeing the changes his baby was making to her body was supposed to have weaned him off this addiction, but instead they only made him want her more.

But as he stripped off his shorts and walked to the cubicle, his mammoth erection leading the way—and watched her fingers trail down to her sex to torture him some more—he shoved the disturbing questions away.

Because he was way too desperate to touch her and taste her and torture her in return than to look for answers to any of them tonight.

* * *

The titanic orgasm cascaded through Bea with more force than the power shower pummelling them both. A guttural moan burst from her lips, her head dropping to rest against the shower tiles as she was catapulted onto the glittering cloud of afterglow.

Her hands slipped off Mason's shoulders, her back wedged against the quartz as he leaned against her. She buried her face into his neck, dragging in the scent of her vanilla soap on his skin, and loved the feel of his forearms flexing under her bare bottom as he held her aloft.

He shuddered violently through the last of his climax, while somehow managing to keep them both upright.

'Don't drop me,' she mumbled, her body massaging the thick length still impaling her.

He grunted in protest. 'Then stop that,' he remarked.

She let out a husky chuckle, still buoyed by the endorphin overload, reliving the memory of him stalking across the bathroom naked, his fierce expression promising retribution for her blatant provocation.

He groaned, then shifted against her, probably attempting a dismount. But as his flat stomach pressed against her belly, she felt the ripple of sensation deep in her abdomen which had started several weeks ago.

'What the hell was that?' He jerked back.

'You felt it too?' she asked, her heart bursting with joy.

'Yeah, what is it?'

She grinned, enjoying his stunned expression maybe a bit too much. She draped limp arms around his neck and wrapped her legs more securely around his waist, to anchor herself in his arms—after all, she was several pounds heavier than the first time they'd christened his shower.

'Answer me,' he said, impatience radiating off him. 'Are you okay?'

She nodded then smiled, pleased even more by his panicked reaction, because it was more concrete evidence of how much he worried about her welfare. Even if he wasn't ready to admit it. Yet.

'Absolutely,' she said, the joy in her heart all-consuming, because she was ridiculously happy they'd shared such an intimate moment. 'It's just the baby protesting at the squeeze on its living quarters.'

'That's...' He stared at the bump. 'Really?' Intense emotion flashed across his features but then his gaze became hooded, and he shifted away from her.

Her joy faded. A little.

The guarded expression was one she'd become accustomed to in the last four weeks. Every time she probed as gently as she could about his thoughts on the baby, or their future, or both.

His gaze glided down to where their bodies were still joined, but she could feel the tension in his shoulders increase—sense him distancing himself from the fierce excitement of moments ago.

'Good to know,' he said, his voice rough with all the things he refused to say.

More of the joy faded, replaced with sadness and confusion. Why did he find it so hard to talk about anything to do with the baby? He listened with interest when she gave him feedback about her antenatal appointments, but he never asked any questions. And he'd refused her invitation to attend her recent scan. And last week, when she'd asked if she could equip the guest bedroom as a nursery— hoping to start a conversation about what would happen once the baby was born—he gave her a gruff yes, then changed the subject by seducing her into a puddle of need on the dinner table.

The next day, his PA Joe had informed her of an account with unlimited funds set up in her name at London's most exclusive department store and supplied her with a list of personal shoppers who specialised in baby equipment and couture, and the contact details for a world-famous interior designer who did nursery interiors.

But Mason had refused to enter the guest room ever since.

Reaching across her, he switched off the still pounding jets. Then levered her off him to deposit her on her feet.

He clasped her elbow firmly, until he was sure she was steady.

'You good?' he asked.

'Yes,' she said, but as he let her go, she knew she wasn't good. Not even close.

Maybe the unshed tears making her eyes sting were the pregnancy hormones. Mostly. And the emotional wipeout of cataclysmic sex followed by feeling her baby move inside her and knowing he had felt it too. But all those qualifications couldn't dispel the ache when he left her standing alone in the shower to grab a towel.

She swallowed down the raw emotion pressing against her larynx as she watched him wrap it around his lean waist.

Why couldn't he let her know how he felt? Why couldn't he even talk about the baby? About them. About their future. She'd tried to be patient, tried to be understanding, tried to give him time to figure out his thoughts and feelings, because she suspected—from the little he'd let slip about his past—he wasn't a man used to having to talk about his emotional needs, or even really having to acknowledge he had any.

But she knew he did, because all the evidence was already there—that he could be a tender, loving, fiercely protective father and partner, if he would just admit it to himself.

She'd seen the way he looked at her when he thought she wasn't watching. Had been able to read all the questions, all the need, in his eyes.

But it wasn't just the things he wouldn't say, it was the small ways in which he showed her she mattered.

He had hardly spent a single evening away from her since that first night when he had told her he needed separation. And he'd stopped leaving her to sleep alone. Now he always stayed the night and dragged himself away at stupid o'clock in the morning, so he would have time to return to his suite at the hotel in Belgravia where he kept all his clothing, but nothing else. He'd been agitated and tense when he found her working late yesterday but had stopped short of demanding she work less.

She'd become used to having him here most nights, used to the incredible sex, but also the feel of his strong arms around her when she slept, and the sight of him doing everything from attempting to cook a stir fry to snuggling up on the sofa so they could watch the romcoms she loved, which she knew he found boring. And she missed him on the very rare occasions when he didn't show.

She had become attached to him. Dependent on his company and his presence, and even on the in-depth discussions they'd had about her job and his work without ever getting a commitment out of him that he would still be here when she would need him most.

She shivered, stepping out of the cubicle. He lifted a towel off the pile and wrapped it around her shoulders.

'Listen, I need to go to an event tonight,' he said as he

turned away to scoop his discarded clothing off the bathroom floor. 'I should probably head back to Belgravia to get changed,' he added.

She shuddered, the chill on her skin piercing her heart.

Was he really going to leave her straight after sex, for the first time in weeks? Spend the evening without her, when he had never done that, not once since she'd been back in London? Right after feeling the baby move for the first time.

'Do you want me to come with you?' she asked hopefully, sure she must have misunderstood.

They'd been to several events when she'd first arrived, and she'd enjoyed being seen with him, but the press attention had been insane, and she'd nearly fallen asleep at a banquet in the Barbican—so she had also been stupidly pleased when he'd stopped suggesting they attend public engagements. But she wanted to go with him now, somehow scared by what this might mean.

He glanced at her, but his gaze darted away again before she could gauge his reaction.

'No need,' he said. 'It's likely to be a late one. And you must be tired. I'll probably crash at the hotel tonight.'

The oh-so-casual dismissal felt like a physical blow, his desire to leave, to pull away from her, suddenly making her question all the assumptions she'd made about how he really felt. About her, about the baby, about them.

Good God, had she been kidding herself all along? Wanting to believe he felt more for her than he did? Wasn't that exactly what she'd done with her father for years? Believed he loved her and cared for her, and that if she just did as he wanted, he would eventually show her she had value to him, instead of just being a means to an end?

'How important is this event?' she asked as her heart

buffeted her chest, making the stinging pain in her eyes intensify.

He stared at her blankly.

'It's just, you didn't mention it until now,' she added. 'And I wondered why.'

But when he continued to stare at her, she knew why. This was just another of his avoidance tactics. Another chance for him not to acknowledge his feelings.

She had seen that moment of awe in his eyes when he'd felt the baby move too, before it had disappeared. But she clung to it now.

Time was galloping away from them. Soon they would have a child, and she still had no idea if he wanted to be a permanent part of its life. Or even how he really felt about her. Because she had failed to ask.

And failed to hold him to account.

There were so many other things she didn't know about him because she had sensed his reluctance to talk about them. And being sensitive to his needs had been easier than facing her oldest fear, that if she asked for more, she would be told she wasn't worthy, she wasn't enough.

Yet none of that had stopped her falling in love with him... The thought blindsided her.

Wow, Bea, fabulous time to figure that out.

But it also galvanised her. Because loving him wasn't enough. She had to know if there was a chance that he could love her in return. Or else she would be trapped in another one-sided relationship—where she was left hoping for the unconditional love she needed, instead of demanding it.

Apparently, her old fear of confrontation had reared its ugly head again over the past month. The same cowardice which had allowed her to live in her father's house for so long and never challenge his agenda. She'd never pushed

Mason about when he was coming over, she'd simply been overjoyed to see him. She'd never asked for a commitment other than what he was willing to give...

How had she allowed herself to slip into that passive role with Mason when there was so much at stake?

Perhaps because she had convinced herself she was different now. But having a fulfilling job, and great sex, and knowing he cared about her—in a way her father never had—wasn't enough. Not for her or her baby.

'Yeah, it's pretty important,' he said. 'I should go.' But she could hear the lie in his voice because she had become much better at reading him now.

A single tear escaped, but she scrubbed it away.

'Beatrice? What's wrong?' he said, sounding pained. And so, so wary. 'It's just one night, okay?'

'Except it's not just about tonight, Mason,' she said, suddenly feeling unbearably weary and unsure of herself.

'What's that supposed to mean?' he demanded.

'You never want to talk to me...'

'I talk to you all the time,' he interrupted her, but she recognised the tactic, although it wasn't one he'd used before—belligerence and indignation to avoid the truth. 'I'm here pretty much every night, *all* night, and I've let my other commitments slide. But I can't keep doing that.'

'You never want to talk to me about the baby, about us,' she said slowly, carefully, determined to pierce the bubble of outrage, knowing she couldn't let him derail her or distract her again.

She had to find her courage now. The courage she'd taken for granted, but which she needed more than ever.

'About how you feel about fatherhood,' she continued. She cupped her stomach, the little flutter there reassuring her and bolstering her determination. 'And what you envisage your role being in this baby's life. In *my* life, after it's born.'

'Why do we need to talk about that right now? We've got months yet before it's even born,' he snapped, but she could hear the fear now too.

'Because I want you to be a part of my life,' she said. 'So much.' She took a deep breath.

She had to tell him the truth too, however exposed it made her feel. Which was a lot.

'Because I've fallen in love with you, Mason. And I want us to be a family.'

CHAPTER THIRTEEN

'YOU DON'T LOVE ME, PRINCESS,' Mason said, trying for flippant, even as everything inside him felt raw and exposed. Feeling those little kicks inside her had shocked him and excited him, but then they had crucified him.

He should have seen this coming, should have realised that someone like Beatrice would make the mistake of thinking he was a good guy. Because he'd been too scared to tell her the truth.

'Don't tell me how I feel,' she said.

'Then don't say stupid things. How can you love me when you don't even know me?' Mason replied as the panic clawed at his throat.

She'd never looked more beautiful than in that moment, he realised, standing in nothing but a towel, her damp curls flattened against her head, her gaze open and generous and direct. And full of an innocence he had always lacked.

But she'd also never looked more vulnerable, her stunning bone structure so fragile, her eyes—those huge blue orbs—so innocent. And so full of hope.

He hadn't wanted to tell her about himself, about his past, about all the things he'd done to survive. The stuff he'd covered up and ignored and never had a problem with until she'd come into his life.

But as he watched her cradle the mound of her belly

where their baby grew, he figured he was all out of options now.

Did she even know she was doing that? Instinctively protecting their child from the likes of him.

She blinked slowly, her eyes blank with shock, but then they filled with the shimmer of compassion which only made the guilty hole in his gut swell. And twist.

'What don't I know about you, Mason?' she said with a confidence he knew she'd worked so hard to earn. 'If it's so terrible, don't you think it's about time you told me?'

He would have done anything not to burst the bubble, not to destroy her hope. Because in his own way he knew he had deep feelings for her too. And the baby. Feelings he'd tried hard not to admit. To himself as well as her. To protect them both.

'You really want to know?' he said. 'I'll tell you, but I suggest we both get dressed first,' he finished, before stalking out of the bathroom.

He took his time getting his clothes back on, his whole body shaking, pathetically grateful when she didn't follow him out immediately. He couldn't do this while they were both naked because it already felt like trying to tear off his own skin.

He was slipping on his shoes when she appeared, wearing a bathrobe, her hair brushed, her face still flushed from her shower and their lovemaking. The thought of never being able to touch her again, to hold her, to make her shudder and moan, to watch her going over with that stunned pleasure on her face felt unbearable. But somehow much worse was the thought of never having her look at him again with that tenderness in her eyes.

He'd always considered himself a selfish man, only interested in dating for the physical pleasure he could get out of it. So why did that thought hurt most of all?

He sat down on the bed. Rested his forearms on his knees. Suddenly exhausted, as all the convenient lies, the easy deflections, the endless avoidance tactics had finally deserted him.

She opened her mouth to say something, but he beat her to it.

'Why do you love me?' The question burst out before he could think it through.

He cringed. How needy and pathetic was that?

He'd expected contempt, maybe even derision, but when her gaze searched his, all he saw was compassion. And that crippling tenderness that made him feel like that little boy again, wanting and waiting for something that he could never have.

'Oh, Mason,' she said. 'Why would I not fall in love with you?' She tucked her hand over her bump. 'You gave me a baby, and in many ways you also gave me my freedom.' She sighed. 'It hurt to hear it at the time, but you were right about what I'd allowed myself to become because I was too scared to stand up to my father.'

'That's nonsense, Beatrice,' he said. 'You would have figured it out eventually, without me seducing you and getting you pregnant, then dumping you the very next day in the most callous way imaginable.'

He'd apologised for the way he'd spoken to her that morning. But the more he'd thought about the way he'd behaved in the last month, the more he'd realised an apology wasn't enough.

She cleared her throat, the pale blue of her eyes sparkling. 'Excuse me, but who seduced whom that first night? Because I'm pretty sure you've got that the wrong way round.'

He let out a brittle laugh. God, she was adorable. But the ripple of amusement faded almost as quickly as it had come.

He looked away from her because he couldn't look at her and explain the rest.

'You want to know why you really had to leave Italy?' he managed.

'Why...' she asked, so sweet, so trusting.

He blew out a breath and pushed the words out. 'I told Joe to tip off the press.'

The murmured confession felt like a gunshot. Her eyebrows lifted but the tenderness remained, because she didn't seem to be able to process the whole sordid truth.

'I forced your hand,' he explained. 'Because I didn't want to wait. And I convinced myself that what I wanted was the only thing that mattered,' he raced on, the hideous reality of what he'd done starting to strangle him. 'So instead of allowing you to make your own decision, I went behind your back to stack the odds in my favour.'

He could still remember her stubborn determination not to give in to his demands in the pizzeria in Rapallo. Her insistence that she needed to be independent. And, in a lot of ways, he'd admired her for it. But when the press hordes had descended the next morning, it hadn't taken him long to qualify his actions and justify doing whatever was necessary to get what he wanted.

It was what he'd always done. Deflect, evade and cover up the truth until things went the way he wanted them to. That was the real man behind the myth. Not the self-made billionaire who had worked his way up from nothing, taken insane risks and reaped the hoped-for rewards, but the boy who even a mother couldn't love. The boy who had done terrible things to escape his fate.

And he could see so clearly now. He hadn't forced her

hand to protect her or the baby, which was what he'd told himself at the time, but because he'd been terrified, even then, that, given the choice, she wouldn't choose him.

He heard her let out a breath and he braced himself for her anger, and her disgust.

But when she eventually spoke, all he heard in her voice was that same compassion.

'Well, I'm glad you told me about that, and it was a pretty sneaky thing to do,' she said, in what had to be the understatement of the century. But then her delicate hand landed on his knee, and she squeezed it softly. 'But FYI, I think you only really speeded up the inevitable.'

He turned to her, shocked by the easy affection in her tone—and the quiet acceptance.

'*Really?* Beatrice? That's it?' he said, starting to feel annoyed now. 'That's all you've got to say? I manipulated you. I ripped you away from a life you loved and had spent months building for yourself and I took away all your choices—and you're just gonna forgive me for it?' Make that a lot annoyed.

'Well, to be fair, I really didn't love scrubbing toilets *that* much,' she said.

'This isn't a joke.' He dragged a hand through his hair, then stood and paced to the window, unable to sit still. And unable to have her look at him like that, as if what he'd done didn't matter, when he knew it did.

He swore softly. 'Is this some leftover from that bastard who fathered you? That you think you have to accept my bad behaviour because you love me,' he said, doing sarcastic air quotes, because he was just that mad.

'No, it's not.'

She jumped up and crossed the room, the quiet acceptance gone. *Finally.*

'And if you ever do something like that again...' Her chest puffed up and her gaze narrowed. 'You will definitely be sorry.'

Which would have been more of a threat if he wasn't so sorry already.

'But it seems to me you've tortured yourself enough so there's not much point in me torturing you too. And the fact you told me what you did is important. Because now we can have trust.'

'Trust?' he murmured. Did she even know what that meant? How could she be so gullible...? He cupped her neck, pressed his forehead to hers, unable not to touch her this one last time. 'How can you trust me, Beatrice, if you don't know who I really am?'

The panic blocked his throat again as she cradled his cheek.

'I think you'd better tell me the rest of it, Mason,' she said softly.

He nodded, knowing she was right. It hurt like hell to know that once he told her all the things he'd done she wouldn't love him any more. But what would hurt more was continuing to manipulate her, continuing to play on her innocence and tenderness for his own ends.

He lifted his head, walked back to the window and looked down at the docks where he'd once worked for villains and dreamed about getting away. Getting out.

Funny to think he'd always remained trapped there without even realising it. The instincts he'd always been so proud of, for self-preservation and self-denial, born of being that boy who would do anything to escape.

'I told you my old man was a bastard,' he said slowly, carefully. 'That he used me. But the truth is, he was just a stupid loser with an addiction he couldn't control. He'd bet on anything—the greyhounds, the horses, on whether West Ham would score in the second minute or the tenth. And because of that, we were always dead broke.'

That life seemed so far away now—being scared in the winter to turn on the heating, eating cereal for tea because there was nothing else in the house, and being the smelly kid in school because you didn't have the pennies for the laundrette. But, in so many ways, that life had always remained inside him. Because he'd never really shaken off the fear of being a failure like his old man.

And wasn't that why he'd worked so hard to get out? Not to be rich, but to be safe.

Her footsteps padded across the carpet, then her cheek rested on his back. He shuddered, the soft touch both reassuring and terrifying. Because he wanted it so much, he needed it, and he wasn't sure he could survive losing it.

'Mason, it's okay. Breathe,' she murmured, but his legs had turned to jelly, the emotion like a tidal wave, threatening to knock him off his feet.

He braced his legs to stay upright as the memories swirled, no longer tethered in the deep recesses of his mind but choking him with guilt and remorse.

The memory of sitting on the wall outside the basement hovel where he had once lived, each day after school, for weeks and weeks, waiting for his mum to come back, shimmered on the edges of his consciousness, damning him even more. But worse was the memory of his old man's face—tired, worn, terrified—years later, the last time he'd seen him.

'Eventually, he owed money to loan sharks. A *lot* of money. And the only way we could pay off the debts was for me to run errands for them.' He forced himself to draw in another painful breath and let it out, her presence at his back the only thing anchoring him to the here and now. 'I did it for a while. I even enjoyed it at first, because they'd give me tips.' He shrugged. 'But then, eventually, I didn't want to do it any more. I was older, smarter. I saw what they did—the people they beat up for nothing, the women they exploited. I was scared of them, and terrified I'd get caught eventually and be stuck in that life for ever. So I told my dad I was leaving.' He stared down at his feet, the polished leather of his designer brogues reflecting his own face back at him. But all he could see in that moment was his old man begging. 'And I never looked back.'

Bea reached around his waist to hold him, her heart shattering as she tried to soothe the shivers she could feel racing through him. She heard the shame in his voice.

'And you blame yourself for that?' she asked softly.

Was this the root? The reason why he had been so determined to hold a part of himself back? Because he had been scared to trust her with his demons?

She'd assumed this was all about her. That she hadn't been strong enough, smart enough, brave enough to demand what she needed from him. That because she'd fallen in love with him, she had been too scared to press the point in case he rejected her.

And there was some truth in that...

But, deep down, she could see now that this wasn't just about her confidence, it was also about his. They had both been broken by things outside their control and plunged into an emotional storm neither of them had had the tools to negotiate without making mistakes.

'Yeah, I do,' he said, his voice breaking. 'They were pretty specific. They told me if I didn't do what they said they'd kill him. So I did what they said. Even though I knew it was wrong.'

He heaved out a breath, his shoulders shaking, his voice a monotone as he continued.

'But when I was fourteen, I'd had enough. I didn't care what happened to him any more.' He turned, the look in his eyes so bleak, she shuddered. 'He begged me not to go, and I left anyway. And I never saw him again after that. I doubt what they did to him was pretty,' he finished. 'How can you love *that* man? A man who would do that to his own flesh and blood to save himself. Why would you want to have a person like that around your baby?'

'Because he wasn't a man, he was a child, Mason,' she said softly, wanting him to see what she saw when she looked at him.

But he simply shook his head. 'I was old enough.'

She saw the hopelessness in his expression and realised she was seeing a window into his past, a glimpse of the boy inside the man. And the impossible challenges he'd faced. The struggles he'd overcome. The terrible price he'd paid for that. Alone and resentful and desperate to find a way out—just as she had been when she'd first met him.

He'd given her a way out, however inadvertently—by challenging her to see who she had allowed herself to become.

She'd discovered in Italy that she could grow and change—by standing up for herself. But she'd never stopped blaming herself for her past cowardice, or she wouldn't have fallen in love with him without accepting he had some terrible insecurities too.

'So now you know,' he said, dropping his head. He rubbed his thumb over the bird in flight etched on the back of his hand. 'I'm a fraud. I built an empire on the back of that betrayal.' His head lifted, the naked honesty in his eyes raw with vulnerability. 'In my defence, the things I did, and the lies I told you to get you to want me, to get you to stay, are nothing compared to the lies I've told myself over the years.'

Her heart broke at the self-loathing in his voice. But, after the pieces had shattered in her chest, she felt the sure, steady beat of her love—and knew it was strong enough and wise enough to see his flaws, as well as her own, and to accept them.

She cupped his cheek, the joy in her chest immense when he leaned into the caress instinctively.

'I guess neither of us is perfect then,' she said softly, her lips quirking. 'How annoying.'

His brows lifted, the stunned disbelief in his eyes almost as painful as the ache in her chest where her heart was pounding so hard she was surprised it didn't burst.

He covered her hand with his, drew it away from his face then threaded his fingers through hers and held on. 'You don't want to leave me?'

Her lips lifted and she shook her head as it occurred to her that this was the easiest answer she'd ever had to give anyone.

'I told you I love you. Now do you believe me?' she asked.

His green eyes turned a rich emerald, the wicked sparkle making her heart hurt. 'If you say so, Princess.'

Lifting her fingers to his mouth, he pressed an earnest, reverent kiss to her knuckles. The familiar awareness sank into her abdomen.

'If it's any consolation,' he added, 'I think I love you too.' He glanced down at her stomach. 'And the bump.'

Her eyebrow lifted. 'You think, or you know?'

He wrapped his arms around her waist and lifted her. She

clasped his shoulders, looking down into his harsh, handsome face as the rich emerald softened with love.

'I know,' he said.

She grinned down at him. Their baby's movements fluttered in her belly, as if it was adding its approval. 'You'd better not forget that when the bump is waking you up at two in the morning, wanting to be fed.'

He laughed, a deep, throaty, relieved laugh which made the joy spread and glow in her chest. 'You do know you're the one with the equipment to sort that out, right?' he offered, the arrogance she had come to adore returning.

He lowered her slowly, then reached inside her robe to caress said equipment possessively—and reiterate his point.

She clasped his wrist, the giddy need firing down to her toes. But she looked him straight in the eye when she said, 'I guess that leaves you on nappy duty then.'

They were both still chuckling as they fell onto the bed to concentrate on tearing each other's clothes off.

EPILOGUE

One year later

'UP YOU GO, Princess Trouble!' Mason grinned. The Riviera sunshine sparkled on the water of the *castello*'s new infinity pool as he boosted his tiny daughter into the air.

Her belly laughs as he caught her again had him beaming back at her. Then his own laughter burst free when she kicked her arms and legs furiously—which was her not so subtle way of demanding Daddy do it again, *immediately.*

At eight months old, Ella Carys Angharad Foxx was an absolute tyrant who had her father wrapped firmly around her plump little finger. Her mother had warned him he was creating a monster. But he adored hearing his daughter's laughter and he hated hearing her cry—so he was usually very amenable to her requests.

But when she rubbed her eyes, while trying to launch herself out of his arms again, he realised this was one of those times he was going to have to disappoint her.

'That's all, Cinders,' he said, touching a finger to her adorable button nose, which was starting to look slightly pink. 'We don't want you getting a sunburn or Daddy will be in the doghouse tonight.'

And he had plans for this evening which did not involve soothing an unhappy baby, because it would be the anniversary of the day he'd told her mother the truth about his past, and she'd decided to love him anyway.

The smile sank into his heart as he tucked his daughter under his arm to wade out of the water. She carried on wriggling and chortling, because she thought this was a brand-new game. There would be tired tears in his near future when she figured out this new game was called naptime.

He walked over to the pool loungers, where Jack Wolfe was reading a book of fairy tales to his oldest son, Luca.

The four-year-old pointed at one of the illustrations. 'Mummy says that's you, Daddy,' the little boy announced.

'Your mother said I was the big, bad wolf? What the...?' Jack frowned, managing to cut off the swearword, while sending Mason a wry look.

'Own it, bro,' Mason replied, laughing as he grabbed a towel and began stripping off Ella's sunsuit.

He and Jack had become fast friends, ever since the guy had offered to walk Beatrice down the aisle at their wedding that spring—because her father had resolutely refused to do it unless Mason paid him five grand for the privilege. He had considered paying the money because he knew Beatrice still struggled with her father's refusal to speak to her, but Jack had advised him not to.

'He doesn't deserve either one of his daughters. I'm guessing, in her heart, Bea knows that, because she's not stupid. And, believe me, you and your family do not need someone that toxic in your life, at any price.'

He'd had to agree with the guy.

He hadn't told Beatrice about her father's demand. She did not need to know the man was still a Class A ass, determined to remain estranged from both his daughters. But he'd been relieved when she had seemed more than happy to have her brother-in-law as a substitute.

The fact that Beatrice and Jack had once been engaged might have made Wolfe 'giving her away' super weird. The glossy magazines had certainly gone into gossip overload when unauthorised photos of the wedding had hit the internet. But Mason hadn't cared how it looked. Because when Beatrice had appeared at the end of the aisle on Jack's arm, dressed in a silk wedding gown which shimmered in the candlelight and made his breath back up in his lungs, he knew his bride had only ever had eyes for him.

And the Wolfes were family now.

Jack and Katherine's three sons—because her second pregnancy had turned out to be twins, to everyone's shock, especially Katherine's—would be playmates for Ella, and all the other kids he was hoping to make with her mummy one day. So they had been more than happy to invite the Wolfes to join them this summer in Portofino, once he'd finished having the old Grande Hotel where Beatrice had once worked converted into a luxury fifteen-room *castello*, for their exclusive use.

Beatrice hadn't been super-keen on the idea when he'd first bought the place as a wedding present for her. Until he'd got her to admit the reason why... She was concerned that her friends at the Portofino Grande would lose their jobs.

So he'd decided to buy a string of resorts in the region to launch Foxx Italia in Liguria and appointed Marta and Fabrizio to head the executive team to oversee the renovations and relocation of the staff. A win-win—not only as a sound business investment but also as a way to show Beatrice that he respected her input and they would always be a team.

'Wave goodbye to Uncle Jack and cousin Luca,' he said, propping the freshly changed Ella onto his shoulder. She was getting fussy. Probably because, being smart as a whip, she had figured out the new game wasn't nearly as much fun as the old one.

'See you later, Ella,' said Jack.

Luca waved enthusiastically, before continuing the in-depth discussion he'd been having with his father. 'The Big Bad Wolf is not a mis-pun-derstood wolf, Daddy,' he said, mispronouncing the word with considerable gravity. 'He's a very naughty wolf.'

Mason was still laughing as he headed into the house.

His daughter got crankier while he had a conversation with the head chef, who wanted to brief him on tonight's dinner menu, and a chat with his sister-in-law, who was looking suitably pleased with herself after having got twins Cai and Dafydd down for their nap with the help of the nanny they'd hired for the summer.

By the time he and Ella arrived in the Presidential Suite, his daughter was making her feelings known in no uncertain terms. And they were not happy ones.

He felt bad about her tears as he tried to soothe her, but it was hard for him to feel anything but a swift kick of joy when her mother rushed out of the bathroom.

Although the suite of rooms looked totally different from last summer, with all the new fixtures and fittings bringing it bang up-to-date, he recognised the fierce emotion that flowed through him as he spotted her. Because he'd felt something similar when he'd first seen Beatrice walk out of that bathroom with a bucket and mop, her hair shorter than it was now, and her figure round with the baby he now held in his arms.

He hadn't understood it then, but he did now as his wife rushed up to them both and scooped the loudly protesting Ella out of his arms.

'Uh-oh, has Princess Trouble got overtired?' she said,

sending him an amused and slightly smug smile over the tuft of blonde hair on their daughter's head—which made her look like a cute, and currently very indignant, dandelion.

'Yeah, a little too much fun in the sun with Daddy again,' he murmured ruefully as Beatrice settled herself and the crying baby on the bedroom's generous sofa and released her breast from the nursing bra.

The emotion he hadn't figured out then was easy to figure out now, he thought as he sat beside them and slung his arm around his wife's shoulders, while his daughter latched onto her plump nipple as if she hadn't been fed in a month.

Shock and awe, fierce pride and total, all-consuming love.

'Success!' Bea whispered triumphantly as she eased the door closed to her daughter's bedroom.

Was there anything more wonderful than watching your child falling into a deep, peaceful sleep?

'That's only because you have all the right equipment,' Mason quipped as his strong arms wrapped around her from behind and he tugged her back against his chest. 'You cheated.'

She turned in his arms and laughed, delighted with them both. And the incredible life they'd made for each other. As well as the fact that their daughter would now be asleep for several precious hours when his hands strayed down to her bottom and squeezed.

'You're just jealous,' she teased. 'Because I am the Queen of the Magic Boobies.'

He chuckled. 'Not true, Queen,' he said, boosting her into his arms and walking her backwards towards their bedroom, the provocative look in his eyes full of the hot promise she adored. 'Because I happen to love your magic boobies too.'

She was still laughing as he dumped her onto the bed, but it wasn't long before he had turned her triumph into a quivering mass of desperate need.

Half an hour later, Bea lay, limp and well-satisfied, in his arms, watching the early evening light turn a rich blue on the horizon.

'So then Luca says, "He's not a misunderstood wolf, he's a naughty wolf". You should have seen the expression on Jack's face, it cracked me up,' Mason said as his fingers stroked her arm lazily.

She chuckled, delighted not just at the conversation between Jack and his son, which did sound hilarious, but also that her sister's family and theirs had become so close. She loved that Jack and Mason had become good friends. She suspected that Mason didn't have many men he could really confide in, because all his friends seemed to work for him. She also knew, from what Katie had told her about Jack's childhood, that the two men had much more in common than Mason realised.

'Katie's hilarious,' she said. 'She told me her and Jack's relationship is *Little Red Riding Hood*, but I wouldn't laugh too hard because she's decided our relationship is a specific fairy tale too.'

'Oh, yeah, which one?' Mason asked. *'The Giant that got the Golden Goose?'* he teased.

She huffed, then flipped over and propped her elbows onto his chest to give him a mock stern look. 'Are you calling me a goose, Mr Foxx?'

His gaze drifted up to her hair, which she suspected was a total mess, but all she saw was rich appreciation in his eyes when his gaze dropped down to hers again. 'I'm calling you golden, Mrs Foxx.'

'Nice save,' she said, and kissed him. Before they could get carried away again, though, she pulled back. 'Apparently, our fairy tale is *Rapunzel*. Because you saved me from my ivory tower.' She brushed her hand over her unruly curls, which she now kept in a manageable bob. 'And I lost my long golden locks in the process.'

He choked out a laugh but then skewered her again with that appreciative look that always made her feel cherished and seen. 'Hey, you know what? I like it,' he announced. 'I think it totally fits.'

'You do?' she said, astonished that he had bought into Katie's whimsical metaphor because, as much as she adored this man, he was far too real and rugged and rough around the edges to be the fairy tale type.

He rolled on top of her. 'Totally,' he said.

The tension at her core clenched and released deliciously as his newly perked up erection brushed against her belly and she calculated if they had enough time for another round before Ella woke up.

She certainly hoped so.

He hooked her hair behind her ear. 'Because that makes me a handsome prince, right?' he added, the smug smile clear in his tone as he nuzzled the sensitive spot on her neck he knew would drive her wild. 'Instead of the Big, Bad Wolf.'

* * * * *

THE FORBIDDEN
BRIDE HE STOLE

MILLIE ADAMS

MILLS & BOON

CHAPTER ONE

HE WAS GOING to kill her.

This was just another stunt in a long line of stunts Hannah had pulled over the past six months threatening to drive Apollo over the edge. And Apollo didn't do the edge. He'd been over it before. Hell, he'd been born over it. He had no intention of going back again.

Least of all, because of a bratty twenty-two-year-old whose well-being was his responsibility.

Taking Hannah in was the only good thing he'd ever done in his life. Everything else had been for his own benefit. Either financially or to feed his own depravity.

He was a strict guardian. When Hannah's parents had died, she'd been a straight A student on the path to certain success. He'd wanted to keep her there. At sixteen, she'd had two years left of high school. She'd gone to a boarding school, and he'd checked in with her often, his best expression of appreciation for the friendship her father had given him—another relationship that he supposed had become about more than what he could get from it—was to make sure Hannah carried on how she might have if they'd lived.

Her finances were in a trust that not even he could access until she was twenty-five or married. He paid for her life while she was in his care, and while he gave her a decent allowance, he wanted to make sure he kept her focused on her studies.

She'd done well. She'd graduated top of her class in high school, then gone on to university, where she'd studied technology and hospitality, which put her in a unique position to work for her father's hotel brand and liaise with his tech company, implementing unprecedented smart tech into the luxury resorts.

That was a reflection of a job well done.

He hadn't allowed her excess funds because he felt that would lead to others taking advantage of her. It would be a distraction. Even when she was in university, he made his expectations clear. No parties. No dating. No drinking.

He'd never had the chance to have an education, and it felt good to see her have a top-tier one he ensured she took seriously.

All had been well until she suddenly had a personality transplant after graduation. She had been living with him since vacating her college dorm, lacking the money to afford her own lodging but apparently making plenty enough to be the life of the party. She had gotten a job—but not at her father's company. At a competitive hotel chain, not as an executive, but as a concierge. She'd suddenly developed a taste for nightclubs, parties, and staying out late.

Last night he'd told her in no uncertain terms was she to go out tonight. And it was past 2:00 a.m., and he'd gone in to check on her, and she was gone. It was rare for him to be bested by anyone, let alone a near child.

The issue was that he hadn't treated her as a prisoner. He would now.

Until she was twenty-five, she was his ward. Perhaps

he should have expected this. Perhaps it was unavoidable that her trauma over her grief would eventually turn into a meltdown of some kind. Was it not his job to protect her from this also?

That was when he heard scrabbling outside. Coming nearer to the second-floor library where he sat, drinking a scotch. He knew she would pass through here because he'd figured out it was how she was sneaking out.

So, he'd decided to lie in wait.

The window opened, and in she tumbled. Ingloriously. Shoes in hand, a dress so short it was more like a glittery T-shirt. She stood straight, her hair cascading in a tumbled, curling mane around her shoulders. The dress left nothing to the imagination. Her curves were out, on full display. And Apollo saw red.

"What the hell are you playing at?"

Hannah was frozen to the spot, pinned by his dark magnetic gaze. Even in the dim firelight, she knew his features, all too well. The sharp cheekbones, the square, granite jaw.

His heritage was Greek and Italian, but he had always put the marble statues to shame. He was broad and tall, well-muscled. She had a map of his body drawn out neatly in her mind, and she could refer to it whenever she wished. She did more often than she'd like to admit.

She'd had a crush on him from the time she was fourteen. When she was sixteen, he'd become her guardian. If those weren't the most confusing, mixed-up authority figure issues, she didn't know what was.

Worse still, from there her crush bloomed inside her and grew like ivy, wrapping itself around every part of her, turning into devastating, paralyzing love.

Now in her twenties, Hannah understood how it had happened. Apollo had been an object of fascination to her already. Then when her parents had died, he'd become her everything. The one who was taking care of her. The one she found most beautiful. The one who had known her most of her life. The one who had known her parents.

Not loving him would have been an impossibility. Loving him was too, though. The more she understood her feelings, the way things were between women and men, the more she resented the dark pull he had on her.

Because at fourteen she'd wanted to marry him. At sixteen she'd wanted to give him her virginity. She'd had foolish fantasies of trying to seduce him—which in hindsight made her cringe because he'd have sent her packing and rightly so.

But now, at twenty-two, she wanted to be consumed by him. Her fantasies were no longer hazy and romanticized. She recognized that what she wanted from him was everything.

It was an obsession.

Also unhealthy. Also why she was desperate—so desperate—to recast her role in his life? To gain her independence. Because how else was she ever going to exorcise these unwanted emotions and needs?

Her whole body went tight with him sitting there.

She hadn't been expecting this.

Not quite, anyway. She was sure Apollo knew she'd been sneaking out because she knew her guardian well enough to know he wasn't an idiot. And he ought to know her well enough to realize she wasn't either.

She hadn't wanted to try to swan past him out the front door, but she had wanted him to notice that she wasn't behaving like herself.

Or maybe she was.

She'd made friends at her new job, and those friends had very plainly and loudly let her know what they thought about her life: That it was effed up.

When she'd explained her situation to the other students at her private university, they'd found it odd, but they'd understood on some level. Because her parents had been wealthy, and Apollo was rich. And it was accepted that rich people handled things differently.

Her friend Mariana thought it was outrageous and hideous and that Apollo was a gargoyle.

And worse, Mariana saw through Hannah and had seen through Hannah, to her most shameful secret.

"You wouldn't go along with his rules if you weren't positively gagging for it where he's concerned."

"I am not!"

But she'd been blushing furiously because, lord have mercy on her soul, she was. Ever since she'd understood what sex was, she'd wanted to have it with him. Who could blame her? He was far too sexy for an impressionable teenage girl to cast her eyes upon. And she could remember him coming over to her parents' estate in Upstate New York and swimming in their pool. In a tight black swimsuit that had left little to the imagination, and dear God, the man's chest.

She'd had her sexual awakening then and there. She'd become a *woman* that day.

Her friends in school had sighed over smooth-faced pop singers and she just couldn't understand the fuss. She'd found the man she wanted. She couldn't get excited over boys.

The wrenching pain and excitement she'd felt when the lawyer had told her she'd be going to live with him...

It had been like being trapped in a strange, gothic fantasy. Her parents were dead, the estate was being cleaned out, and she was being sent to live with the gorgeous, austere man of her dreams, who saw her only as a child.

Because she had been a child.

She was not one now, however.

She remembered her last conversation with Mariana about Apollo, as she'd tried so desperately to hide her reaction to Mariana even speaking his name, tried to preserve a shred of dignity.

"Dieu, Hannah. You're in love with your awful old guardian. What a cliché."

"He isn't old!"

"You follow his ridiculous rules because you're so into him that it's embarrassing. You glow while talking about how he won't let you go out. Like you're a child."

"I can go out!"

"Go out with me then. Dance with another man. Kiss another man."

It had echoed inside her. *Kiss another man.*

She'd never kissed *one.*

Because she'd always wanted to kiss Apollo.

But she'd been the model, well-behaved ward. It didn't make him want her. It didn't make him love her. She had stopped believing he might when she was about twenty.

She could remember, viscerally, watching him come into the foyer of his sweeping Athens home, dressed in a perfectly cut tuxedo, and her heart had just…nearly exploded. She'd been on summer holiday and returning to stay with him was always a mixed bag. One part agony, one ecstasy.

The cliché of it all.

Then a woman in red had come through the front door.

His age. Sophisticated, in her thirties, speaking with him effortlessly.

They'd gone out together arm in arm and she'd understood. It would never be that way between them. She would always be a child to him and he would always be a stratospheric object she wouldn't be able to touch.

That didn't mean she stopped having sex dreams about him, that didn't mean her feelings for him were gone. It was why being around him was still so painful. At least with the agony there had been ecstasy when she'd been able to imagine he might want her back someday. After that, she'd been left with only agony, and as long as she was in proximity to him, as long as he remained in control of her life, it wouldn't stop.

The violent negative reaction she'd had to the idea of kissing another man had been her wake-up call. No matter what she told herself, she was still in love with Apollo. And that needed to stop.

So she'd gone out with Mariana. She'd tried to find another man to kiss, but when it came down to it, she hadn't wanted to kiss anyone.

Then when she'd gotten home just past midnight, he'd told her coolly that she wasn't to do that anymore. No anger, of course. He acted as if she was a wayward child who'd made a mistake.

She'd sat on the edge of her bed with the world caving in around her.

She loved him.

He saw her as a child.

The arrangement wasn't fair or normal.

It was holding her back. *He* was holding her back.

She'd said as much to Mariana the next day at work.

"You have to get him to release you from the guard-ianship!"

"I don't think I can."

"Sure, you can. Drive him to the brink! Make him wash his hands of you."

She didn't want Apollo to wash his hands of her. No matter the twisted-up feelings in her chest, no matter that she needed to get rid of some of them, he was her only real...family. He meant the world to her. He would never be nothing to her. But he couldn't be everything like this. She had to be able to breathe. To be herself.

She needed to have the control of her life, of her money, of her work, so that he didn't have all the power.

She'd told people he was easy. Permissive, even. He wasn't. It was only that she'd never once gone against him because she was so horrifically infatuated with him that she'd let herself be his cheerful little doormat. She hated that for her.

It was like, through the eyes of Mariana and the rest of her friends, she'd gotten a good, hard look at her life for the first time, and she could feel all her certainty, all that she'd ever believed about herself, unraveling.

She was alone. He'd taken care of her, but he'd never offered her anything...emotional, and she was so enrap-tured with him it was like the sun shone out his billion-dollar butt.

She accepted far, far too little from the people she gave love to.

Another problem.

Questioning things with Apollo made her go back fur-ther, it made her question things with her parents. The parents she could hardly remember—not because they'd died six years ago—but because they'd never really been around when they were alive.

They'd loved her. She assumed. Because parents loved their children in theory. An innate instinct that kept them from drowning you when you were too annoying, she'd heard.

They hadn't been cruel. But she'd never been as important as whatever adventure they wanted to take, or business venture they'd wanted to embark on. She'd been lonely as their child, she'd been lonely as an orphan.

Because no matter how much she loved the people around her, they didn't show it back.

And she felt…stuck now. Trapped in the consequences of her parents' actions, their decision to make Apollo her guardian in case they died. Their decision to bind her in the most patriarchal nonsensical trust fund situation she could imagine.

Under Apollo's care until well after she was an adult. Unless she was under a husband's care. And it did say, *husband.* Otherwise, she'd be tempted to ask Mariana to marry her and offer her friend a kickback for doing her a favor.

She wanted to be free of this. Of him.

What she didn't expect was to see…there was more than just anger in his eyes now. This was something else. There was heat there, and she was no expert on the goings-on between men and women, but she was pretty expert on Apollo and his expressions, his movements. There was a fire in his eyes like she hadn't seen before.

And danger.

She sensed danger.

But it wasn't the kind of danger that she wanted to run from. No, it was a predator's gaze. Watchful. Waiting. Hungry. It didn't frighten her, because it mirrored the feelings she'd carried for him for all of these years.

Her breath exited her body in a rush.

He…wanted her.

Or at least for a moment, he had looked and seen her as a woman.

It's working.

No, that's not what she was doing! She didn't want him to be attracted to her, she just wanted to get out from under his authority so she could go on and be a functional, human adult who wasn't hanging on his every move.

She couldn't deny that this moment, being pinned beneath his dark gaze, was the single most erotic moment of her life. It was like everything had stopped around her, yet her body had come alive. Her heart was pounding, a mirrored pulse beating between her legs. Her breasts felt heavy, her knees shaky.

She wanted…

She wanted to go to him. She wanted to touch him. She wanted…

And then, as quickly as that heat had flared in his eyes, it was gone.

If you want him to wash his hands of you, follow your teenage dreams and seduce him like an idiot. Do you really think a virgin's inexpert fumblings are going to make him abandon the Apollo of it all?

No. Apollo was a locked box filled with nothing but honor. If she dared disturb that lock, she would disrupt everything.

She couldn't afford that.

She'd made friends at her new job, and she loved them.

But in the grand fabric of her life, there was one thread woven all the way through.

Him.

This was a very dangerous high-wire act she was doing. Trying to get him to be frustrated enough to let her have her freedom, trying to get him to understand she was too old to be treated like a child.

Then there was the matter of her father's company.

It was being taken care of by a Board of Trustees. Because, yet again, it was another thing that technically belonged to her but could not be hers until she was twenty-five. Or married.

She thought of her friends at the hotel she worked at. Of all the things that she could do for them. If she owned an entire hotel chain, she could give Mariana the hotel to manage. God knew she was better than the frosty manager where they worked. She had ideas. Energy.

And the idea of something belonging to her... That excited her.

The foundation would always belong to her father. But she didn't hate her father, even if she was newly going over some of her resentment.

What she needed was to get her own life.

What she needed was to not be in love with Apollo.

And that brought her right back to the moment.

His burning gaze made her feel as if the flames there had reached out and licked over her skin. Though the fire now was much more apparently anger.

"I think working at this hotel is not good for you. Your friends there are a bad influence on you."

Then her rage matched his own. How dare he?

"You can't tell me where to work, Apollo."

"I am your guardian," he said.

"And I'm an adult. Not a child. But you have failed to notice this."

"The stipulations of the guardianship indicate that your father would not have considered you a full adult until you were twenty-five."

She had kept her emotions locked down for so long. Kept herself in check. And for what? He would never look at her and see why she had done it. He would never understand how much she had loved him. In that way, he was the same as her father. The sharp hook of emotion that curled around her gut at that thought left her gasping.

Was this how it would always be? Her loving men who didn't have the time of day for her? Was she such a cliché that her daddy issues were manifesting like this? She was just so overwhelmed. By shame. By anger. At herself. At Apollo.

"My father wouldn't know," she said, the words wrenched from deep within her. "He didn't spend any time with me. At sixteen, I did a competent job managing my own life because I had to. Because my parents were ever off on adventures. They got themselves killed in a canoeing accident, for God's sake. It isn't that there's… There's nothing wrong with going off and having adventures, but they did it instead of caring for me. That things became more heavy-handed after their deaths just seemed all a bit wrong to me.

"You're not in charge of me," she said. "Not really. I might not have access to my trust fund, but I have a job. I have friends. I don't need you intervening in my life."

"Sadly for you, *agape*, you do."

"No, I don't."

"You do. Because should I decide to withdraw my

support from you, your trust is locked for a further five years."

"What?"

"That is the way of it. If I decide that your behavior is immature and unwarranted, I can hold your money up for five years."

"And what if I marry?"

"If you marry, then your husband is…"

"*My guardian*?" she spat. "You can't be serious."

Yes, her whole life was supposed to be this. Authoritative men telling her what to do, building her little gilded cages. Never, ever loving her the way she wanted them to.

"I am your guardian, exactly. And yes, I am serious. But do not take your rage out on me. I did not create the stipulations of the agreement."

"You're threatening to enforce them."

"For your own good. Your father entrusted you to me. I have done an excellent job with you."

"You have done *nothing*," she said. "You have laid down a series of arcane rules and regulations, and I followed them because I was nothing more than a doe-eyed child where you were concerned for years and years. But I am not that girl anymore. I am a woman. You cannot tell me what to do."

"I can and I will. Go to bed. Go to your work shift tomorrow and give them your notice. Then come straight home afterward."

"I won't." And that was when she decided she would make him unreasonable. She would make him prove himself a liar because he wouldn't do it. Shortly. He wouldn't push it, so he was her guardian until she was thirty. Not even Apollo would go that far. There was no point to it.

But then, she couldn't understand why he was being so unreasonable now.

"I will do what I think is best," she said.

"You know nothing of the world," he said. "That is why your father put me in charge. He was very aware that he had raised a little princess who knew nothing beyond the walls of your gilded cage, and he would no longer be here to protect you. He put me in charge because I know what's beyond the gold and glitter, *agape*. And you do not."

He knew it was a cage. He just didn't care. His use of the word she'd just thought herself made her even angrier. It was difficult for her to hang on to what the goal was right now, not when she just felt...rage. At all the years of being so lonely, so unseen, so unloved.

"He put you in charge because he was a *misogynist*. If he had a son, he would never have done that."

"You're a daughter. The world is not a kind place for women. Surely you know that."

"He might have had some confidence that I was smart enough to avoid—"

"Regardless of gender, avoiding victimization is not a matter of being smart. Believe me. I know."

There was something in his eyes then, something different even than the heat that had been there a moment before. It was a weakness. And it stopped her short.

She had never seen anything half so human in him before. But much like the heat before, it was gone before she could truly grapple with what it meant.

There was no point arguing with him anyway. Apollo was a man who understood action. Not words. She would show him that he could not bend her to his will.

And then part of her wondered...

Wondered if the heat that she had seen in his eyes would make him bend. Would make him withdraw.

He wasn't immune to her body.

Even if he had hidden it quickly. Even if it had only been momentary.

She was going to have to ponder that. What it meant, and how she could use it.

The idea made her heart start beating faster again. It was a risk. For all the reasons she'd thought of already, it was a risk. It could push him away forever. But it could also be the thing that made him realize that now he needed to distance her—just for a time.

Or maybe…

Maybe he would give in.

For one moment she let herself imagine that. His lips, his hands, his body.

She had never tried manipulating anyone ever in her whole life. But the idea that she might be able to make him want her like she'd wanted him…it sent a shock wave through her system.

Get a hold of yourself.

One thing was certain, she couldn't control Apollo. But she could control herself.

She wouldn't be told what to do.

So, she turned on her heel in his office, and when her back was to him and she was near the door, she stopped. "You're not my dad."

Then she swept out of the study.

CHAPTER TWO

"YOU'RE NOT MY DAD!" Mariana laughed uproariously as Hannah recounted the scene in Apollo's office.

"Well," she said, unsure if she was being laughed at in praise or...because she was silly. "He isn't."

"Going to skip the very obvious joke here," their friend Pablo said, leaning back in his chair and grinning. He was wickedly handsome and very gay—a boon for her visually, but nothing more.

"Appreciated," said Hannah. They were sitting in the back of the club, the light swirling around them. Because Mariana worked as the concierge, she got them the best access to the very best places, and that usually at a discount. Because, after all, she had to have experience so that she could recommend things to guests.

They were sitting around a white table, enjoying some delicious champagne, and finally, she had told them everything that happened last night.

"You should get married," Rocco said. He was Italian. Very attractive. *Not* gay. She wished that she could muster up some enthusiasm for Rocco. Of course, it probably wasn't a great idea to date someone you worked with.

"I did think of that," she said. She looked at Mariana. "Actually, I would marry you," she said.

"I'd marry you too," Mariana said, tilting back her

champagne glass and swallowing the rest of it down. "I would literally be marrying my best friend."

"Well, the will says something about a husband specifically."

"How narrow-minded," Mariana said, frowning.

"It may shock you to learn that my white billionaire father wasn't exactly known for his expansive take on the world."

Gigi, the bubbly redhead who was the newest to join their friend group, giggled. "A big shock. Though, it must have prepared you to work in customer service at a hotel."

"Mmm, possibly." Of course, none of their customers could ever hold a candle to Apollo. She had looked at him with rose-colored glasses for so long. And why? Because he was stunningly attractive? Because he was over six feet tall with broad shoulders, arresting features, a square jaw, a blade-straight nose, and lips that looked like they might soften if he smiled. But he never did, so it remained nothing but a theory?

This was her problem. She was a cliché. An absolute cliché. Hideously lousy for the older man who had stepped into her life as an authority figure. Which was problematic and unrealistic. Many would argue that she did not have the agency inherent in the situation to feed feelings like that. So there, stupid heart.

She had never interrogated her life before she'd gotten this job. She was just thankful that she had a group of friends who had encouraged her to do that.

"I googled him," Pablo said. He stole a cherry from her drink and popped it into his mouth.

"Who?"

"Apollo Agassi. Your stern daddy of a guardian. He's a snack."

"Oh, for God's sake," said Hannah.

"I'm just saying," said Pablo. "It's completely valid that you have a thing for him."

"I want to see," said Mariana, taking out her phone. "*Wow.* I'm so sorry I mocked you for wanting to bang him because— OMG."

"Right?" Pablo said.

They passed Mariana's phone around and gaped at the pictures of Apollo.

"He's hot," Gigi said.

"Wouldn't know," said Rocco.

"Yes," Mariana said. "You're straight. We know. Thank you."

"So, get on your knees for him and take control of the situation," said Pablo.

That image was instant, and graphic.

"I'm sorry, *what*?" Her cheeks felt like they'd been scorched.

"There's no way he hasn't noticed that you're an attractive woman."

"He thinks of me as a child," she said, but then she thought of how he had looked at her last night, and she wondered.

"He's a man. And men are simple. Get on your knees, do something better with your mouth than just talking back, and see what happens."

"*What?* You think he'll just… He can't give me access to my trust fund. He isn't legally in charge of that. He's just in charge of me. Kind of? I don't know. It's convoluted." She didn't even bother telling them that he could extend the length of time that she had to stay on the guardianship because it was just unhinged. "I can't just… Do *that*. It would…"

"What? What's the worst that could happen?" Mariana pressed.

Well. He could use that as an excuse to extend the time between now and when she got her money. But, most likely, knowing him, it would make him want to push her away. Apollo was exacting. He didn't expect people to do the unexpected, and it was one of the reasons that he had found her behavior over the last six months so challenging. She knew that. Nobody defied him. And it was why she was fighting him with such intensity tonight.

You wondered about this...

Yes, she had. But that meant like...wearing a low-cut top in front of him, not actually touching him. Tasting him.

She'd wanted a little plausible deniability with her behavior, and something like that would leave no room for her to pretend that maybe he'd imagined it all.

"If you want your freedom," Pablo said. "Take your freedom. In your mouth."

"*Ugh*," said Mariana, taking a cherry out of her drink and throwing it at him.

I'll think about it," she said, and it made her feel all warm and uncomfortable.

"Hannah is a virgin," Mariana said.

"*No*," Gigi and Pablo said at the same time.

"It's true. She's probably the only virgin in here."

"Really?" Rocco pressed. And he looked... Interested. She tried to figure out how she felt about that. She wished she could feel something about that. He *was* attractive. In a more conventional way than Apollo, who was arresting more than he was beautiful. Tall and imposing.

Rocco was in his early twenties. Smooth and pretty,

even. Age appropriate, even. Imagine that. No undue power over her life, even.

She was instantly uninterested.

There was something broken inside of her. She was convinced of it.

"Yes, I am," she said. "Didn't I tell you that he's tyrannical?"

"The issue is that you don't know how to give a BJ," Pablo said.

She sniffed. "How hard could it be?"

Pablo lifted a brow. "It can be very hard, Hannah."

She laughed, in spite of herself.

"You can practice on Rocco," Gigi said, smiling.

Rocco lifted a brow. "I wouldn't be opposed."

It all felt a little bit dangerous. But this had been what she was after, right? Adulthood with no limits. She *could* practice on Rocco if she wanted to. She could do whatever she felt like.

"You should dance with me," said Rocco.

"The way to my heart and a…a—" she couldn't say it, so she cleared her throat imperiously "—is clearly not dance, Rocco, or I wouldn't be a virgin."

"No strings attached."

"Okay."

She took his hand, got up from the table, and let him lead her to the center of the dance floor. She wasn't tipsy. She had only taken a few sips of her drink, and if anything, she had more of a sugar high than a buzz from the alcohol.

Then he pulled her close, and she noted that his body was hard. That he was thoroughly built, even though he had a lean look about him. And she still didn't feel the stirrings of desire. Or anything close. It was blasted inconvenient.

And suddenly, a large masculine hand went to Rocco's shoulder and pulled him away.

Hannah started and looked up. And saw Apollo standing there, looking furious.

"What did I tell you?"

Rage, shock, need, and a feeling of being very small all poured through her. He was here. For her, but not in the way she might have wanted. He was here to scold her like she was a child, and it made her want to weep, wail, and yell at him. And she also wanted to fling herself into his arms. She wanted to take that conversation she'd just had with her friends and make it real.

She wanted that as much as she wanted to run.

She let anger drive her forward, because of all the emotions it felt clearest. Safest.

"What did I tell you?" She took a step toward him. "You are not in charge of me."

The anger she saw in his eyes was just as sharp as hers. It was exhilarating. Intoxicating. Making him respond.

But then he moved. "Let us see," he growled.

He bent down and picked her up, throwing her over his shoulder.

"Apollo!"

She looked around, expecting someone to come to her rescue at any moment because there was no way they were letting this brute carry her out of here bodily.

But nobody came to her defense. Not even her friends.

"Apollo," she shouted, kicking until her shoes came off, hitting his shoulder with her closed fists as they exited the club and made their way outside.

His hands were warm, his hold firm, and it was impossible to feel only anger when he was touching her like this. But it was all the same futile emotion that had had hold of her for all this time. She wanted him to touch her as a man touched a woman. He was touching her like an angry parent would carry a child. But that didn't make *her* feelings change.

"I own that club, *agape*," he said, his words hard.

"You do *not*," she said.

"Yes, I do. As of about ten minutes ago."

"You… You bought the club so that you could carry me out of the club?"

"Yes. All things considered, I think it was worth it."

"You're unhinged," she said. "You're a sociopath. *A psychopath*. Put me down." She wiggled against him, her breasts pressed against his back and sending sparks of arousal through her, even as she wanted to destroy him. Make him feel this same endless need. Make him suffer like she did.

"I am none of those things," he said. "If I were, I probably wouldn't be so angry. I would be looking at this with a cool sort of sophisticated calculation, and instead, I wish to dump you into the sea."

"*Good*. I would rather tangle with the sharks than deal with you."

"The sharks may end up being your only option."

It should terrify her, the idea of losing him. Right now, it didn't.

"*Great*. Find me chilling with the hammerheads. But then you wouldn't be able to control my life, and what fun would that be for you?"

"I will not fail," he bit out.

He set her down on the sidewalk, the ground gritty and cool beneath her feet. "You are a foolish girl," he said.

"I have been tasked with taking care of you. And I will do so. I will do exactly as your father asked me because he is one of the only people who ever did a damn thing for me and didn't expect something in return. With him, it wasn't transactional. And nothing else in my life has been that way. And I will honor that. I will do this with excellence as I have done everything else."

"I am *not a spreadsheet*." She was made of feelings. Of desire and need and aching hunger, and he was turning her into a *thing*. It outraged her. "You can't math out the way that you handle this. And what metric would you even use? The successes that I achieve? And then, would any of them be mine?"

"A question you would always have had to ask yourself, as you come from money. As you would always be standing on the shoulders of your father. So, if that's going to give you an existential crisis, it would have anyway."

"I'm *not* having an existential crisis." Sadly she knew what her crisis was.

"Then what is all this?"

He looked at her, and then he looked her up and down, and she suddenly became very conscious of how her dress conformed to her curves. She had chosen the dress because it was provocative, but now beneath his gaze, she felt naked.

But she saw it then. The masculine appreciation in his gaze, even though he tried to bank it, tried to bury it and deny it. She could see all of it.

She thought of what Pablo had said.

The idea filled her with desire and need.

She hadn't felt any of that when she'd been dancing with Rocco. But the image of getting on her knees before him made her feel liquid. If he dragged her back to the car, she could do that. Slide to the floor, find herself between those powerful thighs, and undo his belt...

She wanted it. So bad. It made her heart throb painfully, and that secret place between her legs ached.

She wanted this man. Even now. She wanted him to tear the dress from her body. And she wanted to wrench the clothes from his. She wanted to have him while they fought. It was like a fever. An illness sweeping through her like a tide.

"What's the matter, *agape*? You look flushed."

How dare he? *How dare he* when he was not immune to this thing either.

"I think you know exactly what I'm thinking about."

"What is it exactly?" he asked.

She was suddenly aware that the street they had gone out to was an alley and deserted. The sidewalk between her feet suddenly felt warm rather than cold, as it had a few moments earlier.

The warm Grecian evening was suddenly hot.

And all of her plans had shifted. In the time since he'd carried her out of the club she'd realized this was more fraught, more perilous than she'd thought before. This was...the end of her sanity. He couldn't have all the power anymore.

She had to take some for herself.

She had to touch him.

She had to make him feel this. Understand it.

She had to.

She took a step toward him until her breasts touched his chest. She tried to suppress a shiver. Trembling.

"Perhaps you're angry with me because you feel I haven't provided adequate compensation." Her voice shook, her heart beating so hard she felt it in her temples. "What if I showed you how appreciative I am of the work you've done for me?"

"You must be drunk," he said, not moving away, staring her down defiantly, his face like stone.

She would not be dismissed. She would not let him do that.

"I'm *not* drunk. I barely had two sips of my drink." She was high on something else. On her outrage. On the clarity she felt now. Understanding that she had power here. That he felt this too. And how desperate she was to force him to feel it. Really feel it. Like she did. "I know exactly what I want."

He stepped toward her, his dark eyes glinting. "And what is it you think you want, little girl?"

He didn't think she would follow through. He thought she would be afraid. She wasn't.

"I would really like to get down on my knees and show my appreciation. You would like that, wouldn't you? I can see that you're not immune to me. I've seen you looking at my body these last couple of nights. You like my dress, as much as you wish you could hate it. If you ask very nicely, perhaps I'll pull the top down and let you see—"

"*Enough*," he ground out, gripping her arms and pushing her back a step. Her eyes widened, fear and triumph warring within her. "You're being a fool. I'm your guardian. You are my ward; you are under my protection. A child."

"I'm twenty-two. I'm not a child."

"You might as well be one to me. I was friends with your father, I've never been friends with you."

"What does friendship have to do with desire? What does it have to do with—"

"Enough," he gritted out.

And she did it, she mustered every ounce of bravery she could and looked down, and she saw. That burgeoning hunger there, pushing against the front of his pants.

"You want me. Your body doesn't lie."

Calling on a boldness she had no idea she possessed, she reached her hand forward, and her fingertips brushed that jutting arousal.

His lip curled as he moved her hand aside. "You think that's significant?"

And suddenly, his face transformed. Pity and contempt were reflected in his gaze. But the need was still there. Regardless of what he said.

"You're hard," she said. "You want me."

"You silly little girl. That doesn't mean quite so much as you would like it to. A man can get hard for anything. Sex is cheap. You have no idea how cheap. It means nothing to a man like me. I've had more lovers than I can readily count. More than I could ever count. Because I don't remember most of them. And why would I? I feel nothing for them. And you… You're young. You have a nice figure—soft skin. A man is bound to respond to you. But don't forget that a man would forget you as soon as he had you, darling. It is not a compliment to make a man hard. It is simply biology. It means nothing about how I feel for you."

"It means that you see me as—"

"It means *nothing*," he said again. "You are a silly child, and the fact that you think it signifies anything reveals your inexperience. No, spare me. Your tantrums and your paltry attempts at manipulation. That you think I would break all that I am for the chance to touch you is the most foolish thing I've ever conceived of. I can find someone to take care of this as soon as I get you locked up in the house."

She had thought he might react badly. She hadn't truly imagined this. His cruelty. The way he cut her with such unerring precision. Hit at everything she felt insecure about.

And it all boiled over.

"*I hate you*," she said. Then she meant it. With every fiber of her being. As much as she had ever loved him.

"Good. Perhaps you should hate me."

He picked her up and carried her to the car then, and she felt scalded by his touch. Outraged. But she didn't wish to protest too much because she didn't want to rub her body against him. They were silent on the drive home, and then she went to her room and locked the door defiantly behind her. She took her phone out of her pocket and called Mariana to let her know she had gotten home safely. And what had happened.

"Rocco told us."

"A lot of good Rocco did."

"Well, you can't exactly blame him for not wanting to have a fistfight in the middle of the club."

It was true. It wasn't like he was her boyfriend or anything. Or her...

"Mariana, I have to call you back." She hung up. And then she dialed Rocco.

Her hands were shaking. And she was desperate. Desperate to get Apollo the way he'd gotten her.

"Thank God," he said. "I was worried."

"Rocco," she said. "I think you should marry me."

CHAPTER THREE

APOLLO SPENT THE next two weeks in a vile temper. He had taken his feral mood off to Scotland to see Cameron, business partner and friend, and his wife, Athena.

"Stop brooding," Cameron said one night. "You're doing a classic impression of me." He grinned, his scarred face shifting with the expression.

"My friend," Apollo said, "it is not an impersonation of you unless I lock myself away in a castle for more than a decade and make my business partner do every last one of the in-person appearances we have scheduled for the company for the duration."

"I am sorry about that," Cameron said.

Then he laughed. It was good to hear Cameron laugh. He had not done so for a long time before Athena came into his life. Truly, he and Cameron had never had much to laugh about. But his friend had always been gregarious and beautiful, so handsome that the people around him paid dearly for the chance to spend time in his company. And when they were younger, had paid astronomical sums for a night with him.

He had seemed unscathed by all of that until an accident killed his lover and stole his looks. And yes, during that time, he had been a veritable beast.

Apollo would love to claim the way he had handled

Cameron as another of his good deeds, but he could not. Cameron was his brother. In all the ways that it mattered. They had come up together on the streets, and they had kept each other from dying. Apollo had spent the early part of his life in Greece with his mother, the bastard child of her affair with an Italian man who'd left before Apollo was born.

She had gone to Scotland on the promise that a man there might care for them, but it had turned out to be little more than human trafficking. His mother had lost herself during those years, and Apollo had run away from home.

It was too dangerous, being around his mother's various clients. He had managed to remain unmolested. Until that was, he had decided that charging money for access to his body before people could take it for free was perhaps the way forward.

It was the kind of work that took pieces of your soul. He and Cameron had not done it because they'd had a vast array of choices before them. They'd had certain assets and had used them how they could.

They were also brilliant. Smart with technology and had begun working at getting their hands on all the pieces of old technology that they could so that they could begin understanding the inner workings of all of it.

The ugly truth was that they had been prostitutes. The uglier truth was that sex was a commodity people paid dearly for. He did not feel guilt over his past actions. He had done what he needed to do. But it had changed him. When your own body was for sale, it forced you to live in your mind. He and Cameron had done so to their own benefit, and with connections they'd built—and some exploitation that verged on blackmail—they had managed to begin establishing themselves in the tech world. Starting their own company. Letting go of that old life.

Yes, he would love to say that staying connected to Cameron during his crisis, keeping him moving, keeping him going, had been an act of charity on his part. It wasn't.

He hadn't known how to live in a world without Cameron, and beyond that, his financial success was tied to Cameron. And he would not allow failure.

They were billionaires. They had more money than a single person could ever spend in a lifetime, but Apollo would never take that for granted. How could he?

The wolves of poverty ever snapped at his heels. The wounds never fully healing. He knew what he would do to survive. He did not have to wonder. He would do it again. But it would cost so much more now. Because, as a boy, he'd had no pride. As a man, he did. And therefore, failure was not an option. Not now. Not ever. He simply could not and would not allow it. But Cameron was healed now. Not because of Apollo, but because of Athena.

The woman who had stumbled upon his castle a few years back, running away from her own troubled past. Cameron had fallen in love with her, whatever that meant.

Apollo couldn't be certain.

He did not understand it. He knew what it was to be bonded to somebody because of flame and fire. He knew what it was to feel as if he owed someone a debt. As far as romantic love went, to him, it looked as if you simply chose a person you wished to have sex with for the rest of your life.

Apollo had never been the playboy that Cameron was. The way that Cameron handled the trauma of their youth had been to shag everything that moved. Once he had money and power. Cameron was always taking delight in how his beauty caused those around him to do foolish things. It was why his accident had taken so very much from him. It had been the way he handled the world.

That face of his.

As for Apollo, he often felt fatigued by sex. The transactional nature of it. The way that it sometimes pushed him into a strange hollow cavern inside of himself. Where his body was moving but his mind was no longer there.

That was another difference between himself and Cameron. Cameron had never cared who he slept with. Other than his wife, who was now the only person he would ever want, he had gotten so much pleasure out of the act of being the desired object that age, gender, nothing, none of it mattered to Cameron.

An advantageous position to be in in a life such as theirs.

It did matter to Apollo. He'd had to do things he had not liked. With people he had not wanted, and he'd had to figure out how to manufacture a response to them.

It was difficult to break old habits. And that was why he found himself sometimes retreating during the act. All these years later. It didn't make sense to him. And it was frustrating, because he liked women. He liked sex. But it could never entirely be divorced from the way he had once used it, and that outraged him. Because he was a man who had defeated the systems of this world. A man who had climbed up from the gutter defied all odds, and in many ways, he had escaped.

And yet, a film clung to him, and he did not know how to clear it away.

And then of course, there was the matter of Hannah. He was doing his best not to revisit that night.

The way that his body had responded to her, because what he'd said to her had been alive. It was true, arousal, desire, was cheap for many. And bought expensively. He knew that better than most.

But for him? He had eminent control over his own responses. Always. Whether he chose to react or chose not to.

But he had chosen nothing with her. When she had looked at him with that beautiful face, her lips parted, her expression earnest, and told him that she wished to get on her knees and thank him for what he had done...

The twist of self-loathing in his gut was intense.

She was offering him payment. He had wanted to take it.

It made him feel... Wrong. All of it was wrong.

He wanted to go back to the night before he'd first confronted her about going out. To before he'd seen her in that dress that had barely covered her body. He did not want to see her as a woman, but as a symbol of his redemption and he was outraged she had pushed things to this point.

As if you did not have a part in it, putting your hands on her body and carrying her out of the club?

He had refused her. That was what mattered.

He had prevailed.

"Are you going to tell me what the problem is?"

"No," said Apollo. "Because there is no problem, Cameron. The presence of a problem implies I'm concerned there is something that I cannot fix. We all know that can't be true. I don't lose."

"You didn't fix me," Cameron pointed out.

"I triaged you. Until your wife appeared."

Cameron laughed again. "You could not have arranged that if you'd tried."

Apollo leaned back in his chair, surveying his friend's castle. It was all a far cry from squatting in vacant buildings in Edinburgh. "When I move, the universe orients itself around me, or did you not know?"

"Your ego is doing well despite the rest of your mood."

He let silence reign for a moment.

"Hannah has become difficult." He shouldn't tell Cameron this. But Cameron was truly the only friend he had in this world.

"Oh, the adult woman whose life you're still in charge of? Imagine that." Cameron's amusement outraged him.

"I did not create the set of rules surrounding the guardianship," he said. "She acts as if I'm the enemy too. And I did not create the situation. I neither wrote the will nor got myself killed in a canoeing accident. That was her mother and father."

"I imagine it doesn't much signify when you are the object blocking her from the things that she wishes to do and have and be."

"I am doing nothing of the kind. I guided her. Through high school, through college. She has a degree, she could get any job she wished. She could get a job at her father's company, and then when the restrictions on her lift in three years she will take an executive position. She's going to be in control. It will be hers."

"Three years when you're in your twenties is an eternity. And after all these years of being under your iron fist."

Cameron had no right to comment. He hadn't been

present for any of this. "I resent that. I have been fair. I have been good."

"Of course you have."

"Cameron, you are a pain in my ass."

"I have been for more than twenty years. Why stop now?"

"I do not know what to do with her."

"Give her what she wants. Give her the respect that she is due."

"I worry for her," he said. Because it was true. Though mostly, perhaps he worried that he wouldn't be able to keep his promise to her father, which would be unacceptable. A failure. And if he put his foot on that path, what then?

"Let her have her freedom. You can stick to the terms of the will, and you can make her happy."

"What makes her happy right now is going to clubs and dancing with strange men." The way he'd felt when he'd walked in and seen that man, with his hands on her, had made him feel a violent surge of possessiveness. It was, he told himself, because she deserved better. That man transparently wished to use her for her body and Hannah deserved more.

The thought of her being used in that way made his lip curl. Made him think of the dark things behind him.

"She *is* twenty-two," Cameron pointed out. "There's nothing wrong with going out, dancing…having a bit of casual sex."

"You can say that after the life we led?"

"Apollo, for most people, this time of their life should be carefree. You and I know nothing about that. My dear Athena knows nothing about that. She was a prisoner, her father kept her from living the life that she truly wanted. Is that what you want to be for Hannah?"

"I am not like Athena's father. I did not kidnap Hannah from her rightful family and then attempt to sell her into marriage after hiding her away for her entire life."

"No of course not. But I'm only saying... There are normal lives to be had out there. Just because we didn't have them doesn't mean Hannah can't."

"But the world is..."

"Dangerous," Cameron said. "Horribly so. But you will be there. To protect her. If she truly needs it. Don't be a monster in the meantime. That really is stepping on my territory."

He pondered his friend's words, even as he went back to Greece.

He moved back to Greece after Cameron's accident because it had felt... It had felt like something he should try. An attempt at finding some of himself. He hadn't found it. At least he didn't think. There was no point going over the past. There was only moving forward. And he was intent on doing that with Hannah.

He arrived home, expecting to find the place turned inside out. Expecting that she would have thrown a party to get revenge on him.

He had left, knowing that she might act out in his absence, but he had felt like it was safer than remaining near her.

He had done what he had to.

But when he arrived home, not only was the house in order, Hannah was standing there in what was a perfectly demure outfit, one that should not have brought his blood to a low simmer and made his body feel set on edge.

"I'm very glad that you've arrived back home. Because I have something to tell you." She sounded placid. He didn't trust it.

Her hands were clasped in front of her, and just then, she moved. And he saw a large diamond on her left hand. "I'm engaged."

"You are *not*," he said, the words bordering on a growl.

Her expression was bland. "I am. You saw the man that I was dancing with at the club. Rocco. I'm marrying him."

That wee boy? That child? Who had pawed at her body as if it was a buffet platter he felt entitled to? Never. There had been no love on his face, no care of any kind.

Most unforgivable of all, he had let Apollo take her. Any man who surrendered a woman so easily did not deserve her in any capacity.

And any woman who had offered what Hannah had offered him could not truly want another.

"You're *marrying* him?" he asked. "When I took you off the dance floor, you offered to get on your knees and pleasure me not one minute after you were in his arms? How can you wish to marry him?"

"I'm in love with him."

No.

The denial was instant and vehement.

"You're in love with him, and yet you offered to take me in your mouth?"

It was a dangerous thing, bringing that up.

"Old fantasies die hard," she said, and the words sparked questions, a fire that tumbled along his skin, and he wanted to ignore all of the implications there.

He had to focus on the issue at hand.

"No. I forbid it. You are not getting married."

"Funnily enough, the guardianship agreement says nothing about you having a choice in who I marry,

Apollo. You can't stop me. We are to wed in two days' time. At the small chapel at the hotel. I hope to see you there. But if you're too angry at being outmaneuvered to do so… Well."

"*Outmaneuvered*. You don't love him."

"I do," she said. "I am prepared to live with him as man and wife for a year. At least. As the will stipulates."

"This is foolish. And childish."

"You think me foolish and childish, and that is why it's what you see. You are not in charge of me or my life. I'm getting married. My trust fund will be mine. And so will my father's company."

"And it could all be his as well. Did you ever think of that? The will gives outrageous weight to the opinions of the person you married. It is set up so that your husband becomes your guardian. Are you that stupid that you would overlook that?"

His words were cruel, and he knew that. He also knew that they would not wound her. They would only make her angrier. But he himself was too angry to be calculated in the moment.

"I'll see you at the wedding. Or I won't."

"It has to be a legitimate wedding. Overseen by the board of—"

"I'm aware. I went over everything with a fine tooth comb. I've known Rocco for eight months. We are in a relationship. We are in love. People have seen us together many times. We have passed our interviews with flying colors, and everyone is invited to the affair. Including you. Even though I hate you."

Rage was a roiling, ugly monster in his gut. He had not felt this sort of anger in many, many years. That she was the source of it made him…he was not trustworthy right now.

"You have not begun to hate me, Hannah," he bit out. "That is a promise."

But Hannah was not cowed. This was not the biddable girl who had been in his care all those years. Not the still, clear reflection of his own goodness that he'd seen as she'd done well in school, worked hard, presented herself with such care.

This was a woman. The one that had ignited his desire so unexpectedly even as she had called up his rage. This woman was on a path of destruction, and he could see in the reckless light in her eyes that she knew it. And was willing to let herself be destroyed if she could claim even a momentary victory.

"You will not best me, Apollo. That is my own promise to you."

With that, she left him standing there in the entry of his magnificent home, the evidence of all his billions soaring around them in the form of clever architecture, high arches and priceless artwork. Feeling as if he had no more power than he did when he was a boy.

But that feeling lasted only a moment. Because it was unacceptable. Because he would not indulge it. Because he would not allow it. He would not be manipulated by a child.

He would see an end to this. One way or the other.

CHAPTER FOUR

SHE HAD DONE IT. She had put the plan together flaw-lessly, and now it was her wedding day.

The chapel was in a beautiful location, on a rock that overlooked the brilliant jewel-bright sea. It was a white building with a blue domed roof and glittering windows. Her wedding dress was a beautiful liquid silk gown that shimmered as she moved, little crystals covering all of it.

The minute the wedding had been scheduled she'd been given access to her trust fund to pay for the affair.

It meant that she and all her friends were outfitted splendidly. And if she had slipped in a few purchases to make her friends' lives better and filed them under wedding expenses, so be it.

She needed this. And she knew she had likely compromised her relationship with Apollo forever but...

She couldn't go on like this. The night he'd carried her out of the club had made it clear. She was lost to him. Willing to debase herself, even as he humiliated her. When it came to him she wasn't rational or reasonable. When it came to him she made terrible choices that could not be endured.

The only power her father had given her was this. She had to use a man to escape another one, and while she hated it with every fiber of her being, she knew it was the only thing to be done.

Apollo had vanished after that night at the club.

Part of her had hoped he would storm in and apologize. That they would find some other way forward, but he hadn't come to her. He'd left town. Hell, he'd left the country. And so she'd moved forward with her plan to get away from him on her own terms.

She hated it. But she needed it.

She couldn't see past the next three years. If she sank deeper into her obsession with Apollo, there would be nothing left of her.

She had to do something.

This was the only something she could think of.

She gathered her bouquet, a stunning coral arrangement with bright blue blossoms sprinkled throughout that matched the blues around them, and looked at Mariana. "This is the right thing to do, yes?"

"Of course it is," said Mariana. "You're getting your freedom. And listen, I can't... You have been extremely generous. Thank you."

"I'm going to get you a job at my father's company. My company."

"You know this is not why I became your friend," said Mariana.

"No, I know," she said. "But I think you're great at your job, and I think you'll bring something to the company. And I understand that... It's not really fair that I've been given all of this. Yes, I have the education to do all of this, but very few people could simply step into this position. Especially not at this stage. I'm not owed any of it. But I do want to have freedom. Agency. I feel like I deserve to at least manage the assets that I was left, even if I'm not entitled to them."

Because the truth was, she could walk away without doing this. She could get a job, be just like her friends. Her anger prevented that. Her anger at her father, at Apollo.

And even more so, doing that wouldn't have the effect on Apollo that this would. She needed him to feel her anger. To feel her defiance. And only this would do.

"It's all right," said Mariana. "You don't have to justify yourself to me."

"Maybe I'm trying to justify myself to me. Because I'm doing a kind of extreme thing to get out of dealing with Apollo for the next three years of my life."

"That's okay. The whole situation is unusual. Could anybody really blame you?"

"I guess not."

"What kinds of agreements do you have in place," Marianne asked. "To protect you?"

"What do you mean?"

"Rocco…"

"He's your friend. He's our friend."

"He is," said Mariana. I've known him for three years. I like him. But… Sometimes… Sometimes he says things that worry me a bit. And I… I would just hate for you to get hurt doing any of this. You could always marry Pablo."

"I can't just substitute a groom at the last minute. And anyway, it's a little bit too well documented that Pablo is not interested in women. And I can't have the marriage looking fake. It has to be legitimate."

"Yes. I get that."

Granted, nobody seemed half as concerned with controlling her life, and what she did than Apollo was.

"What do you think he'll do?"

"It's a lot of money," Mariana said. "And you're being really generous with it. I worry he's going to let that kind of thing go to his head. I'm not going to lie to you, Hannah, it's... It's kind of intoxicating. To have a friend who can suddenly open all these doors for you. But I can't control you, and neither can Pablo or Gigi. Rocco... He's going to be your husband, and I just worry that he's going to start to think he could make a lot of money divorcing you and taking things from you."

"I just..."

"The stipulations of your will didn't allow for prenup, did they?"

"But he and I talked about it and..."

"Yes, you have an agreement with him. But will he stick to it, or will he exploit you as a husband?"

"It's too late to worry about that," she said. "It just is."

Except she was now suddenly worried that she was taking her foot out of one bear trap only to stick it in another.

And Apollo's words echoed in her ears. That she was young and foolish and knew nothing of the world.

Remembering that, the way he saw her...

Apollo was the bigger risk.

She didn't like to think she was naive. She knew that people could take advantage of you. But she supposed that there was an element of naivete in believing that money might not change somebody. Maybe that was the kind of thing someone who'd always had a certain amount of access to money could comfort themselves with. Money was inevitable for her. And she had never had control of it, but she had also never felt the lack of it.

She was worrying about that even as she slipped on

her shoes and followed Mariana to the main part of the chapel.

She linked arms with Pablo and walked into the sanctuary. And Hannah waited. Waited until the music shifted. Until it was time for her to walk down the aisle.

She had no father with her to give her away. And suddenly she felt extremely sad. It was a funny thing, grief like this. Tinged so often now with anger, and yet there was still so much regret. She could go days without thinking of her parents. Weeks. And then suddenly it just wouldn't make any sense to her that they were gone. Not at all.

Right now, though, was one of those times when she was shocked, almost, that they weren't here. For her wedding.

She had never let herself think about that. Perhaps because she had never been in a space where she had really thought about having a wedding.

The whole Apollo tying up so many of her emotions had prevented her from dreaming about that.

She looked up at the white stucco ceiling. "I wish you were here, Dad. But if you were here, this wouldn't be happening." A tear slid down her cheek. Of all the absurd things. She dashed it away and continued into the sanctuary. Rocco was standing there, looking handsome and familiar. And most importantly, like her friend. She tried to push away the doubts that Mariana had just introduced to her. She didn't need to be filled with doubt.

She arrived at the head of the aisle and had just turned to take his hand when suddenly a man in a dark suit melted from the shadows behind him and turned.

Apollo.

Her heart leapt into her throat, thundering like a wild,

trapped creature. His eyes were on Hannah, and only Hannah. He never paused to look at Rocco. He never looked at the crowd, at the priest.

His dark eyes burned into hers with intent, and she knew she had lost. She didn't know how. She didn't know what form it would take. But she knew, beyond words, that he had come to claim victory here, and that no one would stop Apollo Agassi from getting what he wanted.

"Step aside," he said to Rocco.

Rocco turned and looked at him, his expression one of fear. "I said step aside," said Apollo. "You will not be marrying Hannah today."

The words were like a gut punch. She stepped forward, and was about to tell him off.

"Yes," Rocco said, his voice shaking just slightly. "I am."

Well, he'd tried.

"You're not," Apollo said. "You have two choices. I either expose your true identity to all the people here, and call the police, and have you extradited back to Italy, where I think you will find a not very warm welcome waiting for you, or you take the payoff I'm offering, and I will not tell you how much it is. But it is better than prison."

Hannah could only stare, a cold feeling taking root in her stomach and spreading outward, rivaling the heat she'd felt a moment before.

She had been duped. And because of that Apollo was winning.

Her own naivete had hung her, just not in the way she'd imagined it might.

"I don't…" Rocco looked between Hannah and Apollo. Hannah could only stare, shock winding through her.

"What is this?" she asked, feeling sad, defeated.

"I'm sorry," Rocco said.

"I…"

Apollo shoved him aside and came to stand across from her, right in his place. And it was as if Rocco had never been there at all. "You know, Hannah, I considered picking you up and carrying you off down the aisle. But that seems like a bit too much melodrama, don't you think? I think perhaps I could save everyone time by moving into my rightful place. Here. As your groom."

"What?"

"Oh, yes. Your plans have changed. You're marrying me."

It had not taken much for Apollo to dig up dirt on Rocco Marinelli. Or as he was known previously, Rocco Fiore, of Rome, who had a stack of petty misdemeanors that he had committed, minor cons and identity theft. And when the heat had gotten too much, he left Italy and came to Greece, changing his identity and taking a job at the hotel. Where, by all accounts, he had been a good employee, and a good friend. It was entirely possible the bully had truly reformed himself. Or perhaps not.

Apollo trusted no one.

But even if the other man had reformed himself, it did not matter. He was going to see this through. If Hannah needed access to her trust fund so badly, if she wanted to assume her position at her father's company, she could do so, but it would be under his supervision for this next year. This was the best way forward. Cameron had told him not to intervene, but it didn't matter what Cameron said. This made the most sense. He would have to live with her as man and wife in that time, and of course, he would not touch her. He would continue to act as her guardian. Continue to guide her, continue to protect her. To fulfill his promise.

He would not lose hold of her, of this. He had come to that conclusion this morning, and it had driven him to this point.

"I…"

"He can't do this, can he?"

She turned toward the audience, toward the men on the board, and then back to the priest. "He can't," she said.

When she looked back at him, her eyes widened.

He turned to look behind him and saw that Rocco had fled.

"Well, you're without your original groom."

"This is irregular," one of the board members said from the front row.

"I love Hannah," Apollo said. He was very good at manufacturing words of love. The truth was, everyone should be horrified that he had rolled up to confess his long-hidden love for the girl he had been caring for all these years, but they wouldn't be. They would all think it was a boon for her because he was a billionaire, and because her father had trusted him, so what else mattered?

This was the truth of the world. There was nothing Apollo could do about it, except use it to his own advantage.

What they didn't know was that she'd offered to get down on her knees before him in the street, and that he'd been tempted…

No. Not tempted. A physical response was not real temptation. He would never have done it.

"You do not love me," she whispered.

"Little fool," he said, his voice a hushed rasp. "If you

marry me, you will have access to your trust fund and the control of the company. If you don't, things go back to the way they were, and I can opt to have your time under my control extended. So, what will you choose, Hannah?"

He could see her calculating. She already knew she'd lost, but she had to be sure there was no other choice. He respected that even if he did not have the patience for it.

He saw as the defiance in her eyes was replaced with weary acceptance.

Good. He was inevitable. The sooner she accepted that, the better.

"Fine," she said, her cheeks turning red with anger. "I'll marry you."

"There now. That was not a difficult choice, was it?"

She looked as if she would cheerfully eviscerate him with her teeth at the first opportunity, but her happiness in the moment was not his primary concern. His concern was her safety.

And his own reputation.

"Let us proceed," he said.

He took her hands in his and felt that they were damp. Her fingertips were cold.

Reflexively he smoothed his thumb over her knuckles, and her eyes met his again, confusion in those blue depths.

He took a moment to take a visual tour of her features. Wide blue eyes, a delicately upturned nose, full lips, a defiant, pointed chin. Her dark brown hair was styled in the waves that fell down her back, and her dress conformed lovingly to her figure. She was well curved, which was exactly how he liked his women. And she smelled like... Peaches and sunshine. Which was unlike anything he had ever thought he might want to draw nearer to. And yet with her, he found he did.

The words didn't matter.

They both repeated them.

They were lies.

And yet he would never forget the slight shift of her bare shoulder. The way the sun came through the windows and ignited a halo of gold around the edges of her hair. The shimmer of her dress when she shifted her hips and the silk moved like a tide over her body.

And the smell. Those peaches. That was what he would remember. Always.

There were few memories that he felt the urge to try and capture. Hold on to it. And the ones he did have were mercenary. He liked to think of when he had made his first substantial sum of money and had been able to turn down a regular client wanting to meet up for a quick shag. He remembered that because it had made him feel powerful.

He could remember the first time he walked into a party filled with rich beautiful people and made conversation with a woman who was exactly to his taste. He had taken her to his bed, because he had chosen to. Though it had not been the escape, the heady rush of pleasure he'd hoped it to be. He had done it, though. He had chosen it.

They were grim things. Defiant things.

They were not soft and lovely. Not sunshine and peaches and silk.

This he could cling to, not because it felt like a victory, but because it filled him. Every one of his senses, like all the natural wonders around them.

And then came the moment that he had perhaps forgotten for a reason.

"You may now kiss your bride."

Had they married in private, they would not have done so, but they were doing it here in front of the board, and he had professed to love her.

It was no matter. Physical touch could mean very little to him.

And yet the memory of how he had responded to her body two weeks ago lingered within him.

She looked panicked, and he gripped her chin, studying her. "I'm your husband," he said.

She did not relax beneath his touch. He leaned forward, and pressed his mouth to hers, keeping it brief and nearly chaste. And still, the crack of flame that woke within him was like nothing he had experienced before.

He felt her lips go pliant beneath his. Felt that resistance change. So that her mouth clung to his.

Everything was softness. Everything was peaches.

He pulled away.

And then that moment passed, and the ceremony was done. And he let the lingering impression of peaches slip away.

They turned to face the crowd, and the priest announced them. It was silent in the room. Everyone was staring with wide eyes. Uncertain of what they had just witnessed.

They walked down the aisle together, hand in hand. When they returned to the antechamber, he released his hold on her. "Go and speak to your friends," he said.

"But…"

"I assume we have an entire reception to get through?"

"I…"

"We are married, *agape*. Try to look as if you might be happy about it."

"I'm not. I was doing this to get rid of you."

"You had no idea that Rocco was a con artist, did you?"

"No. Was he trying to… Was he trying to con me?" She looked genuinely hurt by that. And he felt the urge just then to soften what he had just said.

For many years he had dealt with her by paying for her life. And with that money he provided safety, structure. She'd had a place to stay when she'd been on holiday. But he'd not had to…contend with her. With her emotions.

It had to change now.

"I have no evidence of that. Only what he did in the past. He was clean as long as he was here. But… Given his inclinations, I would not necessarily want to trust him with a fortune of your magnitude. Or with… Or with you, Hannah. I fear he could've hurt you. I hope for your sake you did not really love him."

"And if I do? If I do love him, you are happy to have separated me from him?"

"If you loved him, then I am extremely happy to have made sure you won't have your heart broken by him."

"That's almost nice. Except you took the whole situation and manipulated it to your own advantage. All of the protections that you're concerned I don't have… Well, now you have access to the company. To all of my money."

The accusation that he was using her for money scraped close to wounded bone, and he found himself snarling in response to it.

"How dare you? I do not need your money. Nor your father's company. I am a self-made man. The company that I built with Cameron is the one that I want, and the one that I care about. But you are my responsibility. And now for the next year I will be able to guide you on this journey."

He'd only just purposed to be more gentle and here he was growling.

She's strong. She's not a girl. If she wishes to be treated as a woman, as an adult, then she will have to deal with your anger when she ignites it.

"You're asking me to trust you when you didn't think that I was capable of figuring out whether or not I could trust Rocco."

"Yes. I do expect that you might have a bit more trust for the man who has cared for you since you were sixteen years old than for the man that you met a few months ago."

"You didn't spend all those days with me. It isn't as if you raised me. Perhaps both you and my parents needed to take real stock of how much you had to do with the way that I was succeeding. I'm sorry, Apollo, but that is the truth. My parents were off on their adventures, and I was at home studying. I was the one choosing to succeed. You put down your rules, but I chose to follow them. We didn't even live in the same country most of the time. I managed my life while I was away at boarding school, while I was away at university. I am the one whose life was completely uprooted, and I am the one who had to cope with it. You weren't there for me emotionally. You think that because you kept me from ending up in an alleyway doing black tar heroin that you've succeeded in some fashion, but you do not recognize that I was the one who was there for myself. And now, because you couldn't stand some other man stepping into your position you... Physically removed him from his."

"If a man is marrying a woman, and it is possible to

physically remove him, and marry her in his stead, he didn't truly wish to be there. Even if he did, he did not deserve to be. Had someone tried to usurp my place as your groom I would've killed them. I don't think I'm being hyperbolic."

The conviction in his words shocked even him. The darkness there.

Murder was one of the few sins he hadn't committed. And yet he knew without certainty he would do it if he had to.

She was his. His responsibility. He would be damned if anyone hurt her now.

"You're a bit of a monster."

"I never claimed I wasn't. You're the one good thing I have ever done, *agape*. I will see it through to the end."

"And I don't have a choice in it?"

"Think carefully about that. Because the truth is you will have more choices now than you ever have. Do not squander it because you're angry at me."

It was then that her friend came through the door of the church. "Hannah…"

"Go and speak to your friends."

And Hannah obeyed, going off with her friend and leaving him there. Nothing would change. This wasn't a real wedding. And it would not become one.

It would be a marriage in name only for a year to protect Hannah and her assets.

He had made the right choice.

Like he always did.

CHAPTER FIVE

"WHAT THE HELL was that?"

"I don't know," Hannah said, her heart still beating wildly, disbelief rolling through her like a freight train.

"He just married you."

"Yeah, I know," she said. "I was there."

Her lips burned; her body burned.

The kiss had been short and chaste and nothing much to get excited about, and yet her nipples were still tight and sensitive, and that place between her legs throbbed. Perhaps it was the memory of what happened between them two weeks ago in the alley. Or rather what hadn't happened.

But either way, the kiss had affected her far more than it should have. But then, how was she supposed to remain unaffected in these circumstances? She had orchestrated this entire thing to get away from Apollo, and now she was his wife.

His wife.

She had dreamed of this.

But never quite in this fashion.

It was like someone had handed her a beautiful snow globe, then smashed it on the ground. All the glass, snow, and the little village still there, but...mangled beyond belief.

And she felt like the broken shards of glass were digging into her now.

"His wife!" she shouted out loud.

"Well," Mariana said. "I suppose that takes us full circle. Because you know, he's not your dad."

"It's not funny." She was maybe *dying*.

"It's kind of funny. I mean, he ended up having to marry you. And he was so furious about the whole thing. You know, when you offered to get down on your knees and—"

"Yes, I remember that. Thank you. I was there."

"Well," Mariana said. "Now he married you. So… Does this mean that you get to have a wedding night?"

Heat burned through her. "I am certain that would be a very bad idea."

"Why? It would probably be really fun. He is so hot."

"I'm aware that he is so hot. That's the problem. But the bigger problem is that he's… He doesn't have any feelings. At least, not the feelings that aren't anger. Every so often, I think maybe he cares about me and that's why he is so intense about protecting me, but I just think it has to do with his relationship with my dad. They were good friends. And it matters to him a lot that my dad trusted him to care for me. He's like psychotically intense about it. But really, that is the only discernible feeling the man has. Otherwise, he's… Unknowable. He doesn't seem to attach much to anyone or anything. He has his friends, his business partner, and he seems to care for them. But… He never has girlfriends."

He'd hinted at dark issues in his past, and knowing him and the degree to which he was locked down emotionally she wouldn't be surprised if there was some ter-

rible trauma he'd endured. But he didn't share that sort
of thing with her, because he didn't see her as a person.

She was a good deed he was doing,

She was already feeling shattered. Sleeping with him
could destroy her.

But he isn't immune to you…

"Well, men like him don't. They're far too sophisticated for that. But then they have wives, and…"

"You don't suppose they're faithful to them, do you?"

"Of course not. I work at a hotel. The things that I've
seen… And a lot of them involve infidelity. Even while
wife goes out shopping for a couple of hours. So, no. I
don't think men like that are faithful. But you're not in
love with him. Not anymore. I mean, you have a little bit
of an infatuation with him, but if you were to sleep with
him, it would get it out of your system."

All of that sounded logical. Except she *was* in love
with him. But she couldn't bring herself to say that now.

"All that sounds very worldly and sophisticated, but
I'm afraid that I'm not that. Especially when it comes to
him. I just get tangled up. I think he meant too much to
me for too long, and it muddies everything. Because I
don't know that I could without… Without having feelings for him."

"You said yourself he doesn't have any feelings. So,
why can't that be the same for you?"

"You've done that, just had sex with people and not
have any feelings about it?"

Mariana shrugged. "I have feelings about it. If it was
especially good, I often wish that he would call. I'm not
*un*feeling. And it's difficult when you have a physical
connection with somebody, but they didn't feel the same,

or it wasn't strong enough for them to want to reach out to you. But you just get over it."

She frowned. "I don't know that I want it to be a thing I just get over. That's the problem. I had to just get over so many things. I don't think I've ever had a lasting connection in my life. Apollo is really the only one. And that's kind of sad."

"Well. Listen, I'm glad that he intervened. Because as much as I don't want to think Rocco was deliberately going to scam you…"

She groaned. "Yes, I know. The facts can't be ignored there."

"Anyway. You're going to be okay, right?" Mariana touched her arm, the gesture of concern touching. She wasn't alone.

Things had felt fraught for a while now. And as important as Apollo was to her, and had been, it was good to know she wasn't alone anymore.

"Yes." She took a breath, determined to weather this without being watery about it. "Hey, I'm still in charge of my money, and the company. So, the offer still stands. I would like for you to manage one of the hotels. Anywhere you want."

"Anywhere?"

"Yes. I've been looking at the way that things are run, and the company has stagnated in the last few years. I think there need to be some top to bottom changeups in leadership. And I feel comfortable saying that you could be exactly what it needs. So yeah. Anywhere you want."

Mariana looked shocked. "I'll look at the catalog and get back to you."

"Good. I just want… You've been a big part of making me see what I needed to do to take control of my own life. And I really appreciate it. I want to pay back."

Mariana smiled. "That is really lovely. But you know, the thing about friendship is that you don't have to."

"I know. I just want to."

And that was her last good feeling for the next several hours. Because after that she was forced to parade herself through the most awkward reception anyone could've ever had, where they ended up skipping cutting the cake, and leaving early.

When she was shut into the limousine that she had arranged for herself and Rocco, with an unsmiling Apollo sitting to her left, she let her head fall back against the seat. "Now what?"

She tried to ignore his closeness. The heat coming off his body. All of it mixing with what Mariana had said to her earlier.

Get it out of your system...

"We go back home. We must live together, and we will do so here. It is the easiest thing."

"We just... Go home? We just act like that didn't happen?"

"No. I'm not suggesting that at all. Of course it will be like it happened. You will now take your position at your father's company. Your day-to-day is going to change drastically. And I will be here to offer support."

"But we won't go on a honeymoon or..."

He looked at her, his dark eyes unreadable.

"I wouldn't think so," he said.

"How come you don't have to make it look legitimate to the board."

"Because I'm me," he said.

"That's not fair. They're just letting you do it because… Because what? Oh," she said. "Because secretly they would rather like it if you were in charge. And that's what they think is happening. They think that you are having a hostile takeover."

"Probably."

"That is horrendously insulting."

"It is. But it is not what I'm doing. You have total control of your father's company. I'm not trying to take anything from you."

"Well, what a boon for me," she said. "Misogyny and classicism are really powering this whole thing."

"Everybody does what they think will be the most advantageous for them," he said. "We all do it. Your friend Rocco was doing it. It seems to me that he had a hard life in Rome. It also seems to me that he might've been trying to make something new for himself."

"You were willing to threaten that."

"Yet again, *agape*. Everyone does what they must. I do not judge anyone for it. But neither will I let them simply get away with it. Not if my needs are different."

"That is a very cynical way of looking at the world."

"Has any part of your life given you a different perspective?"

She shook her head. "No."

"I'm not a cynic. But I have lived. I had lived more life by the time I was your age than you would possibly believe. I had no optimism left in me about people."

"What happened to you?"

Because she had seen it. A kind of hollow desolate sadness in his eyes that she couldn't quite pin down. But she had never asked about his life. She had thought earlier that he had never shared, that he didn't see her as a person. Did she see him as one? For all her feelings about him, had she ever asked him about his life? What his experiences were before she'd known him?

No. Because she'd been so young when she'd met him she'd imagined he existed the moment he'd first appeared in her life and not a minute before. And even as she'd grown older she hadn't challenged that.

"Don't worry yourself about what happened to me. It is the kind of thing you don't want to infect your own thoughts. You did not have to live through it, and therefore you should not have to live with those images in your mind."

"You make it sound terrible," she said softly.

"I survived it. So perhaps it is of no consequence. I survived it, so perhaps it does not matter much if it was terrible. It made me wise. It is why I work so hard to protect you. I trust no one, because I know that every single person on this planet has an end to their altruism. A point at which they must see to their own needs, their own success. I do not judge them for it, but that doesn't mean I'll allow it."

"That's what you're doing with me. You think that what you want, your own success when it comes to your concept of seeing me through to adulthood is more important than what I want."

"Yes," he said. "I do. Mostly because I think you want the exact same thing when you are able to understand."

"You really don't give me a lot of credit, do you?"

"Again, I have no reason to. You've been through some difficult things. But that doesn't mean you truly understand the ways of the world. As I said to you before. The world is not kind to women. Your father knew that. It is one of the things that he and I were both very aware of. The seedy underbelly of things. He had concerns for you.

And the reason he made me your guardian was that he thought I was… Realistic. That he thought I would be able to protect you in a very particular kind of way. Because of what I had seen. Because of what I knew."

"What did my father know about anything outside of his privileged existence?"

"Do you know anything about your mother's family? Surely you must realize that if things were functional in your family there would've been a network of relatives to take you in rather than your father's billionaire friend in his thirties."

"What are you saying?"

"The circumstances your parents came from are perhaps different than you were led to believe. And that is why your father prized my protection of you so much. Your mother and I endured similar things."

"And you're still not going to tell me what that is."

"No."

"Thank God you're not actually my husband."

"I am actually your husband," he said. "It was made legal only a few hours ago."

At that moment, the limousine pulled up to his house. Fury was like a living thing inside of her. He was doing nothing to shed light on anything in the situation, and she felt as if everything had been turned upside down, while he was intent on acting like it was all the same. It wasn't. How could it be? The man she had been in love with for so much of her life had married her today.

And all of her truths converging into one sharp point inside of her. The emotions so big it made her feel like the child she desperately didn't want him to see her as.

The realization her own father had put her in this situation was so painful she couldn't breathe around it. The horrible truth she'd let all this go on for too long because of her own impossible feelings.

Oh, no, she really was going to cry. The car pulled up and she fiddled with her seat belt, frustrated that it wasn't simply coming undone.

She was coming undone.

She hated this.

She hated him.

Maybe as much as she had ever loved him. Except one feeling hadn't shifted the other to the side like she had thought it would. No. It was all just painful.

Because for her this was the twisted perversion of a dream she had never even allowed herself to have, and for him, this was all just a victory. Proof that he was supreme. Proof that he was in control. Emotionally, it didn't touch him. The only thing that had ever come close was when she had challenged him sexually. That he had responded to. That had sent him to Scotland. That was when she had realized she had power.

So perhaps there was something to think about in Mariana's words. But she stood by what she had said. It might be too costly for her. And that was what scared her. Because right now she felt as if she had been skinned and rolled in salt. Right now, she felt like all of the most vulnerable things about her had been brought dangerously close to the surface, and a slight breeze would create a ripple large enough to reveal all.

So, she escaped the car, went inside, and went straight to her room. Where she wrenched her wedding dress off through sobs.

She was married. She was married to Apollo Agassi. And yet wanting that to mean something was as impossible as wishing her father had been there to walk her down the aisle. Because her father was dead. And Apollo's emotions were just as remote, hidden beyond the veil that she could never reach. And neither could he. It was why she had sought to free herself from all of this. But by God, how she had failed. Spectacularly.

And then she stopped suddenly. Her dress was a pool of liquid silk around her feet, and the only thing she still had left on was the white lace underwear she had put beneath the dress. They were so thin they were barely there. The fabric for the gown was so delicate that barely anything could sit under it without being visible. The underwear had been astronomically expensive. Delicate like a web. Her nipples were visible through the cups, and the shadow of curls between her thighs evident. She examined herself in the mirror. She was acting exactly like her father and Apollo would expect her to act. She was acting like a child. When Apollo took control from her she allowed him to do it. It was not her. She was better than that. Stronger than that. If she wanted to be treated as an adult then she had to seize everything she wanted. What would Apollo do, after all? What would her father have done?

They would have taken everything. Not a portion of what they wanted. She was so worried about her own emotions, rather than taking charge and committing to handling them herself. Apollo had taken control today when he had stepped into Rocco's place. But who would take the control now?

She slipped her high heels back on. And she examined herself in the full-length mirror. She didn't look like herself. She looked like a siren. Her legs were impossibly long with the help of the heels, the way they elevated her posture making her breasts look even more prominent.

She was soft. She preferred a lazy day of reading to an afternoon at the gym, but she enjoyed taking walks around the city. And she felt the balance gave her a more pleasing figure than she had previously given herself credit for. But then, she had never truly looked at her body while considering showing it to a man.

What would he see when he looked at her? She had seen need in his eyes when he'd looked at her before. Remembering it now made her heart race.

She might ruin everything. But wasn't everything already ruined? A smashed snow globe. A mockery of her past fantasies.

But her need for him wasn't mangled in all the wreckage. It was as bright and clear as it had ever been.

She wanted to be consumed by him.

He had married her today. Wrested control from her. Taken her own plans and burned them to the ground.

But she could have this.

She was past the point of considering. She was doing it. Her father had been a leader. And she was now going to lead that company. He had clearly doubted her ability to do so. But this was her moment, and she was going to own it.

She took a breath, and opened the door. He did not have staff in the house at this hour, which meant it was only the two of them in the manor now. She also knew exactly where she would find him. In his study. If he was so convinced that things were going to stay the same between them, then his routine would remain the same. It was just like him. To be just so. It was like him, to go right in for a little bit of evening work.

She paused, her heart pounding so hard she couldn't

hear anything but the insistent rhythm. This could destroy everything.

Oh, Hannah. It's already destroyed.

That sad, internal truth made her want to weep.

But she wouldn't weep.

She wasn't a child.

She was a woman.

She was going to show him.

She pushed the door open. He didn't turn. Of course, he was certain that she had come to yell at him. To castigate him. He wasn't even interested.

"Apollo," she said.

"I'm working, Hannah."

"I believe we have something to discuss."

He turned, and immediately, the fire left his eyes.

"There is the small matter of our wedding night."

CHAPTER SIX

SHE SLOWLY CROSSED the room, and rounded the other side of his desk, sitting on his lap. He made no move to stop her, didn't lift his hands to touch her, nor did he push her away. He was warm and hard beneath her. And she was trembling, but doing her best not to show it.

"I want my wedding night."

"Hannah," he said, his teeth gritted. "Stop."

"You act like I don't know what I'm asking for. But I do. I'm twenty-two years old. I know exactly what I want. You have denied me my groom. Will you also deny me a night of passion?"

"You don't get to ask that of me."

"Why not? It seems like it would be an appropriate thing for a married couple."

"We are not a married couple. Not in that way."

"But I want it," she said. "I want to please you. I want to please myself."

He reached up, unexpectedly, and gripped the back of her hair, his hold tight. He forced her head back, tilting her chin up. "And what is it you hope to gain from this? Are you playing with me?"

"No," she gasped. "I'm not playing with you. I want you."

"Is it a *thank you* that you wish to give? Paying me

back for my help? Do you thank all the men in your life that way?"

She tried to shake her head, but he held her fast.

"I don't," she said.

His eyes were like obsidian. Dark and without end.

"Stand up," he said, releasing his hold on her hair.

"But I…"

"Stand up. Take your clothes off. Show me what's mine."

She hadn't expected that. And she wondered if he was trying to call her bluff. If he was trying to prove that she would be too frightened to do what he asked.

This was not the guardian who had set boundaries for her these past years. This was not the man who had taken care of her, or even the one who had stormed the altar today as a method of protecting her.

This was a different side of Apollo. One she had not seen before. She had caught a glimpse of it that night at the club, but it was as if she'd been looking through a cracked window. She had the impression of it but no more.

This was *more*. It was everything.

And so was he.

So she stood, ignoring the thundering of her heartbeat, and unhooked that bra, before pushing her panties down her hips and letting them fall to the floor. She stepped out of them, remaining in her high heels.

"Turn."

She did, in a full circle, letting him see her body, her skin burning beneath his gaze.

"You have been pushing me these past months."

She nodded. "Yes. I have been."

"And you think you know what is out there? You think

you know that you can handle all of this. You know what waits for you. You know what men want. Come here."

She obeyed again.

He beckoned her with his finger, and she found herself sinking down to the floor, on her knees before him, between his spread thighs. A version of what she had fantasized about that night that he had carried her out of the club.

He bent his head down, gripping her hair and pulling her head back, tilting her face up toward him. Then he leaned down and pressed a hot, open-mouthed kiss to her throat.

She gasped. And he captured her lips with his, swallowing down the sound of surprise as he slid his tongue against hers.

She was shaking. Trembling.

His lips were magic, his tongue wicked as he licked deep into her mouth, claiming her. Changing her.

Forever she would think of this. This dark room. The smell of woodsmoke, and the flavor of whiskey, and Apollo.

This would be her wedding night, forever etched into her memories. Not gauze and romance or whatever else a girl might imagine she would get on her wedding night.

But this dark, hot thing that burned between them like a living ember.

He was angry. He did not kiss her out of a sense of passion, but as a punishment. And she was too weak to deny it.

He was giving her what she wanted, but only in part. He was holding himself back, forcing her to swallow his anger down if she wanted any of his desire.

And she did. So she took it. All of it.

When he pulled away from her she was shaking. She could see that he was aroused, and he moved his hands to his belt.

She pressed her knees together, her body liquid.

"Let's see how well you can attend to this task. And then I will tell you whether or not you have earned your wedding night."

"I don't understand."

He unbuttoned his pants, and slid the zipper down, freeing his arousal. It was beautiful. Long and thick and more glorious than she had imagined it could be. She was obsessed with him. His body. His scent. His strength. Even now when he was being cruel she desired him.

There was something about it that called to her. That took all the things that they were, all they had ever been and refashioned it so that it was finally all that she had desired. Because she had spent much of her life with him as her guardian. Giving orders and commands and setting out boundaries. And in the midst of all that she had idolized him. Desired him. Wanted to be the focus of his attention, of his desire. And now she was. All of the things he had ever been to her, all the things she had ever wanted, converging at this moment. Well no. That wasn't entirely true. There was no softness here. Not even a little. Not one bit.

"If you please me with your mouth, then I might give you what you want." He said it again, his voice authoritative. And it made her shiver.

"You like control, don't you?" she asked, looking up at him from her position on the floor.

"Control is everything, *agape*. Without it, what is a man? He is a slave to those around him. And I will never be that."

"Of course not," she said.

She wondered what was beneath those words. He had hinted at his past, but he had not gone into detail about it. So she still did not know exactly what haunted him.

But she could see that he was haunted now. There was something feral in his eyes. And she felt herself responding to it. She wanted to quiet it. To give him whatever he needed to banish those ghosts.

She had set out to do this to please herself, but she realized pleasing him would always be part of that. It was inescapable.

Tentatively, she leaned in, wrapping her fingers around his thick shaft, and then she flicked her tongue out, tasting him.

Desire was a living thing inside of her. She parted her lips and took him inside her mouth. She had never even kissed a man until tonight. This was in many ways going fast. Except, it didn't feel like it. Because even though it had been a formless, nameless thing within her, she had desired him all this time.

He was every fantasy she'd ever had, and the task of being asked to fulfill something for him was so intoxicating she was on fire with it. She looked up, and met his gaze as she swallowed him down. And the strain on his handsome features was everything she needed.

How much she wanted this man. Always. She was desperate for him. Obsessed with him. It was like she had opened the door on it now and everything was laid there before her.

Her need. Her desire. The truth of it all.

Everything. She would have everything.

She continued to lavish attention on him with her lips, her tongue, and he growled, grabbing her hair again.

"Slow down," he said.

"I can't," she said.

"You will. Use your tongue."

She obeyed, licking him from base to tip and back again before taking him in deep.

He made a rough, masculine sound and let his head fall back against the back of the chair.

She reveled in it. In the obvious evidence that he was undone by this. That it wasn't only her.

This was equal ground. Perhaps the first equal ground he had ever stood on, with her on her knees and him above her, his body exposed, his pleasure being guided by her own mouth.

She had never fully appreciated how it could be. The way sex could strip away the layers, could twist and upend the power differentials between them. He was powerful in this, of course he was. Strong and authoritative, the one with experience. But she had power as well. She was the one who had come in without her clothes on. She was the one who made him tremble even now as she lavished attention upon his glorious body.

She was the master of this moment, even as he, rough and strong, revealed his own weaknesses through the way he chose to dominate.

She could feel when she was getting too close when he physically pulled her back. She could sense when he needed to exert himself because she had scraped him too near the bone.

She did not feel young. She did not feel inexperienced. She was nothing more than stardust. Shimmering with need. Beyond age or time.

It didn't matter who had come before. In his case, probably more lovers than she wanted to know about.

And in her case none. But it was as if everything melted away. As if the world had gone to nothing outside of this warm, dim space.

The fire roared. His breath was harsh and jagged, her own heart beating loudly in her ears, her sounds of enjoyment resonating through her as she tasted him.

And then he moved her away from him.

"That is enough."

"You didn't come, she pointed out.

"I know," he said. "But you wanted sex, didn't you?"

"I thought I had to earn it."

"You have," he said, his tone rough, jagged. It cut into her. The realization that he did not surrender to this need between them easily. That even though he wanted her, he didn't want to want her.

It was written all over his face, the stark lines tracing the edges of agony, ecstasy, all at the same time.

But her heart beat with certainty. I want him. I want him. I want him. Every beat, every breath.

It all spoke to the same need.

"It's your turn to sit," he said.

He stood, and she dutifully took her place in the chair that he had just occupied.

He stood two feet away from her, his eyes hooded, unreadable in the firelight.

"Spread your legs," he commanded. And she found herself parting her thighs and ignoring the embarrassment that washed through her.

He began to unbutton his shirt, undo the cuffs. He consigned the shirt and jacket to the top of his desk, before moving slowly to remove his pants and shoes the rest of the way.

He stood naked before her, and she could barely

breathe. He was a glory, with the flames dancing over those hardened muscles. The hollows exaggerated by the absence of light. His shoulders were broad, and so was his chest, well defined with dark hair sprinkled across it. His stomach muscles were prominent, hard. There was no excess fat on his body at all. His hips were lean, and his masculinity hung heavy between his legs. Still hard. Aroused.

Because of her. His thighs were thick, and the strangest thing of all was how intimate it felt to see him without his shoes and socks. His bare feet were somehow an intimacy she had not counted on.

This was Apollo. The man she had known all these years, for she had known him long before he had ever become her guardian. Her father's close friend and confidant. The man who had taken care of her, even if imperfectly all these years.

The man who was giving her what she had demanded of him, even now. Even as it seemed to separate his skin from his bones.

Never was there a moment so suspended in time. One that reached deep within her and seemed to grab her heart, stopping it. It throbbed against the squeeze, making every breath a battle.

Apollo.

She had wanted him all these years. But she had not truly understood what that would mean.

But there he was now, naked and raw, and she could taste him on her tongue. It was no longer a theoretical fantasy. It was happening now.

She had never thought sex would be so uncomfortable. As it was glorious. But her need verged on pain, and she was certain if someone were to touch her skin they would find it feverish.

Her hair was damp where it rested at the back of her neck, and she was not sure whether she wanted to run away from him or run to him. So she sat, legs spread, as vulnerable to him as he had been to her just moments ago.

The look on his face was that of a predator. Sharp and intent.

He moved his hands down to his heavy shaft and curved his fingers around it, stroking himself lazily as he looked at her. She had to look away. Her face was hot, embarrassment rolling through her.

"Look at me," he commanded. She did so without another thought.

"If you're far too embarrassed to see the way that you affect me, then you are too embarrassed to take me."

"I'm not," she said.

Terror streaked through her. Would he deny her even now? As far as they had gone, would he stop this? Would he make her leave? Humiliate her?

Perhaps that's what this was about. Him exerting his control. Perhaps it had all been a lie from the beginning. This idea that they were equal because they were naked. No. She felt so vulnerable then. As if her obvious need for him was written all over her body, and the pleading expression in her eyes, and the obvious slick heat between her legs.

"You must be certain this is what you want. And this is not a payment," he bit out. "When I sink into you it will be because I want to. And it had better be because you wanted to."

Did he want it? Did he want her?

"You will owe me nothing in the aftermath, and I will owe nothing to you. This is not a transaction."

His words were fierce and feral, and she didn't know where they came from, but it was somewhere deep within him. Guttural and fearsome and real. They reached down deep and soothed a wounded place within her, but she felt like she was looking at his scars. At his own pain, and she wished she could make herself fully understand it. Wished she could understand him.

"I hear you," she said.

"Do you? You need to not look upon me with shame. Look at me." He moved his hand over his shaft more times. Swift, decisive.

"This is what you do to me. On that. This is what it does to me to see you naked like this, sitting in that chair with your legs spread wide. If that makes one of us a monster then it's me. But I am far too old and far too jaded to let that stop me. You have pushed me to this point. I know you must accept the consequences. This is your last chance."

"I want you," she said.

"But do you want everything that comes with that?"

"I don't know what that means."

"There is no way to know until this is finished. Are you willing to accept the potential consequences of that?"

"Yes," she said.

"Good. Good, one leg over the arm of the chair, then the other." She did so, the move leaving her even wider open to his examination.

He went back to his desk and opened the drawer, taking a box out. Condoms. It made her scalp prickle. Knowing he had condoms in his desk drawer. In his study. Did he have women here often? It was an uncomfortable realization.

You should tell him that you're a virgin.

She didn't want to. Because it felt like making herself even more vulnerable, and she didn't think that was fair. Already she was the one sitting here legs spread wide. Why did he deserve more? He wouldn't tell her about his past. He wouldn't tell her about the women that had come before her, who had perhaps sat in this very chair. Why should he hear about the lack of lovers in her life?

She did not need to be known by him if he would not allow himself to be known by her.

So she shoved down that desire to share. That desire to find some closeness with him, because that was simply an illusion. They would never have closeness.

He was not promising love. The consequences he spoke of were not a life together.

And she was okay with that. She was.

She had fantasized about him loving her when she'd been younger. When she hadn't understood that a man like him wasn't built for love, marriage, and a family. She knew better now. It hadn't killed her feelings for him, but she did know better.

One thing she knew now with clarity was she could never have handled this before.

This was far too raw. Much deeper, much more feral than she'd imagined it could be.

It was glorious.

And they were glorious.

But it would not end anywhere beautiful.

It would end in ashes. It would end in tears.

Those were the consequences that she was willing to accept. To have him. To feel him moving inside of her.

Instead of putting the condom on, he moved to her again, dropping to his knees in front of her. His face was scant inches from the most intimate part of her and she found herself squirming beneath his close examination. She wanted to run. She wanted to get away.

But she didn't. She held fast. Because he was right. If this embarrassed her, then what was the point of it? It only proved that she wasn't ready. She was not half so worldly as she imagined herself to be.

She would not have that.

He moved his hands beneath her body, cupping her rear, lifting her up from the seat as he laved her with the flat of his tongue. She gasped, her hands going to the back of his head.

And he began to taste her deeply, exploring her, finding every drop of her wetness and taking it for his own.

She gasped as he pushed a finger inside of her, and then another.

He didn't need to hold her up anymore, because she was arching up in the seat, unable to stay still as he licked and sucked her.

Until she was trembling. Until she was crying out. Begging for release.

He moved his fingers quickly, before sucking that sensitized bundle of nerves at the apex of her thighs deep, and she shattered.

"Apollo," she gasped, tugging at his hair as she cried out his name, cried out her release. She felt spent. Shaken.

She was trembling.

He moved up, sucking one nipple into his mouth, and palming her other breast, sliding his thumb over the distended tip there. And then he moved to her mouth, kissed her deeply, letting her taste the evidence of her own desire on his tongue.

He kissed her. And it didn't end. It went on and on,

sending new ripples through her as he traced shapes on her tongue with the tip of his.

And she found another climax rising up inside of her. Not quite as intense as the last, but present all the same, her internal muscles rippling as the unexpected orgasm overtook her. Just from his kiss.

From the carnality of what they had just done.

She was limp against the chair, and that was when he moved away from her, took the condom packet, and tore it open, rolling the latex over his thick shaft slowly.

She whispered something. A curse, maybe. Encouragement, perhaps. She couldn't be sure. She was lost in a haze. Her whole world reduced to this. To him. To the desire that burned between them.

"Please," she whispered as he pressed the head of his shaft to the entrance of her body.

She wanted him. So much. He gripped her hips and pulled her forward, impaling her on his glorious length. She gasped. In pleasure then in pain. There was a slight tearing sensation, yes, and it did hurt. But it was over quickly enough.

She rolled her hips against his, instincts driving her now. And if he had been about to pause, if he had been about to say something, he wasn't now.

He began to move, canting his hips forward, thrusting deep within her.

So deep that she could hardly tell where he ended and she began. This was sex. And she wanted it to be making love, at least a small part of her did. She thought of what Mariana had said. That sometimes, when it was very good, you simply couldn't help wishing it could be more, no matter what you thought when you went into it.

But you got over it. Mariana had gotten over it, and

Hannah would too. This was a rite of passage. She was living a fantasy. She had broken this powerful man, she had made him abandon his principles. For the chance to be with her. It inflamed her. Ignited a need inside of her. It made her feel strong and powerful and like more than she had ever been.

Today was her victory. What he had tried to take and make his own she had reclaimed.

And she would accept the consequences of that. She would not allow herself to cry. Not at the beauty of what was passing between them now, not at the intensity of it. Not at the deep unexpected nature of what it meant to have someone inside of her.

No. This was her victory. Her pleasure.

And she would have it all.

He gripped her hair again, and she tilted her head back willingly as he kissed her neck, down to her breasts, thrusting in time with each kiss.

Then he took her mouth, murmuring filthy promises against her lips that set her on fire.

Her skin was damp all over, the heat from the fire and their own created need all slick and intense.

Her heart was pounding so hard it was as if she had run a race, and she was not done.

He spoke in Greek. English. She had always loved to hear him talk. His accent wholly unique and *his*. Cultured because he had trained it to be, but retaining hints of Greece and Scotland. She liked it even more when he spoke these words over her. When he lavished praise upon her body.

When he gave her everything.

Everything.

No. Not everything.

Just sex.

But that thought did nothing to temper her desire, and finally, she broke. Her orgasm igniting her anew, taking her to new heights as her internal muscles squeezed him tight, drawing a response from him.

He growled, his thrusts becoming faster and faster, losing their rhythm as his own climax overtook him, the unraveling swift and certain, his cry of release a growl, that mingled with her own. She clung to him even as he began to ease away from her.

"There," he said. "You've had your wedding night."

"That... That's it?"

She was still lying on the chair, spent and limp, uncertain of what to do or say.

"It is what you said you wanted."

"Apollo..."

"Did I promise you more?"

Tears pricked her eyes. "No. You didn't. I'll... I'll go back to my room."

"Please," he said.

And she didn't bother to collect her underwear. Why would she? Her dignity was in tatters, and pausing to collect clothes would not restore it.

She held it together until she got back to her room. And then, she broke.

CHAPTER SEVEN

APOLLO STOOD AT his desk, his hands planted firmly on the high-gloss surface. He looked down at the floor. There was a pair of white panties and a white bra, evidence of what had just happened, and if it was not there, he might've thought it was a dream. If not for the spent condom in the wastebasket, if not for the fact that his heart rate refused to come down.

If not for the fact that he felt guilt. Deep, dark guilt that was unlike anything he had experienced for some time.

He had felt used before. It was part and parcel to the life he had led prior to becoming what he was now.

But he had always been very careful never to use a lover. It was possible he'd used her here.

Or that she had used him.

A wall had come down during this and he...he had no defense against it. He had never felt sex in quite this way before.

He had been cruel to her.

He had wanted to punish her for pushing him to the brink, but had that all been justification for being with her? She was beautiful. But why did that matter so much? There were many beautiful women, and they were not in his care.

How had he been so weak with the one woman he should never have touched?

He was reeling. Reeling from the intensity of it all. From the way it had torn down the walls within him.

And he could see them all. Every man, every woman that had paid to use his services, knowing that he was desperate. Knowing that he was poor. Using their power and privilege to gain access to him.

Their faces melted with his own in his mind. Hannah had said she wanted him, yes, but he was the one with experience. He was the one who knew about sex.

She had taken to everything they'd done with enthusiasm, enough that it was easy to convince himself that she had perhaps more experience than he had thought.

He was caught between two sets of beliefs in this moment.

That he had used her, or that she had used him.

That she'd had a few lovers, and that she had been a virgin.

He had felt resistance when he thrust into her. But she barely reacted to it. She certainly hadn't seemed to be in pain.

So perhaps he was wrong. It was entirely possible.

She had gone down on him like a champion, and that made him suspect she knew her way around a man's body.

But perhaps that was just convenient thinking. And maybe it didn't matter either way. Because it wasn't truly about her, what she had or hadn't done, but about whether or not he had taken advantage of the situation they found themselves in.

She came to you.

She had. But he had created the situation.

And she used you because she was supposed to marry someone else...

He poured himself a measure of whiskey and sat down in the chair where he had just taken her.

It could not happen again. She would start her new position at her father's business next week, and he would be on hand to make sure everything went well. Things did not have to change. They could go back to the way they were. It only made sense.

She did not need a lover. She needed guidance.

And there was no reason to think things had to change.

He was resolved. He owed her his service, and he would do everything he needed to do to arrange his schedule so that he could be there for her as she embarked on the next chapter of her life.

He would take the steps needed to continue to act as her guardian. Not her husband.

But she was his wife.

He stared at the white underwear.

She was his wife. And he had taken her on their wedding night.

His bride in white...

No. Just thinking those words opened up a strange cavern inside of him, and it was one that he wished to keep covered.

He had never entertained the idea of getting married. Had never thought that he might have children, or a family of any kind. There were certain legacies that seemed best burned to the ground. The earth salted.

He was happy for Cameron, but Cameron had always navigated the life they'd had differently.

For Cameron, the biggest trauma had been the accident. Of course, through it, Cameron had definitely become a kinder person.

Apollo was fine with his friend's arrogance, but there was definitely less of that now that he had fallen in love with Athena. He was more caring. That made him ache too.

But there was no reason to think along those lines. He was who he was. He had been created from a very specific set of circumstances and there was no use mourning what might've been.

If his mother had not been such a fool over men. She had found a way to stand on her own feet.

If she had not been so easily tricked.

If he had not been so hungry. If he could've found a way to exist modestly then perhaps he would not have thrown himself into the life that he had.

But there was no use regretting it. It changed nothing. There was a version of his life, perhaps, where he got an honest job at a shop and lived quietly in Scotland. When he married and had children. Where his childhood was a sad, regrettable footnote, and not a Hydra that had grown trauma on top of trauma and sprouted many heads.

He had not taken that path. He had taken this path. And because of that, he knew he could not have all things. Money, power, and normality. He had seared his own soul to the point he no longer easily recognized right from wrong. If he did, he would never have done this to Hannah.

All of it. From the wedding today to what had followed. To the aftermath of their passion.

He knew that she had consented. His concern was that she hadn't been entirely aware of what she was consenting to.

And that was not something he had reasoned through in his lust clouded mind.

How could he be half so basic after living the life he had? Hadn't he had enough damn sex?

Had she thought of someone else the whole time? Used his body as a surrogate for what she really wanted?

Dieu. What did that matter? He was the one who was supposed to care for her, and he didn't like these echoes of his own shame, of his past, rattling around inside him.

He poured another drink. Because tomorrow he was going to have to face this head-on. And tonight he didn't wish to think about it at all.

He needed his walls firmly back in place.

When Hannah woke she was sore. That place between her legs was tender, and her skin felt hypersensitive.

She grimaced as she sat up, the memories of the night before coming in hot and fast.

That hadn't been a dream. She knew it hadn't been, because there was no way she could have conjured up any of those images in her mind without actually having experienced them.

Her imagination just wasn't that good.

She lay back down and rolled over, burying her face in her pillow as she groaned.

She was… Humiliated. She had acted a perfect slut for his enjoyment. And then he had sent her away. Was it because he was embarrassed by how much she had wanted him? By how she had acted?

She rolled back onto her back and kicked her feet. Then she pulled her blankets over her face and took two breaths.

Okay. She pushed the blankets down. She was going

to deal with this. She was going to deal with herself. She wasn't a coward. She was about to be the CEO of a major company. She was married to one of the most powerful men in the world. They were married.

That was a whole thing. The whole thing she really wasn't sure how to handle.

"Deal with it. Get a grip. He's probably not even here." Still, when she dressed, it was in a turtleneck and a pair of slacks. It was not flattering, but it covered up a lot of her body. And she just couldn't handle how exposed she felt. It seemed like the best way forward.

She made her way downstairs and then stopped when she smelled coffee. And heard movement.

Was he really still here?

She took the last few steps at a trudge, and then she entered the kitchen. And there he was. Wearing a low-slung pair of pants, his chest bare.

It was a stark contrast to the way that she had sought to cover her own shame.

How nice for him.

"Good morning," he said.

He turned to the espresso machine and began the process of making her drink with what felt to her like an overdramatic dedication to deliberateness.

Not that an espresso wasn't appreciated at any time, but at the moment, she felt like maybe they had something to discuss. Recent experience had taught her Apollo would not instigate. She would have to push.

"Is it?"

"You know, I have never fully understood—and this could be because English is my second language— whether *good morning* was a statement about the fact the morning was a good one, or if it was a wish that the other person have a *good morning*."

"I couldn't say. Nor do I think it's entirely relevant to our present situation."

"Which is?" he asked.

"Well. There's the fact that we got married."

"Yes. And that has changed things. I assume you will be headed to the corporate offices today," he said.

"Not today. They're in New York."

He lifted a brow. "Oh, I'm well aware of where they are."

She scoffed. "I don't have a plane ticket."

"You do have free use of the private jet," he said, waving his hand. "Your father's. Or mine, if you so choose."

"Why?"

"The stipulations of the will—"

She narrowed her eyes. "I am aware of the stipulations of the will, but why are you offering up the use of your plane?"

"Because you have work to do. Do you not?"

"I think we should probably make the team aware—"

"They're aware," he said. "After all, the board had to approve the marriage." He took a sip of his coffee. He seemed so unbothered she wanted to shake him.

"You've already talked to them, haven't you?"

"Obviously. I have told everyone that they are to expect a visit from you this week. I will accompany you, of course."

No. She needed distance from him. She didn't want it, but she needed it, and him going with her to New York was just...no.

"Why? You've never had anything to do with the day-to-day running of the business."

"I haven't, you're correct. But neither have you. And I want to make sure that everything runs smoothly."

"You don't have previous commitments of your own network to deal with?"

"Cameron owes me roughly a decade of service. If I wanted to show up at nothing for the next ten years he would simply have to take it on the chin."

She waited for him to move on to the next thing. To at least acknowledge that last night things had changed between them.

"So… That's all you have to say?"

"Was there another conversation you wanted to have?"

"Yes. There is," she said, staring at him hard.

"About the sex, I assume."

"Yes, Apollo," she said snappishly. "About the sex."

Why not be blunt? Why not say it all? She'd had the man on his knees in front of her with his face buried between her thighs. Where was the benefit in being missish now?

"It won't happen again."

"Did I say that I didn't want it to?"

"I didn't ask you. You got that out of your system and now it's time for us to move forward."

She was angry, mostly because that was exactly how she had thought about it initially, but how dare he say that to her? It was painful, and it felt mean. It felt entirely unfair.

"I don't… I don't understand how you can just say that."

"Hell, I'm your guardian. What happened was wrong."

"You're my *husband*. You're the one that took Rocco's place at the altar. You're the one who changed things between us. You can't sit back now and claim that you're only my guardian. Not when we took the vows. I'm not going to let you do that. Put me back in my place because it's what makes you feel comfortable. You made your choice, Apollo. Your choice was to do this."

"Are you honestly suggesting we live as a real married couple?"

For some reason, those words made her want to retreat. "No," she said. "No."

"I didn't think so. So you will see how things must remain the same between us."

He paused for a moment. "I do want to be very clear that was on a transaction."

"It didn't feel like one," she said.

"Good."

"But you know, you're the one who said some really hurtful things about it all. So why you should care now, and why you should be so concerned with what I think about it is beyond me."

He paused and a strange expression crossed his face. "I suppose that is still about me."

"I guess at least you have some self-awareness."

He lifted a shoulder. "Some."

"You told me attraction was easy. Cheap."

"I did. Because I didn't want you thinking anything about my attraction to you."

He was staring at her, his gaze meeting hers unapologetically, and yet there was shame there. She knew that. It was the strangest thing. Apollo was usually so unapologetic in every way, and yet this seemed to be skirting not only an apology, but an admittance that he'd been wrong in some way. "Is it true then? What you said to me about being attracted to any woman?"

"No. It's not. It's complicated. Desire is common, es-

pecially for men. But cheap… No. Men will pay dearly
for sex. And it is an interesting thing, I find, that something as easy for men to come by as desire is treated with
such reverence. It is given priority over other appetites.
Because men will start wars, destroy their careers, destroy their families, go into debt, and all for what? Sexual
desire. So the truth is, I do not think anyone—a man or
woman should rearrange their life because a man desires
them, because desire is easily created. But at the same
time, men will burn down worlds for the sake of it. It is
very easy for a man to justify hideously wrong acts if they
satisfy his immediate sexual need. What I said was a lie."

She tried to process that. It was an interesting insight,
and true, she supposed. She might not be well versed
in the nature of men, but she did know that men were
prone to risking themselves personally and profession-
ally to have their desires fulfilled. But she didn't know
what that said about him. If that meant he had compromised himself deeply for the sake of sleeping with her,
and if that still made it of little consequence. Because in
the moment his need to be inside of her had been bigger
than his caring about propriety.

She didn't know if she was flattered or insulted by it.
But then, he hadn't connected it to what had happened
between the two of them. Only what he had said to her
at the club.

"Is that true of you? Are you in the habit of burning
your world down to have sex?"

"No," he said.

"Honesty. Let's have that. Maybe for you things need
to go back to how they were. But I don't think they can.
You were my mentor, you were my guardian, and now
you're my… Well, the things we've done, I can't go back.

And so I need you to tell me, the truth. I need you to give me honesty, even if you could never give me that again, I think that you owe me that here and now. I think you owe me a little bit of truth with our coffee, don't you?"

"All right. You can have that. No. I'm not in the habit of burning my life down for sex. I'm too jaded for that. I have watched too many people burn the world down over it. I'm no longer able to lie to myself that if I do that I will find satisfaction on the other side. Because that's how that works. Men lie to themselves. This will be the last time. The best time. At least, they lie to themselves while they bother to continue on with the fiction that they are actually good people held at the mercy of something bigger than themselves. There is a point for many of them where they simply accept that they're debauched and that their own needs are more important than the needs of those around them. But for many, the lies continue. The justification. One last time. And then... And then next time they'll resist."

"What did you tell yourself when you had sex with me?"

"Nothing," he bit out. "I told myself nothing. I wanted you, and I failed in the task of resisting you. I was weak. I can't pretend otherwise."

"Am I supposed to be flattered by that?"

"No. As I said. Never be flattered by the desires of men. But you must know, I am never overcome by desire. It was rare. But it won't happen again."

"Why..."

"Because it won't. How do you see your life, Hannah? What do you want for your future?"

"I want to take my father's company and I want to run it well. I want to grow it. I want to prove that I deserved to be there all along. That I am in charge of my own life, that I know my own mind. That I am not a stupid, silly woman. That's what I want. All of that and more."

"And what do you want in your personal life?"

"What everybody does. I suppose. I want a family. I want to fall in love and have children and…"

"Not everybody wants that."

"No. I mean… I know that. And I don't intend to do it for a very long time. I need to get used to running the company before I go changing things again. But… Surely everybody wants to be loved."

"No," he said. "They don't. And that is what I need you to be especially aware of. I don't want that. I don't want it because I no longer believe myself capable of returning the feelings. I don't want it, and I don't ever want to be the source of someone else's thwarted passion. You don't know about my past."

"No," she said. "I don't. Because you won't tell me."

"It's obvious enough that my last name is Italian."

"Yes. But you're from Greece."

"Correct. My father was an Italian man I never met. He broke my mother's heart. And she never recovered. She looked for love everywhere. She was flattered by the desires of any man. She wanted to feel beautiful, she wanted to feel cherished, and men will say whatever they need to in order to take pleasure with an object of their desire, won't they?"

"Your mother was taken advantage of."

"More than you realize. She fell in love with a man who lived in Scotland, and when he agreed to bring her and me to Edinburgh, she agreed without hesitation. It never occurred to her that it might be a trap. It never occurred to her that the man might not love her because she wanted to believe it so damned badly. He pushed her into prostitution. Manipulated her."

Shock hit her directly in the midsection.

"That's awful," she said, and she could see the way that it haunted him still. She meant it. She felt… Immensely sorry for the young woman who must've had him, believing the best of the world at one time only to have her soft heart used against her.

"Is that why you're so psychotic about me?"

"In part, yes."

"And it's why you need me to know that what happened between us wasn't a transaction."

His shoulders got visibly tight, moving up toward his ears. "In a fashion."

"Why did you do it? I don't understand. You want me, but… Didn't it matter that it was me at all?"

He looked like he was at a loss, and she couldn't remember ever seeing Apollo at a loss before.

"Rarely have I slept with a woman that I know. I think perhaps I was somewhat affected by that."

"You mean you usually sleep with strangers and sleeping with someone you have a relationship with is a novelty?"

"I don't know," he said.

"Well, I'd like to understand."

"Why? To what end? There's no point going over any of this, *agape*. Perhaps it's because you are my wife. And that changed things for me."

"Well, I'd like to know how."

"I can't give you that answer. Because I don't know the answer. I don't… It was different. That's all I can say."

There was more. There was more to him, there was more to this, and he wouldn't tell her. He was hiding behind that icy facade, that insistence that he remain her guardian, that nothing had changed. Even though she had spoken plainly and said that for her it could never go back. Apollo didn't really listen to other people. He played by his own rules. She knew that. Of course she did.

He was determined to frustrate her, she could see that. Exhaust her so she didn't push him here. And yet… She wasn't sure what she wanted. For him to tell her that she was special? He didn't know her. Not really. They didn't know each other. What he had just told her about his mother was completely new to her. They had been part of each other's lives, but in a very distant fashion. He had been a fantasy object for her, but nothing more. It was easy for her to tell herself that she had loved him, but what part of him? His looks, his aura of power, sure. Those were the kinds of things that anyone could see from across a crowded room.

But the substance of Apollo was hidden from her entirely, and she had to wonder if it was hidden from almost everybody. He'd been through horrible trauma, she knew that. But that didn't make this hurt less.

That while he felt significant to her, special to her, there was no real evidence that he was. She knew him as well as anyone in the world who had read a profile about him. Except she slept with him.

He'd been inside of her. And to her that mattered, and to him it didn't seem to. Beyond the lapse of control, that was.

It exhausted her. Caring for a man who might as well be a wall. And now after hearing about his mother she hurt for him too and she was tired. So tired of caring so damned much when he didn't seem to care in return. At least not in the way she wanted him to.

Maybe that isn't fair. Maybe for him this is caring.

Well, maybe the way her father and mother had cared was love, but it still left her feeling like a lonely little husk.

Was it too much to wish that she might be cared for the way she wanted to be? Even once?

"So you really want to just pack up and head to New York?" she asked, because she didn't know what else to say. Because she wanted to push the conversation further and she could sense that she was at a dead end with him. Maybe she did know him. For all the good it did.

"Yes. I will have your things prepared."

"You're not even going to let me pack my own clothes?"

"You're welcome to. If you like. You may want to begin asking yourself what the best use of your time is. There is quite a lot of work to be done."

"I know that," she said, snapping.

"Well. You may wish to start behaving like a CEO. Delegate the task that you're not needed for."

"How is it that I've somehow retained a babysitter."

"Many people would be pleased to have me consult them. They would pay hundreds if not thousands for the privilege."

"Well. They've never met you."

"So certain. And so sharp and pointy."

"Yes," she said, waving a hand. "That's me. Sharp and pointy and utterly ridiculous. Absolutely no merit to the issues that I have with this extraordinarily weird situation."

"If you'd like, you can go in and speak to your manager about the fact you will not be working at your job anymore."

"Oh, can I? Thank you."

"Sarcasm doesn't suit you. You're far too intelligent for that."

"Well thank you for the most useless compliment of all time."

She finished her coffee, and she did go to work, quitting unceremoniously.

"I'd like to manage the property here," Mariana said. "If you don't mind. Because what I would like is to bring the whole team with me."

"Well, that's going to make Rudolfo angry," she said.

"Yeah, but he's a bad manager. So I feel like he's getting no less than he deserves."

"It's true," Hannah agreed.

"When can I start?"

"When I come back from New York. I laid the groundwork for you this week. Because I'm going to make sure that it's known we're going to engage in sweeping reform of the properties."

She wanted to park the big emotions, the complicated things, and focus on business. For a moment. It was an issue, but not one that left her feeling bruised.

The annoying thing was, part of what she wanted was to make sure that she could integrate the technology from Apollo's company into the properties. Which was likely something that he had long been waiting for. It was the best thing for the business, one of the things that would set them apart, and she knew that she would get the best deal out there. Their connection would make it advantageous for both of them.

It was annoying because he was going to get something out of this, and it would be cutting her nose off to spite her face to put a stop to it. She couldn't do that.

She was enmeshed with Apollo whether she liked it or

not. And the problem right now was she wasn't entirely sure how she felt about it. What he had done getting the New York office prepared for her arrival was actually good. She wasn't entirely sure she would've thought of it on her own. What would marrying Rocco have looked like? She would've been given the money and the control, and how would she have handled it? She felt pretty confident and bold, because she had been thinking a lot about what she was going to do to improve the company. She knew that he had been irritated she hadn't taken a job at her father's company, but a lot of it had come down to wanting to familiarize herself with the competition before that wasn't possible anymore. Before her connection to the company made it so no one would hire her.

She was studied up on the history of the business, and what had happened in the years since her father's death. She had ideas, and they didn't come from nowhere. Her business in hospitality classes had given her a good jumping off point. But there was a lot she didn't know about managing teams and big corporations, and Apollo certainly did know how to do it.

The way that he had so easily finessed the board spoke to that.

Though, she thought it was funny. She didn't think she had needed him as a guardian for the last six years. Not really. He was actually the most valuable one now. Because she was fine when it came to dealing with her own personal life. Her studies, her own job, her own ambitions. But yes, she could admit that she was young. And that the responsibility she was taking on was a big one. And maybe a little bit that she had even rushed herself into it because of her anger. That was really annoying.

Having to see that some of his concerns were valid, and that his help was appreciated.

She wouldn't be telling him that, of course.

But she was aware of it.

When she returned from her conversation at the hotel, her bags were packed and sitting by the front door.

There was also a car waiting.

"We'll head to the airport now. We will land in New York midmorning their time. It will be a day we spend getting you oriented to the time zone, and then the following day you'll go into the office."

"I didn't realize that you had signed up to be my secretary," she said.

"If it's what you need," he said. "I am happy to oblige."

"I had no idea you were so accommodating. I feel like I wasted a few years of my life leaving that gem undiscovered."

He lifted a brow. "Is that your takeaway from this experience? That I am accommodating?"

She let the silence lapse between them as she realized he wasn't even going to humor her for a moment. She was tired. Of him. Of this. Of him not reacting when she was a mess.

She'd tried to focus on work. She'd tried to be sensitive to his revelation of trauma. But he wasn't trying with *her*.

So now she was back to wanting a reaction. Any reaction.

"Yes," she said, blandly. "That is one hundred percent my takeaway. You're a secret softie. I could tell when you held me and whispered words of affirmation after you took my virginity in your study."

And on that note she swept into the car and closed the door behind her.

CHAPTER EIGHT

HANNAH WAS SATISFIED at her view of his shocked expression on the other side of the glass. She wondered what part of that sentence he found shocking. If he hadn't realized she was a virgin she would consider that a boon of sorts. At least for her own sense of mystery and her skill set. She'd wrecked it now, of course.

But it was worth it for the shock value.

He got into the car, in the back seat with her and made a slow show of rolling up the divider between them and the driver.

"You were a virgin?"

"Who would I have slept with?"

"You've been going out most nights, it was completely reasonable to assume you might have taken a lover."

"Oh, dear. You were wrong," she said, knowing she sounded cheerful enough to make him grind his teeth.

"Why?"

"Were you wrong? I suspect because you're a mortal like the rest of us and just not always correct."

"No. Why were you a virgin?"

So did she go for honesty or continue being flippant? It was a tough call. But she remembered his moment of honesty with her in the kitchen this morning and she felt some of her rage drain away.

"Do you really not get it?"

"Do I not get what?"

"You can just say no, Apollo. You can say you don't get it. You don't have to engage in questions on questions to avoid admitting you're out of your emotional depth."

"You're a child. I'm not out of my emotional depth with you."

"That's so insulting. Also I know you don't believe it." She took a breath. "So, let's try again. Have you not figured it out yet?"

"No," he bit out.

"I'm a cliché. You're my guardian and I had a massive crush on you for years, which I'm sure a psychologist would argue has to do with childhood trauma and displaced daddy issues, who's to say? Either way do you really think I offered to give you a blow job in the streets of Athens because I just had the bright idea to do it as payment?"

He was staring at her, his eyes dark and fathomless. He did think that. It had never occurred to him that an offer of sexual contact might come from somewhere emotional. That was…a lot.

"Did you think I asked for a wedding night because I was hot and horny for Rocco and thought you'd be a good replacement?"

Two slashes of color darkened his high cheekbones. His rage was visible, even as his expression remained stoic.

"You did, didn't you? You thought I was using you as a stud?"

"I didn't say that," he said.

"But you think it, on some level. It never occurred to

you that I'd wanted you before? That this wasn't a whim for me, or something random?"

"No."

He looked out the window and she saw a muscle in his jaw jump.

"Did it bother you?" she asked.

He turned to her, his expression fierce. "No. I told you what bothered me was the idea I might have taken advantage of you."

"Is it? Or were you afraid I was using you?" It was, perhaps, a crazy accusation to throw out. But she was feeling wild and a little reckless, and tearing off strategic strips of her pride seemed to be an interesting study in gaining some control.

You had to give some to get some, and all of that.

"You seem intent on pushing immaterial issues."

"That isn't a no." She cleared her throat. "So if you were wondering, I wanted you. I always did. I couldn't make myself want other men, and believe me I tried. It's one reason I wanted to get away from you. But that all got turned on its head so I decided to take what I wanted."

"And that was me?" he asked.

She looked at him, his expression utterly inscrutable. "Yes. I thought you must want me too, at least physically. And you know, I did think of what you said. About how cheap male desire is. But knowing what you told me this morning, it's making me rethink it. I thought I could make you want me and it would cost you nothing. It did, though, didn't it?"

He made a low, male sound. "I don't know what you want to hear, *agape*."

"I'm not sure either. Maybe that you were affected by it like I was? Maybe that it was special. Maybe that you care about me, and you aren't just unmoved by it like it seemed you were last night when you sent me away."

"If sex were cheap, worlds wouldn't burn over it. If it were nothing, a sexual assault would be the same as a slap across the face. It is not. If sex was meaningless, indiscretion wouldn't raze marriages, families, lives, churches, to rubble. Sex is dangerous. And it can be heavy, light, transformative. So I've heard." He stared straight ahead. He didn't look at her. "I was not unmoved."

His admission was heavy and she didn't know what to do with it, where to place it neatly inside of her heart. There was nothing neat about this. It didn't make her feel better, either. Not really. Because she couldn't guess what the landscape of his soul looked like, and she felt like she was trying to traverse terrain she couldn't see. Buried beneath the darkened waters of trauma he didn't want to share.

And fair, she supposed, because before this past week he'd been an authority figure to her—whatever she thought about that, and it wasn't very flattering—and now whatever he said things had changed.

Sex had rearranged them.

Everything they had been. Everything they were now.

Apollo was still a sheer rock face, and yet, she'd seen more vulnerability since last night than she'd ever glimpsed before.

"Did I hurt you, Apollo?"

He turned sharply. "As if you would possess the power to do so? And with such a medium."

"Well, I'm sorry if I did," she said. "I imagine nobody wants to feel used. Even jaded billionaires."

"You may rest, Hannah. I did not feel used."

She didn't believe him.

"That's good," she said. "Least of all, I hope you don't now. I hope you understand that I… It was my fantasy."

"Because you…"

"I like you. I mean, I… I liked you. Had a crush on you." She was underselling those feelings, but how could she tell him she'd thought herself in love with him? That even now it felt like a twisted version of something much, much deeper than a crush.

She hadn't known him, not really. He didn't know her, not beyond his need for her to be some token of redemption. How could you love someone you didn't know? Someone who didn't see you as an equal?

Even still, the feelings were…powerful. If they weren't, she wouldn't have had sex with him. She wouldn't have felt so wounded by the marriage. She wouldn't have told him she was a virgin, or that she cared for him at all.

He laughed. The sound filling up the car. "A crush. I don't know that I have ever been subjected to anything quite so anodyne as a young girl's crush."

That hurt. Even though she'd deliberately downplayed it, it felt so…scathing and mean.

"Well, that's probably because you say things like that. Young girls are prone to having their feelings hurt when grown men laugh at them."

He did not look abashed, and she felt that was pretty poor manners on his part considering she had just apologized to him and his own feelings.

"Excuse me, I was concerned about you."

"I did not ask you to be."

"Apollo…"

"You were the virgin, Hannah. Not me. And while I appreciate what you said, I do, and yes, sex is something. It changes things. It changes people. I agree to that. I believe that. I... I'm not wounded. I'm certainly not going to take juvenile feelings to heart."

"I would think that you might recognize that what passed between us was not juvenile."

"No," he agreed. "What passed between us was not. But surely you must understand that any emotional attachments you have for me are... Pointless."

That actually made her want to jump out of the car and swim into the sea. Because how could that be? Okay. Maybe she had never been so foolish as to fantasize that they would get married or have a family or anything like that. But the idea that feelings for him, all the way, were completely pointless after so many years of caring for him just felt... Sad. And it wasn't her she felt sad for. It was him. It was his inability to recognize that he had someone in his life who actually cared for him. Sure, they were spiky with each other sometimes, but he had always been there. He had been a constant. A safe space.

She supposed the real foolishness was imagining that any of those feelings went the other direction. Because why would they? It was easy to imagine that they could, but he really did just see her as a responsibility. A prize to win. A job well done. She had seen him as vastly more.

"Do you care about anyone?"

"Your interrogation will have to wait." At that moment they had pulled up to the private jet.

They were ushered out of the limousine and the stairs were lowered for their embarkation. They climbed the steps and instantly she was awash in comfort. For all that the vehicle was luxurious—because everything Apollo had was luxurious—the jet superseded it. It might as well have been a modern living area. With midcentury furnishings and stonework, that she assumed had to be fake, because surely there was a weight limit on something that had to be airborne.

There was a slim, highly polished wooden bar and gold light fixtures. The walls of the plane were navy and gold geometric design work.

It was lovely. But it would not distract her from the issue at hand.

"Okay. We boarded the plane. So let's continue."

"Cameron and I have been friends since we were boys. Your father trusted me enough to put you in my care."

"You said to me more than once that I was the only good thing you've ever done. So on some level you must have conflicting feelings about your relationships with Cameron and my father."

"Cameron and I helped each other survive. We have a trauma bond more than we have anything else. He is my brother. He is… He is a part of me in many ways. His pain is mine. I don't know that he will ever fully realize that. When he had his accident and concealed himself even from me, it was like losing a part of myself. And yet I felt his agony. I would not call it a friendship. It is something deeper than that."

"Your soulmate, perhaps?"

He chuckled. "If I were built differently, perhaps. He might've been. But it would never have been easy."

"My father?"

"We had business ties. He was a good man, your father, but I was using him for connections, and he was using me for mine. In the end, we did connect in many ways, but it was our isolation that perhaps brought us together the most. He knew that if something happened to him he did not have a long list of people he could ask to care for you. He didn't speak to his family, your mother didn't speak to hers. It was… Perhaps the same sort of thing as I have with Cameron. Lost lonely people who are isolated from everyone else in the world. Could find a measure of comfort in each other as a result. Trust. Because there is no one else. Because there is nothing else."

"And you wouldn't call any of those things friendship. Or even family."

"I don't have the understanding of that that you might. My own mother didn't have the strength to love me or protect me as she should. My own father never met me. I never made friends out of a desire to have companionship, but out of a desire to survive. So perhaps that is the problem. In the absence of comfort, you define things differently. It is not about how you feel, but about how you might live. And so I never knew a relationship that didn't bear a resemblance to a transaction."

She felt burdened by her own experience of love—or a lack of it. But what Apollo was telling her painted an extremely bleak picture of his own experiences. That made her feel…a little guilty. For wanting so much from him. If she was damaged by her experiences, how did she expect him to be any better?

She'd felt ignored. He'd been fighting for his survival. Had felt like every relationship was bought and paid for.

"I find that very sad," she said, her throat constricting.

"Then shed a tear for me, *agape*. But it will change nothing."

At that moment, the plane was consumed by motion and so was she. As it hurtled down the runway and propelled itself into the sky. Her stomach dropped, but maybe it was all related to him. Maybe Apollo was the inertia. It was possible. Maybe it was all her. Maybe everything in her had been so upended by these things between them that she had yet to recover. Her words were reckless, dancing on the edge of something she didn't want to admit to herself, let alone him. It was all fine and good to talk about crushes and girlish longings, and to ignore the fact that he had wrecked her last night in his study. And maybe even more importantly ignore the fact that she had clearly done something to him. It was why he was so set on keeping things the same after all.

Perhaps she did know him. Maybe not all the details of his life, but the substance of who he was.

But she was weighing the cost and benefit of hammering away at Apollo when he wasn't in the mood to admit the truth. Or worse, maybe he would. That was the thing. Of all the things he'd said, which she felt circled truth enough, she did not think that he had actually told her the most real truth of all. Whatever it was.

"Why does it matter to you if you're good or not?"

She asked that, because everything felt circular. She asked that, because she didn't know what else to say. She asked that because she still wanted to dig, but she was tired of talking about sex, her virginity, and getting into her own vulnerabilities.

"Doesn't everyone worry about their soul at least a little bit?"

"I'm surprised you're the kind of man who believes in the concept of the soul, if I'm honest. You seem like the type that might want to believe we are nothing but finite beings who live for today and then die. Take nothing with us, so we might as well embrace hedonism while we can."

He shook his head. "I don't believe that."

"Why?"

"Because I felt pieces of my soul die. I cannot explain it. I only know it to be true. Something has to exist to die. And yet I have pieces of it left. I'm certain of that too. But never more certain than when I look at you."

He was sincere. In that moment, there was none of the cynicism, none of the hardness that was often present in him when they spoke.

"And I'm your redemption?"

She'd found the implication of that upsetting before. But it had new weight now, after what he'd just said. But it still wasn't fair. Not to either of them.

He paused. For a breath. A beat. "In a fashion."

"That is deeply messed up," she said. "Since I'm the person. And I feel like it should matter, what I want."

"I never said it didn't *matter*."

"But your idea of what is right or wrong supersedes what I tell you."

"Not last night."

"Was it about what I told you, or was it about you? I actually can't bear to continue to hammer at this if you're just going to insult me again. But I need to know... Did you want me? Or did you just want sex?"

"I wanted you. And it is the precise reason it will not happen again."

"That is also the precise reason we cannot go back. You're not my guardian anymore. And maybe you can't be my husband. But can we at least stand on equal footing?"

"That would be ridiculous. Seeing as I am a man with much more experience of the world than you and—"

"Fine. I can give you that respect. But you should also respect me enough to treat me as you would anyone who worked with you. Can we find a place between Lord, redemption arc, and wife?"

"All right," he said. "I can try that."

"Am I supposed to be flattered that you're willing to try?"

"It certainly more than I've ever done for anyone else."

She didn't think that was true. She wondered why he was so committed to the narrative that he had never done anything for anyone. That all his relationships were one-sided and mercenary.

She had always seen him as impenetrable. And she wasn't sure how she'd imagined he'd gotten that way. That it was part of who he was. But she knew why she had become the Hannah that she was now. Doing her best to please because she had wanted so much to matter to people who she had difficulty getting attention from.

To the angry rebellious Hannah of the last six months who had been suddenly tearing into the narratives about her life. But she had never stopped and really wondered what had made him this impassable, immovable object.

But he had hinted at enough things in their past few conversations that she had to wonder. He had told her about his mother, about having to run away.

At one time he had been a sad, lonely little boy. There would've been nothing hard or mercenary in anything he had done. And yet, somehow, he had rewritten these things to make himself feel...better? Worse? She wasn't sure. She had never particularly wanted to dig into Apollo as a man. She had seen him as a fantasy object, as an obstacle, but never as a whole man. She wondered how many people ever did. He was rich and he was stunningly handsome. He was more than capable in all these ways, and with certainty, he never seemed like he needed any help.

But she wondered now. She truly did.

"Why don't you take some rest, little one," he said.

"Don't condescend to me, Apollo," she grumped, but she was feeling tired.

"Is it condescending to worry about your well-being? Tomorrow I will take you around the city."

"I'm from the city."

"How many years has it been since you've been back?" He asked as if he didn't know the answer.

"You know I haven't been since my parents died."

"I do. So it will be good to be home, won't it?"

She thought about it, very critically. She thought about Manhattan, and she thought about the estate that her family had had in Vermont. She wondered if either of those places would feel like home now, or if they would simply feel painful. Like a time she could never step back into. There had been a time when she thought of them simply. As happier days. And then she had gone and torn into all of it. Taking it apart piece by piece and she wasn't sure it could ever be put back together.

"You can use the bedroom," he said.

For some reason, she didn't want to. She wanted to stay with him. Defiantly, she lay across the couch that she had been sitting on. "Apollo," she said sleepily. "How old were you the first time you went to New York?"

"Twenty-one, I think," he said. Except she could see that he didn't think, he knew. With precision.

"That young? I didn't think that you and Cameron really found your success until a few years after that."

"We didn't. But we had… A business of sorts. I went with a client."

"I see." But she didn't.

And she was starting to get so tired it felt like a fathomless sea threatening to pull her under. She couldn't see the bottom of his trauma. It was all darkness. She didn't know if she had the strength to swim into those depths just now. It had been such a long couple of days and the subtle movement of the plane over pockets of air was beginning to rock her to sleep.

CHAPTER NINE

WHEN THE PLANE touched down in New York, Apollo roused Hannah. She had slept for the entirety of the flight but he had not slept at all. She was such a strange creature. Digging and persisting into all these darkened corners, as if she was going to find something that would explain away... Him. As if she was going to find something that would give her answers about why he was the way he was. She wouldn't find them. He knew that. It was so simple, he would've untangled all the aftereffects of his youth a long time ago.

He felt raw. After the conversation they'd had and he didn't like that. He wasn't used to it. She might not guess at what he was talking about, but it forced him to relive it. It reminded him of the boy he'd been a long time ago.

Someone he didn't like to reflect on.

A young man who'd still been able to feel guilt and dirt and shame and disgust over what he had done.

And vulnerability. When he and Cameron had first gotten into the business of selling their bodies, many of the others around them who were doing the same took comfort in illicit substances.

"What's the point of wasting the money we just made?" Cameron had asked.

Apollo understood why people did it, because he had

wanted the memories to go away. He had traded himself for drugs just one time. But had felt sick with the feeling of failure after, and had only created a new memory he needed to hide from.

And that, he had realized, could be a dark road. One a bit too much like the one his mother walked. He and Cameron had made promises to each other. After that. They would maintain their control, they would run their own business, and they would keep their wits about them. It was important. So very important.

And gradually, he had learned how to manage his own vulnerability. Without the use of substances. It was just that he had never quite learned how to turn that off.

And if Hannah thought it would be so simple…

"Did I hurt you?"

He shoved that to the side. He had been worried about hurting *her*. That was all. Using her. Because he had been in the space of lost control when he had taken her, and that was singular.

In a way that he didn't wish to speak to her about.

"I like you."

Her words echoed inside of him, along with his own dismissive response to them.

It had been a hideously unkind thing to say on his part. But he didn't know what the hell else she wanted to hear. Something kind, he imagined. The kind words from him would do nothing for her in the end. Because it was nothing that he could maintain. It was nothing that he could spin into something of use to her.

No, he would continue on helping her. That was all he had to offer.

His business acumen. It was easy for him to imagine a world where the ties between himself and Hannah were finally cut. Where she went off on her own, and the only association they yet had was one made of business. But it made him feel adrift. And he hated that most of all. So he didn't spend any time on it. Instead, when the plane touched down he watched her ride sleepily. She was so stubborn. Curling up on that couch instead of going to the bed. He would've carried her to bed, but he feared he would've made a disastrous choice after that. And he had no intention of taking things to that place. Not again.

She'd done something to him. Something painful, something wonderful. He didn't want to experience either sensation so unfiltered ever again.

Even as he craved it.

His issues were his own. Getting that close to revealing them on the plane had brought them up to the surface and he wanted to protect himself.

But he could also see…

He had hurt Hannah. Her father had hurt her. He might want to keep his distance, but that didn't mean he wanted her hurt.

All he had to do was redouble his defenses and he could get back onto better footing with her. Not the same footing they'd been on before.

If she wanted…if she wanted him to treat her like a person he could do that. She was offended by him seeing her as redemption, though for him that meant something. Even if she couldn't see it.

But he wanted her to see it.

Surely he could do that without revealing more of himself?

Hannah was still rubbing her eyes when they disembarked from the plane and got into the limousine that was waiting for them.

"Maybe being jet set isn't for me," she said.

"Some good strong coffee will fix you up nicely." He smiled. "Unfortunately, it will be difficult to find here."

"It's New York," she pointed out. "You can find whatever you want here."

"Spoken with such confidence," he said. "But I find most coffee in America lacking."

But he took her straight to his favorite place in the city, a small hole-in-the-wall that served an eclectic mix of European delicacies. They had baklava and very strong espresso sitting at a tiny table right next to the window, against the busy street. Hannah's eyes were wide and searching as she looked all around.

"What?" he asked.

"I've never been anywhere like this."

"You cannot mean that. You grew up part-time in the city."

"My dad wasn't one for tiny cafés. Especially not…"

"Is this a bit downmarket for you," he said, feeling amused."

"No," she said. "Not at all. It's just different."

"I see. And you and your friends in Greece never went places like this? Not to banish her hangovers."

"No. Mariana is a very good concierge, and she got us into very fancy places. Plus, I'm actually not big on drinking. I did a little bit of it when we went out, but I've never had a hangover."

"Never?"

"No," she said. He felt both envious of her right then, and a bit regretful. Like he had somehow been part of holding her back from interesting parts of life. But also… He wondered what it would've been like to be so protected. To have had choices about these things. Real choices. He had made decisions, difficult ones, it wasn't as if he had no agency in his life. But his choices had been all bad at different points in his life.

Hannah had been able to retain a certain amount of innocence in a world that was unkind to the naive. Part of him wanted to congratulate himself for that, but another part of him knew he could take no credit for it. Not really. Her parents had established that boundary of safety. Something she didn't seem to understand.

He watched as she took a bite of her baklava, a stray bead of honey left on her lips.

He wanted to touch them, to kiss them away. But that wasn't who they were. And it wasn't what would happen going forward.

"Your father did love you, you know," he said.

Softness wasn't a native language to him. But he wanted to try and give her something. All of her actions these past months had demanded what he didn't know how to give. He could at least give her this.

"I know," she said. "I know he did. That's why the things that he did that I don't understand, the things that hurt me, hurt as badly as they do. If he had been awful, if I doubted that he and my mom cared for me, then... I wouldn't be so regretful about not having time with them. I wouldn't feel left behind. I wouldn't... It is that I loved them and they loved me that makes it hard."

"They died before they could finish with you. And I don't have children, obviously. I don't suppose you ever really finish with them. In the fullness of time, they might have made it up to you. The things they did back then. Because they were good people who would've listened to you if you would've said that you wanted things to be different. Your father set that trust up for you with the care and concern of a man looking at a child. Not a woman. He didn't know who you would become, and he never got to see it. Have some forgiveness for him. Think of how much you've changed. He might also have."

She shifted in her seat. "I never thought of it that way."

"I tried to help my mother," he said. He didn't know why he was telling her this, except he wanted her to know. The difference. The difference between parents who loved their children, and those who saw them primarily as a burden. And who could never, ever re-examine their actions because it was far too confronting for them.

"I'm a billionaire. I could change her life if she would let me. But for her to allow me to do that would mean admitting that things in her life are not all that they might be. And she cannot do that. She can't and she won't. I tracked her down in Edinburgh and she refused me. She said that I was just coming back to lord my status over her. She acted like I thought I was better than her, because I had always thought that I was better than her but... We were the same. And she knew it. Your father loved you. My mother grew to despise me. I was an emblem of everything that had ever gone wrong in her life, and she made sure that I knew it. She was too filled with spite and hatred to even allow me to help her."

"I'm sorry," she said. "I really am. You didn't deserve that. No child does. Every child deserves... They deserve to be loved. To be cared for. And I realized that my parents did care for me. But I was lonely. Perhaps if they'd lived until I was older, I would have known how to tell them that. Not that I did a great job of telling you."

I'm sorry for the part that I played in your loneliness," he said.

"It was probably for the best that I got sent to boarding school. I was *less* lonely than I was living at home, even though at the time I resented the change. So in that way, I think you helped. Apollo… How did you get out? What… What happened?"

"That is not a conversation for baklava and espresso and very small cafés."

It was perhaps not a conversation they ever needed to have. But he could feel his resolve to keep it from her wearing thin.

Everything he'd done with her in the past had either produced quiet capitulation or later, rebellion. And she was right about one thing, all of that had been about her occupying a symbolic place in her life. Talking to her, spending time with her, he was beginning to see something deeper.

Lonely.

They were both lonely.

She had hooked into something within him that he hadn't even known was there.

It was strange. And entirely unwelcome. He was used to having control, and she… She stripped it from him. It would be easier if it was only in the realm of sex. But here in this little café, she made him question his own resolve, and that was something he didn't have an excuse or reason for.

"Let's keep you moving," he said. "You want to stay awake until bedtime."

One thing he was certain about, it would be best if they stayed busy. Best if they were able to stay out in public. Because for all the promises he'd made himself about not wanting to touch her again, he could feel himself weakening there.

He did not wish to be weak.

"Will I?" She asked as they swept out onto the street.

"Yes," he said. "And tomorrow when you have to go into the office you will thank me."

They decided that they would see each other's favorite places. And that meant Hannah taking him to The Met, Central Park, and the Magnolia Bakery. While he showed her a gritty art gallery that he had grown attached to as a pretentious new enthusiast of art in his mid-twenties.

She spoke with broad hand gestures about each art piece they stopped at, and her enthusiasm was something more than infectious. Perhaps the thing that hit him hardest was…his own enthusiasm for the art seemed to affect her.

They passed by St. Patrick's Cathedral, and he hesitated.

"Do you want to go in?" she asked.

He felt frozen to the spot. And seen in a way he wasn't used to being seen. He was supposed to be sharing his favorite places in the city but he hadn't counted on this. He hadn't even thought of it, really.

"Come on," she said, linking arms with him and propelling him toward the large wooden doors.

As an architectural marvel, it was stunning. All ornately carved gray stone in the midst of the steel and glass of the city. Archaic to some, he supposed, and yet to him, it had created a stillness within. He had been compelled by it, from the first. He could remember being a young man and wondering if he could still go into a church after everything he'd done. Then he'd remembered his mother always had her rosary, even after everything, and he'd decided that he would go.

He touched the holy water when they walked in and

made the sign of the cross, a reflex. Hannah didn't, but walked in with him. "I've never been here," she whispered. "My dad had no use for churches, and my mom even less."

There were people kneeling, praying, lighting candles. He reached into his pocket and took out a folded American hundred-dollar bill that was there and pressed it down into the slot of an offering box. He'd come in and lit candles in here before he could ever afford to make the suggested offering. He felt compelled to give now, for himself and for anyone else who might need the candle and have nothing to give for it.

"What's that for?" she whispered.

"Payment," he whispered back.

God knew that was too honest. But they were in a church. A lie felt like a sin. A funny thing, that he should concern himself with adding another sin to his vast list.

But here, he always wanted something different.

Just as he did when he was with her, he supposed.

He walked deeper into the building, feeling small beneath the arched ceiling, the massive pillars, and soaring stained glass windows. It had been a comfort then, feeling so insignificant and new. He wasn't sure what it was now.

She held his arm as they walked through, past the kneeling faithful, and back out onto the street, so loud and busy it was like the silence of the cathedral had never been real.

"That's one of your favorite places?" she asked.

He felt…exposed in a way the art gallery had not made him feel. "Yes. The first time I was in the city I felt compelled to stop in. My mother would take me in every cathedral we passed to light a candle when I was young and… I felt like I ought to. I remember I walked in and there was an old woman, kneeling and praying, her dress shabby, her shoulders stooped. A man in a sharp, custom-made suit knelt down beside her. I was struck by the image, that both were welcome. I thought perhaps then I still was too."

"Why wouldn't you be?"

His chest felt twisted up. "By then my life had become complicated. I was not the man I'd hoped to be. But there was something…healing. About knowing I could go there, light a candle. Be in the silence. It's like all the hymns that were ever sung are still in the stone. You can feel it." Perhaps she'd think him insane. "Or at least I can."

"I feel it too."

He worked to lighten things after that. He took her to a Mediterranean restaurant with a glorious dining patio, where you had to queue up out front and pay only with cash. Followed by a walk through The Village.

"I used to wonder what I would have to do to be able to live a life here. There was something so quiet about it. I think it was the first time I really understood that in the middle of a city like this silence costs a premium. A well-preserved home on an old street means you've made it."

He could still remember wandering here when he'd had his free time. Imagining another life. He was living that life now, he supposed, but it didn't feel quite like he'd imagined.

"Did you ever buy a place here?"

He shook his head. "No. By the time I could afford it I wasn't so romantic. This isn't near my office. Therefore it isn't practical. And anyway, I chose to make my primary home in Greece. Perhaps because it felt like taking something of myself back. I never asked to move to

Scotland. I didn't ask to lose my life, my language. That is the problem with being a child, whether your parents are good or not. They make decisions on your behalf. On that, I think we can connect. They choose what they think you need. Or perhaps what they think they need, and you get no say."

It was getting late and the streetlights had come on. They were charming and old-fashioned, though to him, they didn't seem so old. He was from one of the very cradles of modern civilization. With history stretching back so far it was nearly impossible to track.

And still, something about this place would always call to him.

He had never shared these truths about himself with another person. Her favorites were very much New York to the eyes of a child, while his... They were a mix of his missing home, missing his soul, his desperate desire to be part of a class he wasn't. His hunger to escape the scarcity that had dogged him for so many years.

His need to be forgiven.

He wondered if she could see that. Did he want her to? What was the point of it, except that when faced with the idea of not having her in his life at all, he found himself feeling adrift. She was an anchor he had not realized bore so much weight in his world. Though he had to wonder how much of that was just his dislike of change. Of losing people. There were spare few people in his life. And he had attached a great deal of importance to Hannah.

She was his new church, in that sense. The thing he looked at which made him ache. To be whole. To have a soul.

Dieu, he'd told himself he would keep himself separate today. Forever.

But just as the cathedral had enticed him to his knees, to a position of what some would call weakness, Hannah made him vulnerable.

Being finished with her, setting her free, that would be the fulfillment of all the good he'd ever done. And so in truth, it would be a good thing to let her go. In a year's time, when the marriage could be dissolved, he would feel glad about it. And not wistful in any way.

Wistfulness was the province of other men.

As was vulnerability.

They had walked a near impossible amount, and when they arrived back at his Upper Eastside penthouse, they were disheveled in a way he rarely allowed himself to be.

"Well," she said, sinking onto a chair by the expansive windows in the apartment. "I feel like we've done enough."

"Do you think you've defeated jet lag?"

"I do," she said.

When he looked at her sitting in the chair, he could only see that night.

When he had dropped to his knees before her and tasted the sweetness between her thighs.

When he had sunk inside of her beautiful, tight heat.

He had told himself that he wouldn't think of her this way. He had told himself that he wouldn't think of that at all.

And yet, he was.

"I like you."

"Did I hurt you?"

He gritted his teeth.

"What?" she asked.

"I didn't say anything," he said.

"I know you didn't," she said. "But you're looking at me with questions in your eyes."

"I don't have any questions," he bit out.

"Then were you just thinking about the other night?" she asked.

He could see that in his mind far too easily. Could see her, naked and glorious and the redemption he wanted most.

"It was last night," he said.

"Was it? I slept on the plane. And we did change a time zone so I think... Never mind."

"Yes," he said. "Never mind. Because it is nothing."

"It isn't nothing. You said so yourself. It changed us. If it hadn't, today would never have occurred."

That was an unerring truth, hitting him square in his soul.

"You say that with such confidence," he said, his throat going tight.

"Well. I know it's true," she said.

"I don't know how to love anyone, Hannah."

Oh, he wanted...so much. But he was ever a sinner wandering through a cathedral. A man who wanted to glimpse a holiness he could never find or feel.

He said it because he had to be honest with her. He said it because he didn't want her to spin fantasies out of this desire between them. And yet he was desperate. To touch her. To hold her. To have her. It was so far beyond his own experience that he had no idea what he was supposed to do with it. When it came to sex, he had done it all. But it was mercenary. Void of any kind of connection or emotion. With her he had tasted something new, and it had opened up the space inside of him that had been untouched all this time. It had led to today. She was correct about that. He had shown her those pieces of himself that he had never really even trotted out and examined for his own benefit.

But he had done it for her. He had done it because of her.

He wanted to taste it again. This electric, deep connection that he had never allowed himself to have with anyone else.

He could remember the first time he had taken a lover because he had chosen it. Because he wasn't going to pay, and even that had been something twisted. It had not been about connecting with another person. It hadn't truly even been about pleasure.

For him, the act had been so tortured and deformed throughout his life and she... There was something about her. About the genuine strength of their connection that made it feel like it was his first time. And he hadn't wanted to admit that.

He had gone to great lengths not to admit it.

But exhausted from the day, from the years, from holding all of this for so long, he didn't possess the strength to deny it. To deny her. To deny himself.

"I didn't say that I needed you to love me," she pointed out.

"No," he said. "You didn't. But I will not lie to you. I don't..." He wanted to find words. But he didn't have them. He didn't know how to articulate this thing. This desire to connect with her while protecting himself. While making sure she knew that it couldn't become... He had no family.

He had no vocabulary for connection. He spoke so many languages, and couldn't figure out what he wanted to say in any of them. But his chest felt like it was raw and bleeding. His control stretched thin. Because he had been trying to deny himself since he had left her that night, and it was only getting harder and harder to do.

Sex had never been something he'd had to resist. It wasn't about control.

But this wasn't a transaction, and it wasn't about proving himself. It wasn't about the freedom to take sex for free, rather than charge for it.

She was so beautiful it was painful. And yet, she was Hannah, which was painful in and of itself.

He had no words.

All his resolve, all the lies he'd told himself to this moment didn't hold. He had no defenses at all. And he'd walked himself right into this place. Where there was nothing but her. Nothing but wanting to be in her arms again.

To find that place of refuge he had been denied all of his life.

To find that pleasure he'd never known.

That connection he'd thought lost to him forever.

He'd laid a snare for himself to be caught in, and he had stepped into it willingly and even now knowing that, he was nothing more than a raw, bleeding mass of feelings. Of desperation. A mastermind of his own destruction.

"Help me," he said.

They were torn from him, from a place inside of him that he hadn't known existed. They were horrifying, and yet they were honest.

"I want to help you. With whatever you need." She put her hands on his face. She looked at him, their eyes meeting. Intense and long. A deep, shared moment that transcended anything he had ever experienced before.

He looked at her. And he could only hope that she could read what he was trying to make her see. She kissed him. He growled, wrapping his arms around her waist and pulling her up against his body. This was what he wanted. This was what he needed. She had made him feel that night, and he was desperate to do it again, no matter how much he told himself that it was all going to go back to the way it had been before. No matter how much he had told himself that it had to.

He needed her. He needed her like air. He was reminded yet again of the time that he had tried illicit substances to try and change the way that he felt.

She was that.

A drug. A heady hit of something that he had long denied himself. But he had never felt as good as he did that night in her arms. And it really had so little to do with physical pleasure. With orgasms. It was more. It was her.

Because he knew that sex, stripped of its soul, stripped of its intent, could make you feel more alone than anything.

But not her. Not this. Touching her was like holding fire in his arms. And it warmed him, all the way through. She was the most beautiful woman he'd ever seen. And he wasn't certain how he had been blind to that all this time. Something had changed. Well. She had. She had become a woman, and he had been intent on ignoring it. For as long as he could. Perhaps because on some level he had known that it would be dangerous to him. To his redemption arc.

But she wanted this. And he felt… He felt very like he might find salvation in this. Perhaps that was one of those foolish things that men told themselves in order to justify their need for release. He didn't think so. Because this felt more profound. Because it felt deeper. Because it felt more significant. More important. Or maybe he was just the same. As every client that had ever shelled out money for his time.

But she cared for him. She had said so.

He wanted to touch that. He wanted to taste it.

For just a moment, to know what it was.

To be touched because she liked him. To be kissed because she felt something. He didn't know how to feel those things. But the temptation to claim all that for himself was deep. Real.

He had made for himself a world where he didn't need anyone. Not their help, not their money, not their touch. He had made himself a fortress, because before he had to make himself the product. And he had earned that right. That solitude. That ability to stand alone. And yet he felt at seeing now. And perhaps it was inviting the past into the present. Perhaps it had been a mistake to show her all those things. To tell her how the hymns echoed inside his soul.

The way his memories of the two strangers who prayed together lingered.

Maybe it was his own fault for showing her that street he'd once dreamed he might live on. Because it brought her too close to the man he'd been, and that meant it brought him too close to that man.

So he kissed her. Because kissing had always been a game. Because touch had never meant much of anything, but now it did. It did. And what then? What then when he was so consumed by need and desperation, and the kiss did not allow him to retreat?

That's what he was looking for. Oblivion. This perfect, detached oblivion that he often found during sex and could not find it with her. She was the moment. And she brought him right to it. She was everything. Heat and light and innocence. Glory.

And what was he but a man with dirty hands smoothing them over all of this? He did not deserve it.

Did you think I was using you?

That tender question. He pushed it away. Because it got closer to the heart of what had left him seared after their sexual encounter. The sense that he might've been used again. And the shame that he hadn't been able to put a wall up. That it had been real.

Because did he tell himself that every time?

That it wasn't real. It wasn't real because he didn't care about them. It wasn't real because he didn't want them. Because think distant thoughts or even take a pill designed to create physical arousal and perform and so what was happening didn't mean anything. If he could go to a place in his mind where his body was off acting of its own accord, then it wasn't real.

And perhaps, part of him had fought against making any of it real.

For so long that it was no longer an achievement. The achievement would be a connection.

And yet with her... It had been there. Even if it was still behind a layer of glass, because he had been...

Conscious of the fact that she had perhaps wanted Rocco and not him.

But not now. Not now. Her touch was tender, delicate, and yet it was close to pain. It burned his skin like fire and yet he wouldn't have her abandon him. Because he wanted it. He wanted her. "Touch me," he demanded, rough. He began to tear his own clothes off, impatient. For her hands against his skin. For all of it. Everything.

She did, her breath coming in short, sharp pants, her movements jerky and uncertain, and he planted her hand against his bare chest and looked directly into her eyes. He knew that she had no idea what was happening. Between them. Inside of him.

He had a hard time understanding it and it was happening within him.

But she wouldn't know. Of course. She knew nothing about him. Not anything real.

He would have to tell her. But not now. Because he wanted this. All of this first.

If that made him a selfish bastard then that's what he was.

But he wanted this moment. She had seen him. In the church, she had come this close to seeing him as anyone ever had. Anyone besides Cameron.

She wanted him. Him. And it wasn't about a cold, dead transaction that came down to lust. It was something deeper. And just for now, he wanted it. She had lost her virginity to him. And he wanted this for himself. This one time knowing she wanted him. Cared for him. He wanted to be there. All the way.

She wasn't dressed as a seductress this time. Not wearing her white lace. She was dressed in a sweet sundress, one he had seen her in all day, and when she stripped it off she revealed simple pink cotton underwear beneath. She unhooked her bra and flung it off to the side, revealing pale pert breasts to his gaze. She was lovely. More than that. Beautiful. The kind that reached down deep and struck a chord in a hidden place inside of him. The kind that left nowhere for him to hide. And perhaps even more notably made it so he didn't need to.

Then she was naked before him. He could feel the way

that made her vulnerable. She looked soft. Lovely and untouched. In spite of the fact that he had touched her everywhere that first night they were together.

It was a mirror of his own soul. And he realized now why he'd tried so steadfastly to hide it. All that he was. All that he had ever been.

Because the stark truth of the two of them standing there, naked, regarding each other was almost too much to bear. And yet he must. He looked her in the eye, and moved toward her, taking her hand, as he had done on their wedding day. He squeezed her, and then moved to her, putting his hand on her cheek and lowering his head so that he could kiss her. She was glorious. Everything.

And when she kissed him it was that sweet promise of all the gentle things that he had never had in his life.

A taste of what normal might've been.

The anticipation of summer. The night before Christmas. Getting a new puppy. Knowing that when you went to bed that night someone would be there with you, holding you. All these things, these little things that he had never had. His mother had gambled with his childhood, but he had bartered all that he might have in adulthood for...

For all of this.

For this penthouse and this view. For the chance to own a house on a street he'd never even bought a house on the end. Because later he hadn't remembered. Later it hadn't mattered. But the street was still there. And so was St. Patrick's. And there was something strange in that that he couldn't quite put his finger on.

As if all the chances weren't spent. As if he could still go back.

But all of his thoughts were eradicated when the kiss

between them became deeper. Harder. And he did not retreat to a deep place inside of him, rather he was lost in the moment. The heat and fire between them. The slick ride of her tongue against his.

She might not be experienced, but she was enthusiastic. And she more than made up for any inexperience with that.

He put his arms around her and crushed the infinitely lovely creature to him. Hannah. Who was all passion and fire and familiarity.

He picked her up, and carried her determinedly into his room. He wanted her on a bed. He wanted to do this properly. He wanted to do this like he hadn't before.

He brought her into his bedroom and laid her down across the bed, her gloriously lovely body on display for him. He growled as he regarded her. She was simply stunning. Unlike anything he had ever seen. Art living and breathing before him. And he told her so. In all of his languages, to try and make up for his inability to speak earlier. To try and make up for everything. Because he was a miserable guardian. He was the worst man for the job, it turned out. Because the biggest monster out there that he should've protected her from was him. And here he was glorying in her. Taking from her to satisfy this beast inside of him. This needy, desperate part of himself that could no more turn back now than quit breathing.

But he kissed her. Her lips, her neck, down her breasts, and then between her legs. He pleasured her until she cried out. Until her fingernails dug into his shoulders. Until their passion created a new space inside of him. Not to hide in, but to glory in.

This was raw and real. There was nothing between them. Their skin was hot and slick with sweat, their hearts beating hard. She was Hannah, who he had known for half her life. And he was Apollo, who she knew as a friend of his father's. She knew in this strange, broken form he had fashioned for himself.

They had lived separate lives. Served separate purposes. And it was almost a miracle that they came together like this. Primal and urgent and filled with need. Miraculous, even. The way he was desperate to taste her, touch her. The way her cries of pleasure fed something inside of him. The way her own needs surpassed his own.

He hadn't realized. Because he had not truly understood all that sex could be. The purpose of it. The point of it. No. He had never truly understood. Until now. Because it mattered that it was Hannah. And it mattered that he was Apollo. Because it was more important than the final climax. Because sex was more than bodies. Because it involved your soul. And he had kept his own back for so long that he understood isolation more than connection. But here he let it all be free.

When he slid inside of her tight wet heat and she called out his name, it was a healing prayer. And they blended together. Into one. One flesh. One heart. He let his mind go blank. He let himself feel. All of it. Everything. A white-hot blaze of glory that left him burned from the inside out.

Because this was altering. This had changed him. He would never be the same after this. After her.

He welcomed it.

Because she liked him. Because she wanted him.

And because he had been alone for a very long time.

She arched beneath him, her breasts pressed against his chest, her hands moving over his back. He brought her to climax, touching her, tasting her, moving within her, whispering dirty promises against her mouth. And then she brought him over with her.

For one blessed moment, all was still within him. He was with her. Their bodies were pressed together, their hearts beating in time. But there was no thought. There was nothing before, and nothing after. There was only them. And he was not alone.

He knew then that he needed to tell her.

CHAPTER TEN

"I WILL GET you an extra blanket if you want," he said softly, the aftermath of their lovemaking still evident. They were breathing hard, his own heart beating erratically within his chest.

"No," she said, moving against him, pressing her breasts to his back. "I'm fine."

"Good."

"Are you okay?" she asked.

He laughed. "I suppose I am the one who should ask you that. Given that you were the one who only just had sex for the second time."

"I'm not the one who looked like they were drowning inside of themselves only a few moments ago."

"Is that what it looks like?"

"Yes. It is," she said softly, and yet it was ruinous. Because it was only the truth, and he couldn't deny it.

He still felt raw. From the way that they had just... From the heat of it all. The connection of it all. It was far beyond his own experience. And there was no physical act that he could not claim expertise in. But this had been unique. Because it had not been about skill. But about something much deeper.

"You know," he said. "I think to understand much of what happened today, and much of what you've seen from me, and even the reasons that your father chose me to be your guardian, there is something you need to know. I have been in business with Cameron since I was about fifteen."

"You have?" There was a question in her voice, but he could feel the weight of it. She wasn't naive. Not really. And he knew that she had already worked out he'd undergone a fair amount of trauma. Hell, he told her some of it. But he knew she hadn't quite figured this out, even if she was skirting the edges of it.

"Yes. We... That is to say, there was a certain point where we realized we could make a fair amount of money selling ourselves."

"Are you saying what I think you are? That you... That people used you for sex?"

She didn't sound shocked. Or perhaps that was a gift. She was gentle, it didn't sound angry. She sounded... Sad, perhaps, but resigned. Maybe that was what happened when your parents died when you were sixteen, and you saw the harder truth in the world. Maybe you could expand to accommodate many such truths.

"Yes," he said. "We both... We both came from difficult circumstances. I was dodging predators already for half my life. I felt like it was only a matter of time before it was all taken from me by force anyway. I decided... I decided to get ahead of it. We were petty thieves before that. I looked young for a long time. Cameron was tall. It was often my job to charm. To make people pity me. While Cameron would rob them. But... As I said. I was quite pretty. And I did look young. And I hate to tell you this, but that is an asset."

"God," she said, the word torn from her. "That's... It's awful."

"It is. But if I had the choice between being a victim and making money off what I had available to me then I was going to make money. We protected each other. Made a network. Eventually, we graduated from seedier sorts of dalliances to wealthy clientele. Hard-earned connection after hard-earned connection. I was with a wealthy client the first time I came to New York. A woman. Her name was Sandra Fielding. She liked a little bit of company along with sex. She wanted me to be a bit more cultured."

"And she... Treated you like a pet, didn't she? Something to make her loneliness more bearable?"

"Yes," he said. "And if I have one strength it's that I am very good at taking a step back from a situation I don't want to be in and making myself distant. So when things became too difficult for me, I would simply go somewhere else. But I stopped knowing how not to do that, Hannah. Whenever I have sex it's like I'm standing at a great distance from my partner. Until you. And everything in me craves the connection, and yet it's deeply uncomfortable for me."

"I wish I would've known. I... I would've been more... I would've taken it slower."

He had to laugh. At the role reversal. At the way she was treating him like he was the virgin.

"Do you find me different now? Do I disgust you?"

"No," she said. "Why would you? You did what you had to do to survive."

"That's a lie. Many people survive without selling their bodies. I wanted to do more than survive. I wanted to escape. All of it. But you know, I've been living under the delusion that I'm better than my mother. When I'm not. I didn't fall in love with any of my clients, but that hardly makes me better. I fell for the lure of easy money. And once you step into that bear trap you cannot get out of it. With connections, and some investments from Sandra we eventually started the tech company. She was our first major backer. So even in that, it's all sex for money. Sex to get where I am now. So when I tell you that I know sex is not just a handshake, it comes from the fact that I treated it like one for a number of years. At great cost. Do you know how afraid I was to step through the door of that church. Because I hadn't been in one since I…"

"Your mother still went into them."

"Yes," he said. "She did. I decided that I could too. For that very reason. I think I just wanted to feel like maybe I wasn't so broken."

"Did you… It doesn't matter but…"

"You want to know about my clients?"

"A little. But it feels wrong to ask."

"There are more men willing to pay than women," he said, his tone stark. "And I… I am in no way attracted to men. But I do like money. So yes. I did a great many things I did not especially wish to do. And you cannot walk away from situations like that without feeling violated."

"Have you ever talked to someone about this?"

He couldn't help himself. He barked out a laugh. "Like a therapist?"

"Yes. Like a therapist. This is complicated. It's like… It's like untangling years of sexual assault."

"It's not," he said, the denial coming harder than he intended it to. Because he had admitted, even in himself, that there were certainly aspects of it that felt that way sometimes. But for some reason right then he felt the urge to deny it. "I put myself in those situations. I agreed to do those things. Nobody forced me."

"It's a bit more complicated than that, I think."

"Maybe," he said. "But I could never afford to allow it to be complicated. I made my choice, and I kept it in the past. Back then I thought it was worse whatever the consequences might be. And so now I am left with the consequences. But also money."

"Apollo," she said, her voice so filled with compassion that he wanted to reject it. And yet he needed it. "I don't know what to say. It's just… I am so sorry that you were alone. And that you had to… That you felt it was your only choice. Because whatever you say now, I do believe that then you must've felt it was the best and only thing you could do."

He could remember feeling that way. Feeling like he was spinning his wheels. And the amount of money he had gotten offered by some guy in an alley had changed things for him. He had finally seen a way forward.

"I think there are other people who can handle such things better. Cameron is one of them. I'm not saying he isn't his own mess. He is and always has been, but he was never quite so wounded by what we did. I was. It went against my nature, and… I violated myself, Hannah. And it is something I have to live with. I traded myself, my soul, for this life."

She put her hand on him and he resisted the urge to remove it.

"You didn't trade yourself for anything. You're still here."

"Not the way that I used to be. This is a version of me. But nothing more."

She nodded slowly. "I think we're always changed by the things we go through. But that doesn't make us some-one different." She moved closer to him. "I know that you're the one that is supposed to take care of me. And I know you're so much older than me, and honestly, you have lived through so much more. But... You're more than that. You are not going to be that forever. You have to forgive yourself."

"It isn't that easy." It didn't shock him that she couldn't understand. It wasn't a matter of forgiveness, but acceptance. He had proven himself to be the same as his mother, really. And that was the thing that he had to live with. The stark reality of his own weakness. Of the truth that he was no better than the woman he had spent quite a long time despising.

His parents were people he could never truly respect. And he had no evidence that he wasn't ultimately cut from the exact same cloth.

Maybe that was what bothered him most of all. "You haven't explained, though. How it connects to my parents."

Discomfort lodged in his chest. He had talked to her father about this, when he had first made the provision for Apollo to be Hannah's guardian.

"This all seems very out of the blue."

"I trust you. You understand."

"I do. But... Nothing is going to happen to you."

"Hopefully it won't. But if it does, I want you to take care of her. When the time is right, you can explain. Because when she's old enough, Marcy is going to tell her."

"She doesn't have to. She's made it out. She's done well. There's no reason—"

"There is. You know why. Because she needs to be able to protect herself. From the people that would take advantage of her. You want the ones you love to learn from your mistakes."

"I met your father at an event six years or so after our company became very successful. And around the time of Cameron's accident. We met because I had struck up a conversation with your mother. She and I... We recognized each other. Because we had both, at different times, seen each other at events where we were the paid companions of the ones we were with. You know your own kind."

"What?" Hannah sat up, clutching the blanket to her chest. "Are you saying that my mother..."

"Your mother was an escort. For some years before meeting your father. Your father never paid for her services. They met, and fell in love. He didn't care what she had done in the past. And she loved him enough to let go of everything. She loved him enough to let go of any of the pain she might've still felt about it. She loved him enough to let herself be free. Maybe she loved herself enough. But we... We had a bit of a bond. I suppose. Instantly. And your father was so afraid that I was going to judge her, when he realized that I recognized her that... Finding out the truth about me always made him feel like your mother was safer. Having me around. He wanted that for you too. He wanted me to keep you safe because he felt like I understood the way the world works. That I could protect you from the reality of it."

"I can't... I can't believe that."

"Are you angry?"

"Yes," she said. "Because... Because my mother is dead and I never got to know this about her. Because we never got to talk about it. Because I didn't really know how they met. Because I didn't really... I never knew them. I never knew them, and they never knew me. I'm just... I'm angry about it. I don't understand why they had to go off and go canoeing in a river in Africa instead of… Instead of being home with me. We could've been the ones having this conversation and… If we only would have had more time."

"You wouldn't have been left with me."

"No. Maybe you wouldn't have been my guardian. Or maybe you and I would've gotten to know each other and it would've been normal."

"I would never have made friends with you. Because I don't make friends easily." He paused. "I traded in my chance for normal. It was not the death of your parents that created a strange situation for me. Whatever you believe, believe that."

"Well, it is what created one for me. I just… I hate this. I want to talk to her about it. I want to ask her why. And you don't know why, do you?"

"No," he said. "But I can tell you that I do know your mother was a wonderful person. Lovely and caring, and always kind to me. She never acted like I was bringing old pain to her doorstep. And she could have. She allowed me to have a friendship with your father. And no, you can't know why. Except I can tell you the reasons are probably similar to mine. When you have no control in your life you make strange bargains. You do whatever you can to try and make something work for yourself. And you tell yourself you're going to get out, but I will tell you, your mother and I are exceptions. Because it is so hard to be done with that. With the money that it gives you."

"My mother married a rich man. I guess that's an easy way to get out."

He shook his head. "Your mother fell in love. There is nothing easy about that. There is nothing easy about that when you have spent years searing your conscience and your soul. Trust me. Because I don't know how to love. I don't know how to put all the pieces of myself back together that I pulled apart so that I could find it in myself to figure out how to play those games. Your mother did the infinitely powerful and impossible task of surrendering her heart to another human being. Don't downplay it."

"I'm sorry. I just... I'm not upset about her past. I'm just... I'm angry at the universe, aren't I? Because plenty of people travel and leave their kids sometimes, but they don't all die on what should have been a lovely excursion. I've been in this place where I've been just blaming them. And being mad. Because I don't feel like they spent enough time with me. But the truth is, there would never have been enough time. And you are right. Time would've given us a different relationship. It would've given us more. And we didn't have that chance. And it's not fair. But it is. Same as I feel like I'm treading water. And I'm so tired. I'm searching and searching for something around me to hold on to. And it was never them. Because as much as I love them, it was never them."

"It is not me," he said. "I'm sorry."

"It never really should have been your responsibility to be."

"I think we are past responsibility, are we not?"

She shook her head. "I suppose."

"It is them that made you so angry these past few months? That caused you to rebel?"

"No," she said. "It was you. It just opened the door to allow me to be a bit bitter at them."

"Why me?"

She laughed, and rolled onto her back. He looked at her, at her gorgeous form and the smile on her face. "I wanted you. I… I cared about you. And I knew that until I dealt with that I was never going to be able to move on with my life."

"What does moving on look like to you?"

"This, I suppose. Minus the technically being married thing. Being financially independent. Running the company… I have to actually go and do that tomorrow."

"I'll be with you," he said.

"Yes, but that wasn't the idea."

"Was sleeping with me the idea?" he asked.

She tilted her chin up and barked a laugh. "Um. No. I absolutely didn't expect to sleep with you, no."

"Even when you were being an absolute brat?"

"I could see that you wanted me," she said, turning to her side. "But I could see that you were very mad about it."

"I was. At you. How dare you?"

But he didn't ask it with any heat or venom. How could he? There was none left in him. Not now.

"You aren't a monster, you know," she said, softly. "I was angry at you because I was angry at life. I still am, a little bit."

"I thought you were angry because you liked me."

"That didn't help. I wanted to be normal, and on the one hand I do think having a crush on your problematically young and sexy guardian is normal, but on the other hand, I knew I wasn't going to be able to just go out and find someone and hook up. I was a virgin because I was preoccupied with you, and that was annoying."

"I am not a virgin," he said, his voice rough. "Far from it. But I've had the kind of sex that takes more from you than it gives back. For what it's worth, you've given something back to me. In that sense I am close enough to a virgin."

She smiled slowly. "I like that. You've always been good to me, Apollo. And I understand what you've been saying. You can't give me love. I'm not sure I want it anyway. I need to figure all of this out first, I think. But what if we took care of each other for a while? I think that would be nice."

"All right, Hannah. If that's what you want. I'll take care of you; you can take care of me."

He said it as if he was humoring her. When in fact he wanted it. Deeply. He had never been taken care of, not once.

Lying in bed next to her was the closest thing.

He didn't want it to end.

But someday it would have to. He didn't have the stamina to do this forever. She was so firmly beneath his walls, and even now he wanted to close it all off.

Not now, though. Now he would coach her through her beginnings at the company. Now he would be her husband, not just her guardian.

He would be all of these things now, and set her up for success.

And someday, he would simply be a man she once knew.

All the better for her.

CHAPTER ELEVEN

HANNAH LOOKED OUT the office window, down at the bustling New York streets below. The last two weeks had gone well. Really well. Apollo had come with her on the first day, and done formal introductions in the board-room. It had made sense, since the board knew him. Of course, it had been their job—sort of—to present a united front as a married couple. In many ways, she didn't actually think the board thought the marriage was real.

The whole thing had been chaotic enough that she didn't think it looked overly authentic.

And yet, the lines were beginning to blur.

At least, as far as she was concerned.

She was nearly thankful for the reprieve that she'd had the last few days. He had flown back to Europe for five days to deal with something that had come up in his and Cameron's company.

And so she was staying in his penthouse alone, going to work alone.

He would be back sometime tomorrow, and that was good.

She missed him. It was interesting, to feel the footing change beneath her when it came to their relationship. And it was. It had.

After he had shared the truth of his past, things had in fact changed.

He was different. In every way. The first time they'd had sex had been electric, there was no denying that. But since then, it was like a wall had fallen down between them. The time in the penthouse when he had looked at her with those dark, wounded eyes had produced an entirely new sort of dynamic between them.

He had described it as if he had lost his virginity in a way, and she felt awed by that. It was weird to get closer to him with the aim of independence. Because the entire point of all of this had been to create a life for herself that was independent of her parents, of Apollo. It didn't require her to step into the halls of her father's company. And she was still dealing with a lot of complicated feelings around the revelation he had given her about her mother.

In order to deflect the thought she decided to call Mariana. It was late in Athens, but she knew that Mariana would still be awake.

"How is everything?" she asked without preamble.

"It's going well. You're right, the mismanagement at the property is pretty profound. But I have found several ways to improve it so far. I was preparing a report to send to you."

"Thank you," she said. "How is Pablo doing in concierge?"

"Oh, fantastic. The guests love him. Rocco is getting on well managing the outdoor activities."

"Good."

She didn't really have hard feelings about Rocco. In fact, she wanted to prove it by giving him a job. They had spoken briefly last week. He had told her that he didn't ever intend to scam her. She believed him. She also believed that life was complicated, and it was possible that he might've been tempted to take advantage of her had the marriage gone through.

It was for the best that she had gone off with Apollo.

But she still wanted to honor the friendships that she'd made.

"How is your marriage going?"

She sighed. "It's not a real marriage."

It felt like it, though. Or if not perhaps a real marriage, a real claiming, conquering, and consuming rolled into one. She'd downplayed her feelings to Apollo because they'd changed. They were fiercer, stronger than ever.

And had more power to destroy her.

This marriage wasn't the shattered snow globe she'd first imagined it was. But it wasn't...forever either.

"So you didn't sleep with him?"

Her denial died in her throat. "We have."

"Hannah! How come you didn't tell me right away?"

"Because it all felt too big. It still does. And I know that it isn't a forever sort of thing. It's more just fantasy fulfillment. I mean, what's better than getting it out of my system?"

"Is that what's happening?"

"Yes. It has to be. He's complicated. And complicated in a way that I can't... I'm not going to be able to help him."

"What do you mean help him?"

"He's really damaged. By things in his past." She was not going to list what they were. "And I feel for him. I really do. But I have enough issues. And... I don't want forever with him. It would never work. You forget, I lived with the man... Sort of for many years. And it was like living with my parents. This kind of distance neglect. And even worse, that's how he is emotionally. And he's definitely able to connect in some ways."

"Sexually."

She didn't tell Mariana, that for Apollo that was actually a really big deal. In fact, she felt guilty allowing that to stand as something that could be made light of. It wasn't. Not for him. It was a big deal that he could let his guard down for sex. And maybe for a lot of men it wouldn't be. Maybe for a lot of men it would be as easy as chasing an orgasm. Apollo could separate that from his own desire, from his own feelings. And she appreciated that. She appreciated that meant something different to him. That it did something different to him. But she also knew that beyond that wall, was another wall. He had told her himself, and she wasn't an idiot.

"Yes. Sexually."

And in those moments she felt held. For the first time in so many years she didn't feel lonely. And she had spent so much time being lonely. But she knew that if she became dependent on him emotionally it would be just another jail cell.

She couldn't trick herself into thinking that it could be something else.

"Hey, I'm all for taking what you can get in a physical relationship. But you do need to be careful."

"How much more careful can I be?" she asked. "I mean, I am being realistic about it. I'm taking on board what he told me. Which is that he can't fall in love. And again, I don't want him to."

"I just find that sometimes your heart gets tangled up in a way that you didn't quite expect, and then you end up feeling pretty bad about it when you went in with your eyes open and you still get yourself a bit wounded."

"I appreciate it. But I'm just going to keep doing what I'm doing. I'm focusing on the work. And I'll be back in Athens in a couple of months. I'll be able to do the work from there instead of being here."

"Is that what you want?"

"Yes. Greece is my home. In a way that New York just isn't anymore. I'm going to have to invest in a house here, but I'm going to get a place of my own in Athens. I think I'll feel… Whole. Finally. Like something is mine. Like it's coming together."

"What feeling are you looking for exactly?"

"It's like I need to take back all those years. Those years when I was living a life I didn't choose. Those years when I was lonely. My parents mandated loneliness to me. And I will never not be angry about that. Angry at them. I wanted… For a long time I wanted somebody to love me. And it was like I had to sit around and wait for it to happen. I'm never going to do that again."

"You have friends here," Mariana said. "And we love you. For all that we're a pretty ragtag group."

"I know you do. I appreciate it more than I can ever say."

"I would be your friend even without this job. You do know that, don't you? I know that you were stuck with the parents you were born with, and then Apollo was your guardian. I feel like maybe you're trying to create a situation where you force your friends to stay friends with you."

She paused. Because maybe it was true. Maybe in some ways she was trying to continue those friendships in the best way she knew how. Agreements and documents, because beyond the parental relationship it was really the only way she knew to reinforce things.

"Maybe I am doing that," she said. "Maybe this is me trying to make a situation for all of you that was made for me. And that isn't fair."

"No, because you definitely don't make me feel like our actual friendship is contingent on me doing what you want. You gave me choices. And I could've stayed at my job, and I know that you would have stayed my friend. Of course, this is a better job, and it's definitely more what I want. But I'm never going to use our friendship as an excuse to slack off."

That bolstered her. This whole thing had been such a confidence boosting experience. Because she didn't really need Apollo to navigate this job. She didn't need money to keep her friends. She could use it to build her life, and she could trust that she wouldn't have to live in that isolation again.

But then she thought of Apollo. And the furtive nights between them. The increasingly intense feelings that she had whenever he walked into a room.

It frightened her. Made her want to run away.

But she also wanted to cling to it forever.

"When are you coming back?"

"I think probably I'll come back for a visit on the fifteenth."

"Great. Will make sure that we can go to dinner. And give you a tour of the property. I think it's already looking better."

"Great. I can't wait. I'll see you then."

She sat down at her desk. And mused. She and Apollo had a year of marriage left. In a way that was comforting. It would give her time. It would give her time to burn this thing out between them. To maybe figure out what the rest of her life looked like in a personal regard.

She'd been sitting on the truths about her parents. About how the denial of time was the real enemy, much more so than them.

Her mother had been a prostitute. Her father the man who loved her, not in spite of it, but as part of who she was. To hear Apollo tell it they'd been so devoted to each other. They just hadn't known how to show her that same love, but it didn't mean they hadn't felt it.

They'd done the best they could at the time. And they'd never had the time to do better.

If they'd still been alive, she'd have told them what she needed.

Because she deserved to be fully loved.

She couldn't fix that with her parents but...

Maybe after Apollo.

She would date a nice man. One who didn't have all those scars in his past. One who wanted to give her...

Everything she'd been denied.

Without thinking, she called him. He didn't pick up.

She ignored the sinking feeling in her chest.

He was busy. And anyway, why had she called him?

It was so complicated. He was tangled in so many aspects of her life, and they had only made it more complicated, then they had married each other, and she had made it more complicated still when she had seduced him in the library.

She felt so powerful sometimes. The object of his desire.

Especially understanding what that meant.

She looked down at her phone, and then opened up a spreadsheet on her computer, trying to focus.

And that was when the door to her office opened.

There he was. Dark thunder and intense black eyes.

"What are you doing here?" she asked.

"I couldn't stay away," he said.

His voice was rough and filled with intensity, and it was everything she had ever wanted to hear. He couldn't stay away.

It was why he hadn't answered his phone. He hadn't been busy. He had been on his way here.

And right in that moment, a brilliant, bright light of need ignited within her.

He couldn't stay away.

It was all there. The truth of it. He didn't look at her like she was his charge. Didn't look at her like she was a ward to be taken care of. He looked at her like she was a woman, and he was a man who needed her.

He closed the office door, and turned the lock.

"Apollo," she said, looking around the highly polished corner office, the windows facing other buildings and the streets below.

He pushed a button, and they didn't. She knew that they did that, a highly glossed film within the windows that would lower to make it impossible to see inside, but they could still see the outside world.

"Give yourself to me," he commanded.

"I…"

This was heat and fire, this was the opportunity to meet him. As equals. They'd made love more times than she could count over the past two weeks, but there were moments that had shifted things, moments that she couldn't ignore. That stood out in her mind. Of course the first time, had been about her. Her needs, her virginity. He had been skilled, and he had been good, but it had still been different than that time in the penthouse when he had begged her to help him. Because the feelings within him had been so foreign, so beyond his control, and so close to the bone that he had needed her to hold him. That had been about his desire. I desire that went beyond the physical.

And this?

This was about the two of them. Coming together with no walls.

But she had to be brave enough to close the gap between them. Brave enough to banish the anxiety within her.

It was only a year. This thing. It wouldn't last forever. Why relegate herself to a corner of her own soul? Why consign herself to more loneliness?

It was inevitable. It had been a part of who she was from the beginning of her life.

She knew what was going to happen at the end of all of this. And whether or not she threw herself into their thrilling sexual connection, what difference did it make?

It would all be the same. In the end he would leave. In the end, she would ask him to.

They would divorce. Because it was the agreement. They would divorce, because they both had real lives to get back to, and they weren't these.

They weren't this.

And so there was absolutely no benefit to holding herself separate.

She began to slowly unbutton her shirt and let it fall away.

Then she unzipped her pencil skirt, and consigned it to the floor as well. She stepped out of her high heels, leaving herself so much smaller than him.

He watched her, the tension and color mounting in his face. She could see his arousal building. She moved to him, and gripped the knot on his tie, loosening it slowly, her eyes meeting his as she did. She had so many questions. Had anyone ever done this for him? Surely in the years since he had stopped being an escort he had women on hand to service him. To give him exactly what he wanted, and yet for some reason he had never been able to let himself be carried away by it. He had always been held back by those well-crafted defense mechanisms he couldn't disengage.

His trauma was more powerful than the need that he felt. But with them it wasn't. Maybe it was because he trusted her.

In that sense, she did matter. And she could take that. She could use that to soothe some of the loneliness inside of her. It was safe enough.

It was safe enough as long as it was sex.

Because like he had said, it wasn't a handshake. But neither of them were foolish enough to believe that it was love.

This mattered. It was emotional. And it was normal for her to feel things. It was okay. It wasn't something she needed to run from.

Slowly, she began to work the buttons on the shirt, exposing his well-muscled chest to her hungry gaze. He was the epitome of masculine beauty, but it wasn't why she found herself drawn to him. There were many beautiful men. Just like sculptures. You could look at them and feel an appreciation for the aesthetics of them, but feel no passion toward them. What they had was something else. Something elemental. And she grabbed onto that, and held it tightly, because it was perhaps the one thing that made her feel singular in this moment, in her entire life.

There were many beautiful men. Just like there were many beautiful women. But none of them had made him feel this.

And none of them had ever made her feel this.

This was something special between them. It was not a dispassionate, crude coupling simply about release. Though she wanted release.

She prized the journey. The hitch in his breath. The way his heart beat hard beneath her palm. The way her own heart rate sped up, and her breathing became shallow. The slide of fabric as she pushed his shirt and jacket from his shoulders. The anticipation she felt when his hand went to his belt and he began to undo it slowly. When he undid the button on his slacks and lowered the zipper, when he stood naked before her, well-muscled thighs and heavy masculinity sending her brain into a tailspin, an explosion of fireworks popping off within her.

They hadn't touched. Not really. She realized she wanted something more than surrender. To give him something, everything.

And then he wrapped his arms around her and she pulled him tightly to her body, the feeling of his rough, hard body making her gasp. He was so glorious. And this was overwhelming. He kissed her. Consumed her. It was deep and hot and slick, and everything she could have ever wanted. She clung to him, and found herself being walked backward, toward those windows. He turned her sharply, her vision blurring as she looked down at the scene below.

"All of this is still happening," he whispered in her

ear, smoothing his hands down her spine, down to cup her ass. "The world is still turning. Can you believe it?"

"No," she whispered, her breath leaving a cloud behind on the glass.

He kissed her neck, and pressed his body against hers, the cold glass making her nipples tight. She squirmed, unable to find satisfaction, and need building between her thighs.

He continued his featherlight exploration of her body, his lips on her shoulder, his fingertips tracing circles down her spine. Never touching her anywhere intimately. Never touching her where she needed him most. She could feel the hard, hot column of his arousal pressing into her rear, but he did not advance further.

He kissed her lightly, all over her back, knelt down behind her, his large hands cupping the rounded globes there, but he did not kiss her where she wanted him to, and he did not linger. He rose back up, slowly pushing her hair to the side, slowly running his fingers through the silken strands. She was shivering. Poised on the edge of a knife. Ready to come if he breathed too heavily. She was shaking. Violently.

"Apollo," she whispered. Making an even larger cloud against the glass. He moved his large hand around to her stomach, and pushed her back firmly against him, let her feel just how hard he was. She moaned, rolling her hips, seeking something. More of him. More of everything.

"Ask nicely," he whispered.

"You know what I want," she said.

"Yes," he said. "I do. And I want it too. More than anything. But you need to ask."

She breathed out, watching that cloud on the glass

again. Then slowly, she lifted her finger, and began to write. *Please.*

He chuckled. "Please what?"

Slowly, deliberately, she wrote an *F.* And then continued with her request, which was bold and something that pushed her beyond her previously defined limits.

"I want to do so much more than that," he said. "Do you know, I can't sleep when I'm away from you? I can't think. I don't understand how this happened. I don't understand how I've known you all this time, and now everything has shifted. Changed. I don't understand."

There was something about those raw, desperate words that actually terrified her. That pushed her to the brink.

But then she couldn't think anymore because he was kissing down her back again, lowering himself beneath her and spreading her legs wide. He licked her, right where she was wet and needy for him, and she gasped. As his tongue penetrated her slick channel, followed by his fingers. She pressed her palms against the glass and canted her hips back toward him as he moved one hand around to the front where he circled that sensitive bud between her legs as he continued to torment her with his clever tongue.

"That isn't what I asked," she panted, hovering on the edge of a climax.

"You want to end this, because you don't like to live in the space. I understand that. Because in this space, you're wrenched apart. The most vulnerable that you can be. Does it help you to know that I'm the same? I can't think." He licked her then, deep. She shuddered, coming apart at the seams, her climax tearing through her like a train.

Rending her asunder.

"Is it better now?" he asked.

"No," she panted. "You know it isn't."

"You are not my ward anymore. It isn't my job to coddle you. To take care of you. You promised that you would give me what I needed just the same as I gave it to you. So you have to prove it now. Don't get impatient."

He returned his attention to pleasuring her, and she ended up lost. Held there in space. Everything zeroed in on this moment. The dissonance of the whole world moving around out there, in plain sight, while she could fathom nothing bigger or more important than what Apollo was doing between her thighs, adding to the intensity of the moment.

There were no years between them. No gap in experience. They had become one creature, striving toward satisfaction. Striving toward completion. And more than that, reaching. For a connection of their souls. Because nothing else would actually satisfy.

He stood, and moved against her, pressing his hand over hers on the glass, and positioning his hardness at the entrance to her body. He wrapped one arm around her and held her tight as he thrust into her.

"Apollo," she cried out.

"Hannah," he growled in return.

Her body was pressed against the glass, the whole world spread out before her, Apollo at her back. It was like a metaphor for this entire situation, and for just a moment it pulled her from the glory of the pleasure that he was building within her.

It was the truth of it. The whole world was out there. All of the things that she could be. If she wasn't tied to him. If she wasn't continually tethered to the life that her father chose for her.

With what she had now she could do anything. Be

anything. She could have as much day-to-day involvement in the company as she wanted. As much or as little.
She could stay here. She could go back to Athens. She
could go anywhere. She could take a hundred lovers or
decide to take a vow of celibacy. All of it was up to her.
Out there. And then there was him. Strong and solid at
her back, moving within her, and he really was the other
choice. Because there would be no limitless freedom with
Apollo. She would be Penelope.

Waiting at home while he lived his life. Feeling hollow while she waited for him to figure out if he could
love her in return. Truly.

The world or Apollo.

Herself or this all-consuming need that would always
demand that her feelings be tangled around him.

She knew what she wanted. Or rather, she knew what
she wished she wanted. She also knew that in this moment, she had chosen him. For this time, she had chosen him.

Because the board didn't really believe that they were
married, and there was no impetus for them to live together as man and wife. They certainly didn't need to
play games in her office.

But it didn't feel like a game. It felt like he was demanding that she strip herself bare, deeper than clothes,
deeper than skin. It felt like he was asking for her to give
pieces of her very soul, and had she given enough?

Hadn't she given enough? To a man who had promised he could never love her, what would ever be enough?

Just don't love him. Please don't love him.

Maybe it wasn't love. Maybe it didn't have to be.

She repeated that to herself. An endless tattoo that

rolled through her as he thrust inside of her. Taking her.
Over and over again.

Just don't love him.

And then she could no longer fight the rising tide of
need within her.

And it crashed over her like a wave. Endless.

Rolling on and on.

Apollo," she said, or maybe she only felt it. Maybe
there was no difference, here in the space. Between what
they said and what they felt. Maybe it all mingled together
with real honesty, and pain, with real feelings that transcended language.

Just don't love him.

He moved away from her, and she turned to face him,
trembling. "I have work to finish," she said.

"I will meet you at home," he said. She could see walls
come down in those dark eyes, and she wished she understood why.

She knew that he was pulling away. She wanted to
know why he was, but asking would defeat the purpose.

"About tickets to an opera. I thought you might want
to go."

"Are you asking me on a date?" she asked, moving
away from the window with trembling legs and beginning to collect her clothes.

"Yes. I am."

She had never really been on a date. She and Apollo
had been sleeping together for well over a week, but she
had never been on a date. She wondered if she ought to
tell him no.

But you have a year. Just a year.

"Yes. I would love to. I just need to finish here."

"I have had a dress selected for you. It will be in your

room waiting when you return. I have some business to attend to, so I will meet you. A car will drive you to the opera house."

"Okay," she said, uncertain what to make of all of this.

It was like the gesture of inviting her out was a step closer, but there were many other things that seemed like a withdrawal. She wanted to ask him. To what end? Because it would only be defeatist for them both.

So she let him pull away. She let him dress and leave. And she finished her work for the day and went home.

Home. This wasn't her home. She was going to buy a home in New York.

She thought of that beautiful street in the village. The one that he was so enraptured by when he had been a young man who had come to the city.

A young prostitute.

She stopped.

The truth of his past gave a new context to that story. He had come with a wealthy woman who was using him. Who had bought his body.

She really thought about what he must've felt. Being part of that wealthy world without actually being in it.

And the church.

Wanting desperately for some kind of spiritual reconciliation but being uncertain of whether or not you could have it all the world around you was still so… Complicated. Broken. He had done some things he didn't want to in order to survive. To protect himself. To compromise himself to make himself safer in the long run, and she couldn't imagine what that must have been like.

She felt a crack forming in her heart. And it was letting all manner of tenderness in where he was concerned, and she didn't especially like it. It was better when she could push against him. Better when they could oppose each other.

There was so much pain in the world. Her own mother had experienced this same pain. Maybe it had been why she couldn't show Hannah the love she wanted. Maybe it was why Apollo...

She hated that they'd been hurt.

She hated that he'd been hurt.

But she was so afraid of him hurting her.

So afraid that the love she'd felt for him—always— was real, no matter what she tried to tell herself. About how she had been young, how she hadn't known him. That this new, all-consuming need was just that—need.

Because maybe if she could believe that, she could believe that at the end of the year, she would be ready to walk away.

The dress was beautiful. Blue and strapless and form-fitting. Off the back, sheer fabric was attached at the shoulders like a cape that cascaded down in a shimmering waterfall.

On the dresser was a box, containing an elegant diamond necklace that glinted in the light.

She dressed and did her makeup, and went downstairs at the appointed time the car was set to arrive.

The drive across town was slow, the traffic in the city oppressive. But she took a moment to try and steel herself. To try and get her thoughts in order. To get her defenses back up. It was difficult to believe that only a couple of hours ago he had her naked and begging in her own office.

And now he was taking her to the opera.

The driver pulled up to the steps and she thanked him, getting out and walking up to the midway point. And then

she felt heat gather at the base of her spine, and turned.
There he was, standing near the street, wearing a sharply
cut tuxedo, his gaze burning fire.

The crack within her heart widened. And she knew
she was in trouble.

CHAPTER TWELVE

HIS RESOLVE WAS STRENGTHENED. Seeing her like that. Standing there on the stairs like an angel. A vision. The most extraordinary thing he'd ever seen. She was beyond belief. His Hannah.

She had been equal parts innocent and filthy today in her office, and he had loved every moment of it. He had done a lot of thinking while he was away. Or rather, the thinking had been done for him. He had not chosen to have her on his mind every second of every moment of every day when he was trying to work, but she was.

Things had changed. While he was working on his projects with Cameron he found himself wanting to call Hannah and ask her opinion. Because he valued that opinion. Because she was brilliant and clever, and he knew from watching what she had done with the hotel chain and just the weeks since she had taken over and implemented her plans, that she would bring about a fantastic partnership between their companies. He also knew that if he were to bring ideas to her about his own business, she would likely have insightful thoughts about them.

He respected those thoughts. Was curious about them. He had gone to a restaurant he hadn't been to before in Paris during a summit that he and Cameron had to attend. And he had wanted to ask her what she thought about the food, and was annoyed she wasn't there.

He had spent so much of his life in relative isolation, and normally he was used to it. But it felt strange, wrong, even to experience anything without her by his side when she could be there.

More than that, it simply wasn't as enjoyable.

The lights from the opera house were gold behind her, and she was as lovely in that dress as he had imagined she would be. Madame Butterfly. A long-lost duchess. She could have been anything. But she was Hannah. His wife.

The ring in his pocket burned.

She had rings for her wedding to Rocco, rings that she had chosen beforehand, and he had not had one. He still was not wearing one.

He'd decided something while he was away. The marriage should not be temporary. The marriage should be permanent. They were better together. And no, he couldn't offer her love. There was so much inside of him, fractured in the dark, floating around in the endless black sea of his soul, and there was nothing he could do about that. He didn't love the idea of offering her a shattered mirror. He would rather she have something whole. But he was honest about it. He had told her. He felt that the overriding truth was that they were good together. Better together than apart.

And he was confident that she would see that.

They could conduct their business individually, and come back together.

In some ways, he felt that this was inevitable.

She had been part of his life for so long, and the idea of

her not being in his life had never settled well. The image of what things would be like when she wasn't with him was just... He didn't like it. And he had lived enough life he didn't like. He was a rich man now, powerful. Why should he make compromises? He shouldn't. He should keep Hannah as his wife. That much was clear.

He walked up the steps toward her, and she smiled. He offered her his arm. "Come, *agape*. We have box seats."

"Of course we do," she said. "Luxury all the way."

"It is not luxury that I was concerned with, but privacy. I do not trust myself with you." There was a truth to that. One that went much deeper than sex. But she had done something to him. Peeled away the protections as if she had taken a knife expertly to flesh against the bone. Sex with her was not the same as sex with anyone else. He could let his guard down. He could let himself feel. He finally understood about connecting souls. It was like all the pieces of himself were united into one when the two of them came together, and it was unlike anything he had ever experienced before that. He needed it. He could not afford to lose it.

She was soft next to him, and she smelled like violets. He did not truly feel settled unless she was next to him.

Because every time they came together, it was harder and harder for him to put his defenses up afterward, and functionally he was now walking around the world without a shield. At least it felt that way to him. And that was her fault. So it was her responsibility to hold him together now.

"Are you all right?" she asked.

"Why wouldn't I be?"

"You're intense."

"Am I ever not?"

"No," she said. Then she smiled. "You aren't. So, I don't know what I'm worried about. Or why I said anything."

"I missed you," he said.

She stopped walking and stared at him. He couldn't read the expression in her fathomless blue eyes. He wasn't sure he wanted to.

"Thank you," she said.

But it wasn't *I missed you too.*

They continued on into the ornate building, and down the VIP hallway to the box seats. They had a private balcony to themselves with rich red curtains and plush seating. There was a fruit platter waiting for them and two glasses of champagne.

"This is beautiful," she said.

He was glad she thought it was. He wanted to take her out. He wanted to leave her in no doubt that for him, this was not the same as it had been. That there was no holdover to the guardian-ward relationship. She was a woman, and he was taking her on a date. She was his woman.

He didn't watch the opera, he watched her. As the notes soared, and the drama onstage built, he watched as her eyes filled with wonder. Watched as emotion took hold of her. Watched her throat work as it became clear the lovers in the play were doomed. Watched as her eyes filled with tears and one slipped down her cheek. And that was when he reached out and grabbed her hand.

She looked at him, and he felt pierced, all the way down to his soul.

She was the only person that he had ever intentionally built a relationship with. He had chosen to do right by her because he wanted to. And he had chosen to know her because he didn't think there was another choice. She was singular in his life. He and Cameron had been forced together by the whims of life, and he would have said that he and Hannah were much the same. Her parents had died. She hadn't chosen that, neither had he.

But in this moment, he had to wonder if this, this connection, was inevitable. If they would've always found themselves sitting here in this opera box. He would've had to explain to her father that things between them had changed. That it was different than he had planned. That of course he had never taken advantage of her when she was young, and never would have. But that he was rather blindsided by the connection between them.

Perhaps he could have talked to her mother about the ways that you tried to manage the scar tissue left behind by the sorts of wounds they had endured. It was something he could see clearly in that moment. That no matter the road they'd walked on, it would've ended up here. Unless he had chosen normal. Unless he hadn't ever sold his body.

If he would've chosen that quiet life in Edinburgh, then no. He wouldn't be here. He never would've been to New York. He would never have experienced world-class opera, least of all from a plush VIP private box seat.

And that was the tragedy. Because the only way to be with Hannah was to come to her broken. And the only way to be whole would have been a life where they never met.

He felt nothing but deep, profound sadness and regret. But he was going to ask her to be his anyway.

When the play ended, a sob rocked her shoulders and he leaned in, kissing her on the mouth. Softly.

"Are you all right?"

"It was very good," she said. "A reminder, though, that sometimes things are doomed. No matter how much she wished they weren't."

Did she mean them? He didn't like that. He gripped her chin. "I think things are only doomed if you allow them to be."

"I don't know. Sometimes I think there are forces at work that are simply too strong."

It was adjacent to what he had just been pondering. Fate. The fact that had he taken a different road he would not have ended here.

That the cost of this moment had been nothing less than his own hideous trauma.

And yet he was here. He could do nothing about that. He couldn't go back any further. He could only be here.

"I brought you out tonight because I wanted to show you how life can be. How things could be between us."

"What do you mean?"

"I spent these past days without you and I was miserable. I don't like being by myself anymore. I don't like going to cafés and not having you across from me. I don't like going to bed and not having you beside me. I want you in my life. I don't want for this marriage to be temporary. I want for us to stay together."

"What?"

She looked shocked. Confused. He reached into his pocket and pulled out two velvet boxes.

"One is for me. And this," he said, opening the next, and revealing a large, yellow diamond. "Is for you. I want you to wear a ring that I have chosen for you. Not one you chose to have a fake marriage to an Italian criminal."

"In all technicality, Apollo," she said softly. "Aren't you a half Italian criminal?"

"Yes," he said. "And my offer comes heavily connected to that reality. Believe me, I understand. Because as far as all that goes, nothing is changed. I am broken inside. I know that. I can't change that. But I do think that we would be better together than apart."

"You mean you would be," she said, as she reached out, her hand hovering over the ring. His heart stopped. And then she lowered her finger, moving away. "What does this offer me? I have lived life already with people who don't really love me. Or at least, can't do it the way that I want them to. My parents… They didn't give me what I wanted. Not ever. And you… You were my guardian, but you were never there for me. You were there for me financially, but never emotionally."

"Have I not been there for you these past weeks?"

"We had sex," she said.

"No," he said. "Believe me when I tell you, it is not just sex, and it is very different. Very different."

"I do understand that. And I'm not trying to minimize that. But I don't think it's a reasonable reason for the two of us to stay married. I have to choose. A life, freedom, or you. The same sort of thing that I have lived with always."

"I'm not enough for you," he said.

"No," she said, her voice jagged. "It's…it's the feelings that aren't enough. I can't just be a symbol to you. I already know that, because you have been my guardian for all this time, and it wasn't enough."

"Woman, I have given you everything. I married you so that you can have your trust fund, I helped you ease into the company—"

"I didn't need you. I didn't need you for that. I don't need you for this part of my life. I just don't. I finally have some sense of who I am. Some sense of what I can be. Disentangled from the past, and you are asking me to keep myself tethered to you, for what? Why does it need to be me?"

"Because I need you," he said. "Because you have unmade me. Because you have sent me to wander the streets without my defenses, and now you don't want to be with me? You were responsible for this. You have turned me into something that I don't recognize, Hannah. And you must do something about it."

"And what will you do for me?" she asked, her words fractured. "Will you heal? Will you do the work of putting all the pieces inside of yourself back together so that I can be loved. So that I can have what I need. Or will it be nothing more than torrid encounters in the afternoon and beautiful visits to the opera, and then I will sit in our house as lonely as I have ever been. Why would it be any different than all these years past have been?"

He stood, rage pouring through him. "It would be. It would be because I'm promising myself to you. And I am not a man who lies."

"I know you're not a man who lies on purpose. But what do you know about any of this?"

"I know that I spent years wishing that I could connect with someone. I don't understand what is happening inside of me. And you're the only person that can help me make sense of it."

"I'm not your emotional pack mule, Apollo. I have my own feelings. I have my own trauma. I have things that I need."

"And I am too broken for you."

She put her head in her hands, and the sound she made was pained. "I'm afraid you are. Because how will I ever know if you care about me, or your redemption? Am I a person to you? Or am I a symbol? I deserve... I deserve to be loved. I do."

She might as well have shot him. Straight through the heart. That heart that no longer had any protection. That was already so riddled with holes that it felt beyond help now. That it felt beyond healing.

"You are like everything else. Everyone else. You couldn't actually handle the truth of my past..."

"It isn't your past. It's your future. You have told me exactly what your future is. To be a man who cannot love. And I cannot accept that. Why don't you get it. It isn't..."

"You said you didn't need my love."

"I did," she said. "I did. Because I don't see a future with you. So no, I don't need to love. But that's assuming that the marriage ends in a year. Just as we planned."

"If I divorce you your money reverts back to the trust."

The color drained from her face. "Would you really do that?"

He thought about it. It would be ruthless. Decisive. It forced her to change her mind, and it would give him the entire year to figure out how to manipulate her into staying.

He could buy her.

And that was when he let the ring fall from his hand and onto the floor. Because he had become that person. The one who would buy someone else's body. The one who would pay for them to be in his bed whether they wanted to be there or not. Because he was so broken, so damaged, he needed to take from another person in order to be whole.

Time and money had made him the thing that he despised. He would turn her into his whore if he could. And nothing had ever terrified him more.

"No," he said. "I won't do that."

"I can't be alone like that. Not anymore. Please. Don't ask it of me. Let me go, Apollo. Let me… Let me make a life for myself that is nothing to do with you. Let me make a life for myself that is nothing to do with all of the things that have haunted me for all this time."

"Your father's company is good enough for you, but you must cut ties with me?"

"My father's company isn't a human being. It doesn't have the power to wound me. I'm not expecting it to have feelings for me, I just want to do a good job. I want the freedom to find someone who can love me. And maybe no one ever will. Maybe I will never be compelling enough, or interesting enough for somebody to—"

"It has nothing to do with you. The reason that I…" But he couldn't even say it. "I don't even know what love is, Hannah," he said, and he felt foolish, because he was a thirty-five-year-old man admitting that he had no concept of an emotion he was quite certain small children understood. But he didn't. He had no idea at all.

It was the thing that people talked about. Wrote songs about. Poetry. It was something that concerned so many aspects of the world. The power of a mother's love was supposed to drive so many things and yet in his life it never had. Fathers were supposed to love their children and protect them, and yet his had abandoned him. Sex and love were supposed to be linked, and yet for him it had been tied together with money. With the basest of lusts.

He felt something different when he was with Hannah, but what was love?

Was it this feeling that he would die if she wasn't beside him? Or was it the need to let her go free so that she could be happy?

And if it was the latter, then did that mean it was enough to convince her to stay with him? Enough to give her a promise?

He didn't know. And he needed to figure it out. But he didn't know how to do it.

"I will go back to Athens," he said. "I'm sorry."

"Apollo…"

"You are right. This isn't healthy. It's not something I can ask of you. I'm older than you. And I have had time enough to sort through things that I have not managed to fix. It is not your job to fix them for me. And I am very sorry, Hannah. I should've turned you away when you came to my study."

"Don't say that. You shouldn't have I…"

"I should have. It was selfish of me. To take what you offered. I wanted it, and I wanted you. Being lonely is one of the single most terrible things in the world and I will not allow you to be lonely because of me."

He stood, and left the rings on the floor, not looking back as he walked out of the opera box.

She could only sit there, feeling devastated. What had just happened? She got off the chair and knelt down, picking up one of the rings from where it had rolled onto the ground. He had… He had proposed to her. Really. Truly. And she had… She turned him down. She had to. She had to. Because there was no way that he was ever going to stay with her. Why would he? He was an interesting, vital, beautiful man, and in her experience she was…

What was she? She was a lonely child who had never gotten past the isolation of her childhood. She was a lonely girl who had never been able to tell her parents how much she had just needed them to be there.

What is love?

He had asked her, and she didn't have an answer. Except it couldn't be this. It couldn't be the sharp, painful uncertainty. This plunge into the unknown. When she had imagined going off and living her life, taking over the company, doing whatever she wanted, going out and having fun with her friends, and being free to date, it hadn't felt sharp. Love could not be this painful.

And yet she felt like she was bleeding out. And she was afraid she loved that stupid bastard in spite of everything she had told herself. That it was a crush, that was all it was. That she knew better.

"Damn you," she said. "Damn you, Apollo."

Because she might as well be the doomed woman at the end of the opera, consigned to dying in a man's arms. When was it love or was it just a sickness over the chemistry between them?

How are you supposed to know?

She had been shoved into his sphere when she was sixteen years old and her crush had been incubated in the heat of her grief. How could she trust it?

How could she trust him?

She had done the right thing. She had done the strong

thing. She was standing up for herself. She was taking what she needed.

Are you saying I'm too much for you?

She stumbled out of the opera box, the rings clutched tightly in her hand. She didn't see him anywhere. When she got outside, the car was waiting down at the bottom of the steps, and she got into it, half hoping that he would be there.

He wasn't.

She took her phone out of her pocket and she called Mariana.

"Mariana," she said, her voice breaking.

"What happened?"

"I don't know if I've made a mistake or not."

"Tell me everything."

Apollo walked the streets until the pain in his chest became unbearable. Until he had to stop because he was afraid he might be having an actual heart attack. He leaned against the wall of an old, ivy-covered building, surprised to find that he had wandered down to the village. He closed his eyes and shook his head. Was he doomed to be the same idiot, wandering around in the same places forever, never fully being part of them?

Because no matter how much money he had, no matter how much time passed, that seemed to be the case.

He called the one person who had always been there for him. "I need your help," he said.

"I've been expecting this phone call," Cameron said.

"What am I supposed to do? I want to be with her. But I'm… You know what we are."

"Yes. I know what we are. And I'm a monster on top of that, and I am with Athena."

"You're scarred. You're not a monster. It isn't the same thing."

"I wasn't referring to my scars. There are other issues. And she loves me anyway."

"Do you love her?"

"Can you doubt it? I love her with everything I am."

"What is it?" There was a total silence at the other end of the phone. "Dammit, Cameron, I asked you a question."

"I heard you. I just don't quite know how to answer. I'm sorry. I guess I don't understand quite what you're asking."

"No one has ever loved me, Cameron. I told her that I couldn't love her, but the truth is, I don't even know what it is. Is it this feeling like I'm going to die? And what good does that do her? Because she asked me that too, and it's fair. She wants to know what she could possibly get out of being with me, and I have no answer other than good sex. And you and I both know that well can leave you very, very dry."

"I love you, Apollo. Are you absolutely an idiot?"

That stopped him cold. "What?"

"What do you think our friendship is? And what do you think you've shown me in all that time?"

"We were forced together. We're more like brothers."

"Yes. Brothers are notorious for not loving each other."

"It isn't the same. I don't know my life without you. I didn't have to learn how to take care of you. I didn't have to learn how to put my needs second to yours when necessary, it was easy. Because…"

"Because you love me. Which I know is probably a very uncomfortable thing for you to have to hear, given the state of toxic masculinity in the world."

"I…"

"You were patient with me, and kind. When I was at my lowest, you didn't leave. When I gave you nothing, you gave to me extraordinarily. You were patient with me when many would not have been. When many would've tried to buy me out or get me away from the company because I was nothing more than dead weight. You were my friend. My brother. You demonstrated love to me. What do you suppose caring for her is? Love for her parents. Love for her."

"I've been trying…" He closed his eyes and swallowed painfully. "I've been trying to find some path toward redeeming myself."

"From what? You cared for every single person in your life diligently. Without fail. You are one of the truest, most loving people that I know. If you need redemption, if you need forgiveness, it is not from anyone around you. It's from you, Apollo. I think you might be the only one yet who is not confident you deserve love."

"She said I was too much for her."

"Did she say that?"

"She was afraid she could not handle me."

"Listen to her. Don't take it personally. Listen to what that says about her own feelings. I love my wife, and she came with her own specific set of baggage. Sometimes her baggage and mine don't play nicely. And when that happens, she has to listen to me, to where I'm coming from and why I might take something a certain way when she doesn't. And I have to do the same for her. What is she really afraid of? I sincerely doubt it's you and your brokenness. She's probably afraid of loving you more than you love her."

"I don't want to live without her." He felt like he was staring into an abyss. "I am actually tempted to go and walk off a pier."

"Please don't do that. Please think about what you're saying to me. All the things in your life are worth less without her in it. What do you think that is?"

"I didn't like the café I went to in Paris because I wanted *her* there."

"If you don't even like a croissant without her there to taste it with you, I think you can pretty safely say you're in love."

"What do I do?"

Cameron laughed. "Apollo, you and I have been through some pretty hideous things. One thing we always did, though, was fight. To live, to grow, to have more. To have better. Don't fight any less for the woman you love than you would have for money."

"But... Money is only money. This is..."

"Nothing less than your whole heart. Perhaps you are too much for her. Perhaps you are damaged. But it would be better if you were honest. And said that you love her anyway. And then let her decide."

"That sounds painful."

"It probably is. But you should do it anyway. Because the alternative is... Wanting to walk into the sea."

His friend hung up then, and he simply stood there. He wandered the streets until the sky turned gray. And he found himself standing in front of St. Patrick's, just as the doors opened for the day.

There was no early entry or VIP. He came in with everybody else who was waiting to take their place before they went to work.

He thought of what Cameron had said to him, and as he walked deeper into the cathedral old words from his childhood echoed through him. He did know an explanation of love. It was patient and kind. It didn't envy, it wasn't boastful. It wasn't self-seeking. It didn't keep track of wrongdoing. It had seemed, to him, a list of impossible tasks. To love like that was to die to everything within yourself. And nobody could do that all the time. And what he had always seen as a barrier suddenly made sense to him. Every person in the whole world would fall short of such an ideal. People did it anyway. They loved and gave love imperfectly anyway always.

A shaft of sunlight came through one of the impossibly blue stained-glass windows, and it was like a light coming on in his soul. He was broken. But it didn't mean he couldn't love.

Cameron was right. He always had. The thing that had caused him to be the worst versions of himself were his denials of love. Considering manipulating her, making her his through blackmail, that didn't come from love, but from his need to deny it. His need to protect himself.

He knelt down on one of the cushioned benches, his legs just giving out. And that was when he heard footsteps behind him. A figure knelt down beside him, and he turned. Hannah.

She looked up at him, her eyes glistening with tears. And then she pressed her head to his shoulder, her body shaking as sobs racked her figure. He held her. Until the storm between them subsided, because his own rose up like rain and poured from him just as it did her.

"It seemed like the right place to go," she whispered.

"Yes," he whispered. There were no declarations then, no words.

It was a prayer between them. And it joined all the hope, sorrow, and faith that had already sunk into these old stone walls. And something about that made him feel new.

They stayed there like that for a long time, and then he took her hand and brought her to her feet, leading her back outside. They had been in a cocoon in there, and all the silence dissolved the minute they were back outside, people on foot rushing around them, trying to get to work.

"There's a lot to say," she said. "But I suppose the most important thing is that I love you."

He closed his eyes, and he felt it. That he didn't have to wonder anymore. What it meant. "I love you too," he said.

She didn't argue or bring up the fact that he'd said he couldn't do that. He appreciated it. But he wanted to explain anyway. "I couldn't understand the idea of love because I had decided that no one could love me. And that no one should. I am deeply ashamed of the things I've done. I felt like I had broken myself. That everything that was wrong with me was something I had done. It was a pain I had caused. And that meant I didn't deserve to be healed. If I had just gotten a job when I ran away from my mother, I would just be one of the many people in this world who had a parent that neglected them. I didn't. I made a different choice. The choices I made hurt me. They left me feeling used, they left me feeling assaulted. They left me detached from myself, and most of all, ashamed. I could not fathom love because I cannot fathom anyone loving me."

She shook her head. "I do. And I'm sorry. You were

never too much for me. I needed… I needed to know you could love me. Because I spent so many years being lonely. While everyone prioritized their own needs over mine, I just needed to know I wouldn't be lonely like that again. I'm sorry I said you were too broken. I love you broken. I just want you to love me broken too."

"I'm just a fool," he said. "I didn't understand that I had everything I wanted. I just had to stop being so afraid. Had to let go of things that kept me safe. It's why I was different with you. Vulnerable with you. You made me feel that way all the time, and it made me angry. But of course it didn't occur to me that it was just falling in love. I'm not going to be perfect at it. Nobody is. But we can try. We can try, and I think that's the important thing." People from the streets kept going into the cathedral, moving around them. "Nobody that goes into those doors is perfect. It's all people trying. And I think part of me always wanted that. For my trying to be enough. And I was afraid that it wasn't."

"Your trying is beautiful. And it is more than enough for me."

"What about your freedom."

"Being with you can still be freedom. It only ever felt like a prison when I imagined myself still existing in that loneliness. I called Mariana last night. And I told her I was so upset with myself because I had gone and fallen in love with my first lover. And that wasn't responsible. It wasn't the right thing to do. She said what's the point of limitless freedom if everything you want out there means less than the thing you already have? I have the freedom to choose, Apollo. And I'm choosing you. I'm choosing this. Our love. No matter if we aren't perfect at it."

"Thank you." As declarations went, it wasn't a great one. It was just nothing more than the truth. From the bottom of his heart. Because he knew all about loneliness. They both did. And what neither of them had ever known before was this. And he was just so grateful.

He took her into his arms and kissed her.

He was going to love her. Forever. There was no doubt in him about that.

* * * * *

COMING SOON!

We really hope you enjoyed reading this book.
If you're looking for more romance
be sure to head to the shops when
new books are available on

Thursday 28th March

To see which titles are coming soon, please visit
millsandboon.co.uk/nextmonth

MILLS & BOON

MILLS & BOON®

Coming next month

THE KING'S HIDDEN HEIR
Sharon Kendrick

'Look... I should have told you sooner.' Emmy swallowed.

She was biting her lip in a way which was making warning bells ring loudly inside his head when suddenly she sat up, all that hair streaming down over her shoulders, like liquid gold. She looked like a goddess, he thought achingly when her next words drove every other thought from his head.

'You have a son, Kostandin.'

What she said didn't compute. In fact, she'd taken him so completely by surprise that Kostandin almost told her the truth. That he'd never had a child, nor wanted one. His determination never to procreate was his get-out-of-jail-free card. He felt the beat of a pulse at his temple. Because what good was a king, without an heir?

Continue reading
THE KING'S HIDDEN HEIR
Sharon Kendrick

Available next month
millsandboon.co.uk

OUT NOW!

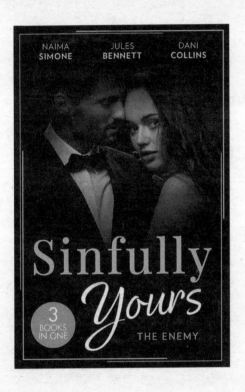

OUT NOW!

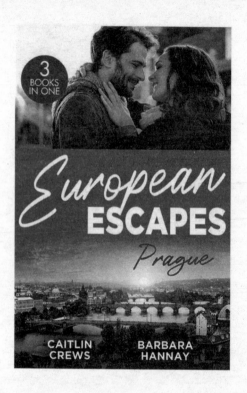

Available at
millsandboon.co.uk

MILLS & BOON

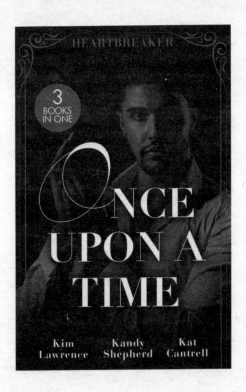

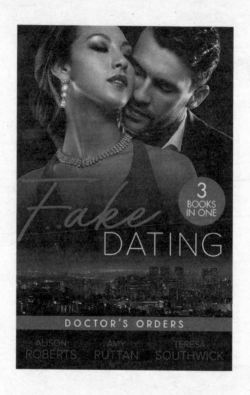

LET'S TALK

Romance

For exclusive extracts, competitions
and special offers, find us online:

 MillsandBoon

 @MillsandBoon

 @MillsandBoonUK

 @MillsandBoonUK

Get in touch on 01413 063 232

MILLS & BOON

THE HEART OF ROMANCE

A ROMANCE FOR EVERY READER

MODERN

Prepare to be swept off your feet by sophisticated, sexy and seductive heroes, in some of the world's most glamourous and romantic locations, where power and passion collide.

HISTORICAL

Escape with historical heroes from time gone by. Whether your passion is for wicked Regency Rakes, muscled Vikings or rugged Highlanders, awaken the romance of the past.

MEDICAL

Set your pulse racing with dedicated, delectable doctors in the high-pressure world of medicine, where emotions run high and passion, comfort and love are the best medicine.

True Love

Celebrate true love with tender stories of heartfelt romance, from the rush of falling in love to the joy a new baby can bring, and a focus on the emotional heart of a relationship.

HEROES

The excitement of a gripping thriller, with intense romance at its heart. Resourceful, true-to-life women and strong, fearless men face danger and desire - a killer combination!

###

From showing up to glowing up, these characters are on the path to leading their best lives and finding romance along the way – with plenty of sizzling spice!

To see which titles are coming soon, please visit

millsandboon.co.uk/nextmonth